Jersild, Per Christian, 1935-

Animal doctor [by] P.C. Jersild.
Translated from the Swedish by David
Mel Paul and Margareta Paul. Pantheon
Books [c1975]

I. T.

THE ANIMAL DOCTOR

THE ANIMAL DOCTOR

BY P. C. JERSILD

Translated from the Swedish by
David Mel Paul and Margareta Paul

PANTHEON BOOKS

A Division of Random House, New York

First American Edition

English translation Copyright © 1975 by Random House, Inc.

All rights reserved under International and Pan-American
Copyright Conventions. Published in the United States by
Pantheon Books, a division of Random House, Inc., New
York, and simultaneously in Canada by Random House of
Canada Limited, Toronto. Originally published in Sweden
as *Djurdoktorn* by Albert Bonniers Forlag, Stockholm.
Copyright © 1973 by P.C. Jersild.

Library of Congress Cataloging in Publication Data

Jersild, Per Christian, 1935–
    The Animal Doctor.

    Translation of *Djurdoktorn*.
    I. Title.
PZ4.J567An3   [PT9876.2.E7]   839.7′3′74   75–10360
ISBN 0–394–49464–4

Manufactured in the United States of America

INTRODUCTION

1

The Alfred Nobel Medical-Surgical Institutes, or NMSI, is Scandinavia's largest educational institution for physicians and medical researchers. It originated as an appendage to one of Europe's oldest military academies, the War College at Karlberg. In connection with Sweden's loss of Finland in 1809, the military medical apparatus had taken on proportions impressive for the time. This led in 1810 to the establishment, under the aegis of King Carl XIII, of a separate school for military surgeons. The Academy of Military Surgery was located in Stockholm, one of the few European capitals that lacked a university.

In 1901 this military medical facility was made civilian and placed on an equal footing with other medical faculties. However, this did not take place without resistance from the universities at Uppsala and Lund, which is why His Majesty's government decided, in 1906, that it would be just as well to grant the school's nagging petition to be allowed to take the name Alfred Nobel Medical-Surgical Institutes. Thereby, the school fastened to itself the name Alfred Nobel—a concept as weighty in international carats as Carl Linnaeus or Emanuel Swedenborg.

Ever since, the Nobel prizes in medicine and physiology have been given out on the tenth of December each year by the faculty of the Institutes—a circumstance which has provided the rock-solid foundation for Sweden's self-assumed position as a medical superpower.

NMSI's financial position has always been precarious. On the profit side can be entered education budgets and re-

3

search grants from the national treasury's slender resources. Certain fixed resources also exist, in the form of over a hundred buildings and a number of civil service positions. Yet without large contributions from private funds NMSI would not survive. Therefore it surrounds itself with a circle of philanthropic financiers, a group of rich relations who can be bowed and curtsied to and consulted privately and, in especially hard times, might possibly be sent some honorary medical degree or other.

In an earlier day, the relatives were called Aunt Alice and Uncle Kurt Wallenberg, Aunt Marguerite and Uncle Axel Wenner-Gren, Uncle George Eastman, Cousin Astra Pharmaceuticals and Cousin-by-Marriage Folksam Insurance. In recent years, the clan has been fortified with younger, fresher blood from Europharm, Medinvent International, and Dow-Know-How.

In the 1940s, NMSI was moved from central Stockholm to the ring of graveyards, railroad yards, parklands, and colleges that make up a no-man's-land between the city of Stockholm and its suburbs. Over an area half a mile square, the many institutes and annexes are dispersed among stony knolls that have been partially blasted away and solitary pines that forgot to leave when the woods were forced to retire into Uppland County.

The heart of NMSI is a quadrangle. Bounding it on the north is the Administration Building, on the east, the famous library, on the south, the Student Union, and on the west, the cafeteria. At the center of the quadrangular lawn is a foot-deep pond. The pond is shaped like a white blood cell or a fried egg, with irregular bays and peninsulas. At the center of the pond—in the position of a cell nucleus—stands a tall metal sculpture. It is a mobile with a number of upright rods. Mounted on every rod are a number of rotating wind vanes. In profile, the vanes look like airplanes: pointy nose, slender body, shark-fin tail. They are made of silver clad in weatherproof plastic. Every wind vane bears on its fin the name of a Nobel prizewinner in medicine. There are names like N. Finsen, I. Pavlov, R. Koch, S. Ramón y Cajal, A. Gullstrand, W. Einthoven, Charles Sherrington, E.A. Doisy, and U. v.

4

Euler. From more recent times, the names of such leading researchers as B.F. Skinner, Anna Griebe, Richard Studsman, P. Klevsjin, J.J. Bandura, and Rollo Ray, Jr., can be recognized.

The mobile is a gift from the Nobel Foundation to NMSI, honoring the Institutes' seventy-fifth anniversary. Today the number of wind vanes approaches 250. Most of the time the vanes are free to respond to wind, gravitation, friction, or whim. But on the hour a magnetic field is induced in the mobile so that all the vanes line themselves up and point in exactly the same direction. When the clock strikes twelve, all the arrows point north, at three they all point east, and at six they mass a phalanx, like a company of pikemen, against the Student Union to the south. In this way, the mobile is a combination of individual academic anarchy and systematic pooling of energy—a combination weather vane, work of art, clock, and compass.

2

Now the Nobel Clock strikes ten in the evening. Just as if somebody off in the west-northwest blew a whistle pitched too high for any but dogs to hear, all the wind vanes suddenly swing their greyhound muzzles around to ten o'clock.

In the heated waters of the pond around the mobile, big goldfish are swimming. These lazy carp, clad in sequins and lamé, are the only captive animals in all the institutes that are kept alive solely for their looks. As for the rest, the Institutes keep a many-thousand-footed menagerie going that includes guinea pigs, quail, rats, coypus, rabbits, hens, dogs, frogs, apes, goats, doves, sharks, mice, pigs, hagfish, and insects, to name a few. All of them—except for the dressed-up goldfish —are there to be at the service of science with their pain, their guts, their fluids and molecules and hormones and fetuses and cells, and with their more or less marked relationship to man.

As Swedish agriculture has become mechanized, the number of cows and horses has steadily diminished; instead, the country has been invaded by a rapidly swelling army of smaller species. In the 1950s, several hundred thousand experimental animals were consumed annually in Sweden by high schools, colleges, institutes, and hospitals. By 1970 the figure approached a million. Today their number hovers around 2.8 million. But numbers don't tell the story—the higher they are, the less they tell. The difference between 150 and 200 traffic deaths a month is obviously significant. But whether 19.7 or 20.1 million Soviet citizens died in the Second World War—that difference lies wholly within the framework of margin for error.

It is late on the evening of the thirteenth of December. The quadrangular lawn surrounding the Nobel Clock is rimmed with torches. The flames blacken in the wind and the thin frosting of snow melts in circles of black water around the burning canisters. The cafeteria and Student Union are lighted up. From the Student Union's broad steps, a worn red carpet has been laid on the slush and leads to the pond. The Nobel Clock's 243 silver vanes turn lazily in the driving smoke of the torches and in the steam from the heated pond.

Old tradition dictates that the year's Nobel prizewinners take part in the students' Lucia celebration. Since the seventy-fifth anniversary of the Institutes and the creation of the Nobel Clock, the tradition has been augmented: just before the clock strikes midnight, the prizewinners and their families rise and leave the Student Union and promenade the short distance to the pond.

This year's winner, oddly enough, is alone in copping the $215,000. His name is Wang and he works in the USA. He has no family with him. With the students' Lucia on his arm, he advances in small steps over the red carpet. After Dr. Wang comes the president of the Institutes. After the president, several recent prizewinners. Then comes a tall student bearing the standard of the student body. Wang inscribes his signature with an engraving gun on the fin of the new wind vane that is about to be mounted on the mobile. First he writes his name in American. The Lucia shivers in the freezing wind. Then Wang writes his name in Chinese characters. For this he receives spontaneous applause.

A workman in high wading boots steps out into the pond and screws Wang's wind vane fast to one of the rods. The vane begins at once to spin around like a propeller. No one applauds, everyone is waiting breathlessly. The president consults his watch. Precisely at the moment that the date indicator on the president's watch clicks from 13 to 14, all the arrows on the mobile stop, pointing due north. Dr. Wang giggles delightedly and claps his hands. Forgotten are the long hard years in the basement laboratory. It's as if he'd accomplished his magnum opus right here, tonight, by successfully inscribing his signature on a metal plate.

3

When the company returns, with the blue-frozen Lucia several yards in the vanguard, three persons leave the celebration and trudge out separately into the darkness.

Assistant Professor Björn Johansson, hunching his shoulders against the cold, walks down toward the Physiological Institute. The building is dark except for the second floor, where two windows give off a cool violet light. When he reaches the door, he presses his right thumb against a little eye right next to the handle. The eye reads Johansson's fingerprint. It recognizes the fingerprint and the lock opens with a click. Being late, he races up the stairs.

Up on the second floor, he throws a white lab coat over his tuxedo and puts on dark protective goggles. He goes through the first laboratory door, shuts it behind him, and waits ten seconds as prescribed—then passes through door number two, entering the brightly lighted laboratory.

The room is filled with huge glass boxes that are interconnected into a bewildering looking maze on several perpendicular planes. Within the glass labyrinth are a multitude of metal pegs and little lights of various colors. The wavy grained plywood floors of the boxes are covered with colored ribbons of tape which run through the whole labyrinth system like guide stripes on an exercise track. There's a red track, a black, a green, a yellow, and a blue. Five pigeons are at various points in the glass maze. It is the pigeons' assignment to find their way through the labyrinth with the help of the tapes. But they are not to work undisturbed. Sometimes a colored bulb lights up, causing the tape track to change its color. Thus the pigeons are subjected to stress. With short-circuited sensory impressions they are continually led deeper into the maze; the metal pegs keep them from turning back.

Every other hour each pigeon's excrement, which has accumulated in a little condomlike sack stretched over its tail, is collected. The excrement is subsequently analyzed for its stress hormone content. In this way an "objective" measurement can be made of the pressures the pigeons are exposed to in different parts of the maze.

Sleepily Johansson changes the condom sacks on his pigeons with automatic movements, like a mother changing diapers at midnight. He knots the neck of each sack, marks it with red, black, green, or blue tape, and then places the little balloon in the freezer. Tonight he's ten minutes late— but he doesn't note that in the lab record. When he approaches the glass box with the yellow pigeon in it, he sees that it is lying on its side with feet drawn up and clenched.

He stands perfectly still, staring at the dead bird. Then he begins to weep quietly behind the dark goggles. It's the fourth time this has happened to him. Now he must set the experiment back to zero and train a new pigeon. That will take him two weeks, or at best ten days. If any more pigeons die, his grant won't cover completing the set of experiments.

The second person who has left the Lucia celebration at midnight is a woman, Birgitta Wennström. She is a graduate student and assistant to a professor in the Institute of Bioengineering. Her coat is thrown over her shoulders. Lifting the hem of her long dress, she trips in gold slippers between the puddles. She lets herself into the institute through a back door with an old-fashioned key and goes down into the basement. Birgitta Wennström is twenty-three years old and

8

finds this a bit scary. Back in August there was a burglary here; they were looking for alcohol.

The reason she's left the party is that the professor has assigned her to keep a heart experiment going. In a warm, damp little cubbyhole in the basement stands an incubator with a rounded plexiglass cover. Inside the incubator is a test stand, and from the stand hangs a beating rabbit heart with a drooping lung on each side. The heart is the size of a walnut and quivers energetically while pumping a colorless salt solution in place of blood. The sutures leak here and there, so the salt solution sprays out and drops down to be collected in a bowl at the bottom of the incubator. Next to the incubator is a rack of equipment for x-ray photography and a mingograph for recording an electrocardiogram.

The experiment goes like this: When the heart beats, its shape changes. This can be recorded on film; in this case, the film is exposed by x-rays. The motion picture which results can later be translated into an ECG-track by a little computer of the kind that has been used for some time in warplanes. The goal is to be able to record an ECG while doing an x-ray examination of a patient. Then one would not need to use annoying and time-consuming electrodes for taking the ECG. Besides, within a few years it might be possible, with the help of other rays than x-rays, to take "remote ECG." Then it would suffice for the patient to be located within a few hundred yards of the machine.

A heart-lung preparation carefully removed from a rabbit should continue to beat outside the body for at least forty-eight hours. This preparation is hardly six hours old. Birgitta Wennström backs up onto the lab bench beside the oscilloscope, kicks off her shoes, rubs one reddened foot against the other, and lights a cigarette. She's not especially sleepy, but her false eyelashes make her eyelids stiff. Suddenly she sees that the heart in the incubator has stopped beating. She hops down from the bench and pads over in stocking feet. The rabbit heart hangs dead, like a big gleaming teardrop. Quickly she opens the clamp that shuts off the adrenalin supply. The adrenalin is released directly into the left ventricle. The heart shudders as if it were trying to shake something off, but it's just a slight trembling. She releases a new dose of adrenalin. But now the heart hangs flaccid and lifeless.

She swears—low, but with emphasis—"*Oh shit . . .*" There's a plan prescribing what she should do. In the next room are about a dozen rabbits. It's difficult, but she can manage to remove the heart and lungs of a rabbit by herself. She puts on an operating gown that buttons up the back and starts setting up: the operating board with clips to restrain the rabbit, scalpels, scissors, forceps, needles, needle holder, vascular tape, compresses, spreaders, and anesthetic appliances. Before pulling on the gloves, she opens one of the boxes and takes a firm grip on a pair of rabbit ears. The rabbit she pulls out is a black-and-white spotted one. It hangs quite still. Then it pees a fine stream against her leg.

She looks at the rabbit. Then she wrinkles her nose and mouth, exposes her front teeth, and chews rapidly on her lower lip. The rabbit doesn't recognize itself. The big dark pupils seem not to see her. She bends over and drops the animal back into the box.

"*Oh shit . . .*" she says again, turns off the equipment, and hangs up the operating gown.

What the reprisals will be, she doesn't really know. But there's going to be trouble. She's going to catch hell because she hasn't done what the professor has a right to expect of an ambitious student and co-worker. She's a deserter. That's dangerous when there's an oversupply of students. When she realizes this, she gets very exhilarated. Whistling happily, she picks her way through the slush with lifted skirts.

The third person who leaves the party is named Hasse Rubenick. He's not having a good day. He was already drunk at the Lucia luncheon. And if a guy's made a start he ought to go right on, Hasse's always thought. It took a couple of shots of whisky to ward off the grayness of the afternoon. Then there was a big dry martini before supper. And aquavit with the herring appetizer—with a beer chaser. Of course red wine was included in the price of the Lucia buffet, along

10

with hot spiced wine. But cordial with the coffee had to be ordered extra. At the dance, a bar was set up in the foyer and there Hasse got himself a Drambuie and two rum and cokes. Before it was time to go out in the snow and applaud Dr. Wang, Hasse had to get his overcoat from the checkroom for an extra nip of the needful. Now Hasse is sitting, three-quarters drunk and maudlin, in the Pharmacological Institute and trying to ingratiate himself with a light-brown beagle with a white chest named Maecenas.

When he left the party at midnight, his path was not as straight and purposeful as Björn Johansson's or Birgitta Wennström's. First he jogged over to the Anatomical Institute, where he had once been a temporary assistant, and pressed a wobbly thumb against the eye-lock. But his fingerprint has been washed out of the Anatomical eye-lock's memory long ago.

Then, with arms flying, he stalks over to the Institute of Forensic Medicine, where he filled in as a messenger one summer. He has no thought of going back to the Student Union and the Lucia Ball. There's a young lady there who, just before eleven thirty, told him to *Go to* . . . He fishes his ticket for the midnight supper out of his breast pocket and, a little halfheartedly, holds it up before the door-telephone at Forensic Medicine. Then he tosses the ticket in the air. The slip of paper spins away at once in the wind.

Hans Kristian Rubenick, thirty-three years old and a premed Bachelor of Science, decides to make a third attempt, this time at the Pharmacological Institute. There, he's never been employed. But on the other hand, he's taken his exams there—three times. He sinks to his knees before Pharmacological's double glass doors. With his lips a quarter-inch from the eye-lock, he slowly breathes out his alcoholic breath. Then quickly up with the thumb! The lock opens with a frightened hiccuping.

Inside, in the first-floor corridor, he tries to remember how the institute is laid out. He knows that the course laboratory used to lie to the left but has now been moved to a central laboratory building. When he grasps the handle of the door

11

that formerly led to the course laboratory, a dog begins to
yap and whine. A mutt! he thinks. Really, why haven't I got
a mutt?

He steps in and turns on the light. In a basket on the floor
lies a beagle, wagging its tail. Hasse bends down and strokes
the dog's back.

"Yes-*yes* . . . nice doggie, yes-*yes,*" he says, and lets the dog
lick his face. It feels great—really fantastic. Really great.

This dog isn't just any old dog. It's over eleven years old,
is named Maecenas, and is proudly displayed to foreign
and local visitors including Bachelors of Science. Upon
Maecenas's gastric juices no fewer than seventeen doctoral
candidates have defended their theses. Not only at Pharmacological and NMSI is Maecenas a phenomenon; on his
birthday, the thirteenth of January, the dog gets greeting
cards from far and near, from Lagos, Princetown, and New
Delhi. It's part of the courtesy expected of those who have
taken their finals at Pharmacological to send birthday greetings to the institute's valued mascot.

But not even Maecenas is kept alive in gratitude for faith-
ful service or just for fun. When the dog gets up, Hasse sees
the implanted rubber tubes hanging down from its belly.
Every tube is closed with a screw-clamp. When the dog wags
his behind, the tubes wave like extra tails. But unlike the
regular tail, the rubber tails droop dejectedly.

"You 'n' me," says Hasse, scratching the dog under its
muzzle where the skin sticks together. "You 'n' me, we
oughta go places . . ."

The weight of his rump gets the upper hand. Without
meaning to, he sits down on the floor. The dog climbs out of
the basket and sits down next to him. Now they both sit there
with hanging heads, staring down into the empty basket.
Carefully Hasse puts his arm around Maecenas's shoulders.

"Listen," he says, "listen . . . I'm just a late bloomer, thass-
all. Like, I mean, some people have sort of a different life
curve 'n others. Like, some kinds of trees grow slower. Yes.
Oak!" he exclaims proudly, thumping his chest.

He turns his face to the dog, which attentively directs its
sharp nose right against Hasse's nose. The dog has its mouth

12

half-open; the tongue wags against its teeth in time with its breathing.

Hasse notices he's sitting on something lumpy. He feels for it in his back pocket, and coming up with a flattened and crumbled piece of French bread, he breaks off a bit and stuffs it in his mouth. He chews on the dry bread and looks down at the dog basket again, as if somebody had just placed it before him without his noticing. I'm drunk, he thinks, and massages his forehead with the ragged end of the bread.

The dog begins to whine low and stir with its front paws. Hasse again puts his arm around his four-footed friend.

"Are you hungry?" he asks, and holds the bread under the dog's nose. But the dog doesn't want to take the bread. It turns its nose away as if offered something evil-smelling.

" 'Course you like *bones* . . ." says Hasse. "Nice, juicy . . . *marrow.* Yum-yum!"

He wets his lips and tries to get his tongue to hang out as far as Maecenas's. Then the dog gets up, walks under the window seat, and lies down behind a stool. It whines pitifully and scrapes its dull claws on the worn parquet.

"Get in your basket . . ." says Hasse; then he realizes that dogs must be handled with a certain firmness. He rises unsteadily and points into the basket: *"Sit!"*

There's a peculiar sound from the dog, who's lying out of sight beneath the window seat. A sobbing sound.

"Listen, Maecenas," says Hasse. "Some day you'll see! A birthday card's going to come to you 'n' it's going to be postmarked Sundbyberg 'n' it's going to be from *me!"*

He drops down on all fours and peers under the window seat. Maecenas has half-risen. On bending, rickety legs the dog stands there and vomits. Long convulsions advance from its belly forward. The tubes under its belly fill and stretch in time with the cramps.

Flickeringly—like a fluorescent tube lighting up—the realization dawns in Hasse's befuddled brain: I'm killing this dog! When the dog is waked up in the middle of the night and offered bread, all the juices and enzymes start bubbling out, there in the dogbelly. But this animal doesn't have its normal anatomy any more. Through ingenious operations, its normal

13

tracts and ducts have been detoured, linked up in parallel, or blocked off. The dog has been transformed into a milk cow that's stimulated by the sight of food and then can be tapped for its juices and secretions through the rubber teats.

He lies down on his stomach and tries to get at the dog, which presses itself backward into the gap between the window seat and the radiator. Hans Rubenick gropes for the clamps on the tubes under the dog's belly. He gets hold of a leg, he grasps the tail. The dog vomits on his cuff.

Quickly he sits up. Idiot! he thinks. Damn stupid fumbling idiot! What if I pull a tube loose—all the guts may come out along with it!

He gets to his feet, stuffs the bread in his back pocket, and tries to pick up some crumbs from the floor. Then he goes to the door, opens it, and turns out the light. Before he goes, he says apologetically, "Just like I promised, it's going to come . . . Remember: from Sundbyberg."

When Hans Kristian Rubenick returns to the Student Union, music can no longer be heard. Most of the torches have burned out and begun to freeze to the ground. He shudders when unexpectedly the Nobel Clock strikes two and all the silver vanes avert their faces from him.

4

Several days have passed since Lucia, the festival of light. It's Friday afternoon and the faculty are assembled in the meeting room of the Academic Council, which is very crowded. The rectangular table with the green billiard cloth can't accommodate all the professors. At the table itself sit the president, the head of administration, the chairman of the Labor-Management Committee (who in mufti is a laboratory animal caretaker), representatives of the employees' union and the professionals' association, and the delegate from the student body, as well as some twenty-five from the inner circle of professors.

The inner circle consists of representatives of the basic science disciplines in the Institutes, such as medical chemis-

THE ANIMAL DOCTOR

try, bioengineering, tumor biology, molecular physiology, radiohistology, and related subjects. It is the inner circle who have the best contacts with the Office of Education, the foundations, and UNESCO, and who actually give out the Nobel prize in medicine and physiology. It is no coincidence that the prize seldom falls to a representative of one of the more "diffuse" clinical subjects.

In a ring of chairs more loosely surrounding the table sit a mixture of newly appointed professors and professors in the "harder" clinical specialties, that is, internal medicine, surgery, gynecology, and diagnostic radiology. As the president puts it, this placement a short distance from the table is not to be regarded as any kind of discrimination; on the other hand, it cannot be denied that the presiding officer has a slightly harder time seeing and placing on the agenda those who sit in the disorder of the outer circle.

The third circle consists of professors who have been preserved, rolled out flat on canvas, varnished, framed, and hung on the wall. The portraits hang on several levels—it's as crowded as the walls of the officers' mess of a venerable crack regiment.

There's a fourth circle too: the window sills. There sit associate professors, acting professors, and representatives of the absolutely lowest rated subjects: child psychiatry and industrial hygiene.

This is an assembly under the pall of fatigue. During the autumn, all the usual trivialities of the agenda have had to be put aside in favor of the many intricate gyrations and bold advances of Nobel candidates. Then the members of the inner circle play against each other, making sudden alliances, falling out, finessing a point, delaying the vote, wielding sanctions, or insinuating favors. This game is followed by the outer circles, the public. That public which would love to join in and try its luck on the green baize cloth, but which has no chips. The Nobel sessions are concluded by the president's dealing out little casques containing medallions to all those present. Being present at a Nobel conclave is as weighty a matter as winning a national championship in orienteering or a district championship in competitive skeetshooting.

15

But today's assembly meets under the pall of fatigue. Uninteresting duties will be assigned, vacancies announced, messages answered, housekeeping reformed, and a complaint to the Ombudsman answered, in which a former employee claims that his thoughts have been recorded and are now on file in the Nobel Library's Data Search System.

The participants in the meeting sit there, their knees loaded with mimeos, folders, catalogs, dissertations, and writings that none, except possibly the person submitting them, has read, but that all, in democratic order, are going to take personal and insightful positions on.

The last point on the day's agenda is Other Business. A preannounced Other question is *What to do about the Institutes' veterinary medical problems?* It's a question that has come up a number of times over the last fifteen years. The whole thing began with an attack by some young "radicals" at the Veterinary College in Uppsala who, without incontrovertible evidence, declared publicly that a lot of the dissertations that came out of the Alfred Nobel Medical-Surgical Institutes ought to be rejected. The reason given—on very dubious grounds—was that many animal experiments were carried out by researchers who hadn't the faintest idea of experimental animals' behavior, normal or abnormal, sick or well. The doctors at NMSI were indicted for regarding animals as test tubes or litmus paper, as neutral experimental material without its own inherent physiology, psychology, or pathology.

Such a senseless attack obviously could only be met with the total silence of a united faculty. And that's what happened—though not without Solomon-like exertions by the president, who was obliged to calm down some hot-tempered colleagues. Colleagues who wished to wield counterfire and sanctions at once, maybe not publicly but via channels to the Research Council and the foundations. Or to quote one biochemist of Nobel caliber: "Don't let those goddam rat-doctors get a damned red cent in grants from here on in."

Some time later, the same question bobbed to the surface in the very highly respected journal *Science.* The article also brought out the fact that two of the finest American research institutions, the Mayo Clinic and Stanford University, had put veterinarians on staff specifically to keep the laboratory animals in good shape. This issue of *Science* was read with a certain skepticism and put aside.

Four years later, the NMSI auditors suddenly requested information on "the consumption of laboratory animals, broken down by consumption in connection with experiments and consumption in connection with other things, for example waste." A report was cooked up in which "involuntary consumption" was generally attributed to defects in the animals delivered. At that time, the Institutes still obtained large quantities of cats, rabbits, and dogs from small private operators and farmers in the trade.

The person who has revived the question of veterinary medical problems this afternoon is neither a recognized troublemaker nor a featherbrain, but the professor of pharmacology, who is on the verge of retirement. From his place right up at the table he says, "Maecenas died yesterday."

A murmur goes through the assemblage, a murmur of surprise and sympathy, and a giggle here and there from the younger group on the window sills.

"Naturally, this isolated occurrence is nothing more than one example," the professor of pharmacology continues. "It proves absolutely nothing. *But,* ladies and gentlemen, let us look upon it as a reminder that *the problem exists.*"

"Maybe it's time to do something about it," the president says. "During my last visit with Haberstein in San Diego, the question was put to me directly: *When* is NMSI going to establish a special chair of *Preventive Veterinary Medicine?*"

"Chair? Kiss my . . ." says the professor of thoracic surgery.

"Folksam Insurance isn't exactly the Ford Foundation," says the professor of chromatography.

"But we can't overlook the fact that the Institutes suffer serious financial losses because our lab animals don't get expert care," says the professor of bioengineering.

"You sit here and suggest we're publishing faulty experimental results!" says the professor of anatomy with such intensity that the president begins groping for the gavel, a gold-plated thighbone dating from the barbaric epoch of military surgery.

"No," says the professor of bioengineering. "So far I'm *only* talking about financial losses . . ."

"So far?! Whaddyoumean, so far?" demands the choleric anatomist. "What do you plan to propose next—that we rewrite all our dissertations?"

The question hangs in the air. After a few moments, it dissolves into a cloud of deliberation that slowly descends like tobacco smoke upon the green cloth.

"Let me advance a specific proposal," the president says. "I wish to propose that the faculty establish a working group, made up of a number of the graduate students who are assistants to professors, to look into the question more closely."

"On behalf of the student body, I object!" says the student delegate. "I reject even the thought of students being used for any unpaid labor of a nonscientific nature that has minimal potential for improving our qualifications!"

The president sighs and twists the thighbone gavel with Oscar I's personal greeting on it: "To Sweden's Military Surgeon Corps from its Royal Patron."

"We haven't got any money . . ." says the president, and stares gloomily out over the assembly.

The administrative chief, whose title is Department Head, pokes up his nicotine-yellow index finger with a certain embarrassment.

"Yes?" says the president, looking at the clock.

"I suggest we use the WOLMB budget," says the department head.

"WOLMB?" asks the president.

"LMB stands for Labor Market Board and WO for Women's. To get right to the point: LMB will pay the wages if NMSI gives work to an unemployed female college graduate who has reached the age of forty-nine no later than the year she is employed. The grant is made for twelve months at a time."

18

"May we assign the Administration Department to explore our chances of getting a female veterinarian here for free?" asks the president, and looks out over an absolutely silent and slightly skeptical assemblage.

Nobody answers, which is tantamount to consent.

DISSERTATION

1

It's one of the weekdays just before the Christmas season gets rolling, and it's not yet 8:00 A.M. Evy Beck climbs down from the express bus right at the entrance to the Nobel Institutes. The sky is purple and the lawns around the Institutes' buildings are as black as wet asphalt. A heavy mist hangs in the air, swathing all the streetlights in angel hair.

Evy Beck is fifty-two years old and a Doctor of Veterinary Medicine. She's done it the hard way: first lab assistant, then lab technician, and then, at the age of forty-four, veterinary doctor. She's never had a permanent position with regular advancement. Instead, she's managed to get along on research grants, as a temporary replacement, by taking miscellaneous assignments, and for the last sixteen months, on unemployment compensation.

Evy Beck has a nickname for herself, "Quotia." When she writes a letter to somebody she knows well, she signs it "Quotia." This morning, when the timer in the bed lamp turned it on at 6:00 A.M., she gave her brains a shake and said out loud to herself, "Up with you, Quotia. Old ladies have to have time to do their hair when they're going job-hunting!"

Nearly her whole adult life she's been part of one quota or another. A retraining quota, an education quota, an exemption quota. And when they called her late last week and said she could go up to the Nobel Institutes and let them look her over, she didn't ask, "Is it for a regular job?" Because even this time it was, of course, about a quota. A letter came yesterday confirming that the quota was called WOLMB, one

23

of LMB's selective techniques for getting women over forty-nine into the regular world of work.

She puffs up the long slope toward the administration center of NMSI. Astonished, she stops short before a silver-gleaming mobile that seems to be a metallurgical attempt at a perennial Christmas tree. It's eight o'clock and suddenly all the ornaments turn in the same direction.

Evy Beck takes a couple of turns around the lawn surrounding the goldfish pond. As usual, she's come too early. Not till eight fifteen will she meet Assistant Administrator Hörrlin for an employment interview. Inside her heavy brief case she has her transcript, her certificates, her publications, her dissertation, and four new passport photos. What she'll do with the photos, she doesn't know. She had them made just to be on the safe side.

At ten after eight, she goes into the Administration Building. The outer glass door is unlocked but the inner one doesn't budge. Between the doors, a microphone hangs from the ceiling. On the microphone it says: *Please give your name and whom you wish to see.* Evy Beck goes up to the microphone and says, "Evy Beck, to see Assistant Administrator Hörrlin."

"Do not understand," says the microphone with a slightly nasal synthetic voice.

That's just what she expected. She's tired to death of these door-telephones that rasp, *Do not understand, do not understand . . .* The trouble is, she has a rather deep voice for a woman. When she says her first name, "Evy," it's understood as feminine—but at the same time it's spoken by a voice that on a phonogram could be understood as masculine. In that case, the computer has to question, *Do not understand.* Feminine and masculine cannot coexist.

She sets her right index finger and thumb against her throat, presses lightly, and pipes in falsetto, "Evy Beck, to see Assistant Administrator Hörrlin."

"Step in and follow the green arrow!" the microphone raps out so quickly she hardly has time to finish her sentence.

A green arrow is blinking on the ceiling. She follows the arrow's direction and steps into a corridor to the right. The

24

arrow comes along, running along the ceiling just ahead of her, like the star leading the three wise men. Suddenly it stops. It is no longer blinking but instead shines steadily in red. Evy Beck is standing before a door marked 560314–0356 As. Ad. S. Hörrlin. A light in the doorframe flashes, "Come in."

The room is empty. It's a small room with a desk, a built-in file cabinet with hanging folders, a visitor's chair, and a metal cart with dictaphone, telephone, calculator, hot plate, and TV screen. She takes off her raincoat and lays it over the cart, then seats herself in the visitor's chair with her brief case on her knees.

When she's waited almost ten minutes, a tall, skinny, red-headed man comes in and shakes hands without looking her in the eye. He's somewhere over thirty, and his breath smells of coffee.

"Thanks for coming," he says, and tilts backward in his springy swivel chair; then he looks at her, but without seeing her. His eyes cross slightly, as when one sniffs at a flower or examines a bent paper clip.

Evy Beck fumbles at the straps of her brief case and Assistant Administrator Hörrlin looks at it with interest.

"Well, I brought along my papers," she says tentatively.

"Papers?" he says, and puffs out his cheeks.

"Yes, my transcripts and . . ."

"Look at my desk," says the administrator, and spreads his arms out over the empty surface. "Not a single paper!"

She leans forward and looks politely at the empty desk top. The surface is dark green and appears to be made of hard rubber. There is absolutely nothing on it: no pencil, no note-pad, no paper clip.

In his breast pocket, Assistant Administrator Hörrlin has a little black plastic box the size and shape of a cigarette pack. He fishes it out and presses it against his chin. The little box has a gleaming metal grid on top like an electric razor.

"May I have your I.D.?" he asks, and extends his free hand across the deserted desk top.

Evy Beck hands over the stiff little identification card, and Hörrlin slips it quickly into a slot on the bottom of the gadget.

25

It's not an electric razor, but a microphone; he blows into it a couple of times, as if trying out a trumpet, and says, "Hello, Personnel ADP! Display professional data on the screen!"

Beneath Evy Beck's raincoat—which she has dropped over the metal cart—a buzzing and crackling begins. Embarrassed, she snatches up the raincoat. The nine-inch screen on the cart is lighted up. First her identity number comes up in white; the figures are shown backwards. Then an unsteady picture that rolls a couple of times before it stops. They both sit there a few seconds looking at a five-year-old telephoto of Evy Beck.

She stares at the screen in fascination. She's heard that many places nowadays have a direct connection with a central data bank, but she's never actually seen it before.

After the photo come her blood group and a condensed health record, then weight and height: 196 pounds and 5 feet 8½ inches, respectively. The health record concludes with a body type: *athletic.* The assistant administrator clears his throat, a little embarrassed.

Then follow, in quick succession, school attendance, grades, experience, higher education, and job history. The title of her dissertation rolls up, in English. Then the machine seems to get stuck, for it blinks anxiously, like a failing neon sign: *Not offered teaching position, not offered teaching position, not offered teaching . . .*

"Thanks, ADP!" says Hörrlin into his microphone.

They face each other again, and again Hörrlin seems to lose his gaze somewhere among lifeless objects, though he's looking right at her.

"Do I fit the job?" she asks; absurdly enough, she speaks in falsetto, just as she did when addressing the door-telephone. She's embarrassed, and coughs to clear her throat.

"Of course, of course," he says, and continues to stare at her with his gray eyes that have no depth.

"Then I'm hired?" she asks.

Hörrlin picks up the microphone again and presses it like a shaver against his chin: "Evy Beck, access key C."

A little dull glass pane lights up beside the hot plate on the metal cart. Hörrlin holds up his right thumb and demonstrates with an exaggerated pedagogic gesture how she should put her own thumb against the glowing glass surface. She does it, a little hesitant, as if she's afraid of burning herself. But the glass is cold and darkens at once.

"Now you have access to all the locks that are marked with a big C," says the assistant administrator. "All you have to do is press your thumb against the eye-lock."

Before she stuffs her thumb back behind the brief case, she looks at it hastily, as if it's suddenly acquired a new and magical significance. It's a short, thick, not very feminine thumb.

There's no trick to holding the assistant administrator's gaze; his eyes look like a pair of flat cufflinks. She looks right at them and says, "What kind of work is it?"

For the first time, he seems a little confused—as if she'd just tried to tell a joke but spoiled the punchline.

"I'm just in charge of the employment interview itself," he says with a trace of apology.

"I see," says Evy Beck.

Assistant Administrator Hörrlin suddenly seems upset, and feels around on the desk top for a paper clip that doesn't exist.

"Don't get me wrong," he says emphatically. "You're going to get instructions, introductions, information, tours, visits, policy manual, personnel portfolio, maps, contact with the Recreation Association . . . We have a *very* progressive personnel policy here at NMSI!"

He swings around as if he were looking for material in the file cabinet behind him. He doesn't seem to find anything, but swivels around to the front again.

"My assignment is *only* the employment interview itself," he explains.

Three minutes later, she's standing outside the Administration Building again, looking at the silver mobile. I've got a job, she thinks, and shakes her head as if she didn't quite believe her own thoughts. Then she looks down at her heavy brief case: You're getting to be a scatterbrained old lady, Quotia! Bringing along passport photos when you're looking for a job.

27

2

Two days later, at three thirty in the afternoon, Evy Beck is standing there again, looking at the Nobel mobile's wind vanes, which stick out lazily in all directions under the floodlights. Some yards above the mobile, the cones of light are clipped off short by the December darkness, which lies like a huge sopping woollen blanket over the campus.

She has her brief case with her and has placed it between her feet to keep her from walking away. Her body is restless but the concrete block between her feet keeps her at anchor. She's supposed to meet the Labor-Management Committee at three thirty and doesn't want to arrive too early—not wishing to seem anxious.

Her watch shows thirty-three past, but it's usually set a little ahead—for safety's sake. She watches the mobile and expects it to strike. Her feet twitch and she drives the tips of her shoes in under the brief case.

Her watch now shows thirty-five past, but still the mobile doesn't strike. Then she realizes that it doesn't strike on the half-hour; her heart leaps into her throat and hits the base of her skull, bong! She almost falls over the brief case. Regaining her balance, she sets out almost at a run toward Lindgården. Lindgården is the name of an old red farmhouse with a Dutch roof and white corners. Right up to 1913 there was still a farm here.

Lindgården is the Labor-Management Committee's own building and the only wooden structure on the NMSI campus. She scoots around the corner of the library and into the grove of closely grown lilac bushes surrounding the crooked, warped, and tottering cottage. The door is standing open and she springs into the vestibule. From outside, Lindgården looks as though it will fall to pieces in the next autumn storm, but inside, the building is slickly renovated. The walls of the vestibule are covered with

28

coated burlap stiff enough to function as load-bearing construction.

She tears off her overcoat and scarf and steps into the room to the left. There, in the living room, three men are sitting by a long table that takes up almost all the floor. They get up and shake hands.

"Department Head Håkan Rosenquist, in charge of administration. How do you do!"

"Lab Animal Caretaker Edwin Karlsson, chairman of the Labor-Management Committee. Welcome!"

"Hakvin Hansen, student representative. Hi!"

"Hi," she answers a little bit lamely, and sinks down in a chair at a little distance from the rest.

The three men sit with their hands folded before them on the table. All three smile.

"This house is called Lindgården," says the chairman of the committee, nodding at her encouragingly. "Here, you're always welcome. This is *our* house. The employees'."

Evy Beck wonders fleetingly whether there are others besides employees at NMSI, but doesn't ask.

"Well . . ." says the department head. "How nice that you could come."

He smiles, and she feels that if they don't stop smiling soon she's going to get a facial cramp, not being very practiced.

"So. We three are the Working Panel of the Labor-Management Committee," continues Rosenquist. "It's we who hire people here at NMSI."

"But I'm on the WOLMB budget," says Evy Beck, afraid of presenting herself under the wrong label.

"That's just a question of bookkeeping," says the department head. "Everybody's here on one kind of appropriation or another."

"Then it's all arranged," she asks. "It's all set that I'm to work here?!"

"But of course," says the department head, and looks smilingly at his comrades. "You are absolutely one of us now," he emphasizes, winking meaningfully at her.

Relieved, she leans back in the chair and presses her brief

case against her stomach; the stomach she is always trying to hold in. Either with her hands, with a book, with a brief case, or by buttoning her coat too tight. The hard, solid stomach that really has looked the same ever since she gave birth to Erik, twenty-seven years ago. She sees Erik's face before her, a smooth tanned face with absolutely frank blue eyes and a deep cleft in the broad chin. Erik dear, she thinks, now Mama's gone and got herself a job . . .

She gives a start; Hakvin Hansen is standing right behind her, and places a typed paper on the table before her. The paper is ornamented with the emblem of NMSI, a laurel wreath with a medallion of Alfred Nobel in its center. Nobel's head is mounted on the snake-entwined rod of Aesculapius —as on a spit. She reads:

ORIENTATION PROGRAM
FOR DR. EVY INGA-BRITT BECK, D.V.M.

First Day   General introduction. Visit with the President. Tour.

Second Day   Briefing by the Chief Safety Officer. Visit with the Chief Librarian.

Third Day   Review of social benefits. Luncheon for new employees. Security regulations.

Fourth Day   Film on History of the Institutes.

She lays the paper down again.

"When do I really get down to work?" she asks.

"Get down to work?" says the department head. He has stopped smiling at last.

Karlsson, the lab animal caretaker, is smiling now with only one corner of his mouth, and shifts uneasily in his seat. Hakvin Hansen takes over.

"Getting oriented is *part of* your job. The first two weeks are a very carefully thought-out preparation. It's something that will benefit you many times over in the future."

"Oh!" she says, and is deeply ashamed.

The chairman of the committee clears his throat: "We've fought for many years to get this, to get sensible orientation procedures."

"Aw, you don't have to dramatize it," says the department head. "Fought? We, the administration and the personnel,

30

have *jointly* fought to get money for it from the Office of the Chancellor of the Swedish Universities."

"Well, y'know, I'm really not so used to getting employed," Evy Beck essays.

All three laugh deprecatingly, after which the department head tries to sneak a look at his watch; he plucks his coat sleeve as if to remove a hair.

"We-e-ll," says Hakvin Hansen, pressing his palms together and propping up his nostrils on the tips of his middle fingers. "Did you have any questions?"

"I think you're going to get answers to all the questions you can possibly think of when you go through the orientation program," clarifies Karlsson.

Evy Beck looks at the three men. They have shown clearly that the meeting is over, but perhaps she dares to keep them just a minute longer.

"Maybe I'm a little stupid," she says, "but I haven't quite understood, really, what my work is going to be about."

The department head now looks openly at his watch, and then glances quickly at the other two.

"A good question," he says, and feels whether his chin is properly shaved. "A good question."

Edwin Karlsson and Hakvin Hansen are now looking down at their knees as if they were deeply absorbed in an urgent memorandum that had to be read through right away during the course of the meeting.

"Maybe I'm bringing it up too early?" she says, prepared to take it back.

"One ought to try to distinguish between *introduction* and *instruction,*" says Rosenquist with friendly but teacherly emphasis. "So far, we've been talking about introduction, that is to say, a general orientation concerning your working environment. What instruction comprehends, then, is, in much more detail, what you, in particular, are expected to do . . ."

"Yes?" asks Evy Beck.

"And that's not the Working Panel's bag. *We*'re not specialists, *we* can't interpret your working assignment from a lot of veterinary-medical angles."

31

"Veterinary-medical angles?"

"Yes, for crying out loud," says the department head teasingly. "Surely you understand that if they've brought someone like you here it must, for pete's sake, have something to do with *animals.*"

MEMORANDUM TO ADP CENTRAL DATABANK
CLASSIFIED INFORMATION OFFICIAL USE ONLY
OBSERVER ASST ADMINISTR S HORRLIN NMSI
KEYWORD EVY INGA-BRITT BECK WOLMB
CONTINUOUS WORK REVIEW 1
VERBAL REPORT B HAS GONE THRU EMPLOYMENT I
NTERVIEW ORIENTATION GOTTEN SETTLED APPEAR
S POSSIBLY SOMEWHAT OVERAMBITIOUS INTENTIO
N NOW TO ALLOW B OBTAIN OWN OVERVIEW FOR
BREAKING IN ON ASSIGNMENT ANTICIPATED DIFFIC
ULTIES WITHHOLDING PROGNOSIS BECAUSE OF SH
ORT TIME EMPLOYED
RATING 1–5
COMPETENCE 4
ADAPTABILITY 3
SOLIDARITY 4
MOTIVATION 5
COST NONE

3

It's Sunday, the nineteenth of December. Evy
Beck is visiting her father in Roslagstull Hospital. Papa sits in
a wheelchair and presses his cheek against the headrest. He
doesn't look right at her, just gives her sidelong glances from
profile. His head is skinny and bald, his nose, long and
pointed. His nose goes down so far that he has a hard time
raising his upper lip over his teeth. When he talks, it's out of
the corner of his mouth.

"Job??" he says. "What the hell kind of job?"

She's glad to hear his prickly, aggressive voice. Papa's on
the road to recovery. He's not so yellow-skinned any more,
either.

He sits and mutters and rubs his chin against the little
pillow and looks out the window. Then he nods sagely, as if
he was really talking with somebody else about his daughter
Evy—some invisible but sensible person sitting on the window sill.

"A job?? Can it be she's got a job??" he says with the
deepest suspicion.

She notices that his ears have gotten longer. The lobes
hang down like flat wax teats. Long narrow ears that are
beginning to bend back are a sure sign of age in men. Papa's
just had his seventy-ninth birthday. The knuckles on his blu-
ish hands stand out like the teeth of a cogwheel. He sits there
pressing his knuckle-cogs together, meshing them up and
down, up and down.

"Papa . . ." she says cautiously and not daring to pat him
on the hand, "Papa, you really do look a little more chipper."

"Bullshit!" he wheezes, looking at her sharply with one
little black eye. Not even now does he turn his face to her.
On the contrary, he presses his hip against the wheelchair as
if he would really prefer to turn his back on his daughter.

"Maybe you could get leave for the holidays?" she asks.

He doesn't answer. Instead, he winks at his invisible sym-
pathizer on the window sill; winks craftily, as if confirming

34

a now fully revealed conspiracy to evict him from Roslagstull Hospital.

Silently and carefully she lays the bag of grapes on the wheelchair's book rest. He won't show any interest in the grapes so long as she's there. But the nurse has told Evy that as soon as she's out the door the old man gobbles them up, spitting seeds over half the room.

"What can she, a veterinarian, do that is socially useful?" he questions the window sill.

"You already know, Papa," she says quietly. "I've explained a thousand times that veterinarians inspect foods, do lab tests, and keep watch for disease carriers among animals . . ."

"A thousand?" he says. "How can you be sure it's *exactly* one thousand times?"

"Many times," she corrects herself.

"So somebody, we won't say who, hasn't got the least grain of comprehension? Has to have every little thing explained *one thousand* times?!"

"Not a thousand. But sometimes more than *once.* Probably I'm a poor explainer."

"Worthless," he declares, with the grace of someone conferring an undeserved compliment.

She smiles, hoping he won't notice. Now old Papa's on his way back to health. No longer the voiceless and deep yellow-colored bundle she's seen lying on the bed these last months. He's got back that gleam in his eye, too. Not exactly a rascally gleam, more like the intensive glow of the chronically persecuted.

"Babysit house-pets, that's what you might be able to do."

"It's a position at the Alfred Nobel Medical-Surgical Institutes."

"Alfred Nobel Medical-Surgical Institutes," he repeats with heavy emphasis, extending one blue hand toward his invisible companion in the window. "Ha!" he says then, overcome, and declares that his daughter has finally reached the absolute bottom.

But she knows he's curious now—the eye narrows uneasily in its socket.

"The so-called Nobel Prize," he pronounces. "The lackeys of capitalism wiping each other's asses with thousand-dollar bills."

"Medical progress can't be made unless someone makes sure the lab animals live under hygienic conditions," she tells him.

"Is that what you'll be doing? Shoveling rat shit and cleaning cages?"

"I really don't know yet. Not in detail."

"Don't know? She really doesn't know!" he says, smiling at the window. "My daughter goes and takes a job without even knowing what it is. Godalmighty!"

There's a knock on the door.

"Yass, come in!" bawls the old man with unsuspected strength, though without turning his face away from the window.

Erik walks in. Erik Beck, Evy's son and Rodion Beck's grandson.

"Hi, Evy. Hi, Grandfather," says Erik, advancing.

Erik is a very well-turned-out young man. Perfect suit of short camelhair, necktie shining discreetly. Cuffs extending precisely one and a half inches below the sleeve. In the right-hand cufflink a little watch with a curved magnifying lens over it. Erik Beck is twenty-seven years old and a Doctor of Technology. He's six feet tall, crewcut, close-shaven, and well-modulated. Evy Beck loves her son, and yet: How could *I*, bloated frog, have given birth to this perfect creature?

Grandfather undergoes an instant transformation. He turns and slides down in the wheelchair and fondly stretches out both hands to Erik. Now his bone-hard old man's face is softened. His eyes beam warmth. The corners of his mouth rise up on each side of the pointed hanging-down nose.

"Sonny!" he cries. "Come here, Sonny!"

Erik bends politely over Grandfather and gets clapped eagerly on both lightly padded shoulders.

"You look peppy," he says.

"Poo!" says the old man, making light of it. "I'm not quite dead yet."

Erik turns to his mother and pats her quickly, absentmind-

36

edly on the cheek. It's the kind of a pat an older person gives, while thinking about something else, to someone of lesser years and tenderer understanding.

"Well, Erik," she tells him proudly. "I've got myself a job."

"Congratulations, Evy," he says, and puts out his right hand.

She takes his hand between both of hers and holds onto it. His appearance is strange to her, his voice is strange, his maturity is strange. There must be something left—maybe the feel of his skin?

Erik coughs lightly so as to have reason to take back his hand and use it for something else, to cover his mouth.

"Great," he says. "Really great that they're using the WOLMB budget for something sensible."

No one has said a word about the WOLMB budget. But she knows you can't fool Erik. Erik knows everything. Erik has no illusions. Erik's never surprised. Erik, who is a Doctor of Technology and Assistant Professor of Budget Technology at the National Institute of Technological Economics.

"Sensible?!" says the old man. "How d'you know she's going to do anything *sensible?!*"

Erik goes up beside the wheelchair and lays his hand, still tanned from his vacation, on the old man's bald head. Grandfather's tight jaw muscles slacken immediately.

"How's it going with the liver, Grandfather?" asks Erik. "Have you tried it out yet?"

"No. The chief physician said it had some bugs in it. They had to ship it back to the factory."

Rodion Beck starts rolling up the hospital gown, which is far too big for him. A wrinkled yellowish-brown belly appears. The navel protrudes. To the right of the stomach, under the rib cage, two tubes are sticking out. The bases of the tubes are wound in gauze. The right tube is marked with a broad red arrow pointing inward. The left tube has a blue arrow pointing outward.

"It itches," the old man tells them, and plucks at the gauze.

"Please, Papa. Don't pick at it," says Evy.

Erik doesn't say anything. Instead, he strokes the old man's bald dome with the back of his hand. The old fellow drops

37

the tubes and lets his arms slide down over his belly. He ends up sunk down in the wheelchair with knees ajar and eyes half-shut.

"You're not in a rush, Erik?" Evy asks.

Rodion Beck's eyes darken at once with three shades of mistrust.

"Naturally he's in a rush! Erik can't squander his time like just anybody."

"As a matter of fact, *I've* got to rush today," says Evy, starting to get up from her chair.

"You??!" says her father, gaping so wide that his shiny, thin-skinned old man's tongue shows—then he recovers, and sees his opening: *"We* won't keep you! Not when you're in a little-bitty bit of a hurry for once!"

She goes to the wheelchair and leans over toward his cheek. But she stops in time. Stops before Papa falls into a fit of rage because she is leading a conspiracy with the express purpose of attacking him with a kiss on the cheek. Instead, she lightly pats the armrest of the wheelchair.

"Okay, Papa. Take care," she says.

Erik leans forward and, wind-swift, grazes both her cheeks with his nose.

"Keep well," he says. "Good luck with the job!"

She leaves the room with Eric's aftershave lotion in her nostrils: lemon, salt water, and a hint of leather? Before shutting the door she turns and waves. Erik waves back indulgently. But Papa doesn't see her. He's engaged in hauling in Erik's lion-yellow jacket sleeve to pull the boy down beside him in the chair.

4

I'm free, Evy Beck bangs out on the typewriter, using her index fingers. *A middle-aged matron without obligations, passions, or aspirations . . . Homely, healthy, fat, free, and willing to work.*

She's sitting in her two-room apartment in a twenty-year-old building facing Roslag Street. On the balcony, a vacuum-dried Christmas tree pokes up in its plastic bag. Just in case Papa should, after all, accept Christmas leave—or Erik should not, after all, go away to Florida on Christmas vacation.

"Free?" she says out loud and quickly X's out what she's written.

Instead, she hammers out: *What does NMSI expect of me?* She lets her index fingers glide lightly down the edges of the keys; it sounds like running your fingers across a xylophone. Beside the typewriter stands a bottle of white port wine. She half-fills a tumbler and sips.

Has any goal been formulated? she types next, while the sweetness ebbs on her tongue. *Or have I been hired just to shut somebody up?* She crosses out *to shut somebody up* and types instead, *for tactical reasons?* She takes a swallow of port wine and composes: *What resources are going to be placed at my disposal?*

"Idiot!" she says half-aloud. "Asking about resources when you don't even know the goal."

But what if it's true, she thinks, that you have to cut the coat to fit the cloth? What if first you scraped together some small resources, and then you looked around for the place they could best be applied? She pushes away the thought and decides firmly to: *Press them for what they're really after!!* Press whom? she thinks with resignation.

To the left of the typewriter she has a pile of professional journals she has borrowed from the library of the Veterinary College. They are *The Vet Journal, Acta Mammalia, Swedish Veterinary Medical Journal, Science,* and the *Vertebral Gazette.* She counts the journals and lays them aside. If she opens them, she'll be swamped. Ten thousand problems will pop out and clamor for immediate attention, like so many greedily gaping beaks of baby birds.

The number of conceivable problems is unlimited, she types out. Seeing as they haven't hired me for any specific institute, she thinks, the point must be that I'm going to have some kind of general assignment, something that affects many or most parts of NMSI. For example, it may concern small species as disease carriers; or how one can eliminate the risk of allergy in people who come in contact with lab animals. And then, too, it might concern the problem of selecting among incoming lab animals. Or the setting up of a standard of weight and size. Or maybe breeding—how can one most quickly inbreed thirty generations of rats?

She drinks a little wine and writes: *First, overview; then, choosing priorities.* It looks a little silly, like a first-grade reader. She poises her right index finger, about to X it out— no! It *is* a first-grade kind of thing. All the obvious logical questions that usually get passed by. Much misery is caused not by missing subtleties, but by neglecting the obvious.

"Quotia," she says to herself, and yawns heedlessly. "It's just as well you toddle off to bed now, Quotia, and go to sleep. Before you get absolutely unbearable . . ."

She drinks the rest of the wine, turns off the lamp, takes the glass with her out to the dishwasher. Then she goes into the bathroom, pees, brushes her teeth, walks back into the bedroom, gets undressed, sets the lamp to go on at six thirty, climbs into bed, tucks one pillow under her cheek, and hugs the other.

Then the telephone rings. Papa! she thinks, snatching up the receiver.

"Dr. Beck?" a sprightly male voice inquires.

"Yes, this is Evy Beck."

"Mats Sundell here! Hope I didn't wake you?"

"Oh, no," she answers.

"I happen to be professor of naval medicine. We have a monkey here who's giving us some trouble."

"At NMSI?"

"What?!" he asks confusedly, as if she had asked whether he was calling from Skansen Zoo.

"You said you've had some trouble with a monkey," she says.

"Right. Your name's given in the Nobel Notices. It says there you've started taking on our veterinary medical problems . . ."

"Not exactly," she says. "The whole thing is still in the planning stage."

"Oh, hell," he says, disappointed.

40

"What symptoms has the animal got?' she asks. "Has the patient eaten today? Drunk?"

"Oh, sure. But he refuses to get into the pool."

She begins to get the picture: naval medicine, pool, reluctant monkey.

"Does he have to?" she asks. "Does he have to get into the pool right now?"

"Yes, for crissakes, that's what he's here for. We've been preparing for it since right after lunch."

She looks at the clock that's set into the center of the telephone dial: 1:13 A.M.

"Naval Medicine? Professor Mats Sundell?" she says. "I'd better come over, then."

He puts down the receiver at once, as they do in American movies. No "thanks," "good-bye," or "great."

5

Twenty minutes later, she's paying the taxi outside the Institute of Aviation and Naval Medicine. She walks up the steps to the door, stamps the wet snow off her boots, and presses her thumb against the eye-lock. Nothing happens. The eye-lock is clearly marked with a C.

"Damn," she says, and looks around for a doorbell; there is none. She dries off her thumb with a handkerchief and once again presses it against the eye-lock. Nothing. She retraces her steps to the pool of light under the streetlight. When she scrutinizes her thumb, it looks just as usual . . . Then she understands: Left thumb! If you're lefthanded, you put your left thumb against the lock. But the lock's only programmed for right thumbs.

She unlocks the door and enters the foyer. Surely they could have sent somebody out to show her the way. She runs her eye down the building directory: Professor, Prof. Secy., Prof. Laboratory, Elec. Control Room, Dolphin Aquarium . . . *Diving Tank*. She turns to follow the arrow that points toward the Diving Tank.

She goes down long, empty, well-polished corridors. A few

steps up, a new corridor, a few steps down. This labyrinth of corridors must have resulted from several more or less unplanned additions made at different times. She swings around a corner and enters the airlock of a big air-supported tent. When she goes through the door, heavy, damp, chlorinated air hits her.

Evy Beck stands in the big tent and feels like the prophet inside the whale's belly. The walls of the belly are olive drab, and they expand and contract lightly in time with the breathing sound of the fans. In the middle of the tent is a covered tank. Around the sides of the tank are ladders and bracing cables. Next to it is a little building that looks like an igloo of armor plate. Outside the igloo are two directors' chairs. In one sits a man in a white coat, in the other, a young chimpanzee in a scuba suit; the monkey's eating a banana.

"Hello," says the man in the chair and raises his hand limply; he doesn't get up.

She goes up and shakes his hand.

"I'm Evy Beck," she says.

Professor Sundell is about her own age. A well-barbered man with tinted glasses in gold-plated frames, a gold watch, and two rings on his left hand.

The chimpanzee begins to whine, and stretches out an unnaturally long right arm to pull on her coat.

"Jocke wants to say hello, too," says Professor Sundell.

She takes Jocke's rough hand and opens her mouth to introduce herself, but stops in time.

"Let the lady sit down, Jocke," says Sundell.

The monkey swings over to the professor, seats itself on his knee, and glowers at her when she takes its chair.

She judges the monkey's age to be about three years. It's dressed in a black scuba-diving suit of thick rubber. On its feet it has long black flippers, which it sits and pulls on. Around its neck hang diving goggles and an expandable black tube. But what catches her attention is the monkey's scalp. Sticking up in the middle of its skull, which in shape and texture looks like an unshelled coconut, is a white plastic plug. The plug is square and about an inch on each side.

Evy Beck leans over toward the monkey and looks into the

plug. It is pierced with many small round, hexagonal, or oval holes. In the holes is a glint of brass contacts. She knows at once what this means: the chimpanzee's brain is full of hair-fine silver electrodes. Through the plug, a weak electric current can be sent to the various brain centers. The monkey smells of rubber and the professor has the same aftershave lotion as Erik: lemon, salt water, and leather.

"I think it's something mental," says Sundell, and scratches Jocke under the chin.

"Mental?" she says. "I thought his mind was under control."

"Monkeys are tricky devils. No matter how many wires you stick into their skulls, there's still a tiny bit of willfulness left. Squeezed up under the edge of some bone."

"What am I supposed to do about that?" she asks wearily.

"Well, you're a *vet.*"

"What do you want? For me to come here in the middle of the night, look down the monkey's throat, and give a diagnosis?"

"Forgive me," he says. "Please forgive me. I'm asking the impossible."

Professor Sundell looks beaten-down and worn-out, as though the gold-plated glasses, the gold watch, and the rings have lost their grip on him.

"I don't have very much experience with chimpanzees," she says. "But I could check with someone in Stockholm who's worked with monkeys. Tomorrow morning early. You might also consider taking Jocke in to the Veterinary College in Uppsala for observation."

"Listen, I *am* sorry I asked you to come out here in the middle of the night."

He lays his hand on her coat sleeve. It's a small hand with pretty, square nails. It could be a young man's hand were it not for the veins as thick and twisting as the roots of a tree.

"Maybe it isn't Jocke who's the main problem?" she suggests.

He doesn't answer, but takes his glasses off and rubs his eyes. Jocke snatches up the glasses, puts them on, and peers through them at Evy Beck.

43

"Go and play!" says Sundell.

The chimpanzee climbs down from his knee with the tinted glasses still on. Quickly he lopes away on his knuckles over the floor to the ladder leading up to the pool. Jocke pulls off the flippers and claps them together, like a sea lion. Then he swings himself up on the nearest cable, hops onto the roof of the pool, and disappears from sight.

"No, it isn't Jocke who's the problem," says Sundell, looking helplessly at her with naked gray eyes. "Probably it's me who's off the track. And when Jocke notices that I'm out of sorts, he gets worried. He doesn't trust me. And then he refuses . . . The last time I was divorced, I had a dolphin that didn't perform. They're damned sensitive creatures."

The heavy port wine has nearly evaporated now. Evy Beck feels clearheaded.

"Maybe *you* know what NMSI had in mind for this veterinary setup?" she asks.

"No. I was absent from the meeting. I'm not so eager to show my face there nowadays. Probably somebody just got a bright idea."

"Like what?"

He doesn't answer. Instead, he sits and stares with widened eyes, trying to get his eyeballs out of his skull again after just having rubbed them into their sockets.

"The trouble is," he says, "we've been robbed of our motivation. For thirty years I've worked on submarines and how you get people out of 'em . . . Then suddenly Parliament says, Now we're not going to have any more submarines! It feels like they've let the air out of you. Not just that: the appropriation disappears. You're not worth anything any more. Soon you'll have to be thankful if your colleagues even say good morning to you."

He leaps up, enumerating on his fingers one by one: "I've built up this institute. Eleven doctor's diplomas I've held in these hands. I've had four scheduled double lectures during the physiology course . . . And now? Only idiots apply to this institute. I am fifty-three years old. I have no desire to go out and lie down on the trash pile yet! Or hold lectures on the history of medicine, like those other sway-backed professors and senile doctors."

Evy Beck ends up sitting there until three thirty in the morning. It turns out that while Professor Sundell is baring his sorrows, Jocke has quietly and purposefully disassembled the diving tank's intricate feedback system for automatic pressure regulation.

6

She's seen the chief physician of Roslagstull Hospital only once before. That was when she learned that they would have to take out Papa's liver.

"You *are* a veterinarian, Mrs. Beck," says the chief physician, and picks at his nails with a letter opener.

"How is my father really doing?" she asks.

"You can see for yourself," he tells her. "As full of sparks as Lucifer."

She gets a little offended on Papa's behalf. Papa is mean—but she doesn't like outsiders pointing it out.

"So now he's ready to go home," says the chief physician, and taps his forehead with the handle of the letter opener.

"Home?"

"He can't stay here. As soon as we've checked out the apparatus, he can get along all right at home."

"He hasn't got a home to go to," she says. "He hasn't had a fixed address since Mama died. He's just traveled around giving lectures. Lived in hotels or stayed with supporters."

"Lectures on what?" asks the chief physician.

"Papa has always been politically active," she says.

The chief physician scratches his neck with the letter opener and looks annoyed.

"We've taken for granted all along that you'd take care of your father after his release. Otherwise we would have put him on a waiting list for a convalescent home. Now he hasn't even got a place on the waiting list."

"What does he want, himself? Has he said?"

45

"We-e-ell, probably nobody's exactly asked him. But if a man has a daughter who's single, has a two-room apartment, has a medical education, and is in good health . . ."

"And what if I'd been his *son* instead?"

The chief physician doesn't answer. He waits impassively until the question dissolves of itself, as if it had been written in smoke rings.

"Papa will never agree to it!" she says.

"Oh, yes," says the chief physician. "Oh, yes, Mrs. Beck."

"I have a job to do," she says, and stares hard at the letter opener to get him to put it away; he has worked it into the top buttonhole of his lab coat and is balancing it like a scale.

The chief physician stretches over to reach a pile of computer print-outs. The knife slips out of the buttonhole and clatters to the floor. He lets it lie, and begins to unfold the data sheets.

"In the patient's record, it says you have no regular employment. Census records aren't usually wrong."

"On the first of December I had no job. Now I have."

The chief physician takes a thick lead pencil out of a special case in his breast pocket. He makes some marks on the record.

"Now we're up to date," he says, then raises his eyebrows. "But still single?"

"Yes, still," answers Evy Beck.

The chief physician sucks in his upper lip and folds the print-out's paper concertina back together. Then he takes a pencil and begins to draw, explaining pedagogically: "A mechanical liver functions in a way similar to an artificial kidney. It takes out of the blood the substances a normal liver takes care of. The patient needs to be connected to it only at night. During the day, he can move around freely."

"What happens to the liver's function as a storage place for sugar? And for blood?"

"Oh yes. You're a veterinarian . . ."

He lifts neither his eyes nor his pencil, but continues to draw. He's drawing on a big envelope imprinted UPJOHN MASTERPIECES OF THE RENAISSANCE, SERIES III.

"The blood reservoir he can do without. Blood sugar usu-

46

ally stabilizes after a few months. Of course, he has no re-serves of strength. Mustn't go up stairs, among other things. He's getting pills that replace the bile."

"Will he need constant attention?"

"Then you're prepared to take him home?"

She sighs, resigned.

"Nobody's ever put Rodion Beck any place he didn't want to be."

"Oh, yes," says the chief physician.

"I suppose he has to have a special diet, too?"

"Exactly, Mrs. Beck. I'll give you a special cookbook de-signed for those with liver problems."

The chief physician takes a thin pamphlet out of his desk drawer and tosses it in front of her. The pamphlet is called *An Invitation to Dine, from the Chef at Merck.* She takes it, realizing that now she's given in: she's taken Merck's chef to her bosom.

"Then we'll release him the day after tomorrow," says the chief physician. "We'll send out a technician from Westing-house to install an Auto-Hepar. Your wall plugs will have to be grounded. And you'll also need a filter on your TV cir-cuit."

"I don't have a TV," says Evy Beck. "You'll talk with Papa?"

"Won't you do that yourself?" he asks, looking weighed down with responsibilities.

"Oh, no, he'll get mad."

"Well, I'll try to get the social worker or the physical thera-pist to prepare Mr. Beck, then," he tells her. "Is there any-body home during the day who can let the technician in?"

"No, no one's home during the day," she responds, holding back her irritation.

"Regularly employed and living alone," he says, and nods.

"And the prognosis?" she asks.

He looks at her a long time, as if estimating what she can take.

"You must find it odd to be asking that. As a *veterinarian.*"

"Will he be able to last another six months? Or till next Christmas?"

The chief physician doesn't answer, but sucking in his upper lip again, lifts his hands almost as if to give the question back to her; then he lets them fall heavily back to the arms of his chair.

7

Fairy tales are long-lived. There's an old and widespread tradition that on one night in the year the dumb animals gain the gift of speech. The dream that Evy Beck dreams seems to be in technicolor:

Late on Christmas Eve, the temperature suddenly drops a couple of degrees and the rain and sleet of the preceding days become a soundless cloud of wafting feathers. Snow flutters down upon the Alfred Nobel Medical-Surgical Institutes, covering the roofs, padding the bushes and trees, and spurting thick strands on banisters and window sills.

In the stable behind the Immunological Institute, the serum horses stand stamping in the straw, while the cynomolgus monkeys and rhesus monkeys slumber in the calf pen, intertwined. Around midnight, the temperature sinks farther and it stops snowing; when the snow-curtains open, a new-washed purple sky appears. The star of Christmas takes its place just above the stable.

The rabbits over at the Chemicum start semaphoring with their ears. There are Flemish giants, New Zealand whites, French lops, silver-grays, English checkereds, blue-and-tans, and some other varieties. Like eager able seamen, they signal each other: "Silent night, holy night," the message goes. "Let us gather in the stable!"

The dolphins over at Aviation and Naval Medicine cruise around in their aquarium. They squeak and crackle to each other like excited ham operators: "Able to Baker, Able to Baker: A child is born this night. Come!"

The Pharmacological Institute is crowded; in no other institute do so many animals work. Even in the sixties, the cat kennel was too small and the cats had to move out to the three retired circus wagons in the rear of the institute. The bright colors on the sides of the wagons faded long ago, but tonight the frost comes and draws out the old designs—the ice crystals are attracted like iron filings to old suns and constellations, whirling parasols and tossing waves.

The cats begin to purr and hum to each other, soon blending into a swaying Negro choir from the Mississippi delta: "Oh Lord Jesus! Oh Lord Jesus . . . Oh my Holy Lord!"

The dogs inside the main building at Pharmacological get restless over the cat concert. A dachshund with two heads begins to bark like a badly tuned up two-cycle motor. But then the chairman of the canine chamber—a Saint Bernard —rises in all his stately bulk. Under his throat is a little cask that draws saliva through a plastic tube driven into the salivary duct. In a rumbling bass voice, the huge dog says to the two-headed dachshund, "Tonight all beasts are brothers. On this night, there's no difference between dog and cat, between wolf and lamb!"

It's as if Walt Disney's magic wand whirled among the institutes like a Fourth-of-July sparkler. The sheep in the cellar of Anatomical are waked, combed, and lined up to go tripping over to the manger in the serum horses' stable.

The sticklebacks in the aquarium at Physiological suddenly notice that legs are growing out from under their bellies: little red tubelike legs with three-cornered webbed feet. Gills flapping, they start a slothlike progress up the glass walls.

The tar-painted rats in Tumor Biology find themselves fitted out in stocking caps, short pants, and green patent-leather boots. They rise up on their hind legs, grasp each other's hands, and spread out in a dancing row like a long paper cutout of Santa Clauses.

Disney's magic wand hovers like a sparkling dragonfly over the Nobel mobile and the goldfish in the heated pond. The dull fishy faces come to life, the lips thicken and pout, long wavy eyelashes grow out above their eyes, and the pupils grow as big as portholes. The goldfish girls wiggle their tails coquettishly, and modestly cross their breast-fins over their bosoms like tender little mermaids.

The pigeons in the Stress Laboratory suddenly stop pecking at the blinking instrument panels. Instead, they crane their slender necks together, puff up their feathers, and coo: "Peace, peace be with you!"

Joy bubbles up among the tens of thousands of creatures, among the white rats, the Syrian golden hamsters, the beagles, the baboons, the NMPI-mice, the green guenon monkeys, the ducks, the Vietnamese miniature pigs, the lizards, and the tiny marmoset monkeys. They form into lines, collect in groups, herds, and delegations to burst the doors, the gates, and the lids, and march in procession to the stable with the winking star on its roof.

But in every animal area, in every loft, in every cellar and rat closet there are microphones and surveillance cameras. All the wires converge at a central watch station, where a single night watchman sleeps with his head on his hands. Alert!! The night watchman—an inexperienced one because this is Christmas Eve—reaches out sleepily and picks up the phone to Central Command's automatic telephone-answerer.

"Phase One—extra rations! Phase One—extra rations!" rasps a voice in his ear.

"Thanks," says the night watchman to the telephone-answerer, because he's inexperienced.

Then he presses the button for release of extra rations. And in all the cages, boxes, pens, and aquariums the automatic feeders spew out a storm of brown rice, hemp seeds, soybean meal pellets, dried larvae, Grix, dog biscuits, live shrimp, and concentrated fodder. All the animals eat, belch, and doze off in the holy night. The Nobel mobile strikes one and the silver vanes gleam in the cold. After that, it becomes utterly still.

Evy Beck wakes up drenched in sweat. Then she is seized with a deep thankfulness that it was only a dream.

8

It's early on the morning of the day after Christmas. Evy Beck tiptoes into the living room, where Papa's big hospital bed is standing. Papa looks like an emaciated dwarf

50

within the wide, high bed structure; the bed that can be lowered and raised, leveled and tilted in every imaginable direction. Papa's little head lies sunken in the bulging pillow like the navel in a fat belly. He wheezes slowly, at the same pace as the mechanical liver on the night table. Papa's feeble breath almost completely drowns out the effectively sound-insulated liver-box. The liver is no bigger than an ordinary electric typewriter. It clicks and hums quietly inside; about every fourth second, its pump slurps.

She presses the Stop button. Two black tubes, accordion-pleated, run under Papa's covers. First she unloosens the tubes from the sockets on the liver marked "input" and "output." Then, very carefully, she lifts the covers and detaches the tubes from Papa. She tucks him in again and hangs the tubes over her shoulder. Then she slides out the little drawer of ashes on the back of the mechanical liver. The liver's waste products have been heated and collected as a gray-white powder in a self-sealing paper container. She places an empty container in the drawer and slides it back in.

Out in the kitchen, she puts the tubes into the dishwasher and tosses the filled container into the incinerator. The container isn't quite sealed; it smells. The smell reminds her of singed hair.

She sits down at the kitchen table and writes: *Papa dear . . .* Then she tears up the paper and writes on a new piece: *Rodion: Your protein-free breakfast is in the microwave oven. You just have to push the green button (the oven is already set). I'll be home at five o'clock. You can try calling 980–1000 if anything should come up. See you later, Evy. P.S. Don't forget the bile pills.*

Fifteen minutes later, she's standing at the entrance to NMSI. It reminds her of the entrance to a cemetery—along both sides run walls with benefactors' names in gold: The Anderson Foundation, the Wallenberg Fund, the Herman Miller Trust, the Erlander Foundation for Art and Science, Draco Pharmaceutical, the Volvo Chair, the Red Feather Fund . . .

Where to start? she thinks, shows her thumb to the eye-lock, and enters the grounds. She's been employed for over a week now, and still hasn't got a working space. After New Year's, they've said, after New Year's we'll really try to get you an office. Probably a shared office, but anyway a room with a telephone. She has tried to get the use of one of the student lockers for the time being, but it hasn't proved possible. For a while she thought it might work out for her to sit in Lindgården—the employees' place—but that, too, turned out to be impossible. Mr. Karlsson, the lab animal caretaker, responded to her telephone inquiry that the Labor-Management Committee could not under any circumstances grant the use of the premises for *pure and simple* working assignments *into which consultative procedures cannot be regarded as entering.*

But she has her brief case. In the big satchel she has pencil, paper, sandwiches, and a roll of toilet paper so as not to impose on anybody. Today—which is Day Seven—there's nothing special arranged on her Orientation Program, it just says: Time for Individual Study. Probably she's stepping out of line, but she's reached the decision that today she is going to visit the areas in the institutes where animals are kept. Since it's the middle of the Christmas recess, she counts on being able to work undisturbed.

She's tried to arrive at some kind of "functional" system, but hasn't been able to think up anything better than to take the institutes in alphabetical order. This isn't satisfying. It would be more reasonable to begin with the big consumers first, with those institutes that have the largest number of experimental animals. But she has no access to a statistical summary. Such a thing can probably be found in the Purchasing Office, but it's closed.

The Anatomical Institute is one of the oldest buildings. It is a three-story red brick structure overgrown with clinging vines which at this time of year look like tangled rusty baling wires on the façade. The brick building has been altered and enlarged several times. Only the front part, with entrance hall and lecture hall, dates from 1941.

She goes into the building and looks for stairs to the basement. The corridors and stairways are dim. NMSI draws

52

great quantities of electric current and the ration of electricity has to go primarily for other things than lighting up empty corridors. She comes into a round building with a dome like an observatory. It's more than fifty feet high, and she is standing on a narrow balcony that runs around the walls. She looks down into a huge circle divided by plasterboard partitions into pie slices, like the exercise yard of a prison. In every pie slice stands a minimal desk and one chair. The whole pie-system is covered with plexiglass so that light can reach the rooms from the glass roof of the dome. She realizes that she is standing in what, some decades ago, was meant to be an anatomical theater.

She enters an alcove that looks like it contains a toilet; instead, she finds an elevator there. Practicedly, she presses her right thumb against the elevator's eye-lock, and the sliding doors glide open. She steps into the elevator and presses the button marked 3B.

In the deepest basement, there's no lack of light. Blue fluorescents in double rows run across the ceiling like tracks. It's cold down here—when she breathes out, she smokes like a car starting. She turns up the collar of her coat and, shivering, presses her brief case against her side.

The corridor she's standing in has walls of raw cement, enlivened by the imprint of unplaned boards. She draws the cold air into her nostrils. It doesn't smell of straw, rat pee, or rabbit droppings. The low temperature also argues against there being any animals kept here. Just to be sure, she goes a little way down the corridor and steps through a low door that looks like the hatch between two watertight bulkheads deep down in a huge ship.

Behind the low door, the corridor widens into a large room with a vaulted ceiling of gray-sparkling bedrock. The floor of the room is taken up by high gray steel shelves standing very close together. In the few gaps between the shelves, she glimpses narrow rails in the cement floor. On the end of every shelf is a large wheel. She's seen this type of movable archive shelf before, in the rock vault below the National Archives. But this rock chamber differs markedly from the National Archives vault: a white mist rests on the cement floor and swirls up to her knees. As she wades through it up to the shelves, the mist billows in slow motion.

She looks into the narrow space between two shelves. The mist is streaming down from the shelves themselves, which seem to consist of frosty pipe grating. On the grating lie large, oblong, foil-wrapped packages. This is no library, it's a deep-freeze charnel house.

A card is fastened to the end of the nearest shelf. It says, *A–E, Men born 1900–09.* She goes fifty or sixty feet farther to the right and reads, *V–Z, Women born 1970–.* There are twenty-four shelves in the rock vault. How many do the shelves contain: five hundred? seven hundred?

Evy Beck follows the fluorescents' blue tracks on the ceiling back to the elevator. She doesn't feel especially creepy. She knows very well where she's been. The frozen corpses in the rock vault are donors who have bequeathed their bodies to science. The custom of donating your body began as a fad in California some fifteen years ago, and now has spread over the whole Western world. But NMSI is not especially delighted. The dissection rooms were already being remodeled into offices at the end of the sixties, when instruction in anatomy was cut back. There's no real use for all these bodies that don't meet the standard for transplantation. If the laws aren't changed soon, the institute is going to have to rent space in someone else's deep-freeze.

She's had enough of the basement and rides up to the old anatomical theater again. Following along the walls, one comes to the corridor with research labs. Nobody's in any of the rooms. Plastic that has turned brown with age covers microscopes and test tube racks. The glass doors of the storage cabinets stand ajar to air them out, and in the sinks lie used test tubes, slides, bowls, and stirrers immersed in orange-red picric acid.

When Evy Beck turns from peering into the labs, she catches sight of a white-clad figure waddling toward her from the other end of the corridor. It's a pregnant woman whose belly is so distended that the buttons on the white lab coat can barely keep their purchase on the buttonholes. Her face is splotchy, as after a quickly fading sunburn. The woman holds her hands clasped under her belly. Her wedding rings no longer fit on her ring-finger but have had to be shifted to her little finger.

"It's nice to meet somebody in this place," says Evy Beck. "Happy holiday to you."

The woman looks tired, and brushes a wisp of thin blonde hair back from her forehead.

"I was just going to take a look at the animal areas," Evy Beck explains.

The woman nods, her mouth open.

"First I went down in the basement. But that was obviously wrong."

"I'm on my way to the animal loft right now. If you want to come along, you can."

"Are you the lab assistant here?" asks Evy Beck.

The woman nods again, brushes back her hair, and begins to scuff wearily along in her sandals. As they are riding up to the loft in the elevator, Evy Beck notices that the assistant's abnormally white throat is swollen around the larynx.

"When's the day?" Evy asks brightly.

The lab assistant stares at her as if she didn't quite understand. Her eyes protrude slightly. Then she says, "I was due two days before Christmas."

"Why haven't they induced you, then?"

"Oh, no. I got an injection so I could hold out till after Christmas. There's nobody else who can feed the animals. It's my turn on the schedule."

They step off the elevator in the loft. The air up here is dry and hot and smells like a circus. Evy Beck takes out paper and pencil and puts down her brief case. First they go into a crowded room with a skylight of chicken-wire-reinforced glass. The little chamber is filled with shelves, and on the shelves are rat cages made of steel wire. The rats—black-and-white spotted—lie with their noses plowed into the wood shavings. The narrow wormlike tails are twined in loops and circles. On top of every cage sits a little glass bottle from which the rats can suck water. For solid food, they get hard graham-like biscuit threaded on a steel wire. When the feeding is done, the lab assistant sprays chlorophyll over the shelves.

"No time to change the cages more than once a week," she says.

Evy Beck takes notes. Then they go through six identical rooms of rat cages. A rat here and there has died and is fished out by the tail. Evy Beck wants to know how many rats there are in the whole institute, but the lab assistant doesn't know. They agree on "around two thousand." The assistant suspects that single cages can be found here and there in the various laboratories.

When they enter the first room of guinea pigs, Evy Beck notices a bit of paper on the doorjamb on which is lettered in red marker: WARNING! CONTAGIOUS DISEASE??

"Who wrote this?" she asks.

"My boss, Assistant Professor Nagy."

"Do you know what kind of disease?"

The assistant shakes her head.

"He told us to put on rubber gloves when we go in here."

She takes a pair of rubber gloves that hang on a hook glued to the door.

"There was a girl who got some funny kind of pneumonia," she says. "They're going to make an investigation, of course."

She looks at Evy Beck and brightens. "Are you from the Safety Committee?"

"No. But I can contact them."

When they've gone through the animal loft, Evy Beck has noted down: around 2,000 mice, probably Japanese waltzers, *Mus vagneri*. 60 black rats. 200 white rats. 500 guinea pigs. 3 rabbits. 2 pigs. 36 bats.

By four thirty, she's had time to go through two of the 108 Nobel institutes. When she's ready to take the bus home, it turns out that there's a breakdown in service: a bus has skidded on a patch of ice and blocked the bus lane that runs like an aqueduct in a wide circle out toward Roslagstull. She must walk home.

When she is standing, puffing, outside her own door, she

looks at her watch: 5:13. No use rushing any more, she's not by any means going to be home before five o'clock as she wrote in her note to Papa. He's extremely precise about time.

She lets herself into the apartment quietly, pokes one shoe off with the other, and goes in stocking feet toward the living room. The door is shut. She turns the handle; Papa has locked himself in.

Out in the kitchen, a piece of paper is lying on the floor. Papa's custom is to lay his messages where one will stumble over them. *Erik called and wants gasoline coupons,* it says. There's no signature.

MEMORANDUM TO ADP CENTRAL DATABANK
CLASSIFIED INFORMATION OFFICIAL USE ONLY
OBSERVER ASST ADMINISTR S HORRLIN NMSI
KEYWORD EVY INGA-BRITT BECK WOLMB
CONTINUOUS WORK REVIEW 2
VERBAL REPORT B NOW FULLY INTRODUCED ORIEN
TED DURING XMAS RECESS MADE TOUR OF ANATO
M INST NOT NECESSARY IS PUNCTUAL CERTAIN A
MOUNT OVERTIME 168 PASSAGES WITH THUMBPRI
NT-C EXPECTED DIFFICULTIES OF SOCIAL NATURE
CARING FOR AGED FATHER WITH CONTINUOUS LIV
ER DIALYSIS AT HOME HAVE NOT YET CAUSED ABS
ENCES CONTINUED RISK OF OVERAMBITION OTHER
WISE OK PROGNOSIS OK
RATING 1–5
COMPETENCE 4
ADAPTABILITY 4
SOLIDARITY 4
MOTIVATION 5
COST NONE

9

Papa's sitting at the kitchen table playing solitaire. Evy's trying to sew buttons on her fur-lined coat—an almost hopeless enterprise. The old buttons took with them, when they pulled off, nickel-sized chunks of leather. How do you go about stopping up a hole in leather? She sighs, and feels her barrel of a belly. She buys all her clothes one size small, *though there's no real reason to.*

Suddenly Papa shoots his chair back, hoists his eyebrows, and rakes her with a withering stare.

"Oh no, Papa," she says. "I haven't swiped a card!"

He remains unmoved, and teeters like the scales of Fate on the chair, as though he hadn't heard her and still awaits a full confession. She looks back at him, trying to appear innocent. It goes badly. Since she was a child, she's learned over and over that when Papa looks like that, you've got to look guilty. Long ago, when he had hair on his head and strength in his face, he could be a dead ringer for Stalin—minus the mustache.

The coat slips out of her grasp. She bends over to pick it up from the floor. Between her feet lies the Ace of Diamonds, glowing like a stolen ruby. She snatches up the card and lays it on the table.

"It was lying on the floor," she says.

Papa looks at the coat with interest, trying to tell from which sleeve she drew the card, right or left.

"Who said anything about a card?" he says.

"I guess I'll have to take this coat to a furrier," she says, without the least hope of distracting him so easily.

Papa doesn't bother to repeat his question, "Who said anything about a card?" It would be completely superfluous. The question fills the whole kitchen anyway, scrawled in brilliant green loops of neon that run across the table and the drainboard, over to the stove and above the cupboard door, ending with a yard-high question mark on the kitchen window.

He's after something else—but what? The harmless question "Who said anything about a card?" is a trap. He has surely sat here all evening waiting for the right moment to spring it. To spring the first innocent question which will then be followed by a minutely thought-out interrogation. An interrogation made up mostly of gaps and trick questions. Papa has the same technique as a psychoanalyst: he works subtly, cheering up the patient with a pinprick here and a pinprick there until he is seething with loquacity and lets it all out: dream interpretations, fantasies, guilts, and confessions as black as night.

"Would you like some tea?" she asks—there's a slight chance he'll tire if one behaves in a completely ordinary way, acting completely relaxed and beating down his plans for the interrogation with ordinary trivialities.

"Why not?" he says firmly.

She goes to the stove. When Papa's in his best form, he has already reckoned in from the very beginning the trivial attempts at distraction. Obviously he plans to take his own sweet time about it.

Evy drops the lid of the teakettle in the sink with a crash. It shoots through her body as if she'd hit the funnybone in both elbows at once. She has an urge to scream till the porcelain falls out of the cabinet, till the forks and knives leap up, and till the kitchen windows *and* storm windows shatter.

"Papa dear," she wails, surrendering. "What *do* you want?!"

"Tea," says he, and lays the Ace of Diamonds farthest up on the fourth row of cards so that the solitaire is complete.

Neither of them says anything for the next few minutes. Evy pours the tea and sits down, tastes it, and tries to concentrate on something pleasant, on Erik. Erik, who hinted that he'd probably be made a full professor this spring when she called to say she'd put the gasoline coupons in the mail.

The timer in Papa's watch buzzes suddenly. It's ten o'clock. She looks at him. He hasn't touched the tea.

"Papa . . ." she says gently. "Time for you to go to bed."

"No," he says in a neutral tone.

She begins to suspect what's going on. The nine evenings

60

he's lived with her have gone beautifully—with respect to going to bed at ten. It's critical that Papa go to bed exactly on time. Otherwise the mechanical liver won't have time to detoxify him during the night. If he's sloppy about this, he can go into coma again.

"Papa dear, if we're going to keep our schedule, you'll have to be nice, now, and climb into bed. We can go on talking when you've lain down."

"And why should I let myself be connected to that damnable purification plant?" he responds sharply.

The pattern emerges: This time Papa has chosen to build up his drama of persecution around the mechanical liver. Who's conspiring to get him out of the way this evening? Westinghouse? Roslagstull Hospital? Or the power company that delivers the current?

"Oh, Papa . . ." she says. She feels so tremendously sorry for him—the energy, concentration, and imagination he's compelled to invest in this persecution mania would under other conditions have made him a poet or inventor.

"Who knows who's connected to whom?" Papa demands, but his question is not directed to Evy. When he really gets going, all his questions become rhetorical. They leave his mouth, rise toward the ceiling, swing into a landing approach, and then slip handily back into his brain via his ears.

"To get those goddam machines to function, they've got to find suitable human beings for 'em to parasitize on. Preferably old and feeble. D'you think I don't know why they've made two holes in my gut?" he demands, descending momentarily to direct the question right at her.

"My dear. You would have been dead by now . . ."

"Dead?"

"Excuse me for being so blunt, but you don't have any liver of your own any more."

Papa nods and grimaces for a time, wholly absorbed in his inner monologue.

"Experimental animal," he says then, sarcastically—at first allowing the statement to spin freely up in the air, then directing it with his gaze so that it bursts right in front of

Evy's face like a remote-controlled missile.

"Do you mean to say that I've had something to do with it?!" she demands angrily.

"Sure, why would you get so upset otherwise?"

She gives up, hangs up the coat in the hall, and goes into the living room to begin making Papa's bed for the night. She checks the tilt of the bed: the tubes that go into his belly must lie horizontally on a level lower than his heart. Otherwise the suction and pressure in the venous blood interchange will be disturbed.

When she returns to the kitchen, Papa has pulled his shirt up over his stomach and is regarding the tube stumps with distaste.

"Papa," she pleads. "I have to get up and go to work early tomorrow!"

"And I? All night I'll be lying here being sucked dry by that tin vampire!"

She sits down and kneads the wrinkles of her forehead.

"If it doesn't work out, taking care of you at home, you'll have to go back to the hospital," she says.

"Great. Call a taxi."

"Tomorrow, Papa," she says, shutting her eyes. "I'll call the chief physician tomorrow morning."

Papa brightens, drops his shirt, and stuffs it into his pants.

"A fine man, the chief physician. Well-educated, efficient. I regard him very highly!"

"Sure," she says, without enthusiasm. "Do you promise to go to bed if I call him tomorrow?"

With unexpected willingness, Papa gets up and goes into the bathroom. She sits down on the edge of the big bed and waits, tubes in hand, repeating silently to herself the instruction book's exhortation: "Always connect the evacuation tube first to the patient, then to the Auto-Hepar's input."

Papa returns from the bathroom with his pants at half-mast. She puts down the tubes and blows on her hands to warm them—Papa can get very irritated if she touches him with cold fingers.

Carefully she frees him from the shirt, pants, socks, and undershirt. As usual, he wants to have the undershirt pressed down over his private parts when she pulls off his long johns. There are things a daughter shouldn't see.

When he's all tucked in, with the blanket up to his nose and the liver connected, he suddenly tears his hand free from the covers and grips her arm hard: "I don't care any more about you being an unmarried mother!" he announces, and the little yellowish head beams reconciliation from the depths of the pillow.

10

Today she'll *know.* Evy Beck has spent the first six hours of her workday at the Nobel Institutes trying to track down a telephone for the room she's been given temporary use of, mornings. The Administration has okayed it--but when she gave the Administration's telephone-requisition form to the clerk, the answer was: As soon as we get one in. In the lunchroom, she found out that no one with half a brain contents himself with that. Anyone who needs a telephone goes out and hunts for one. An unused telephone in an empty office is fair game. But in six hours of searching she has yet to see a single available telephone. At NMSI, the minute you leave your office you pull out the jack and lock up the telephone in your desk.

But today, anyhow, she'll *know.* She steps into the elevator in the lobby of the Wenner-Gren Center, faces the elevator microphone, presses her fingers against her throat, and pipes: "Evy Beck, with a three o'clock appointment at CSUPC."

"Yes, ma'am!" the elevator drawls in American, lazily closing the double doors and starting to haul itself upward in the skyscraper. It bumps to a stop on the top floor and announces in the best high Swedish: "Chancellor of the Swedish Universities Program Committee, right this way!"

She has been here before, long ago. But then there was a banquet room up here on the top floor. Over twenty years ago, along with thirty-one other brand-new laboratory technicians, she celebrated her graduation in the Wenner-Gren

Center's banquet room. She surveys the soiled and battered walls—buildings wear out as fast as cars.

She leaves her overcoat in the cloakroom and follows the spiral staircase up to the skyroom. Through the huge windows she looks down on the city—though several panes have been replaced with chipboard. The lighted bus ramps below look like long, narrow bridges.

Five minutes later, she's sitting in a little darkened room in the heart of the building. There are four chairs in the room. In them sit Evy herself, Program Director Ulfsson from CSUPC, Seth Steel, who is a professor of Medical Administration, and Laboratory Animal Caretaker Edwin Karlsson, representing the Nobel Institutes.

Professor Steel draws on the overhead projector's acetate roll with a magic marker and explains: "Every activity is called a *program*. A program is not to be initiated without a statement of the *goal*. Besides the goal, the *budget* is decided up to the point of first *review*. In a *program* of this kind, the *review* must take place no later than twelve months from inception. In the review, the *accomplishment* to date is compared with the goal identified at inception, and from this we determine the *effectiveness*. It's no more complicated than that."

Evy Beck scribbles frantically; this is hard to do because the ceiling lights are turned down to groping level.

"Dr. Beck, you needn't take notes," the program director says kindly. "All this is printed in the CSUPC manual."

"Actually, I was beginning to wonder if my job had any head or tail to it at all," she says cautiously.

Ulfsson and Steel chuckle encouragingly.

"Administrative instruments are just as essential as traditional tools," Steel says. "What good's a carpenter without his hammer?"

"You need only to make yourself familiar with these concepts: P, G, B, R, A, and E, and you'll never go wrong."

"Just remember that there is $+E$ and $-E$," Steel adds. "Though $-E$ means one hasn't succeeded. And we don't expect that to happen. Not in this case."

Evy Beck relaxes a little; this doesn't seem so complicated,

64

really. Maybe even a middle-aged WOLMB can handle it. P, G, B, R, A, and E. She closes her eyes and tries to make the letters into a word her memory can hang onto: PABREG, PEGBAR, REGBAP . . .

"There's an answer for every question in this manual," the program director says, and lays a thick blue looseleaf binder on her knee.

"But we still have ten minutes left to take up oral questions," Steel says obligingly.

Evy Beck glances sideways at Edwin Karlsson. He is sleeping in a very practiced way, with subdued breathing and one eye half-open but extinguished. She feels dumb. Seldom has she been able to squeeze searching questions out of herself right after a briefing. She's slow-thinking, needs time to ruminate . . .

"So I'll be getting the actual content of the goal statement from somebody else?" she says cautiously, sort of trying it out.

"Correct," says the program director. "We merely offer you the *pattern* itself."

"Who from?" she asks.

"Pardon?"

"Who will I get the goal from, the goal for the activity?"

"From the parties concerned, of course," Professor Steel answers. "Goals must not be formulated just anyhow."

"Exactly!" says the animal caretaker, Karlsson, who has hastily awaked at the signal "parties concerned."

"Well, who are the parties concerned in this case?" asks Evy Beck.

"If we expressed ourselves on that, we'd be steering your program," answers Ulfsson.

Professor Steel is not so worried about his neutrality, and says, "The parties concerned are, for example, the directors of the Nobel Institutes, the grant-supported researchers, and the Institutes' accounting office."

"How about the animals?" she asks.

The three men are totally silent. Only the fan in the overhead projector tries to hold out against the silence. It grinds and grinds. A teasing smell of fried dust begins to spread through the crowded, dark little room. Edwin Karlsson closes one eye entirely and switches the other to parking lights. The awkwardness comes closer and closer to pain . . . then Steel starts to guffaw!

Program Director Ulfsson soon chimes in, like a laggard chorister. Edwin Karlsson blinks a couple of times with the half-closed eye—then squeezes both eyes shut and begins laughing so hard that the saliva sprays out as from a humidifier.

Evy Beck doesn't know what they're laughing at. She didn't ask about the animals just to be funny. Nor did she mean to be annoying. She didn't for a minute believe that the animals would be considered "parties concerned." It just popped out, one of the two dozen possible questions. If you don't have much information, you're willing to use the process of elimination. She has a powerful need to sort out a number of more or less conceivable "parties concerned"— simply to try to clear the equation. There are plenty of factors already: BEGPAR, GAPERB, GRABPE . . .

When the men have had their laugh, both Ulfsson and Karlsson feel a need to stuff their shirttails back into their waistbands. Steel returns enlivened to the acetate roll.

"If I were to guess, a program outline might look something like this: The goal would be to bring down the cost clear across the board, maybe to diminish the number of different animal species so that more unified maintenance becomes possible, to control the incidence of the most common animal ailments, maybe to make recommendations on how the more costly experimental animals—for example, monkeys— can be used for several different kinds of experiment. A monkey without a cerebrum can very well be used for demonstration experiments with liver-damaging substances . . . yes, why not consider a zoo-brary?!"

"I don't quite get you?" says Evy Beck, scribbling eagerly.

"Yes, that was an idea that popped into my head just now . . . A central zoo-brary would function like a library. A researcher would borrow an animal and then return it after the experiment. There's a damnable *throwaway psychology* in medicine nowadays!"

Zoo-brary???? writes Evy Beck on her pad.

66

"Seth, Seth. . . . !" says the program director admonishingly.

"Okay, sure," says Seth Steel. "I'm altogether too easily enthused. That's dangerous when you're working with administrative processes."

The program director calls *"Lights!"* to the wall switch and the ceiling lights brighten. The men stand. The laughter remains, and bubbles behind Edwin Karlsson's closed lips.

"Just one more question," pleads Evy Beck.

"Yes?" says Professor Steel, who's just discovered that he's laughed his shirttail right out of his pants.

"It sometimes happens that people on staff get allergic or pick up diseases from the animals—"

"Who's been shooting his mouth off about that?!" says Karlsson with unexpected heat.

"Well, nobody in particular. But are such questions a part of my program goal?"

"Little lady," Karlsson says and gives her a hard look. "I'm going to give you some damn good advice: Keep clear of the Safety Committee's territory."

11

Evy Beck doesn't dare go home. She's promised Papa to call the chief physician at Roslagstull. But in her hectic pursuit of a telephone, she forgot. Though it would have been even worse to have to come home and tell Papa that the chief physician had categorically refused him readmission.

She's walking down the frozen sawdust-strewn footpath around Bellevue Park and over toward the old Veterinary College. Ice covers Brunns Bay. A freakish winter with sudden changes of temperature has made the ice uneven and shifting: gray windblown snow-strands wind among pools of India ink, and, in some places the ice has been forced together, floes have tilted and piled up on each other. Here and there, the ice heaps are garnished with juniper bushes and spruce branches as if to warn of abandoned fishing holes.

Right out in the middle of a rugged field of frozen glass a ski pole is standing straight up with a red mitten on it.

Evy Beck is used to being alone. But she's never sought to be alone. She's had to adjust to it, just as over the years one accustoms oneself to Sweden's inhospitable climate. The cold loses its bite, you kid yourself that the goose bumps come from feelings of pleasure.

Sometimes she's afraid she'll talk to herself where others will hear. When she's entirely alone, it doesn't matter that a sentence or two gets said out loud. It's a way of checking that one's voice is still there—something like a test call on the Hot Line. Several times she's dreamed that she fell into the sea and tried to scream for help, but the little hinges in her larynx were rusted from lack of use.

Now and then, she's been obsessed by someone outside herself—by Erik or Papa or somebody who's written a book that impressed her. Most often it's been Hans-Olof. Hans-Olof Rehnman was Assistant Veterinarian at the National Veterinary Institute when she met him, twenty-nine years ago. She herself was a lab assistant. A dumpy but good-humored kid of twenty-four. A kid who had discovered that if you laughed a lot, people didn't notice how you looked . . . that you happened to be rather homely. That you had calves like barrel staves and breasts like a matron's.

She laughed a lot with Hans-Olof Rehnman, when they sat late into the night doing autopsies on ptarmigans that had been flown in from Jämtland. He was married, but she hadn't had an especially bad conscience over their sleeping to-gether occasionally. It was a kind of colleagueship—some-thing like two co-workers going out to lunch together. Then she got pregnant. She hadn't the least thought of telling Hans-Olof. It wasn't sad at all, no, to the contrary. Neither before nor since has she ever felt such a heartfelt happiness as when she was expecting Erik.

Her lover emigrated to Australia in 1961. Since then, she's never seen him again. But he's the most regular partner in her solitary dialogues. If I do this, what will Hasse think? Does Hasse think I look like an old frump in this dress? Hasse is very chatty. At this point, he's also much younger than Evy, somewhere between thirty-five and forty. With the years, he's become more and more like his son Erik. Yet while Erik has become so terribly busy, Hasse has come to devote ever more time to Evy. He's almost always there, listening, commenting—and at long intervals, as a lover just flown when she wakes from a sweaty dream with pounding heart and the bedsheet tangled around her legs.

"I wish you could have a talk with Papa," she says.

"Now's the time," laughs Hasse. "To come home with me in tow now, after twenty-seven years!"

"I've always seen Papa as strong," she says.

"Invulnerable?"

"Exactly. Someone who's got a world of his own is sort of out of reach."

"But now you're worried about him?" says Hasse, and nuzzles her cheek, light as a snowflake.

"I'm not afraid of his dying, it isn't that. I mean, it's plain that he's going to die. I'm resigned to that."

"Is he really off his rocker now?"

"I don't know. What I'm afraid of is that he'll lose his sharpness. That he'll get dull, sloppy, turn into a pudding."

"What then, Evy?"

"Just that if Papa loses his sharpness . . . Well, what'll become of me? We're so close. Like razor and strop."

Hasse nods gravely. Hasse is good—he keeps quiet when he has nothing to say. He'd rather be silent than come up with well-intentioned platitudes. About Papa, there's no easy advice to give.

"Then there's this job," she continues. "I can't make head or tail of it."

"Don't be so darned ambitious," says Hasse. "Evy, do you always have to excel? First lab assistant, then lab technician, and then defending your thesis at the Veterinary College. You *are* clever."

"I don't look at it that way."

"We won't love you less if you don't succeed," says Hasse, maybe a shade too feebly. She feels a little hurt.

"Who's we?"

"I. Erik. Rodion too, though in his own funny way."

69

She feels pacified. Sometimes she needs to hear Hasse say that Papa needs her. That Papa's scared stiff he'll lose her. Papa's like a seventy-nine-year-old two-year-old. It would feel enormously empty for her, not to get bitten on the cheek or have her hair pulled out in tufts.

"Love?" she asks.

"Wrong word?" asks Hasse.

"Maybe. Feels more like a possibility. Up to now, 'love' has seemed pretentious—like walking around in oversize boots. I don't want to even use the word unnecessarily. The best things are what you save for last."

Evy Beck has walked around the bay and entered the grounds of the old Veterinary College. The red brick institutes are close together. The styles of their architecture differ. The oldest buildings have vaulted roofs and windows, and white indented squares ornamenting their façades; they must date from the turn of the century. The youngest, flat-roofed pavilions were built in the early seventies, meaning that they were prefabricated barracks. She took only her pre-med courses here. By the time she really got rolling, the Veterinary College had already moved to Uppsala. She did her doctorate at the branch campus in Skara. She has hardly any memory of her first two years of study in Stockholm, remembering only her isolation among the other students, who were so much younger. The girls who came directly from high school with but one interest: horses.

What's the old college used for now? Everything seems to be boarded up and locked, nobody has scraped off the snow or strewn sand on the ice. She remembers reading in the paper that the college is used for some kind of warehouse. Oh, yes, now it comes back! All the old stalls and pens are full of automobiles. Over seven thousand cars are in storage here, just standing in wait for better times. Waiting for a more generous distribution of gasoline.

It's past seven when she gets home to Roslag Street. A light is on in the kitchen. On the table lies an upended empty port wine bottle.

"Papa!" she cries, and rushes into the apartment.

70

What she hasn't considered is that he might do something to himself—it's so utterly out of character for him. Yet spirits and wine are as dangerous for someone who's had his liver removed as lye or hydrochloric acid for an ordinary person.

"Papa dear?!"

She stands in the living room in her wet boots and stares at Papa. He has dragged the rocking chair over to the night table, and has a bottle of cognac in his hand. At first he doesn't seem to notice her. Intent and smiling, he sits there pouring the cognac into the mechanical liver's "input." The machine slurps and sputters.

He catches sight of her and brightens.

"I thought the Tin Woodman needed himself a spree!" he says, raising the bottle in a toast.

12

A whole month has gone by. Evy Beck has begun to settle in. Nowadays she has her own room in the cellar of the Pharmacological Institute. She was able to get it thanks to a famous dog named Maecenas. When Maecenas was found dead one morning, having crept in between a lab bench and a radiator, the head of the institute decided to push for having a veterinary medical consultant at NMSI. He also realized that it could be useful to have the consultant located within his own institute.

During her first month, Evy Beck has succeeded in making a rough estimate of the number of experimental animals within the Nobel Institutes. It hasn't been easy. She's gone from institute to institute, counting. Then she's tried to find other counts to cross-check her own: invoices, feed consumption records, wastes of animal origin at the NMSI central waste treatment plant, and so on.

The complications have been many. For example, what is meant by "institute"? On paper, NMSI comprehends 108 independent institutes. But in reality, two or three institutes turn out to have vanished—they've been nothing more than bookkeeping entries whose right to existence the bursar has patiently tried to explain to her; eventually she hopes to find the wit to comprehend why two or three "ghost institutes" are necessary to give the economy of NMSI sufficient "elasticity."

Then, she has come upon buildings or parts of buildings that don't exist. These have been various branches or satellites, whose connection with NMSI hasn't been altogether easy to discover. A few enterprising professors evidently carry on wholly or quasi-private research on the grounds. Nearly all the larger pharmaceutical firms own or lease space, in their aspiration toward more intimate contact with the researchers. She has asked, she has read, and she has looked. In fact, a tangled skein of transactions occur within research, a kind of primitive barter economy. A mortgage can be acquired on a research name of Nobel caliber for a contribution of a million dollars. Then the company can put the Nobel-caliber name on its books as part of its "scientific advisory board." But since cold cash is impractical in many ways, the mortgage is paid for with a laboratory setup, a radio microscope, a lecture tour around the world, or a complete research facility including equipment, operating expenses, and lady lab assistants.

Evy Beck has nothing to do with any of this. She tries to keep strictly neutral. But if one wants to count the number of lab animals in the Nobel Institutes, it is reasonable to ask which animals work for NMSI and which are part of the private sector.

As a first specific step, she's begun setting up a card index. She sits printing information by hand on stiff little cards. One card system she's set up according to institute, another according to species, a third according to type of experiment, and a fourth according to the most usual animal diseases. When she's fiddling with her card index, she locks the door to her cellar cubbyhole. She doesn't want to be surprised by any of NMSI's many computer consultants.

She's tried to make the room a little more comfortable. The window is framed on both sides by wide Easter yellow curtains which cover up the cement. From the ceiling hangs not only a lamp but also two glazed pots with lushly growing ferns in them. On the walls she's taped up the pictures Erik made as a boy: the four-year-old's watercolor flowers and elephant-droppings, the seven-year-old's Lucia procession, the nine-year-old's death's-heads, the twelve-year-old's space stations—and the gifted fourteen-year-old's first discovery, the electrostatic paper clip. On the walls of her cellar cubbyhole, Erik never grows older than fourteen—the drawings he's made since then, he's kept.

Anytime she leaves the room, she locks up two things in the drawer: the old-fashioned card index and the telephone receiver she's bought at her own expense over at the Telephone Company's surplus warehouse.

Around the first of February, Evy Beck sets up an old-fashioned PERT chart on the inside of the door. She's no great shakes as a draftsman: the lines are wavy and the symbols on the flow chart—the squares, diamonds, and triangles —tip every which way. At the bottom of the paper, she's written down the most vital problem areas.

Selection. How are the Institutes' experimental animals selected? Are they purchased as needed or do the suppliers control the selection completely? Why is a specific species selected for a specific experiment? How many suppliers are there? Who monitors the suppliers? Who monitors the suppliers' raising of the animals? To what extent are the various institutes self-supporting, i.e., carry on their own animal raising?

Housing. Are there any standards applied? Who supplies cages, boxes, containers? Are there standard procedures for cleaning? Ventilation? Temperature? Is there a general awareness of the risk of overcrowding? Is consideration given to the animals' territorial requirements in nature? Needless changes in the animals' environment?

Diet. Is the diet adapted to each animal species? How about regularity of feeding times? Overfeeding—undernourishment? Vitamins—minerals? Composition of diet in relation to natural cycles? What's done with leftover food?

Condition. Are the animals kept passive? What possibili-

73

ties exist for exercise? Diet/exercise? Do ways exist for animals to get stimulation? How is general physical condition checked before an experiment?

For long periods she sits with her back against the desk and stares at her PERT chart. She tries to sense patterns and connections, combinations and short-cuts. Countless times she has erased the big paper that covers almost the entire door, drawn it over, and rubbed it out. An obvious main track doesn't seem to exist, only a number of equivalent paths and a great number of sidetracks.

Sometimes she sits staring into the bulb in her lamp. When she shifts her gaze back to the PERT chart, colored rings and balls follow along, yellow or violet light phenomena that dance across the network. Then she realizes that the real problems haven't yet been identified, that the key questions can barely be sensed, and that the colored spots of light go away quicker when she tries to fix them with her gaze.

She shuts her eyes and is about to despair; she thinks herself incompetent and unenterprising. In short, rather slow, far from bright, a little cowardly, and maybe a bit naïve. One thing is going to be needed more than any other: *patience.* Then she feels in a slightly better humor; if there's one quality she's been forced to cultivate and depend on, it's neither amiability nor analytical quickness, but just waiting, stubbornness and stick-to-it-iveness.

13

In the beginning of February, she makes a discovery. By chance, she comes into one of the labs at Pharmacology just as they're cutting up some guinea pigs that have been sacrificed by being put into a container with ether-soaked cotton. Two graduate students are pinning the dead guinea pigs to a board and cutting open their bellies, then taking out the intestines and the contents of the chest cavity.

Evy Beck asks to borrow a scalpel and slices through the lungs of a few animals. She wants to check whether there might be some small yellowish-white spots in the guinea pigs' lungs, small infiltrations that show that the highly susceptible animals have become infected with tuberculosis. Instead, she finds something else: Davies' lung fibrosis. The lungs are hard and inelastic, the edge of the slice is tough and dry. She goes through a total of thirty-one animals. In every one of them Davies' lung fibrosis is more or less developed.

Guinea pigs that are fed for a long time with feed that "dusts up" easily get this special disease of the lung. She checks on how the guinea pigs are raised—yes, exactly: they've been fed flour mill wastes. When the powder is dropped from the automatic feed-meters, a stubborn dust whirls up. In open cages that doesn't matter so much, but at Pharmacology guinea pigs are kept in plastic boxes, which are easier to keep clean and shelter the sensitive animals against cold and drafts.

Animals that suffer Davies' lung fibrosis can't be cured. On the other hand, it's easy to prevent the disease by going over to pressed food, which doesn't dust up. The following week, she goes around to all the institutes that, according to her card index, work with guinea pigs. She tries to get in to see the institute director or at least leave a mimeographed sheet on Davies' lung fibrosis. Coming to them in this way, with a cheap and specific action to be taken, yields her good will. She no longer feels too slow to be accepted. She begins to feel that people think she's accomplishing something.

Her best contact with the medical men becomes the Saturday meetings she has with the head of the Pharmacological Institute, Professor Nils Rosén von Rosenstein. He himself never uses anything but the first part of his name, Nils Rosén. He's named after an ancestor who was a famous physician and cultural eminence at the close of the eighteenth century. Evy Beck has noticed that few academic careers seem so often to be passed down from father to son as the profession of medicine.

Every Saturday at eight o'clock, she has coffee with Nils Rosén in his office. The professor of pharmacology is sixty-five years old, and is one of those old characters who have never understood why one shouldn't work on Saturdays. Evy Beck, on the other hand, needs her Saturdays for housecleaning and for keeping up with the large quantities of wash that Papa leaves for her. But she doesn't complain—she considers it a real break to have one of the influential professors to herself for an entire morning. Nils Rosén has clout; he's part of that minority who sit nearest the green table at meetings of the Academic Council.

Rosén is a big man and powerfully built. His face is bright red and a little bit blue-veined, like that of an old farmer. A ring of white hair rests like a silvery wreath around the polished ruddy dome. Despite his relatively advanced age, his eyes are bright blue—there are no blood vessels or other blemishes in the whites. Despite his size, he moves quite gracefully. Despite his proletarian appearance, he speaks the most beautiful high Swedish she's ever heard. She feels a strong common bond with him, and feels perfectly at ease in his company.

On Saturdays, no scheduled activities go on; there are no lectures, seminars, or exams. With the exception of a researcher or two, nobody is there. Not even anyone to look after the institute's animals; that assignment, Professor Rosén himself takes on. After coffee, Evy goes around with him and feeds the animals.

"It's a nuisance with this automatic system," says Nils Rosén. "Animals don't need just water and food, they also need to feel somebody cares about them."

Evy goes along and helps. They stay the longest in the institute's dog yard. Maecenas wasn't the only dog here. There are about a dozen beagles, Swedish foxhounds, a Saint Bernard, dachshunds, and some dogs that aren't thoroughbreds. Several of the dogs have been here for many years. The institute's researches center on studies of digestive juices and enzymes. A very highly specialized operative technique has been developed for dogs. They are scrupulously taken care of and often live as long as ordinary dogs out in the community.

For exercise, the dogs are let out into big monkey cages in the back of the institute. During the summer, the staff usually take them out on a leash when they go to get the mail, carry a message, or simply take a ten-minute walk at lunchtime.

"Any comments?" asks Nils Rosén each time they leave the dog yard.

But Evy Beck has no comments. In no other scientific institution has she seen such well-cared-for dogs.

Other laboratory animals at Pharmacology are also well treated—but no other species is given such attention as the dogs. The dogs are, incomparably, Pharmacology's upper crust.

For lack of room, a number of cats live in three former circus wagons. It sounds worse than it is. The wagons have electric heat as well as water and drain connections. In a real cold snap, the bare water and drain pipes can freeze, of course, but that happens extremely seldom. So the circus wagons are more an aesthetic than a hygienic problem.

The rest of the Pharmacological animal collection, the rabbits, guinea pigs, and mice, live in one wing of the building. Here, too, order and acceptable hygiene hold sway.

"They're too tight here," Evy has said a number of times. "Animals suffer from crowding more than one may think."

"Give me seventy-five thousand!" says Rosén sadly.

It's a little script they run through every Saturday. Evy Beck mutters about crowding. But Nils Rosén hasn't got any money to expand with. The central administration is unresponsive. Other institutes, for example Bacteriology, have it much worse.

But this Saturday, Evy Beck has a concrete proposal to offer when they return to the professor's office after making the rounds.

"If we could shorten the holding time, then we'd get away from some of the crowding," she says.

"Tell me how, Evy?"

"The animals that are to be used within just a few days ought to be separated from those that are kept here much longer. One ought to set up two sections, one for short-term and the other for long-term."

"But we want them to stay with us for a while. Animals suffer from being transported," says Rosén.

That's a standard argument. Evy Beck doesn't believe it's

so very important if the animals' immediate surroundings are held constant. Small animals have a limited experience of the larger world.

"If we could get the suppliers to use Pharmacology's cages," she says. "So that the animals have gotten accustomed to the new cages *before* they come here. Change of cage is a far greater disturbance of their environment than being carried here from another building."

Nils Rosén nods. He never wrangles with her. Either he understands at once or else he asks her questions. Nothing is allowed to remain unclarified. She envies his intellectual sharpness. The only thing she's tempted to criticize is the excesses he falls into in anything relating to the care of the dogs. Pharmacology's dogs could very well give up a little room in favor of the small animals. But Nils Rosén takes no personal interest in the small animals, and she has told him as much to his face.

"The animals that stay here a long time ought, in principle, to be treated just as well as the dogs," she says.

"If possible, yes. But on the condition that we succeed with the first part of your proposal. To set up a section with a very short rotation period."

"Whom do you buy from?" she asks.

He goes into the outer office to fetch the invoices.

One of the actions Rosén has taken is to have everyone who uses animals in his research sign a special agreement. An agreement in which the undersigned solemnly promises not to undertake painful animal experiments. No younger colleague is allowed to work alone with lab animals without having done an apprenticeship with an older one. It is also an absolute requirement that colleagues must have come far enough along in their studies to have had course instruction in administering both local and general anesthetics. To the extent that painful experiments must be undertaken, they are only to be undertaken after application to the head of the institute.

He returns with a bundle of invoices.

"The larger deliveries have to be made through Central Administration," he tells her. "It's not like the old days, when one made deals for stolen cats and runaway dogs . . . The chief NMSI supplier of smaller laboratory animals is Findus Pharmafarm, Inc. Do you know them?"

Evy Beck certainly does recognize the supplier that has snared over eighty percent of the Scandinavian market.

"If you have no objection, I'd like to contact the Findus animal agent for the Stockholm district," she says.

14

Erik has a permit for driving in the downtown area. He comes and picks her up at the main entrance of NMSI. Erik is so *useful*. He calls up to ask if they can have lunch, whether he can drive her any place, or whether she'd like to watch him play squash. It's been a very long time since Erik dropped in and merely sat.

"Thanks for the gas coupons," he says when she gets into the car. "How's Grandfather doing?"

"You might look in on him once in a while."

"I was up there a little while last Thursday."

"During the day?"

Papa hasn't said a word about it. Apparently he prefers to meet Erik in secrecy.

"Did you two have a nice time?"

"Sure," says Erik. "We spent two hours tuning up his mechanical liver."

She doesn't approve of Papa's messing with the Auto-Hepar. But you can trust Erik. Mechanical things seem to love Erik—like the birds adoring Saint Francis.

"What did you talk about?" she asks enviously.

"Oh, everything. Grandfather's a good listener."

"Yes," she says, but means "No."

They pass Roslagstull and swing onto Valhalla Street. Erik drives well; he talks without looking away from where he's going, even for a minute.

"I'm a little surprised that Grandfather and you seem to have so much in common," she says. "I mean, him being a totally convinced old Communist and . . ."

"And?" he says, grinning.

"And you," she says.

"What do you mean?" Erik asks. "What's the big difference between me and Grandfather?"

She wishes she hadn't brought it up. Such conversations with Erik usually go badly. She doesn't like being teased by her own son.

"D'you mean I don't believe in anything?" he continues. "Unlike Grandfather?"

There are qualities in Erik that both frighten and attract her. That he's clearheaded and hard-working, she likes. It's also good that he's never been sloppy. But he is so *clinical*.

"It's the same with society as with any other administrative system," Erik tells her as they pass the Stadium. "Any administrative system can be guided if you can only get at the keys, get hold of the right instruments."

"It's nothing more than a technical problem, then?"

"Socio-technical."

"Have you told Grandfather that?"

"Of course. We agree pretty well, really. Oh, sure, he's a little irritated that I don't believe in the class struggle as an explanatory model. But otherwise we agree completely. Grandfather represents *scientific* marxism."

"And you?" she asks, and looks at him; how one could know so little about one's own children.

"I advocate socio-technical science."

"There's no risk of high feelings, then?"

"Not when we're discussing sociological theories. I just cannot fathom what *feelings* have to do with it. The moment anybody brings up how society functions, a general overflow of feelings is expected. Why?!"

"Politics has always raised people's tempers," she says.

"Exactly. And that's why I dislike the word politics. Let's look at it as social technology instead."

They reach the outermost end of Valhalla Street, where Swedish Broadcasting is located. Next door rises the newly built skyscraper of the national federation of labor unions.

"The Kaknäs Tower?" says Erik, and cranes forward over the steering wheel to look up the square cement-gray TV tower with its orange-tinged windows at the top. "Is it true they once had a restaurant up there?"

"That was many years ago," she says. "It would be nice if you'd drop in some *evening*. So we could all three have a little chat."

Erik stops the car and lays his gloved hand on her knee. "I've told Rodion that he really could take a friendlier tone with you."

Startled, she looks at him. Up to now, Erik has seemed completely blind to the way Papa exercises his bad temper.

"What'd he say?" she asks uneasily.

"That he can't make you out."

"Thanks," she says, stepping from the car. "And so long."

"Take care of yourself, Evy!" says Erik, half-absently; he has already lifted the receiver of the mobile telephone halfway to his ear.

She goes into the Kaknäs Tower's entrance, which is like a vault—or like the entrance to the Lenin-Brezhnev mausoleum in Moscow, where she visited two years ago. She'd won a trip in the Internal Revenue Service's Tax-Refund Bingo.

In the entrance is a very discreet sign: Findus-Nestlé International. There is no door-telephone. Successful companies prefer to have live receptionists. Evy Beck seats herself in one of the deep armchairs provided for visitors in the foyer. The room is dim, the only light coming from the aquarium tanks that make up its three sides. In the tanks swim not goldfish or guppies, but the company's own products: pollack, Arctic cod, tuna fish, and fat herrings. A receptionist suddenly materializes from the shadows, like a photo image in a developing tray.

"Welcome, Dr. Beck," says the receptionist, and extends a silver server the size of a playing card toward her. On the tray is a cognac glass full of avocado juice.

The receptionist has a very tiny nasal voice, the same voice that Evy Beck remembers all the dumb blondes had in the films of the fifties. She feels a little envious. It must be very practical to have a naturally piping voice. It must be pleasant and comforting to one's self-esteem not to have to put on an act for the door-telephone.

The very moment she finishes the avocado juice, the receptionist is right there to take the glass.

"Mr. Pedersen, our manager, is ready to see you now," says the receptionist, and follows Evy Beck toward the elevator.

The empty glass and the silver tray are suddenly gone—how was that done? Evy Beck is seized with a bizarre feeling of finding herself at a magicians' convention. The frosted glass doors of the elevator glide apart and the receptionist takes her in by the elbow. In the center of the elevator is a visitor's armchair which she sits down in; the receptionist perches on the arm. The whole elevator is made of glass. Outside it is water. She seems to be floating up through a water tower. After a few floors, they acquire the company of some playful dolphins, which swim spirals around the rising elevator.

The elevator stops very gently; it's the first time she's ever been in an elevator with liquid springs. The receptionist takes Evy Beck's hand and walks with her down a short corridor, then out into the Kaknäs Tower's observation deck level, where the restaurant used to be. Mr. Pedersen, the manager, is waiting for her behind a column—he steps out suddenly and kisses her hand. Evy Beck turns to thank the receptionist—she's gone!

"I am truly delighted," says Mr. Pedersen; he's Danish, by his accent.

She pulls her right hand away and for safety's sake, pushes it deep down in the pocket of her jacket.

"Yes, Professor Rosén von Rosenstein called . . ." says the manager, and leads her to the wide floor-length windows so that she can look down on Stockholm, spread out below in slush and cutting winds.

She shuts her eyes and tries to convince herself that she's really standing down there on solid ground, but it doesn't work, and she's unable to suppress the trembling in her thighs. She quickly retreats several steps, and her back strikes glass—still another aquarium?

"It's about the deliveries to Pharmacology," she babbles. "Would you consider using our cages?"

"We've always had the very, very best of relations with the

Alfred Nobel Institutes," says Pedersen. "We are really and truly delighted that now the Institutes have their own expert veterinary medical consultant. Our veterinarians have sometimes tried to lend a hand with this or that small question out there—when they happened to be there. But in the long run an institution of that size really *must* have its own specialists. It is very important."

She opens her eyes again and looks at Mr. Pedersen, to avoid looking down. She's forgotten what he looks like! Is it the same man? Just like the receptionist, Pedersen seems to be instantly changeable, floating, projected in slow motion. His age swings back and forth between thirty and fifty, his height between five-six and five-eleven . . . She yanks her hand hastily out of her pocket and holds it under her nose. Yes, he is *real:* her hand gives off the strong fragrance of lemon, sea water, and leather.

"We all have our problems, more or less," says Pedersen, and smiles; when he opens his mouth, he leans forward slightly so that his mother-of-pearl teeth end up in the nearest spotlight.

"Would you take Pharmacology's cages, then?" she asks again, and tries to fix his gaze with hers—but his eyes slide away, as when you try to look right at a grain of dust that's gotten caught in your eye.

"Pharmacology's cages?" he repeats in his Danish accent; he speaks in a peculiarly flexible and elastic way. It's as though somebody had gone over his replies with water and sandpaper to wear away all the letters that stick out or up. What's left is a smooth acoustical gruel.

With her hands, she feels the aquarium she's leaning against. Then she looks over her shoulder: it's not an aquarium, but an oblong glass box with a stuffed guinea pig in it. And it's not a common kind of guinea pig; it has slightly thicker fur than a suckling pig and is as large as a rabbit.

Mr. Pedersen walks by her and places himself beside the glass box.

"The real answer is here, Dr. Beck. You see before you our new container."

She turns and stares stupidly at the lighted glass box. Suddenly she's unsure whether the giant guinea pig in the aquarium is stuffed or alive. It stares at her without blinking, as frightened rodents do.

"You mean our old cages might give you some trouble?" she asks.

"Oh, no, on the contrary, it would be truly rational for us to use the same containers."

"Which would mean that we went over to *your* containers?"

"In that case, Findus is prepared to place our new shelf system at your complete disposal as well. A new shelf system perfectly adapted to the containers," says Pedersen, and lays his dry palm lightly on Evy Beck's sweaty fist, which is steaming its own image upon the glass box.

"Free?" she asks.

He doesn't say, Of course, but is satisfied merely to nod slightly while patting her hand three times with his.

"But what that means is, Pharmacology's committed to buying all its future lab animals from Findus," she declares.

"Oh, not at all," says Pedersen. "I'll tell you a little secret: the Felix Cat Company is also going over to the same containers."

She has a question on the tip of her tongue: Has Findus bought out Felix? But she swallows it. The question wouldn't fit in with these surroundings. Any more than Evy Beck fits in with these surroundings, she thinks.

"Dr. Beck," says Pedersen, looking at her seriously; his India-rubber face assumes for the moment the same rough-hewn honest aspect as a hand-carved head of Abraham Lincoln. "Allow me to advise you, as a very intelligent woman, that this means something more than cages and containers. We're now talking about the central problem of how the entire laboratory animal sector is going to look in the future."

The manager shows her around the observation terrace. Glass boxes are exhibited here and there on plush-covered pedestals, with no apparent plan. Everything is very artfully arranged. The illumination comes from individual concealed spotlights and from within the aquariums themselves. This gives one a muted and substantial sensation—like silently tiptoeing around to look at the crown jewels behind bullet-proof glass.

They stop before a glass box with a stuffed rabbit in it. Like the guinea pig, it has very sparse fur—really only the long upright ears distinguish it from the giant guinea pig. Perpendicular to the rabbit box stands a container with another animal in it as big as the rabbit and with the same sparse gray-white fur. By the hanging ears you can see that it's a dachshund.

"At the same time that we go over to the containers, we introduce a truly much more significant improvement," says Pedersen. "I mean that we launch our new line of animals with genetic guarantee."

Evy Beck leans over the rabbit box and scrutinizes the details. In one corner lies a shattered test tube—it gives a very sloppy impression.

"Carelessness?" asks the manager brightly. "Tell me please, Dr. Beck, do you truly believe the test tube got there entirely by chance?!"

She gathers that it was not by chance, but just to go along with him she answers, "Yes, I did think that, as a matter of fact."

"It's there because the animal never leaves its container."

"Never?!"

"No. The animal remains—from conception to consumption, may I say?—inside the *same* sterile container. In truth, the container *never* needs to be opened."

"How does the animal get food and water, then?"

"You see, dear lady, food and synthetic water are inserted into the container at the very beginning. Enough to last the animal's entire life."

"Wastes, then?"

He points with the back end of his gold fountain pen: "They fall down into this gutter, where they're chemically transformed into food and synthetic water."

"I still don't understand what that broken test tube is doing in the container," says Evy Beck.

Pedersen holds up the pen and his fingers, and draws pedagogically in the air: "This rabbit, for example, comes from a cloning mother. All our rabbits come from the same cloning mother, that is what makes possible the *genetic guarantee.* The unfertilized egg from the cloning mother is placed in the test tube together with a drop of cleavage inducer, which divides the egg so that it starts growing in the tube. Then the container is sealed. In the test tube is everything the rabbit fetus needs. When it is fully developed, it breaks open the test tube and crawls out into the container itself. Inside the container, the rabbit grows and thrives under entirely sterile conditions and *without ever being touched by human hands.*"

"Till it's ready to be used," says Evy Beck.

"Exactly, Dr. Beck. And if you should want to anesthetize the rabbit before taking it out of the environment it has grown up in, that's really a very simple matter!"

The manager points to a turn-switch in the base of the glass box, sealed with a lead wafer for safety. Beside the switch is inscribed "Halotane—Stages I-II-III-IV." The switch can be turned to four different positions depending on the desired depth of narcosis. Stage IV means that the animal is anesthetized to death without ever being touched by human hands.

"But this means each animal can be used only once. That it will be sacrificed after that."

"Really no problem," Pedersen assures her. "Should one wish to repeat an experiment, one just takes the next rabbit. They're all identical twins. Now do you see what we mean by Findus's Genetic Guarantee?"

She feels slightly ill. It must be some trace of vertigo that's lingered—or maybe it's because the four-hundred foot Kaknäs Tower sways a few inches in the strong February winds.

Mr. Pedersen shows her the rest of the collection. All the animals are thin-furred albinos and weigh exactly the same, but their specific distinguishing marks remain: long ears, drooping ears, long naked tail, short stubby tail, curly tail, hanging tongue, pug nose, straight horns. A few animals have feathers instead of thin fur. The high point of the exhibition is a perfect dwarf horse, a full-blooded white Arabian steed.

She tries to pull away in the direction of the elevator. Out of nowhere, Pedersen has materialized a gold pen and a

diplomatic-style brief case filled with brochures and docu-
mentation. He hands over these promotional gifts ceremoniously, and holding her hand a long time, pumps it up and
down as if presenting her with the Nobel Prize.

"Thank you, thank you. I'll talk to Professor Rosén," she
says.

"Give him my very best regards, my very best regards,"
says Pedersen.

The elevator doors glide apart as though someone had
tapped them lightly with a magic wand. In the elevator, the
receptionist is sitting on the chair arm with a welcoming
smile.

"Dr. Beck," Pedersen says at the elevator door. "It would
really make things much easier for us if in the future Findus
Pharmafarm could regard you as purchasing agent for *all* the
Nobel institutes."

"I have absolutely no such authority," she says stiffly.

Mr. Pedersen smiles deprecatingly, as if he's just heard the
commander-in-chief declare, with false modesty that he has
no influence whatsoever on the armed forces. Then, swiftly,
he seizes her hand, which she's again forgotten to hide in a
safe place. He draws it to his lips and implants a kiss precisely
on the center of her little fingernail—which must signify
"ground floor," since the elevator quickly takes her there.

15

For as long as she can remember, she has de-
tested long, lazy Sundays. She's never been able to get relaxation and enjoyment from leisure. Either she has worried
about having to get up and go to work on Monday morning,
or she has felt entirely annihilated by knowing there's no
work to go to when the week begins. During those long
jobless periods, Sundays stretched out lengthwise into a sev-
en-day chewing gum.

Yet this winter, she finds herself wishing for a long, dull,
solitary Sunday. The long Sundays are the worst, giving Papa
the chance to carry out his intrigues in full detail: first merely

hinting at them; then steaming at high speed onto a sidetrack to divert her; then twisting the scene ninety degrees around so that everything said so far assumes a new significance. Then all that remains is to work out the drama whose plot, at this point, is as inevitable and as time-consuming as Jesus' progress toward Golgotha.

Yet at the beginning of March, to her surprise and delight, she notices that Papa no longer gives her the leading role in his paranoid dramas. She's certainly in the cast, but she no longer stands in the center of the spotlight like the Virgin Mary. Instead, she's moved out to the edge of the altarpiece, like Mary Magdalene or Mary, wife of Cleophas.

Sunday mornings begin at exactly six thirty, like any other morning. Papa must be disconnected from the artificial liver at just that time. At seven fifteen he has to have breakfast, so that his metabolism doesn't get out of balance. The tubes must be washed and the liver output emptied. Also, the machine has to be calibrated once a week—on Sunday. For the space of an hour, the liver is fed synthetic blood with a known composition; then one can judge whether it is out of whack, whether it's going too fast or too slow. The liver is the body's clock and completely controls maintaining the daily rhythm.

Then follow a few hours of relative calm while Papa scrutinizes the Sunday news in minute detail and Evy catches up on the wash she hasn't gotten to on Saturday. At eleven o'clock comes the radio worship service that Papa *always* has to listen to. Without Morning Service, he can't recharge. When he's sitting there with the radio on his knees, he's like an old car battery that has suddenly been connected to a high-tension circuit. If it's a good service, it keeps Papa occupied nearly till evening. If it's a bad one, Evy has to take her place as substitute target right after lunch.

This Sunday, she's standing in the kitchen sorting out the sheets, her ears closely tuned to Papa's room. If he's in a bad mood, he turns the radio down so low that she can hardly distinguish anything but the hymns. But today he's relatively kindly; toward the end of the service he even turns up the volume, and she begins to think this may actually be a bearable Sunday.

88

Quite so. Just after twelve Papa comes charging into the kitchen.

"That devil of a bishop!" he bawls. "Can you believe that that dumb theologian succeeded in violating *four* of the proofs of God's existence in a sermon of twenty-two minutes forty seconds!"

"Tell me all about it," she encourages him.

Papa swings a kitchen chair around, places himself behind it, and bellies up to the back of it. With one hand he tries to press the chair down into the kitchen floor, while the other flies around his head with two fingers extended as if he were a boy scout or an excited pope.

"First the bastard goes and declares that it don't matter whether the world is designed according to a fixed plan or not, because God exists anyhow. That's a violation of the *physiotheological* argument for God's existence. Then he says right out from the radio pulpit so the whole Swedish nation can hear it: The Lord God ain't cause and effect, the Lord God is our Omnipotent Father in Heaven . . . *Cosmological* argument, he's stepped over the line, plain as day. Three and a half minutes later, here he comes again, a bishop, talking about the life to come, about the infinite soul of man . . ."

He looks challengingly at her and slowly sinks his right fist into his open left palm, like an auctioneer preparing to close the bids.

"Say it, Papa," pleads Evy.

He grants her wish: "The *anthropological* argument tells us that man's soul is finite, while the Creator himself is infinite!"

But then, when Papa's about to act out the fourth proof of God, it looks as though he's forgotten his lines. He digs into his sweater, into his pants pockets . . . Then he plucks out a bit of paper he's had tucked inside his wedding ring all along. He holds the paper a yard from his face and reads squintingly: "*Ontological* argument. The bishop stated . . ."

Here, Papa seems to have lost the thread; he turns his Argus eyes up into his skull, ransacking the crannies of his brain. Things are becoming critical.

89

"It's the bishop who's giving the morning service all next week," Evy says.

"Beg your pardon?!" Papa bursts out, disturbed, and turns one eye on her.

"I said it's the same pastor who's giving the service tomorrow morning."

Papa slowly closes his gaping mouth and brightens up.

"Then there'll be somebody layin' for him!"

He leaves the kitchen and goes into his room to write down a reminder to listen to the morning service.

Evy starts preparing lunch: new potatoes and canned herring in dill sauce for herself, acidified bread and CIBA omelet for Papa.

Papa's interest in Christianity is nothing new. He's always been a fanatical opponent of religion. Many of his lecture tours have had titles like "Marx's View of Christianity," "The So-Called Socialism Among the First Christians," "Lenin and the Russian Orthodox Church," and so on. He's fought religion doggedly.

When Evy was a child, Papa used to soak up textbooks of religious history and Christianity. She's still got the books stored in a trunk up in the attic. Books in which every other sentence has been clipped out, so that a page looks like some kind of paper comb.

Nowadays she doesn't dare to question his interest in religion. But earlier, when they lived together, she would sometimes ask him to explain, ask for his views on marxists who were also devout Christians. She herself has always found it hard to see the contradiction. Marxism aims to build a better society on earth; Christianity's goal is for people to get to heaven. Only if Christianity sabotages a more just society does it become dangerous. Otherwise it's complementary. Marxism's no religion.

But in Papa's philosophy, Christianity is still equivalent to the Holy Synod, the Vatican, or the Swedish clergy's militarism during the Finnish wars of the forties. With the years, he's gotten deeper and deeper into "textual criticism," as he calls it. With a bookkeeper's avidity, he tots up contradictions between the Old and New Testaments, searches for quotations from Jesus that might throw a doubtful light on the declaration "My Kingdom is not of this world," and now in recent years, denounces violations of the proofs of God's existence. Those proofs that were formulated by the fathers of the Church and the Christian philosophers. It's very convenient for Evy that Papa gets himself involved in something that doesn't lead to conflicts between them. But at the same time she feels sorry for him.

After lunch, it's time for Papa's Sunday stroll. Usually they go a few blocks toward St. Stephen's Church, where Papa pauses to rest a moment and to launch a few of his opinions about the watered-down derivativeness of Swedish church architecture. When it's icy underfoot—like today—she'd like to hold his arm. But then he gets furious and brandishes his cane. Evy must walk ten feet ahead of him "so he knows where he has her." It's become her habit to pretend to herself that she's chatting with "her Hasse" while she walks— that makes it easier to hold her pace. If her attention is held by Hans-Olof, she isn't turning around unnecessarily to check that Papa's keeping up.

16

The old Nobel prizewinner B.F. Skinner has had a decisive influence on the Institute for Clinical Psychology. Of course. For a professor of *psychology* at Harvard to be awarded the Nobel Prize in medicine and physiology was a spectacular departure from tradition. The tradition that for seventy years had reserved the prize for physicians or, to put it plainly, test tube physicians.

Skinner's research has two sources: Mother Russia and Papa America. The maternal tribe was represented by the giant Ivan Pavlov, the fellow with the dogs, who was professor at the Academy of Military Medicine in St. Petersburg from 1890 to 1913. On the paternal side were the American "behaviorists," who made such a rumpus around 1930.

B.F. Skinner's ideas are best expressed in his novel *Walden Two*, in which his major thesis is that mankind cannot afford the traditionally cherished liberal ideal of freedom. Skinner sees an absolute contradiction between individual liberty and society's chances to survive. Instead, he sees only one possible alternative: communal ownership of land and buildings, equality between men and women, devotion to art, music, and literature, reinforcement of constructive behavior, freedom from jealousy, freedom from gossip, *and* freedom from the traditional ideal of individual freedom.

That may sound like a thin broth, a very long simmering in ten quarts of water of one pinch of salt and the marrowbones, tail, and claws of the Communist Manifesto. But B.F. Skinner's writings are based on no such values and ideals as Justice or Brotherhood—instead, they concern "behavioral technology."

Burrhus Frederic Skinner was born in 1904. As a child, he was mechanically inclined but also strongly attracted to animals. He also liked to go to the circus. In 1922 he entered Hamilton College in Clinton, New York, majoring in English, but his real intention was to become a writer. By chance, during his school years, he read Bertrand Russell's articles in *Dial* on John B. Watson, the father of behaviorism. It was with Watson that psychology broke its ties to philosophy and became an independent *materialistic* science whose fundamental axiom is that men and animals are machines. In their construction, of course, men and animals are somewhat soft and elastic, having cogwheels of cartilage and pistons of bone. Yet they can be mapped out and understood from the vantage of mechanical principles. The Watsonian psychology took upon itself to show scientifically that the man-machine can be directed and controlled in every respect. Or if man *could not* be programmed, then man was no machine, and this, in turn, was equivalent to rejecting the whole scientific world view.

In 1928 Skinner gave up his writing career and began to study psychology at Harvard. During the years that ensued, he taught rats to live like Spartans and pigeons to pace off figure eights, play ping-pong, or dance. During World War II, he designed a missile—called "Pelican"—that was steered by pigeons, whose pecking at white spots on a radar screen directed the missile toward its target. "Pelican" never came into use, because the complex guidance system left no room in the missile for more than an insignificant quantity of high explosive.

In 1945 his daughter Deborah was born. She quickly became the USA's most talked-about infant as the "baby in a box." The box was an insulated, air-conditioned wooden box with glass windows. One of the problems of raising infants— Skinner reasoned—was simply keeping the child warm. Clothing was a poor solution, since it constricts movement, may cause overheating, and even poses a risk of strangulation. So Deborah went naked in a pleasantly warmed box. Skinner noticed that the baby was extremely sensitive to changes in temperature. Small changes could be used to get her to laugh—more or less like tickling or squeezing. In six months, the baby cried on only two occasions.

As an adult, Deborah has given only positive judgments of her two-and-a-half years in the box. In an interview with *Time,* she said: "It wasn't really a psychological experiment, but what you might call a happiness-through-health experiment. I think I was a very happy baby. Most of the criticisms of the box are by people who don't understand what it was."

Skinner's methods have since been developed and have achieved importance in pedagogy, in psychiatry, and in the handling of prisoners. That Skinner eventually received the Nobel Prize came to affect the Nobel Institutes' own clinical psychology, for an important recognition isn't a one-way street, it affects the giver as well as the receiver.

The Institute for Clinical Psychology is one of the units that have welcomed Evy Beck with open arms. The veterinary-medical angle is especially important to an institute that works with learning and training as prerequisites for experiments. If a pigeon dies—a pigeon that after eighteen months' training has learned to play "Twinkle twinkle little star" on the recorder—it is a catastrophe of entirely different dimensions than if a completely unschooled white rat falls on a cement floor and breaks its spine.

The head of the Institute of Clinical Psychology is Acting Professor Bengt Orvarsson, a quiet, very likable researcher with wide contacts in applied conditioning research in industry and defense. These contacts mean that the institute finds it relatively easy to get money.

In mid-March, Evy Beck's benefactor, Professor of Pharmacology Nils Rosén, proposes that their Saturday morning sessions be enlarged.

"Who would you like to add, Evy?"

Her usual irresolution doesn't trouble her this time, the answer is easy: "First of all, I'd like to add Bengt Orvarsson. He's one of my best 'customers.' And besides, he's very savvy about an area I have a poor grasp of myself, animal psychology."

"Makes good sense," says Nils Rosén. "And then?"

"Maybe Mats Sundell, at Aviation and Naval Medicine."

"Isn't he a little bit in the backwater?"

"Yes, but that means he's got lots of time," she says.

"I'll speak to him," says Rosén.

"Wouldn't it be a good idea to pin this down somehow in the Academic Council?" she asks. "I mean, after all, that's where the important questions are decided."

Now Nils Rosén gets a little troubled; he runs his fingers through his wreath of white hair and looks out the window. Then he collects himself and looks directly at her with his clever, cornflower-blue eyes: "We can't make our little Saturday morning session into an official institution . . . If we *organize* ourselves in any way, we'll be required to follow the apportionment principle, to the last comma."

"The apportionment principle?"

"We don't have the right to sit here and pull together a working group *ourselves*. As soon as a group exceeds two people, it falls under the apportionment principle," says Nils Rosén. "That means that for two specialists there must always be one lay representative or personnel representative."

"Aren't we personnel ourselves?"

"Not in the meaning of the apportionment principle. When we are operating from our professional knowledge, then we're *specialists*, not personnel."

She realizes her question has been a dumb one. Of course

94

NMSI applies exactly the same regulations that are applied everywhere else in society.

"We'll keep this to ourselves," says Rosén. "If Edwin Karlsson, for example, gets wind of our little session, he can make difficulties."

Evy Beck doesn't like to play secrecy games—yet she has to get a grip on her work assignment somehow. The chance to work with three friendly institute directors mustn't be missed. To pass it up would also be a kind of betrayal.

MEMORANDUM TO ADP CENTRAL DATABANK
CLASSIFIED INFORMATION OFFICIAL USE ONLY
OBSERVER ASST ADMINISTR S HORRLIN NMSI
KEYWORD EVY INGA-BRITT BECK WOLMB
CONTINUOUS WORK REVIEW 3
VERBAL REPORT B HAS GONE THROUGH CSUPC B
DISCOVERED ANIMAL DISEASE DAVIES FIBROSIS IN
SEVERAL INSTITUTES SAVING MINIMUM 3000 DOLS
STILL WORKING OVERTIME GENERALLY SUCCEEDING
HAS COMMENCED CLOSER COOPERATION WITH
ROSEN PHARMACOL INST AND FINDUS PHARMA FA
RM ACCORDING INFORMANT PEDERSEN MADE POS
IMPRESSION BUT POSSIBLY NOT WHOLLY UPTODAT
E NOTE THAT B TOGETHER WITH ROSEN SUNDELL
ORVARSSON HAS FORMED IRREGULAR WORKING GR
OUP WITHOUT CONSIDERATION GIVEN TO APPORTI
ONMENT PRINCIPLE HOWEVER NOT ON B'S INITIATI
VE W RESP TO HER FATHER SEE SECURITY POLICE
FILES HOWEVER NOTHING CURRENT STILL CERTAIN
AMT OVERAMBITION BUT PROGNOSIS OK
RATING 1-5
COMPETENCE 4
ADAPTABILITY 4
SOLIDARITY 3
MOTIVATION 5
COST NONE

17

Every other month, Papa's Auto-Hepar has to be taken back for factory adjustment. Papa himself has to spend the time in Roslagstull Hospital. The first factory checkup takes place at the end of March. Papa is admitted for Saturday-Sunday-Monday, when the hospital has a surplus of laboratory capacity.

Evy Beck has looked forward to a three-day holiday. Papa has been crankier than usual during this last part of March. She's been worried about him. The magnificent aggressive and paranoid outbursts have turned into a tired whining, a fretting and whimpering like that of a sick infant. When the ambulance came for him, he was so weakened that she was able to kiss him on the cheek.

Saturday is spent on the usual session with professors Rosén, Sundell, and Orvarsson. In the evening, she has her major housecleaning to do. It isn't till early Sunday morning that she can get around to an assignment she's put off all too long: reading through the current laws and regulations concerning the treatment of experimental animals.

In her program at the Skara branch of the Veterinary College, she studied the required legal subjects, of course, but that was some years ago. Besides, it's easy for the study of legal texts to be just lifeless memorization until the moment one confronts their application. Now, after studying the books for fifteen minutes, she's seized with great fright: that she's forgotten nearly everything—and that NMSI seems to be unaware of long passages of the law.

There is no unified "Law on Animal Welfare," but instead a number of regulations, ordinances, and administrative actions collected under that heading. The decisions, too, are from very different times—some as old as 1958, the newer ones written in the seventies. Current decisions on newer problems—for example, genetic manipulation—are entirely lacking.

She sits at her desk and with a marker tries to draw up a

97

schematic diagram. At the top she writes: *Law on Animal Welfare,* then draws a long vertical line down to a circle in which she prints: *Institutions with Laboratory Animals.* After that, many arrows and lines come to cross the paper. *Heads of institutions have primary responsibility,* she prints in smaller letters in the circle. But the head of an institution has to be able to consult somebody—she draws a long diagonal arrow up to the paper's upper righthand corner and writes: *Commission on Experimental Animals.* This commission consists of a number of specialists. The chairman is Olle Höjer, Justice of the Supreme Administrative Court, which handles taxation and civil service regulation cases. The secretary is Magnus Poussette, Consultant on Experimental Animals to the Chancellor of Swedish Universities. The other members of the commission are Professor Jan Yttergren, Acting Professor Yngve Larsson, Vet. Dr. Katarina Gren-Cederlund, Chief Chaplain Helge Vogelhielm, Director Pierre Allansson, Manager Gorm Pedersen, and Laboratory Animal Caretaker Edwin Karlsson. Advisory: Milan Topinka, Experimental Animals Veterinarian to SVA, and Roger Ellis, Chief of Research for Astra-Nestlé.

She draws a heavy arrow up to the top lefthand corner, where she prints *Supervisory Authority: Board of Public Health.* Then suddenly she discovers that she's left out an important outfit; she crowds it in edgewise between "Law on Animal Welfare" and "Board of Public Health": it is the *Reviewing Commission: Parliamentary Auditors.* She draws a number of triangles in free-floating positions with labels like *Veterinary Board, National Medical Research Council, Medical-Industrial Cooperative Committee, Agricultural Board,* and *Department of Industry.*

Then she does something she regrets, which robs the schematic diagram of its sharpness and clarity; she looks up the names not only of those who sit on the Commission on Experimental Animals but also of those on the other boards. She writes down the names, and now discovers that many of the same ones reappear. Between those, she lightly draws dotted lines, because it must be true that if Olle Höjer sits on not only the Commission on Experimental Animals but also the board of the National Veterinary Medical Institute as well as among the Parliamentary Auditors—well then, that means some form of *connection*, it's unclear what. But Olle Höjer isn't the worst. Research Chief Roger Ellis gets his name crucified by four perpendicular lines, while Director Pierre Allansson ends up being surrounded with a burst of radiating lines like the eye of God gilded above the pulpit. The record is held by Lab Animal Caretaker Edwin Karlsson—such a multitude of lines converge on him that he appears to be not a person but a great international airport.

Before this more or less completed diagram, she feels a great powerlessness. She goes out to the kitchen and takes a bottle of white port wine out of the refrigerator. When she has nudged the refrigerator door shut again with her knee and is standing there with her hand around the neck of the bottle, she feels someone else's hand grasp her wrist: it's Hans-Olof's. "Yes, Hasse," she says, "you're right—it's too early in the day." She looks at the kitchen clock: just ten to two.

When she returns to her desk, she takes the thick red marker and writes right across the diagram: AND WHERE AM I?!

That afternoon, she decides to write down the regulations that people at the Institutes seem to be violating. She feels like an accomplice, and is ashamed. Of course she shouldn't have come to the Institutes without having read up on the regulations. If you hire a specialist in veterinary medicine, you have a right to expect her to be grounded in the judicial decisions that affect her work. If you hire—?

Obviously Pharmacology breaks the law on the *quarantine period*. According to law, at least seven full days must elapse between purchase and experiment. Besides, they violate the *tattooing requirement:* "Every experimental animal shall, as soon as possible, and unless special reasons to the contrary exist, be tattooed in some fur-free location with an identification code (letter and consecutive number)." What really worries her is the requirement for keeping a purchase record and testing record on *every* animal. That doesn't seem to happen. But then she realizes that this requirement must be transferred to the Administration's Data Processing Section. In the data bank of NMSI, either on magnetic tape or in ionized-helium memory cartridges, are stored all the animals' weight, size, age, and estimated suffering.

One circumstance pleases her, namely, that the Nobel Institutes seem to restrict themselves to suppliers approved by the Veterinary Board. The primary supplier is Findus Pharmafarm, but also on the list are Ytterby Cat Farm, the Anticimex farm in Sollentuna, SAAB-Udevalla, Felix, Astra-Ewos, Konsum Medi-Kennel, and the United Workshops of the Åkers Powderworks. There's only one question mark. Through the grapevine, she's heard that a couple of institutes have set themselves up as animal raisers. It's said they subsequently sell the animals to other institutes below the market price to improve their own finances.

After supper, she relaxes with a book. Books of reportage depress her, she can never follow the thread of the plot in detective novels, but lovestories she devours like candy. She has had a treasure tucked away against this "mini-holiday" for a long time, Guy de Maupassant's *Bel-Ami*. She's just begun to get involved in Georges Duroy the hero's shaky finances when the telephone rings.

"Good evening, we're calling Mr. Rodion Beck," says a trained female voice.

"He's not home," she answers.

"At what number can he be reached?"

Evy doesn't know whether she ought to answer that Papa's in Roslagstull Hospital; it's not really everyone's business.

"Well, who is calling?" she queries.

"The Central Statistical Bureau," says the woman.

"At this time of day? And on Sunday?"

"Unfortunately, we have to call at a time when people are at home," the woman says. "And we are very anxious to reach Mr. Rodion Beck."

"Oh, really? Well, this is his daughter speaking."

"Are you his nearest relation?"

"Yes, I am."

"In that case, there's no objection to our explaining," says

100

the woman brightly. "I'm trying to reach Mr. Beck because he's *lotted.*"

"What do you mean, *lotted?*"

"Mr. Beck is part of our sample of ten thousand Swedish citizens, chosen by lot, who are going to decide through an opinion survey our next year's parliamentary election."

"Mr. Beck is ill," says Evy.

"Is he mentally ill?"

"Hardly. He has a liver ailment."

"If Mr. Beck has not been declared incompetent by a psychiatrically trained physician, there is no objection."

"I'd appreciate it if Mr. Beck could be left in peace," says Evy. "He's an old man . . ."

"There is no upper limit to the voting age," says the woman.

"It would be better if you'd ask somebody else, anyway."

"No, that absolutely cannot be done! We cannot manipulate the selection. If Mr. Beck does not participate in the opinion survey, he will be counted as *discard.*"

"Oh. I see. But I would still be very grateful . . . He gets so wound up!"

"To vote is both a right and a *duty,*" says the woman.

"I really think he's done his part in that respect."

There is silence on the receiver. Evy gets an unpleasant feeling that she's just conversed with an automatic telephone-answerer—but then the theatrically trained female voice comes on again: "Mr. Beck himself has to decline. In this case, a refusal from the nearest relative does not suffice."

"I beg you, leave my father in peace," says Evy.

"You did say liver ailment and not mental ailment?"

"They've removed his liver."

"So sorry . . ." says the woman. "We'll have to try another day. Mr. Beck ought to answer yes or no *himself,* if possible. Good-bye!"

When she puts down the receiver, she's lost all interest in love stories. She stuffs the open book under the cushion of the armchair so as not to lose her place. For a long time, she stands by her desk, leaning over, staring at her ambitious doodling. With a green marker she draws a double line under Edwin Karlsson and writes: *Lotted or discard?*

18

On Monday morning Evy Beck does something she's never before been able to bring herself to do: she stays home as "compensation" for working Saturday and Sunday.

For permanent employees there is a comprehensive and meticulous "compensation system," a system of overtime compensation so hard to handle that each institute has a special clerk for the purpose. Every kind of provable overtime is to be compensated with time off. But one doesn't get an hour off for every hour of overtime. Depending on when during the year it occurs, the overtime is to be multiplied by a "compensation constant." If you work Christmas night, you can take off the number of hours you worked times 5.18. But if you've skipped lunch on an ordinary weekday, you can only multiply your overtime by .975.

For people who aren't permanent employees but instead are employed on the WOLMB budget or otherwise belong to the so-called lower productivity sector, there is, of course, a special compensation schedule. However, it can't be applied so long as the Labor Market Board isn't allowed to fill the vacancies in the Compensation Office. SACO, the professional union, has blocked any appointment to the chief's position until the pay is raised.

Evy Beck has not, on the whole, thought very much about compensation. But on this particular Monday morning, while she's preparing her morning coffee, she feels delightfully heavy, and at the same time as if she were floating a couple of inches off the floor. "Hasse dear, sweet dear Hasse," she murmurs, "today we'll stay in bed till lunch!" Hans-Olof makes no objection. Evy thinks it's terrific that Hasse can stay when, for once, she's out from under the parental thumb.

For a moment she considers pulling out Maupassant's *Bel-Ami* from under the armchair cushion, but she's feeling too lazy even to read. The watery chicory coffee hardly makes her any more alert. By eight fifteen she's already deep in slumber. Just after eleven the telephone rings.

"Evy? Are you ill?" Nils Rosén von Rosenstein asks from the other end of the line.

"We-e-ell . . . no. My father's coming home from the hospital today," she answers somewhat blurrily.

"Sorry to disturb you. But it seems they've got some kind of epidemic at the Physicum. I met our colleague Nilson-Roth at the Grants Committee meeting today. He lost fifty gerbils over the weekend."

"Have they escaped?"

"No, died."

"The worst problem with the gerbils, or Mongolian desert rats, is that they get away. They spread their diseases so easily that way."

"Evy, d'you think you could come? This couldn't have happened just by chance. Of course gerbils aren't really high-priced animals, but Nilson-Roth says this has already cost him nearly two thousand dollars."

At half past twelve she's standing in the Physicum's Small Animal Area looking at a black plastic bag that by this time contains over seventy dead gerbils. Something doesn't figure. On Friday all the gerbils were healthy. They don't seem to have had any real symptoms. Suddenly they turn restless, get a high fever, become listless, and die within a few hours.

"How many people have been in this room since Thursday?" she asks.

"I can't say for sure," answers Professor Nilson-Roth. He's at least sixty-five years old, crippled by polio, and uses two big black canes with the largest rubber caps she's ever seen.

"There's you and I," she calculates. "And somebody who looks after the animals."

"Gimlund."

"Unfortunately, I've got to propose that you isolate this room," she says, "till we know what's killing the gerbils."

"I'll see to it," the professor says, and starts out of the room;

his hips wiggle in an almost obscene way and he seems to be screwing the canes into the floor.

"Just a minute," she says. "Unfortunately, that also applies to us."

He turns around as laboriously as a paddle steamer.

"Are you sure it's also contagious for humans?!"

"It may be," she says. "Is Gimlund in the building?"

He nods toward the intercom and Evy Beck goes over to the little screen-covered hole in the wall, presses one hand against her throat, and says, "Evy Beck calling Mr. Gimlund."

There's a crackling and hissing on the intercom. Then it sounds like it used to when the dial of an old-fashioned telephone went around. It's a few more minutes at least before he answers.

"Gimlund."

"The professor wants you to come to the Small Animal Area right away," she says.

Nilson-Roth shoves his powerful torso into a corner and crosses the canes before his undersized legs.

"I hope you know what you're doing," he says. "I *really do* hope you know what you're doing."

She paces back and forth among the galvanized cages. Thank God they have modern cages with a double layer of wire mesh. *If* she's right . . . then it would be catastrophic if these rodent escape artists broke out.

Gimlund comes. He's a tall, slender man of about twenty-five. He's got his skull shaved clean in the latest style. The only hair on his face is his eyebrows and the whiskers that hang like a bunch of grapes.

"It's probably some kind of salmonella infection," he says, and starts rolling up his sleeves to open a cage where two dead gerbils lie.

"Stop!" Evy says. "Don't touch that cage!"

Slowly and wearily Gimlund rolls down the sleeves of the gray lab coat.

"Are you talking about total isolation?" he says in a tone that suggests he doubts her sanity.

104

"This is no common intestinal infection," she answers. "The symptoms don't check."

"We haven't got authority here to isolate totally," Gimlund says. "That's the safety officer's bag."

"I know that. Who's your safety officer?"

"The machinist," says the professor from his corner.

Gimlund goes to the intercom: "Mattias Gimlund calling Yerganian."

"On the way," says Yerganian.

Gimlund advances on her. She only comes up to his breast pocket, where he has six different pens and pencils.

"Just what kind of disease is it they've got, then?" he says from high above her hairline.

She doesn't want to answer. She has a very firm and intense conviction that she is right, that the gerbils have been struck down by a dangerous and very rare virus disease. The stupid thing is, though, she can't remember the name. It's been thirteen years since she had her exams in rodent diseases. She remembers the page in the textbook, she even remembers its number: 2013. The next page, 2014, is occupied by a photo of a little monkey scratching himself. She remembers the symptoms, she remembers the incubation period: 6–9 (25) days. But she cannot to save her life remember *the name*.

"It's probably one of your rare viruses," says the professor.

"Got any monkeys in this institute?" she asks him.

But it's Gimlund who answers instead, and heatedly, as if in defense: "Yeah, but they're conditioned!"

Conditioning means that the monkeys—who are often captured in the wild—have been sitting in quarantine while being wormed and checked as to condition. At that moment she hears ringing steps made by shoes with metal heel-taps out in the corridor.

"Don't come in!" she calls around the corner. "Stop where you are!"

"What's going on?" says a hoarse voice with an east-coast accent.

"I've got good reason to suspect that a virus disease dangerous to humans has broken out here in the Small Animal

Area," she says, and notices that her voice is squeezed up into the treble just as if a couple of invisible thumbs were pressing on her throat.

"Oho," says the calm easterner, as if she'd announced that a faucet was leaking.

"I have to ask you as safety officer to close down this working space."

It is quiet out in the tiled corridor.

"She won't tell us what the disease is called . . ." says Gimlund quickly, and leans his long frame out in the corridor.

"Somebody really ought to talk it over with the chief safety officer, Edwin Karlsson," says Yerganian thoughtfully.

"Edwin Karlsson? No, he's sitting as an expert on the panel that's filling the new professorship in stress research," says Nilson-Roth. "They're meeting this afternoon."

"Couldn't we consider . . ."

"No!" she says, now nearing panic; the grip on her throat has tightened. "We have to isolate immediately and check if anybody else has been in here."

Yerganian doesn't answer. When the silence gets too hard to bear, she sneaks over to the doorway and peers cautiously around the corner. About fifteen feet away a man somewhere over forty-five with unruly blonde hair is sitting on the floor. She'd expected him to look like an Armenian. Yerganian tucks a big pinch of snuff under his lip and looks at her pleasantly.

"Hi," she says.

"Hi yourself," he says with bulging lip and widely flared nostrils. Then he looks down at his heel-taps again: "If you shut down the animal area as an unsafe working space . . . If you do that and it turns out to be unnecessary . . . then you can lose your job . . ."

The pressure on her throat returns; the responsibility is hers—it's she who *knows*. But it's Yerganian who's supposed to make the decision, and Yerganian who has to pay if the investigation shows that she's sounded the alarm by mistake.

"I don't want anybody to die . . ." says Evy Beck.

Yerganian nods slowly, then looks up and grins: "Maybe

I've been rattling around in these tunnels too long. Probably it's time I changed jobs. Time for MELMB to take care of me."

She pulls her head back so he won't see that she's almost ready to burst into tears.

"Call on the 'com," says Yerganian in the corridor. "Call down to the section head and notify him I've closed down Physicum's Small Animal Area as a dangerous work space!"

19

It's late afternoon. They've brought three easy chairs into the Small Animal Area. Evy Beck isn't sitting in hers. She's been standing up for over an hour, scraping her right shoulder against the wall where the intercom is.

"Roslagstull Hospital on the line," says the operator.

She straightens up and massages the numbed shoulder.

"Evy Beck calling the chief physician," she says.

Silence again. She hates this new type of intercom where a person is never sure whether it's turned on or off. But she's glad that a supply space like the Small Animal Area is not given priority for telecommunications; had this area been judged "critical," there would have been a TV screen set into the wall next to the intercom. The mere thought of that causes Evy Beck to comb her fingers through her unwashed hair.

"Yes?" says a familiar voice right by her ear. The quality of the connection is so perfect that in spite of herself she has to look behind her to see if the chief physician is standing there.

"Hello, this is Evy Beck," she says. "I'm sorry to bother you, but something has hap—"

"Hello, Mrs. Beck," the doctor says pleasantly.

"I'm so worried about Papa, because I've got a kind of problem here . . ."

"Mr. Beck is just fine," the doctor says, with a slightly weary professional optimism. "All the blood values are at a proper level. Serum potassium was a little high, but we've adjusted that. General condition, satisfactory. There isn't very much more to tell, Mrs. Beck. You really *needn't* worry."

"Unfortunately, I can't be home to receive him this evening," she says. "I'd be awfully grateful if you could keep him for a couple more days."

"There's no medical justification for further hospital care. Are you claiming some kind of justification of a social nature, Mrs. Beck?"

"Whatever you like, but I'm unable to leave my place of work . . . There's nobody at home to take care of Papa when he comes!"

The chief physician doesn't answer. Has he hung up? Erik. She mustn't be afraid to trouble Erik, she thinks. For once I'll have to ask Erik's help. Of course he is busy . . . Still, this concerns his grandfather, so . . . She goes and seats herself in the free armchair. To her right sits Professor Nilson-Roth reading yesterday's Sunday *News,* which somebody kindly put on one of the armchairs. To Evy's left sits the lab animal caretaker, Gimlund, reading a paperback. She takes his hand and raises it to see the cover. It's Maupassant's *Bel-Ami.*

Without waiting for her to ask, and without looking up from the page, Gimlund says, "Actually, I'm a literary scholar."

Without warning, the intercom spits out the chief physician's voice: "Mrs. Beck?" He sounds slightly tentative, as if he stood inside the wall and was peering out through the little speaker aperture.

"Here!" she cries, leaping up.

"Yes. Mrs. Beck, our allotment of beds for social cases is unfortunately completely full. I've just checked with the Medical Board's computer."

"Where can I turn?" she asks shrilly. *"Somebody's* got to take care of him?!"

"The way I see it, just about your only choice is for Mr. Beck to be admitted to an emergency shelter."

"Where do you apply?"

"The Metropolitan Police Department's Emergency Center."

"Yes, but Papa . . . I mean, Papa's sort of . . . special . . ."

"Your father's in good condition."

She gives up. She starts to say "Thanks anyway," but she doesn't know if the chief physician is still on the intercom. She puts her ear against it to listen for an electronic hiss. Suddenly there is a powerful whine. Frightened at first, she stares at the intercom, and then realizes that the sound is coming from the corridor. The piercing whine rises higher and higher in pitch as it approaches.

"It's the fork-lift," says Gimlund, getting up from the arm-chair. He raises the gray lab coat and stuffs *Bel-Ami* in his back pocket.

She realizes that the National Veterinary Institute has finally come to take charge of the black plastic bag of dead gerbils. The dead animals have to be dissected to determine the cause of death. Probably nothing definite will be an-nounced before the virus tests are complete. How long do they take—twenty-four hours or two weeks?

Gimlund stands six feet away from the plastic bag and looks at it with distaste: "How do you catch it?" he asks.

"Probably only by direct contact," she says. "Give me the gloves."

He gives her the long-sleeved monkey-gloves he has in his pocket. She pulls them on, takes a deep breath, and advances toward the sack. There isn't any string so she has to try tying a knot in the plastic bag. It's hard to get a real grip on it. She tries again. Her lungs are bursting with old air that wants to be let out. When the pressure becomes unbearable, she re-leases the used breath a little at a time, like a diver. At last! She turns around, nearly nauseated, and breathes greedily.

"Administration calling Dr. Beck!" says the intercom, as though it had been standing there waiting for her to turn back around again.

"Yes?" she answers, and goes toward the wall with her gloved hands held straight out at each side, like a penguin.

"We've just gone through the microfilm records of the eye-lock on Physicum's animal department."

Why hadn't she thought of it! Fingerprint locks aren't just impossible for outsiders to open; all the thumbprints are stored in the lock memory and can later be transferred to microfilm.

"We have narrowed it down to four possible persons," says the intercom. "At 7:03:35 A.M. the lock checked in machinist Peter Yerganian . . ."

"It can't be him!" says Gimlund. "He's got no business here."

"—At 9:14:20 A.M. Dr. Kihlman went through the lock. At 9:23:06 A.M. laboratory animal caretaker Gimlund—"

"That's *me*, of course," says Gimlund.

"At 10:10:25 A.M. we find that custodian Helene Bernadotte checked in."

"That's the cleaning woman," says Professor Nilson-Roth.

"You must get hold of her at once!" says Evy Beck. "She can put everyone around her in danger."

The intercom says neither *Roger* nor *Willco*—it merely becomes silent.

Evy and Gimlund together shove the black plastic bag toward the corridor. They don't touch it with their hands, but use their feet. It feels repulsive to kick a sack filled with dead animals. When they give it a last shove so that it slides out in the hallway, the electric fork-lift whines into motion and a grasping fork covered with transparent plastic comes into view. It takes a careful grip on the dangerous sack and raises it a foot or so above the floor. Then the machine backs out.

There is a shallow pan of chloride of lime in the corner— Gimlund and Evy go there and stamp around in the powder like two athletes before a try at the record.

"Edwin Karlsson calling Evy Beck," says the intercom.

She's been expecting that; sleeping dogs seem to have waked.

"Yes," she answers, and braces herself.

"Calling back at six," says the intercom.

She waits a few minutes, then says, "I've got to get someone to take care of my papa."

Gimlund says nothing, he's deep into *Bel-Ami* again. But the professor—who up to now has taken no part—wakes up suddenly.

"Rodion Beck," he says. "I remember him. He shook some

110

sense into us when we were hardly dry behind the ears . . ."

"When was that?" she asks, though she can guess what he means; but she'd like to hear something good about Papa.

"It must have been just before you were born," he says. "It was during the Spanish Civil War. A group of the students here had gotten up a collection for the Franco side. Went around begging money from the big pharmaceuticals manufacturers. Yes, Franco was considered a guarantee that the Reds wouldn't get a foothold in Western Europe. A meeting was arranged in the old Student Union, a kind of Franco rally. It was my first term as a medical student. Then Rodion Beck came in, unannounced. He not only succeeded in getting in, he also succeeded in getting to speak. That speech was one I'll never forget. I have seldom been so ashamed . . ."

The professor looks down at his crossed black walking sticks, then says, "He was interned during the war, wasn't he?"

"Yes," she says.

"Couldn't have been much fun to have your father in jail?"

What answer is there to that? Instead she goes to the intercom: "Evy Beck here. I want to send a telegram to Dr. Erik Beck, at the Technological Economics Institute."

"Hello? Telegram office here. Is this official?"

"No, private," she says.

"Then you must pay in advance at the office," says the intercom.

"But . . ."

Behind her she hears the professor getting to his feet. The rubber caps squeak on the tile floor as he approaches.

"It's *official*," he says.

"Who countersigns?"

"210113–1357 Wilhelm Nilson-Roth."

"Go ahead," says the telegram office.

"Erik, you must take care of Grandfather who is coming home tonight at eight. Signed, Evy."

For the next few hours they wait. She can't seem to stop probing between her shoulder blades to see whether she is stiff, whether her neck muscles ache, whether she might be

111

getting a fever. When beer and sandwiches are handed in from the corridor on a big shovel, she doesn't feel hungry, just slightly nauseated.

At six fifteen Edwin Karlsson finally has time to talk with her on the intercom: "Well, miss," he says. "This is Edwin Karlsson . . ."

Obediently as a schoolgirl she trots up to the intercom.

"Now what kind of a sickness is it that our little girl has gotten so tremendously upset about?"

"A virus," she says. "Very rare, but dangerous."

"And it is called—?"

"The name is not important," she says. "Have you got hold of Helene Bernadotte?"

"We can't send out an all-cars alert on just our own say-so," says Edwin Karlsson paternally.

She gets so angry she stamps the floor hard.

"What?" he says. "What was that?"

"Nothing," she says; suddenly she remembers the name of the disease. "I implore you to search for Helene Bernadotte. She is suspected of carrying the Marburg Virus."

"Is that so?" he says, a little set back. "Marburg, is it? All right, I'll talk it over with the Experimental Animals Commission, which I happen to be on."

"I know that," she says.

"But I just want to let our little girl know she's going to have to answer for this before the Production Committee. Young lady, you'd better get ready to explain in detail this hasty interruption of the Physicum's production."

20

The clock approaches midnight. Gimlund has just finished helping the professor go out to the john; now they are both asleep in their armchairs. Evy hunches over, knees ajar, and counts the tiles in the floor. Even though they are placed with mathematical regularity, she gets a different total every time. She counts over and over. A child ought to be able to add up tiles that are set edge to edge. But it's impossible—her eye isn't capable of distinguishing a large number of precisely identical white squares.

Should she call Papa? She's been on the verge of getting up to call home at least fifteen times. But each time she has sunk back again: I'll call him when I've got the tiles counted right. But she realizes that this is just a fit of ambivalence, of both wanting and not wanting to. She doesn't like to gamble but wants a rational basis for decision. She can't find one: either Papa's home but won't answer or he won't answer because he's not home. Or he does answer—and then she's waked him. If the telephone rings, he can jump up and in his hurry forget that the tubes are clamped to the mechanical liver. And Erik . . .

An unfamiliar voice is heard over the intercom: "Situation report from Metropolitan Police: missing person Helene Bernadotte has not yet been located."

Evy tries to make contact with Hans-Olof, but it doesn't work. Instead, it is Erik who establishes himself as superego; it is clever Erik who has perched himself on the roof of the animal area and peers down through one of the plexiglass skylights in the ceiling. She licks her finger, smoothes down her eyebrows, and looks up.

"Hi, Erik!"

"Hi, Evy!"

Then she doesn't know what else to say—she just stares at the ceiling and tries to smile. Erik smiles back; he smiles naturally, without looking strained. Then his hand rises and waves with two fingers. She clears her throat.

"Your mom's got to learn to take responsibility."

"Sure, Evy . . . but you really could have called up the National Veterinary Institute first."

"But I did that, Erik! They said that no decision could be expected on their part before they'd had a chance to examine the gerbils."

"You could have asked *somebody. Somebody* in this country must know more than you do about this Marburg Virus disease."

"But Erik, I just couldn't remember what it was *called!*"

113

She looks intently at the skylight to get support from Erik. But Erik has nothing more on this mind this time. He waves, just perceptibly—still with only two fingers. Then his handsome regular features fade away. As he's disappearing, Erik smiles very slightly; the same one-inch smile he put on as a five-year-old when she hired a baggage porter to be Santa Claus . . .

Of course she could have looked for somebody, for example at the Veterinary College. Called up and said: The symptoms are such-and-such, I don't remember the virus's name but the page number was 2013 and the picture showed a monkey. A monkey!! Suddenly she's on her feet and shaking Gimlund awake.

"Yuh—yuh—'s time go to the john . . . ?" says Gimlund. Then he wakes up, looks at her hostilely, and says with distaste, "Yes?!"

"You said before that you've got monkeys in this institute?"

Gimlund looks sourly at her, as if she had waked him up just to tell him that the sun sets in the west or that Sweden is a neutral country.

"Who takes care of the monkeys?!" she asks fiercely.

"The mammal caretaker is Jan Norén."

"I want to get hold of him. Immediately!"

"At this time of night?" he says, and tries to start a yawn by just gaping; it doesn't work. He looks as though he's simply trying to call attention to a bad tooth.

Ten minutes later she has gotten the Communications Department to call Norén. She stands and waits by the intercom hole and looks for Erik in the skylight overhead. But Erik doesn't show. Instead, she glimpses the flashlight of the quarantine watchman on the roof who is pacing back and forth to keep warm.

"Hi-ho-o-o-o! Hi-ho-o-o-o!" comes howling out of the intercom.

"Jan Norén?"

No answer. Instead, someone begins singing "Asleep in the Deep" in falsetto.

"I'm trying to find Jan Norén," she says.

114

"Me too!" says a voice that immediately breaks up in giggles.

The man is drunk, but she *must* get an answer.

"Please pull yourself together," she pleads. "I've got to find out how the *monkeys* are feeling!"

"Shu-u-ure!" says the voice. Then the speaker seems to turn away toward the room he is in: "Tell ya in a minute . . ."

She hears heavy breathing which becomes panting, then the voice sneaks right up to the microphone and says with the greatest confidence, "They feel *great!*"

"I mean the monkeys at the Physicum!" she says.

Mattias Gimlund has finally realized that this is serious. He comes up next to her and says, "Johnny? This is Gimmy."

"Come on over and bring the broad with ya!"

After a while Gimlund succeeds in changing the tone of the conversation by thrusting stiff key-words into the intercom: quarantine, police, alarm, epidemic.

"So what is it with the monkeys . . ." says Norén, tired and uninterested.

"Are they completely well? Have you noticed any symptoms whatsoever in the last few days?" asks Evy Beck.

"They've been scratching themselves."

"Where?!"

"Yeah, where do monkeys usually scratch themselves?"

"It's important! Where?"

Again there's panting, as if the speaker was trying to run away from his own drunkenness or air it out.

"Oh, on the inside of the arm . . . Sickan and Selma have gotten eczema on the inside of the arm."

"They're two baboons," Gimlund explains.

"Just Sickan and Selma?" Evy asks. "None of the other monkeys?"

"We haven't got any more monkeys in the Physicum," Gimlund says. "They've mostly been replaced by pigs."

The Marburg disease is regarded as most common among monkeys. Where it comes from nobody knows—she sees the whole of page 2013 before her now. The disease begins with skin eruptions on the inside of the arms. Death usually follows within forty-eight hours. The disease is communicated by direct contact with sick animals or by contact with the urine or saliva of sick animals. It does not infect at a distance. Besides monkeys, the disease can occur in hamsters, mice, and men. It got its name from Marburg in Germany; an epidemic there killed seven people some time around 1970.

By 2:00 A.M. the monkey room at the Physicum has been put under quarantine, Jan Norén has been brought to the Communicable Diseases Hospital, and Helene Bernadotte has been found. For the past two days she has been in the South Hospital for observation because of high sedimentation rate, fluctuating temperature, and unexplainable fatigue.

Evy Beck sits in the easy chair, scratches her neck against the backrest, and tries to shut her eyes. It doesn't work. Her neck is sore and her whole body feels stiff in the joints as after unaccustomed exercise. She squints up at the ceiling, looking for Erik: "Mama was right, Erik . . ." she mumbles. But Erik isn't there. As usual, he's probably got something more important to attend to.

Then, she tries to summon up Hans-Olof. It's hard—but after all, he's way off in Australia. In the end he does show up, though, as dim as a reflection in rippling water.

"Hasse . . ." she says. "Hasse, can't you come, just this once . . ."

But Hasse's image fades away before she has had time to say anything. Another face presents itself. It's a sharp and crystal-clear image, it's Papa. Papa is between thirty and forty and has a funny big gray hat with a black band and a wide brim that turns up. He's dressed in a trench coat. In his hand he has a cardboard suitcase.

Evy, says Papa. *I'm going to be away for a while. Take good care of Mama.*

No, Papa! You don't have to go to jail! she cries. *They're wrong, we're right! It* is *Marburg . . .*

Papa laughs with his mouth, but not with his eyes. Then he reaches out and pulls her braids.

Sure we're right, Evy, he says. *But that doesn't help.*

A locomotive hoots tremulously . . . She wakes up and looks

at the clock: 5:35. Then she hears a voice coming from the intercom. It must have been talking a while. It is Edwin Karlsson.

". . . according to what the doctors at South Hospital have just told me, little girl."

"What's that?" she cries. "What have they said?!"

"There's no reason whatever to suspect Marburg. It's perfectly clear that this cleaning woman is suffering from jaundice. From a perfectly common *hepatitis,* if the little lady knows what that is? In other words, you were *wrong!*"

Evy Beck does something she hasn't done since she was eleven and had her first menstruation—she faints.

21

It's Good Friday and spring has come. The snow, from the first a light sulfur-yellow in color, has been packed down by the warming temperature, and now the drifts look like saffron dough. Erik comes with his car to pick her up at the Isolation Hospital on Ship Island. The frozen earth is also melting and the few cars have plowed patterned furrows in the gravel. Evy wonders if they can't stroll for five minutes in the spring sunshine before he drives her home, but he thinks she has to take it easy now, after nearly two weeks in the hospital.

Evy doesn't feel at all weak or washed-out. She feels strong, optimistic, and happy. She can't remember that she's ever before in her life had such thoroughgoing *luck.* It's as if she'd been depositing her own personal allotment of luck in a bank ever since she was born and now, with interest on top of interest, it's all come pouring out at once. Is it sensible to take it all out at once?! The thought fills her with bubbling laughter . . .

"Quotia," she says half-aloud before she has time to press her hands over her laughing mouth and laughter-filled cheeks.

"What'd you say, Evy?" Erik asks.

"Well, I'm just sitting here thinking of what terrific *luck*

117

I've had," she says. "First a job—and not just any old job, but a job in my own field. Then the job turns out to be both independent and interesting. And then I think a Marburg epidemic's broken out . . . Erik, that's *hard* to diagnose," she says, glancing furtively at him for a little credit.

But Erik happens to be wholly occupied with steering the wide car over the much-too-narrow Ship Island bridge.

"How's that? What luck?"

"I sound the alarm. And then sit there and get sick and think . . . well, how is Papa going to make out when I'm not around any more. Then Edwin Karlsson calls up and says it's *not* Marburg. And then I faint away, go to the hospital, lie there two weeks, feeling pretty good and thinking it's nothing much, nothing to worry about. Not till they're releasing me do they tell me, *You've had Marburg but now you're recovered.*"

"There's luck and luck," says Erik. "You were *right.*"

"Maybe so. But I've never experienced such a chain of lucky circumstances before."

She sits enjoying herself as they roll through downtown. They're wending their way through the central shopping streets: Library Street, Birger Jarl Street, Sture Plaza, King Street. Not for several years has she felt any urge to stroll here. While she was unemployed, she easily fancied that people could see her joblessness on her, almost as if it were some kind of skin disease. But now she's not one bit embarrassed—if Erik hadn't been in such a hurry, she'd gladly have stepped out and strolled a little while on Library Street, now owned by NK, the Nordic Corporation; or on Sture Plaza, owned by the Domus chain; or on King Street, with all its gourmet food shops, which is part of the Agricultural Consortium.

Erik roars on, along Roslag Street. They have to drive around the block twice before he catches sight of the parking attendant to pay for an hour in front of Evy's door. Up to now, Evy has pushed away all thought of Papa. She knows he's been well cared for by a practical nurse while she's been in the hospital; Erik arranged that. The only question now is whether her luck will hold all day, so that Papa won't have lain there loading up for some especially well-planned kind of indictment against her. Maybe he is lying in wait up there with a pair of psychological thumbscrews under his pillow. It's been eighteen days since she's seen him, and she's worried that she may have gotten out of the habit, that she won't be able to control her temper.

When they go into the kitchen, the table is full of flowers. The practical nurse must have put them in water. She almost gets tearful reading the cards: "Welcome home, from the Saturday bunch, Nils, Mats, and Bengt." "Thanks for your extraordinary help! Wilhelm Nilson-Roth." The next card puzzles her: "Thanks, Evy Beck—Georges Duroy." Then she understands. Georges Duroy is the hero of Maupassant's *Bel-Ami*. The flowers must have come from the laboratory animal caretaker and literary scholar Mattias Gimlund. The last and largest flower arrangement comes from Gorm Pedersen, manager of Findus Pharmafarm.

But where's Papa? Is he sitting in the bathroom ready to pounce? Or is he lying in bed pretending to be asleep? Cautiously she opens the door to Papa's room. He certainly is lying on the bed. But he is sleeping peacefully. It's no phony sleep he's trying to pull this time. She can see that at once; Papa has always been a hopelessly bad actor.

"Erik?" she says in a theatrical whisper in the kitchen. "You have to go now, of course?"

Erik comes in from the vestibule. She's surprised to see that he's hung up his topcoat.

"Mind if I sit down for a while?" he asks, and seats himself by the kitchen table.

She moves all the flowers to the drainboard and puts on the coffee.

"Aren't people fantastically *nice*," she says.

"What d'you mean?" Erik responds neutrally.

"That they go and send flowers, of course! And that they sent get well cards to the hospital!"

"You really think you're lucky, do you?"

"Yes. *Really.*"

"And also you imagine that people send you good wishes because they are *nice?*"

119

"I'm happy, Erik," she says.

"It's not because they're nice, and it's not because you've had luck. It's because you were *right.*"

She understands perfectly what Erik means, though she doesn't like the message: Had everything that's happened in the last two weeks happened exactly the same—except that it *wasn't* Marburg, then Quotia would have been wrong. Not only been wrong, but made a fool of herself. And the difference between right and wrong in this case is a matter of sheer chance. She would have been exactly as smart, professionally competent, responsible, and skillful even if it hadn't been Marburg. Yet Erik is probably right: Everyone might have turned their backs on her if she'd been wrong. It would have been entirely natural—and she would have had no appeal whatsoever.

"Did I make you sad?" asks Erik.

She shakes her head and puts on a smile.

"Evy, aren't you ever going to grow up?"

Then Erik says something that causes her to sit down by the table without even pouring the coffee.

"I think you should leave NMSI."

"Now?! After all this?"

"Next time it may not turn out so well, Evy. You can't count on it."

She doesn't understand. At last she has good prospects—admittedly, by pure chance—but now she has the opportunity to achieve some practical results.

"You know it's not a real position," says Erik.

"I'm content to be on the WOLMB budget. There aren't any funds for a regular position."

"But don't you realize that you haven't got any *clout?*"

That, she has realized. That she's there on sufferance has been plain from the beginning. On the other hand, it's perfectly understandable. If you take somebody in from outside, put him on the Labor Market Board budget doing work that isn't considered obviously useful by the directors of the institutes, then he's going to lack clout.

"What's going to happen when the WOLMB money is gone?" asks Erik.

120

"If I'm lucky I get a renewal."

"It hasn't really got anything to do with luck, Evy. Don't you see that it's a budget question. And a question of market conditions. If the wind's blowing in the wrong direction when your budget's up for renewal, luck won't help. Neither will people being so nice."

She doesn't like Erik's way of saying "nice"; there is an undertone of cynicism in Erik that she despises. When he was twenty-two years old and at the top of his class in the National Institute of Technological Economics, he also seemed cynical in a way—but subsequently Erik has matured and grown up to the level of his intelligence. At least she's wanted to believe so.

"Evy," he says, placing his hand on hers. "It was well done, discovering that epidemic before it had time to spread . . . But you did something that really lay outside your work assignment. If NMSI employees are exposed to infectious disease, then it's a question of working environment, not a problem of veterinary medicine."

She pulls her hand away from Erik and looks at him sadly.

"Don't get me wrong!" says Erik, taking back her hand. "You made a very valuable contribution. But it was really the Safety Committee's responsibility."

She knows what Erik means. And she'll gladly share the glory with anyone who wants. But in practical terms this has given her strength and increased her opportunities in her work.

"I know you, Evy," he says. "For you, the *animal welfare* angle is just as important as protecting people who work with animals."

"Sure, Erik."

"That's why you're not going to make it."

She's thought about that too. Only an idiot would imagine it was going to be easy to push animal welfare at NMSI. Or more generally, to push through actions that are not required by law or not profitable in one way or another, either from a crass financial point of view or in terms of research progress.

"If I have people's good will, I probably can accomplish a

little something," she asserts; for once she thinks it's she who's right and Erik who's wrong.

"Marginal accomplishments," says Erik with a trace of contempt. "I'm sorry to have to say this, Evy . . . but you're old-fashioned."

She doesn't mind that a bit—she's felt old-fashioned and exaggerated ever since she was a teenager. Over the years, the feeling has been transformed from a handicap to a security, an inner stability. At certain moments she has thought with gratitude that she would never have been able to adjust to "the society of continual change" without that peasantlike slowness.

"Anyway, I can't leave now," she says. "Why should I choose unemployment over an insecure job?"

"I might be able to help you get a research grant."

"No, Erik. Maybe I'll just end up beating my head against the wall, but I'd hate myself if I quit."

Erik looks at her for a moment, then brightens, stretches across the table, and squeezes her shoulder.

"Let's forget this conversation, Evy. And listen . . . hold your ground!"

Instantly she gets back her good humor. Erik has only been worried. He's sharp and penetrating. He has vision. She herself has always had a hard time seeing things in a larger perspective. Sometimes she's wanted to blame that on being a woman. Naturally that's wrong, but it feels better to blame being a woman than to have to admit to being a dunce.

22

Never before has it been such fun to work. Everybody at NMSI seems to know who she is. Many people greet her spontaneously in the lunchroom, on the bus, in the ladies' room. On her fourth day back, she gets a new office in what's known as the Administration's "penthouse," a long wooden pavilion atop the flat roof of the old nineteen-fifties-vintage Administration Building. The penthouse is a popular place to work. Every room has its own door opening directly onto the roof terrace where evergreens are planted. But maybe the greatest advantage is that the penthouse isn't connected with the main building's continually malfunctioning air-conditioning system; those who work in the penthouse have access to an old-fashioned, almost sinful luxury—windows that open.

Her new office is two units in size—that is, twice six square yards in area and with two windows. That's the most concrete evidence to date of NMSI's esteem. It signifies plainly that if she'd been a regular employee, she'd have had a salary grade corresponding to department director.

The room's three blind walls are covered with white-enameled tin. This isn't for fire protection; the white tin makes it possible for her to draw on all three walls with different-colored magic markers. She has seen researchers' rooms where the walls were scribbled over with numbers, integrals, and symbols—rooms where the researcher himself sat like a kind of thinking spider inscribed at the center of his own three-dimensional coordinate system.

The furniture is brand-new: the minimal desk, the "thinkalounger," and the instrument cart. It's just like the instrument cart she saw on her first visit to the Nobel Institutes when she was interviewed by Assistant Administrator Hörrlin. Compactly installed on the little wheeled cart are a telephone, a dictaphone, an electronic calculator, a nine-inch TV, and an electric coffee maker. When she comes lumbering in with her bulging brief case and her rolled-up PERT charts under her arm, she feels at first delighted and then alien. The feeling of strangeness diminishes somewhat once she has carried up her potted plants. But the walls bear down on her; it's like staring somebody right in the whites of his eyes. At last she plucks up her courage and writes in huge red letters right across the longest wall: WISHING YOU A VERY MERRY FIRST OF MAY!!!

With legs aching, she sits down in the thinkalounger. This chair is made like a dentist's chair. It can be raised or lowered, tilted, reclined, and even made to rotate with four pushbuttons in the armrest; in recent years, it's been scientifically demonstrated that many people are stimulated and excited by riding a carousel—something carnival operators have known for five hundred years. But she doesn't dare spin the chair. Nobody in the Beck family can ride a carousel. Nobody? Oh, yes, Erik can take it, Erik, who is a reserve officer in the Air Force, checked out on both loops and rolls.

She would have liked to show Erik her new office. But that's hardly possible before summer. Papa's illness and then her own have put entirely too great a burden on Erik during April. Now he must be left alone to look after his own affairs. In her wallet she has a photo of Erik. She raises the overhead projector out of its compartment in her desk, turns it on and directs the gleaming square against the white wall, then slips the photo into place. Erik, in a six-by-six-foot magnification, looks down with a Mona Lisa smile on Mama Evy in the thinkalounger.

After lunch she has to be present as a witness before the Production Committee. She leaves the cafeteria, passes the Nobel mobile—where some tourists stand waiting for the clock to strike one—turns around the corner of the library, and steps in among Lindgården's high lilac bushes. Startled, she stops to stare breathlessly at a single titmouse. A bird here, right in the middle of Stockholm!

Lindgården's porch is draped with red banners and Swedish flags, in preparation for the celebration of Mayday tomorrow. Inside, in the entrance hall, her "accomplice" is waiting, the machinist and safety officer Peter Yerganian.

"That we should have to meet *here*," she says guiltily.

He tries a devil-may-care grin but it doesn't work very well because he's just stuffed a big pinch of snuff under his upper lip.

They're immediately called into the big room where the Production Committee has seated itself around the end of the large oval conference table. The committee consists of Edwin Karlsson, chairman, Administrator Håkan Rosenquist as representative of the employer, and the Nobel Institutes' legal counsel, Max Ehrendorffer.

Evy and Yerganian remain standing.

"Well, sit *down* for Christ's sake!" says Rosenquist peev-

124

ishly, as if standing up amounted in itself to some kind of demonstration.

When they've seated themselves, all three committee members come forward and shake their hands. They sit down again and the lawyer coughs to cue the chairman.

"Comrades," says Edwin Karlsson. "I presume you're fully informed why we have brought you here?"

"Actually, I'm not," says Evy Beck.

"Haven't you received the xeroxed memorandum?" asks the lawyer.

She feels very guilty; the memorandum must be lying somewhere in one of the big envelopes she hasn't gotten around to opening yet.

"A prerequisite for this meeting is that the parties have familiarized themselves with the prerequisites," says the lawyer sourly.

"*I've* read the paper," says Yerganian. "And Evy Beck, here, is just a witness."

The three committee members look at each other, then Edwin Karlsson says, "That's right. Has anybody got any objection to our proceeding . . . ? No one. Then I request the counsel to give an account of the situation."

Max Ehrendorffer seems to be reading from the air and not from the paper that's lying in front of him: "On the afternoon of March twenty-nine, Safety Officer Peter Yerganian was summoned to give a ruling on the prospective isolation of a contagious work space located in the Small Animal Area of the Institute for Medical Physics. The person who requested that ruling of Yerganian was the WOLMB employee Evy Beck. As justification it was stated that the animals in the area might be infected with the Marburg virus. On the said afternoon, Yerganian ruled on the isolation question. Pursuant to special instructions for safety officers, Yerganian decided that the aforementioned work space should be *isolated*. Are the parties agreed on these statements?"

Yerganian mumbles a thick "Yes," while Edwin Karlsson contents himself with drumming on the edge of the table.

"Seeing as we have now established that the parties concerned are in agreement, the Production Committee has appointed the undersigned to submit a proposal of penalties, which is as follows: In accordance with special instructions for safety officers, the local safety officer is to bear the entire responsibility for production-curtailing actions taken by him. In the present case, the safety officer has arranged for isolation before sufficient investigation of the facts could be effectuated. In response to a written inquiry from this Production Committee, the National Commission on Experimental Animals has responded that 'sufficient investigation' in this matter cannot be regarded as having been undertaken before such a time as to the said investigation has been attached the report of results of the virological analysis undertaken by the National Veterinary Institute. In this case, the safety officer has therefore, not assured himself that sufficient objective grounds for decision existed before the isolation on March twenty-nine. Inasmuch as the safety officer disregarded the intentions of the law on working environments, the Nobel Institutes have been caused an interruption of production amounting to fifty-six hours; that is to say, the time which elapsed from the decision to isolate to the completion of the virological analysis. The cost of this production curtailment has been calculated, in accordance with the scale which applies under the agreement between the Union and the Swedish Employers' Association, to amount to 3,950 dollars. Restitution of this sum in full is required."

Now Edwin Karlsson takes the floor; he seems to be in an unusually jovial mood. "Now, comrades, we shouldn't take this so seriously. There happen to be no less than *two* extenuating circumstances. First, veterinary-medical expertise incited you, Yerganian, to close the animal area . . . Second, as it later turned out, you *were right.*"

Evy Beck raises her hand exactly as she once learned in elementary school: her left forearm is laid upon the table, her right elbow is rested on the back of the left hand, then the right forearm is extended straight up with hand out straight and fingers together.

"But it *was* Marburg," she says, and reddens over her whole throat.

126

Administrator Rosenquist now seizes the floor.

"Exactly, Evy! Really damn clever of you. You've rendered us an *invaluable* service."

"However . . ." the lawyer begins, but is immediately interrupted by Edwin Karlsson.

"But you see, Evy, what we're analyzing is the situation on the twenty-ninth of March . . . what basis for decision existed *then."*

"Do you mean we should have let the Marburg virus spread through the institutes? The last known epidemic took seven lives."

"Certainly not, Evy," says Håkan Rosenquist. "That's not what we're discussing."

"You seem to follow all this?" says Evy, seeking support from Yerganian.

"Well, I've been safety officer for eleven years."

"Now as you know, comrades," says Edwin Karlsson. "It's Mayday Eve today. So it would be good if we could reach some agreement."

"You mean Yerganian's got to pay 3,950 dollars!" says Evy with an indignation of which she hadn't thought herself capable.

"Easy, easy . . ." says Rosenquist. "We're not there yet."

"I now ask our counsel to read the Production Committee's proposal of penalties," says Karlsson. "It is my express wish that the parties be able to agree on this proposal."

"Proposed penalties," Max Ehrendorffer reads, still gazing at the empty space above his paper. "The Production Committee of the Alfred Nobel Medical-Surgical Institutes shall abstain from requiring repayment from safety officer Peter Yerganian. It is proposed instead that the sum of 3,950 dollars be jointly paid by the Labor-Management Committee and the Nobel Institutes. Peter Yerganian is to be sentenced to eighteen months' suspension from his post as safety officer and his job as machinist. During the suspension there is no impediment to Yerganian's receiving salary from special funds administered by the Labor Market Board, Section M."

"I'm satisfied," says Yerganian, after which all parties present quickly shake hands with each other, and Yerganian and Evy Beck go out in the cloakroom.

"I'm just so damned sorry on your account," says Evy. "The only fair thing would have been for me to take responsibility for the isolation."

"Can't go along with you on that," says Yerganian. "I mean, it's the principle of the thing. You're talking about going back to the days when the employer and his specialists alone could do whatever they damn pleased with the working environment."

She feels both astonished and stupid.

When they're both standing on the porch under the red, blue, and yellow banners, she asks, "Well, what will you turn to now? For the eighteen months."

"They're going to charge my salary to the MELMB budget."

"Yes, but what are you going to *do?*"

He looks at her a little surprised.

"I'll stay in my old job, of course. The only difference is, I get less pay. I've really been damn lucky. Eighteen months on the MELMB budget is a very mild punishment."

23

She's awake nearly the whole night before the First of May. Papa went to bed right at eight thirty, just like an obedient child, but then he couldn't sleep. For the first time, she uses the Auto-Hepar's selector. With the selector the artificial liver can be instructed not to break down certain compounds. She punches in the chemical code for the sleep substances of the midbrain on the liver's control panel. Within fifteen minutes Papa has fallen asleep.

There's lots to be done before the sun rises on the First of May. The graham cake must be baked, the pike has to be marinated, and then there are all the birch twigs to be trimmed and put in water. She scours the kitchen table, pushes it up against the wall, and lays out the runner with a design from the Great Strike of 1909. She stacks up plates, glasses, and plated silverware on the table. The big brass medallion has to be shined. The polish hardens and sticks in the relief like pink putty; she can't get at it with the rag, but has to sacrifice a toothbrush for the purpose. It's after three in the morning when she tiptoes out into the hall and fastens the medallion to the outer door—the big brass coin with Marx and Karl XVI Gustav in profile.

When she's standing in her nightgown by the sink in the bathroom and looking with distaste at the spoiled toothbrush, it suddenly strikes her: THE BANNER! Where in hell did she tuck away the rolled-up banner last year? She goes through the closets, lifting out Papa's old and now four-sizes-too-big suits, rooting through heaps of old shoes and Erik's abandoned hockey skates. She's so sleepy that while climbing up on the kitchen stool, she almost loses her balance—at the last moment she catches hold of the fan housing above the stove.

But there's no rolled-up banner in the upper kitchen cabinet either. She tiptoes into Papa's room—he's sleeping deeply—and looks helplessly at the empty varnished flagstaff, stuck into the clay pot in the corner, gathering dust. Then she's got it! The banner is in the attic. After last year's First of May she figured there wouldn't be any more of these celebrations for her. It seemed silly to put out all the decorations when you were completely alone. That was before Papa got sick—and Erik had just announced that *he* most certainly didn't intend to celebrate the First of May in the future, as a protest against the commercialization of it.

She pulls on her coat, takes the key to the attic, and lets herself out into the chilly stairwell. Up in the attic, she unlocks the chicken-wire door to Unit 773. The banner's leaning in the corner, just inside the door. She picks up the long paper tube and shakes off the dust . . . then she nearly has a stroke: she's forgotten Papa's present! She sinks down on a box of books with the rolled banner between her knees. How utterly silly! For weeks she's been thinking about Papa's First of May present. He was to have a new dark-blue demonstration cap. Naturally there's no question of Papa's taking part in any First of May march, nor even of his being present at the wreath-laying at Gärdet. But when their household belongings got inventoried after Mama passed away, Papa's old First of May cap went astray; she realized that, for him, it was like losing a wedding ring.

Three thirty in the morning . . . Of course, she could take a taxi down to Åhlen's and buy something or other. Listlessly she pokes the banner tube among the stuff in the attic, lets it fall against the different objects—ploonk! the cardboard strikes an old hollow bust of Joseph Stalin. Behind the moth-bags with Mama's clothes, she finds a shoebox of photographs. And under the box lies her battered schoolbag from the forties. The imitation leather is worn down to the white, and one tin corner-shield has fallen off. A frayed red ribbon is sticking out. She picks up the schoolbag and seats herself on the chest. In the bag, she keeps Papa's letters, written to her between 1941 and 1944. Letters that she was too young to understand.

In the first letters—all of them lack any indication where he is—Papa writes to tell her how it is to be "called up." In the autumn of 1942, the letters go right to the point: Papa writes about the camp authorities, the barracks, and the logging they do. The last letters, from 1944, are written without any anxious deference to the mail censorship: Papa pours his white-hot contempt over the German sympathizers, the black marketeers, the iron ore shipments, and the "hastily contrived caresses for that old worker-tormentor John Bull Churchill."

She takes the letters downstairs with her, sorts them out by date, and packs them in an empty typing paper box; she wraps it in wine-red First of May paper, pastes on a label, and writes, "To Papa from Evy, age 9." She carries the package and the banner into Papa's room. The red banner, she fastens to the flagstaff and the packet, she lays in the clay pot the staff is standing in. Before she goes out, she arranges the banner so that the folds fall straight down.

The hour is almost four in the afternoon of the First of May. They've listened to the King's First of May speech at Gärdet and eaten their way through a ridiculously ample meal. Papa has retired to have a nap and get in an extra purification-hour on the Auto-Hepar. She herself considers taking a walk to look at the birch-leaf-clad city and the dressed-up crowds of people, but she's too sleepy. Instead, she takes a splash of sweet white port wine—that's me all over, she thinks, there's no better sleeping potion than sweet fortified wine.

Then the doorbell rings. Erik! flashes behind her forehead until she remembers: it's Erik's habit nowadays to make a trip to Gambia over the First of May. Outside the door stands a girl in her early twenties. She's dressed in a blue suit and a little white hat, and on the lapel of her jacket she's got a May Day cockade in yellow, red, and black.

"Rodion Beck??"

"He's busy. May I ask what it's about?"

The girl has a large, well-filled shoulder bag; she seeks support from it by fiddling with the flap.

"Voting!" Then she says, "Today is the First of May, you know."

Evy Beck understands that very well; she says wearily, *"Yes.* But I thought I had made it plain that Mr. Beck is *not* interested."

"Oh, yes," says the girl.

"But wasn't it you I talked with on the telephone? Or was it somebody else? I'm quite sure I *pleaded* with you to leave my father in peace."

"But Rodion Beck has answered our postcard inquiry. He has agreed to CSBIFO's opinion poll. Unless he's gone and broken a leg or—?"

"Mr. Beck can't see anyone before five o'clock. He's having a liver dialysis."

"May I come in till then?" the girl asks.

She lets the polling worker come into the kitchen. When they met with resistance on the telephone, the Central Statistical Bureau must have sent something through the mail instead. And since Papa hasn't been placed under the control of a guardian, she can hardly prevent a political interview.

"After five o'clock?" says the girl. "That will just work out. I have to have time to telephone in the result before six."

Evy knows. On the First of May, CSBIFO's polling workers go around interviewing the selected ten thousand. The election results go into the computer that same evening, so as to be ready for the TV news at seven thirty. Then the party leaders come forward and answer for the numbers.

"I think that somehow it felt *fairer* back in the days when *everyone* got to vote," says Evy after they've seated themselves.

"I have heard several people say that," the girl answers sententiously. "But the truth of the matter is, the new election simplification gives a more dependable result. Considerably fewer will evade the vote. In the past, voting participation was just over eighty-seven percent at its highest. In our three last opinion surveys, the discard was 3.8, 3.3, and 2.9, respectively. Our goal this time is to get below 2.5. That means a voting participation of over ninety-seven percent."

"Yes, it's purely emotional, of course," says Evy. "I mean, you have the statistics on your side."

"Honesty's on our side too. Before, all adult Swedes got to vote, of course. But it was largely a charade. With more or less conscious thought, people went and *stuffed a piece of paper into a box behind a screen.* Not to mention all the election posters that littered . . . And the expense of the more and more unfactual party campaigns."

"As a matter of fact, this is the first time anybody in our family's been chosen."

"Lotted."

"That anyone in my family has been lotted. I don't actually know, really, how the voting itself is done."

The girl opens her heavy letter carrier's bag and takes out a sheaf of brochures and questionnaires, photographs, schedules, a pair of dice, and a test tube with a balloon attached. She holds up the balloon and points to it.

"First the voter has to blow into the alcohol test balloon. The regulation that intoxicated persons may not enter the polling place still applies, of course."

Evy looks guiltily at the port wine bottle.

"Then I assure myself that the lottee is able to read, knows what year this is, and seems generally collected."

"Don't you eliminate the retarded and psychopaths from the beginning?"

The girl sits with her mouth half-open for a few seconds, looking blankly at Evy Beck. But she quickly gets rolling again.

"Then we go through the three parliamentary parties' election brochures together. The voter gives reasons for and against the parties' arguments."

"Who produces the election brochures?"

"We produce them ourselves at the Central Statistical Bureau. We look back over the preceding three years and find out how the party in question has acted. Then we combine that with the current party program—well, of course we wash out obviously unrealistic elements first."

"Ah, that makes it more objective, of course."

"Exactly."

"And then the voter decides on a specific party?"

"Not so fast, not so fast. We were going through all the parties' arguments and trying to estimate the voter's antipathy versus sympathy toward the various stands the party has taken."

"And if a person doesn't know?"

She takes the dice between her nicely shaped thumb and forefinger, with their long curved wine-red nails.

"In that case, we decide the question exactly the way they do in Parliament, by chance."

"And if a person doesn't want to?"

"Want to??"

"Go on, please. Papa will be awake in a few minutes."

"Yes. Then we put down plus and minus points for the parties' different proposals. Well, then we have only to add it up."

"And that gives you which party the voter wants to vote for?"

"No. You've completely misunderstood the procedure: We get two counts for every party, a minus-count and a plus-count."

"So a person votes a little bit for every party?"

"Exactly. The outcome of the interview is a count-combination. For example: the voter puts twenty percent on the Right, five percent on the Left, and seventy-five percent on the Center. So we have what we call *differentiated* voting."

"I see!" says Evy, amazed.

"Do you understand now?" says the girl, pleased. "You see, the old voting system's lack of objectivity is gone, the unrealistic promises are gone, the extra wear-and-tear on the polling places is gone . . . And above all, the occurrence of *manipulation* is gone! In the future, we can really and truly say that the voter knows what he or she is doing."

Suddenly Papa is standing in the doorway. He's dressed in his best black suit with vest, and in his buttonhole he has a wine-red carnation. He hasn't looked so vital in years.

"I think I'll go out for a little walk," Evy says.

Papa rubs his scaly hands together and grins from ear to ear.

"Now, by God!!!"

24

The brave sun of late spring blossoms out. A pleasantly tempered glow pervades Evy Beck's penthouse office—the windows are so made that when the sunlight strikes the panes directly, the glass darkens to a smoky brown. When the sun goes down, the color of the windows lightens, just like pouring soda into a highball.

She's sitting in the thinkalounger leafing through a short paper, "Classification Norms for Experimental Animals," written by a lab animal assistant, Hedda Sjögren. She's heard the name Hedda Sjögren brought up parenthetically several times. For several decades, a position called Laboratory Animal Assistant existed at NMSI, just as at other institutions of higher biological learning. But for some reason that position hasn't been filled for a number of years. The reason might possibly be one of qualifications—Lab Animal Assistants are only junior college graduates, not veterinarians—they're called "band-aid vets" by licensed veterinarians.

Purely by chance, Evy Beck has found Hedda Sjögren's memorandum in the Administration's own library. She feels like an archeologist who suddenly confronts the remains of

134

a vanished civilization—a civilization that seems in many respects to be comparable or even superior to the present one. She's filled with a kind of reverence. The things that this lab animal assistant writes about in her introduction are precisely the same problems Evy Beck faces: the difficulty of knowing what the work is really about, the false expectations, the rebuffs, the problems of getting information, the homelessness, and the paralyzing feeling that all the most important events are taking place on the other side of an impenetrable glass wall.

What ever happened to Hedda Sjögren? Why did she make such a slight impression on NMSI that hardly anyone even remembers she was ever employed?

"Classification Norms of Experimental Animals" proves to be something entirely different from what the title seems to promise. It's not a taxonomy laid out in columns according to invertebrates, cold-blooded vertebrates, mammals, rodents, hoofed animals, or birds. Instead, Hedda Sjögren writes: *The guiding principle of this classification has been function, as opposed to species. A functional classification should prove more useful to one who must distribute veterinary medical support by institute.* In line with this, Hedda Sjögren divides up lab animals into *Individual Animals, Recyclable Animals,* and *Consumable Animals.*

Evy Beck hardly needs to read the text—it's as though her predecessor had communicated in just a few syllables the value of a symbol in an equation that had long withstood every attempt at solution. Learning what A stands for, one need only pull lightly on both ends of the equation and it opens up as elegantly as an artful sailor's knot.

The identifying characteristic of consumable animals is that they are used only once, most usually for standard tests or routine diagnoses. Consumable animals seldom need to be prepared and are never trained. Such an animal is useful only as a biological system, never as an individual.

Consumable animals are often cheap and are raised in huge numbers. Their lifetime is short. The guinea pig is a typical consumable animal, though as highly evolved an animal as the rhesus monkey can also be considered consumable; that is, those rhesus monkeys that are raised simply for the purpose of extracting their kidneys for virus cultivation.

At the opposite pole from consumable animals are the *individual animals.* The identifying characteristic of the individual animal is its high development capacity. That is to say, one invests resources in the animal more or less as one invests capital in an enterprise: the capital can be either in the form of training or in the form of transplantations. The period of investment may be long, it may take years before the animal can be placed in an experiment and begin to return a profit. The animal's value, therefore, rises swiftly: an untrained chimpanzee in puberty may cost around 1,500 dollars to purchase, but should it die three years later, after having learned to operate a lathe on an eight-hour shift, with one brain lobe replaced by an electronic copper-circuit memory, the loss can be reckoned in the hundreds of thousands.

Recyclable animals occupy a middle position. Here we chiefly number those animals that undergo tests that, rather than being single-incidence interventions, extend over time. No substantial investment is made in recyclable animals, but certain provision of resources is required, for example, to maintain an environment suitable for the animal between an operative intervention and the sacrifice of that animal. Other animals that are included in this category are those that are maintained for longer periods of time for the purposes of serum generation or hormone extraction. Recyclable animals are distinguishable from individual animals chiefly in undergoing a moderate rise in value, and in being relatively easy to replace. Cats are a common recyclable animal.

Hedda Sjögren admits in her memorandum that the drawing of boundaries can be diffuse in this as in other biological contexts. Further, she points out that it should be obvious that categorization by function is not entirely independent of classification by species: experimental animals that are most closely related to man do most often belong to the individual category, though notable exceptions exist, such as dolphins and whales.

After Sjögren has described classification, she turns to discussing the allotment of veterinary medical resources. She rejects assigning priorities in accordance with diseases or the need for attention. Instead, she starts from the return-on-investment principle and draws a diagram, an equilateral triangle with its point downward. She cuts the triangle into three slices of equal thickness. The upper slice represents the individual animals, the middle one, the recyclable animals, and the point, the consumable animals. *A person who has a given quantity of resources,* writes Hedda Sjögren, *needs only to compute the sector areas of the divided triangle in order to get an approximate measure of a balanced division of resources. According to this formula, the veterinary medical budget for a medical college ought to be divided roughly 5:3:1 for the clients to feel that they are being offered optimal service.*

Evy Beck takes out her card file, with all its notes made on many institute visits. It's spooky how closely Sjögren's formula matches her own observations. The space devoted to the dogs at Pharmacological is 7,381 square feet; to the cats, 3,980 square feet; and to the small animals, 1,205 square feet. *However,* she wonders, surely there's some connection between the number of animals and the space assigned? If an institute has five thousand golden hamsters and two orangutans, the division can hardly match Sjögren's formula? To check, she takes up the Institute of Aviation and Naval Medicine, the Marine Biological Division—*it matches:* a cachelot whale requires a basin cubic volume over five times greater than 2,600 little dogfish.

Slowly she reads through Hedda Sjögren's memorandum once more. She feels she has an "administrative instrument" in her hands as weighty and convincing as a formula that haunts her dreams: PABREG, PEGBAR, REGBAP, GRABPE . . .

Before she closes the pamphlet, her eyes are caught again by the line *to be divided roughly 5:3:1 for the clients to feel that they are being offered optimal service.* She reads the words through several times, and every time the meaning seems to glide farther away from her. "Feel" is a subjective concept, while 5:3:1 is a numerical-objective one. What just

137

appeared to be an open and fully visible landscape now disappears beyond the text, so that now she only glimpses a beautiful garden concealed behind the letters' richly ornamented iron fence.

25

One rainy evening in May, she goes to her first animal welfare meeting. Nils Rosén has suddenly been detained and Evy Beck takes over as replacement. She doesn't escape Papa's prying eye when she sneaks into the bathroom with her overcoat on and takes a tranquilizer. But Papa doesn't say anything, he just watches her so that she can't swallow the pill. Her whole mouth tastes bitter before, out on the sidewalk, she finally succeeds in getting it down her throat.

It is the Anti-Vivisection League that has called the meeting, which is to be held in the basement of the former headquarters of the Swedish Employers' Association on Blasieholmen. When she comes half-running down Hovslagar Street, she sees the meeting room through the basement windows. Twenty-five or thirty people are sitting at a long table. To the right is a little table with a water carafe and a dried carnation. If she's going to back out, she'll have to do it now! Nothing simpler than to go over to a telephone booth, call, and say that she's suddenly been taken ill. But what's the phone number of the meeting room? And has she got seventy-five cents in change? She clambers down the half-flight of stairs, knowing it's not the practical matters that prevent her —it's her inability to lie.

A cheerful man in his forties greets her. He's Love Ahlin, a high-school teacher and chairman of the Anti-Vivisection League. He introduces his wife, who's secretary of the League. Then Evy is introduced to her "opponent," as Ahlin puts it. She greets Henke Kihlman, an engineer. Now that aggravating reddening on her throat starts. She hadn't conceived of this as a debate, but as a question-and-answer session.

138

Together with her opponent Kihlman, she's led into the room she saw from the street. Mr. Ahlin introduces them.

"Friends, on behalf of the League I want to welcome you all warmly to the fifth evening in our series 'Meetings with Science.' We're especially happy that the Nobel Medical-Surgical Institutes have been willing to let us have their Chief Veterinarian, Dr. Evy Beck!"

She bows, somewhat halfheartedly, toward the assembly, and puts her hand over her blazing throat as if she had an infection.

"This evening's other speaker shouldn't need any further introduction: the League's Treasurer for lo, these many years, Henke Kihlman! Henke has asked if he can begin with a few pictures."

Evy Beck sits down at the end of the long table. Before the lights are dimmed, she has time to make a hasty survey of the audience. All ages are represented. Opposite her sits a very old lady wearing an antiquated appliance: hearing-aid glasses. Next to her, a couple, twenty-five, loosely and elegantly clad in tunics. Then there are some teenagers and a lady her own age with pageboy-bobbed metallic-tinted hair that looks like a helmet. Then a man in a watchman's uniform. A thirty-five-year-old woman with a doll face and rosy cheeks that are no longer quite dewy fresh. The lights fade out and she thinks: Quite ordinary people!

The slides that Kihlman shows are of pretty blurry quality, the details hard to make out. First comes a monkey undergoing a space experiment in a Paris laboratory. Then a tobacco-smoking dog from America, a goat with electrodes imbedded in its sleep-center, a rabbit equipped for measurement of crash injuries, one of the famous W.R. Hess cats, the branding of shaved cats with a branding iron, and two sewed-together rats.

All the pictures are between ten and thirty years old. They show experiments Evy Beck has almost never actually seen. She is a little irritated that the information hits off-target, and feels no empathy with the animals in the pictures. Instead, she's disturbed by the poor quality, by Kihlman's generally wandering commentary, by his using facts wrongly, and by the very distinct impression she gets that those present have seen these pictures countless times before.

The lights go on and she realizes it's her turn. What should she say? She's prepared herself to answer specific questions, not to give any comprehensive analysis or considered defense.

"Please, Dr. Beck!" says Mr. Ahlin, waving her toward the little table with the water carafe and the vacuum-dried carnation.

She sits down, again puts her hand in front of her reddening throat, and begins: "I'm not going to try to comment on the pictures that have been shown. For a person to do that, he would reasonably have to know quite a lot more about the experimental situation itself than what the pictures show. Than what one thinks the pictures show."

Her throat feels burned from the bitter pill, and she has to store up saliva. The people around the table give no sign, not the least sign at all, of how her introductory phrases have gone over. Whether she's aroused their aggressions or their understanding. She thinks they are looking at her as if she's an object, a television set, for example.

She swallows and continues: "Instead, I would like to say a few words about the veterinary-medical activities at NMSI. We will soon have had an expanded veterinary service under way for six months. Of course, it's entirely too early to say anything about the results, other than that we've met with a very positive interest."

Why am I sitting here saying "we," she thinks between the lines. As if there were a whole staff and not just a single woman on the WOLMB budget.

"First time around, we've begun to take a close look at the suppliers of experimental animals; we've also done a general survey and have offered some advice concerning the places where animals are housed. I can also say that we're trying to set up a 'model institute,' in this case the Pharmacological Institute. There, we're trying to concentrate our efforts to gain experience that can later be applied to the other institutes."

Where has she heard this before? She's frightened to dis-

THE ANIMAL DOCTOR

cover how *easy* it is to speak. It's not laborious, like building up a pattern or a weave—instead, it's like ripping out knitting: crimped yarn running out of her mouth without a break. All the words and sound waves have existed, ready, inside her body, though she's been unconscious of it. Now all she has to do is pull.

"The Nobel Institutes constitute the largest medical research center in Scandinavia. Changes can't be carried out overnight: you've got to know what it is you want to accomplish and you've got to know how the organization functions. You get no place by beating your head against the wall. Obviously the budgetary aspects of things always have to be kept in mind, the funds for animal welfare must be balanced against other funds, there's no way to avoid that. Let me get down to some specific examples."

She talks about the Marburg epidemic, about the Davies fibrosis among the guinea pigs, about Professor Rosén's extremely restrictive position on animal experiments that are considered painful, how these must only be carried out when he himself is present.

When she looks at the clock, she discovers that she's been going on for three-quarters of an hour. And there are still hundreds of yards of chatter-yarn to roll out. She closes her eyes and says that now she's going to wind up her introduction so that she won't take too much time away from the discussion.

There's a pause before anyone asks a question. Mr. Ahlin, the teacher who is chairman, looks out, smiling and with eyebrows raised, over his congregation—finally he himself asks, "How much money is there for animal welfare?"

"That's nearly impossible to say," Evy Beck answers. "Each individual institute has to allot sufficient funds out of its own budget."

"I thought it was like what they do with artistic decoration of buildings," says Ahlin. "That a certain percentage of the building's cost always had to be set aside for art or in this case animal welfare."

"Not at all," she replies. "We have to calculate according to *need*, not some fixed percentage."

141

Then the man in the watchman's uniform asks if she feels that the Animal Welfare Law is observed at NMSI.

"That question ought to be directed to the Board of Public Health, which is the supervisory authority," she begins, and then draws the complicated diagram she composed so laboriously several months ago: the Board of Public Health, the Commission on Experimental Animals, the Veterinary Board, the Agricultural Board, the Parliamentary Auditors, and the Department of Industry.

"And what's your own personal opinion?"

"That a great deal of work has been done on animal welfare," she answers. "But nothing is so good that it can't be improved."

For some time Henke Kihlman, the engineer, has looked as though he wanted the floor: he's grimaced, nodded, looked in turn questioning and enlightened—just now he shifted his chair away from the big table and nearer the small one.

"Henke Kihlman!" says Ahlin, and after that seems to slump down in his chair.

She leaves her place—almost reluctantly, for she is experiencing a kind of giddy invincibility. Whatever questions she may get, long interconnected arguments are lying ready to be pulled out.

Kihlman takes off his jacket and hangs it on the chair, pours out some water, and shifts the carnation before he folds his hands on the table and begins.

"Do we have to have painful animal experiments, do we have to have animal experiments at all? It's a question that ties right into the development of science. And since we've got to look at science as something that exists to prevent mankind from getting plagues and diseases, we've got to ask: What do the so-called human diseases come from? Let me answer that with a quotation from what Dr. White said as long ago as 1956 . . . As you know, Dr. White was President Eisenhower's personal physician when he was President. Dr. White stated this about our most serious diseases: 'I believe that another diet could do more to cure heart and circulatory diseases than any new drugs. The key is in a person's life style.' "

142

Evy Beck notices that she's getting angry and upset, that she's irritated by the amateurishness and the inaccurate simplification. But the tranquilizer makes her a stranger to her own aggressiveness. She puts it coldly: Kihlman is talking nonsense, which makes me justifiably upset. Kihlman is dangerous, he is ignorant and misleading . . . But she doesn't follow through with any action.

"It's modern man's artificial life style that's got to be changed. Drugs and surgery don't get us anywhere. I tell you, medical science has gotten off the track, it's on the way to even greater destruction of man's inner environment and a huge increase in so-called scientific animal experimentation. And this is happening even though leading scientists have explained time after time that it's often hard, yes impossible, to transfer the results from animals to man."

Evy Beck's legs feel weak, her relaxed body tingles pleasantly. Does this man really know what he's saying? Does he really wish us back in some kind of Bronze Age existence, when men lived in mud huts, ate roots and berries, and at best, for their most important occasions, roasted an elk they had clubbed to death . . . A civilization that lacked painkilling drugs and antibiotics and had an infant mortality rate of eighty to ninety percent?

Kihlman continues, speaking now of the tens of thousands of chemical substances that pervade modern society—and cannot be checked with animal experiments because the methods of animal experimentation are too poorly developed.

But the man is standing there contradicting himself! Granted that in some far-off paradise one could be free from the multitude of chemical substances. Nevertheless, for the foreseeable future, we are going to have to live with them. And are going to have to try to keep them under control by, among other things—alas!—animal experiments.

She looks at the members of the Anti-Vivisection League. Even now, they don't seem to react at all. It's understandable —is this the twentieth or the thirtieth time the League's treasurer has given this lecture? She turns back to Kihlman and suddenly sees him as a naturist agitator, a prophet promising all will be well if only we dare to show ourselves naked.

Kihlman doesn't run down until nearly nine thirty, just at the time when Evy Beck realizes she has to rush home and help Papa. But she has a hard time getting away from the cheeriness in the cloakroom. It's as though there had never been any difference of opinion. When Kihlman says good-bye he pats her shoulder, as though one must avoid a real, serious confrontation at any price.

Mr. and Mrs. Ahlin take her aside when good-byes have already been exchanged twice.

"Well, Dr. Beck. The League's financial resources unfortunately won't allow any monetary honorarium . . ."

"I don't want any pay," she answers, surprised and annoyed.

"But we would really like to show our appreciation with a little present."

"Is there any particular kind of liquor you prefer?" asks Mrs. Ahlin.

"Port wine, then," she tosses to the well-meaning pair, in order to pull free at last and hurry back home to Papa.

The next morning, which is Saturday, she meets with the Saturday bunch.

"You did a good job yesterday evening," says Nils Rosén.

"How do you know?"

"Love Ahlin called up. He was very pleased, as a matter of fact."

"Do you two keep in touch?" she asks.

"Ye-e-es. I think it's much more peaceful if we try to work together. Then you have a better idea of what's going on out there on the fringe. You probably didn't get paid?"

"They said something about a present . . ."

"Those miserly bastards. They've got government support for their lectures. Just like all the other study circles."

26

More and more seldom does she address herself as Quotia. There's no real factual ground for the change: she's still a female academic over forty-nine years of age who lacks permanent employment. Sometimes she will stop short suddenly, look up from a book, drop her pencil, or halt when she's out walking—like people who suffer from a very mild form of epilepsy, so-called "absences." Her consciousness disconnects and her mind goes blank. What's remarkable is this: a few months back, *Quotia* was always written on the smooth surface of these sudden blanknesses. Now they're simply blank.

Nor is she as afraid as she was before that menopause will show on her. For several years now, she's gone around with her hand ready to cover her throat so that those around won't notice that she's boiling over.

White throat and blank spaces in her mind. Even as early as her late teens, she'd relinquished the conventional female role. There wasn't any point in trying to keep up, not for a girl who was as round as a barrel and had a face that might possibly have found grace in the eyes of a Rubens or a Rembrandt, but never in the eyes of *Mademoiselle* or *Vogue*.

A person who's homely, a little jolly, and obviously not sexually attractive is less likely to experience aging as something especially dramatic. If even as a teenager one is matronly, then one has already passed the test of maturity. Evy Beck has never experienced what other women have described: realizing one day that you're no longer standing in the center, that men look right through you—if they look at you at all.

But these last months—since the job got going well—she's felt *free*. There's nothing ecstatic in this feeling of freedom, nothing like *Now by God it's my turn at last!* It's just that despite the fact that Papa, NMSI, and Erik fill almost all her thoughts, she feels that she's without ties.

One Saturday afternoon, she strolls toward downtown

145

Stockholm. Papa has suddenly gotten the notion that he needs some new ties. It's been like that for as long as she can remember: Papa declares abruptly that now he needs a new hat, a new tie, or a new overcoat. No consideration for the family's meager finances; Mama had to learn that bitterly over the years. There wasn't any way to stop Papa. His sudden purchases of clothes have nothing to do with vanity. Over time, she's come to understand that it's something else: Papa has always lived in roles. For a period of months it seems as though he's trying to imitate or live up to an image. He changes his sleeping and eating habits, he starts using new expressions and gestures. Then, one day, the role has been used up and he has to shed his skin. Usually he's done that by buying a new hat or a pair of gloves. Evidently this has helped him to get over the discomfort and temporary crises of identity.

She thinks that maybe she's unfair to Papa. He's never for an instant been an opportunist. It's not his values that keep changing, only his outsides, the everyday little tricks that enable him to put up with himself. And so this time it's ties. "I'd be extremely grateful if you'd hop downtown right away and buy me a couple of ties," he said when she came back from the Saturday morning session to catch up on the washing. If Papa weren't so touchy about displays of affection, she'd have liked to say, "Dear Papa, I think you're worth a whole mountain of neckties!"

Just six months ago, she would have asked Erik to do it. Even if she'd have felt guilty for taking up his time. She'd have asked him rather than go down herself to the commercial center of Stockholm. From being an unemployed nonperson, she has become Evy Beck again, with the right to plant both feet on Sweden's soil.

She takes the deserted pedestrian path across the Domus Company's Sture Square and stands at the entrance to Library Street. The guard, who wears NK's light-blue beret, salutes her when she goes by. He doesn't salute everyone—it must mean that she belongs here. She strolls along Library Street, looking fleetingly into the glass display cases that stand in the middle of the street. Overhead, a banner stretches clear across: WE HAVEN'T HAD A ROBBERY IN 7 YEARS!

Suddenly she notices how warm it is—as warm as inside a department store. Then she remembers Erik's description of the way the street has been sealed at both ends with a layer of motionless air. She didn't understand the details of how it was done. Erik called it "utilizing the surface tension of the air." Really it's obvious, the air behaves just like diluted water. If man had a lower specific gravity, we'd all be able to swim in the air.

She doesn't hurry. She has a legitimate errand and Papa's not going to care what the ties look like—it isn't the tie as an object that matters to him. It's the change he needs. It has sometimes happened, in later years, that he accomplished this change by getting rid of this or that instead of buying something new. While Mama was still alive, Papa suddenly up and burned every album in the house. Only a few loose snapshots were left. It's for safety's sake that Evy carries the key to the attic storage room on her person.

The privately owned streets in the downtown area enjoy a tax-free dispensation for liquor, tobacco, and candy. But the tax-free merchandise can't be taken away, it has to be consumed on the spot. Everywhere on the shopping streets are little bars and vending machines. Yet you never see any drunks, only a well-dressed public a little high on tax-free booze and ready to buy.

She turns into an entrance where there are three bar stools covered with angora. The pale girl in Tyrolean costume behind the counter presses the glass against the mouth of the upside-down port wine bottle and draws sixty grams. Evy Beck pays four dollars. The wine you buy duty- or tax-free never tastes as concentrated as what you buy in the government liquor stores, she thinks.

With a light heart, she crosses the street and enters NK's necktie center. Like all big shops, the necktie center is divided not into men's, women's, and children's departments, but according to the makers of the merchandise. Just as, in the past, one could go into an automobile emporium and choose a Buick, a Chevrolet, or an Opel. In the necktie center, imaginative counters stand here and there on the marble floor. Around every counter is a shrubbery of embalmed palm trees, and above these oases the trademarks of tie makers shine like a mirage: ERREDIECI, SILJA, ENRICO ROBERTO, DPF, and RONSONSILK.

She goes up and looks into the display cases. Silent gentlemen in corduroy jumpsuits pretend not to see her until she looks up.

"I'm interested in a tie for my father," she says to the man behind the Silja counter. "But I've forgotten his size."

"I would recommend that you try it on him. But perhaps it's to be a surprise?"

"Yes."

"Is your father taller than I am?"

A little embarrassed, she looks at the salesclerk, a man of barely thirty-five with a shaved head, slim, hipless, and dressed in a wine-red corduroy jumpsuit, a gold tie patterned like alligator hide, and a penis case of black glove leather.

"Actually, I don't know."

"What's his collar size?"

She doesn't know that either. Papa has a whole raft of shirts that all look five sizes too big in the collar. She puts her index finger on a glass-topped casque in which a necktie crocheted of metallic thread lies on red plush.

"How much is this one?"

"Sixteen dollars down and six fifty a month for twenty-four months."

She realizes it was dumb to go to one of the more expensive shops.

"I'll look around," she says, and for the sake of form looks over still more ties. They are of the most widely assorted materials: leather, metal, mesh, water-filled transparent plastic, and rare natural wool. There are also ties so long they function as penis cases. Right up front-and-center stands a metal sign nearly nine inches square with the trademark SILJA on it, followed by the degrees of quality, Admiral, Commodore, Captain, and Cadet.

She goes out onto Library Street again. She has to buy something or she'll get funny looks from the checkout cashier

148

at the end of the street. She goes to the book accessories department and walks between the counters of paperknives, bookplates, protective covers, book vacuum cleaners, and aerosol spray cans of anti-static. Finally she finds the counter with bookbands, thin colored bands of various materials that are used for bookmarks. She buys two eighteen-inch lengths of Lapp handiwork.

When she displays her purchase at the exit checkpoint, the checker says teasingly, "You're not planning to use these for neckties?"

"Of course!" she says cockily. "I buy all my family's ties at NK's book accessories department."

Two months ago, she thinks, I would never have dared. They would have put me down like that.

27

The Student Union still displays traces of NMSI's heyday. The copper plating on the entrance doors hasn't been entirely torn away by souvenir hunters: some still remains, around the edges of the doors and doorknobs. The lobby is battered and the painted walls almost entirely papered with bulletins and posters, so that the greasy spots are hidden. At lunch break, hundreds of medical students crowd in here to eat their sandwiches. Few can afford to go into the cafeteria.

One flight up, there used to be a magazine reading room, a billiard room, and a library. The billiard table remains, but the grass-green covering is so worn that white spots show through, like a soccer field after play. Half the upper floor is taken up by the Student Union's store: cans of tuna fish, soya meat, corn, and barley stand in high toppling piles on the ping-pong tables. The other half of the floor looks like an old furniture warehouse. Crowded together here are a leather sofa with spiral springs hanging out, presented by Ferrosan Vitamins, Inc., in the Year of Our Lord 1957; a monstrous color TV with coagulated picture tube; sixteen armchairs whose armrests have been reupholstered with oilcloth so many times that they have grown fat and begun to crowd the sitting space; a bookcase with locked glass doors containing a forgotten display of Bonniers' first novels from 1961—nobody's broken the glass because no used book dealer would give a red cent for any of them; and a card table for checkers and chess from which the pieces disappeared as long ago as the seventies. These have now been replaced by eight hazelnuts and eight sugar cubes, four thread spools of which two have been sadly disfigured with blue ink, two dusty green jujubes and two dusty red jujubes, two paper clips and two key-rings, and two little plastic squeeze bottles—one white one for Intima-Hygiene, one violet one for nail polish remover—and finally, two wooden pepper shakers—one dark-stained, the other light mahogany, and both stolen from the student cafeteria. The furniture warehouse's weightiest item is a piano without a lid, its insides like a loom: somebody's begun setting up warp and woof of steel wire, suddenly tired, and departed without trimming off the curly ends of the wires.

The silver clock out in the Nobel pond strikes six, so that the reflections sparkle. Evy Beck leaves the proud rubbish heap on the upper floor—what was once the country's swankest Student Union lounge, its furnishings supplied by drug firms who nowadays have no interest in medical students. The distribution of medicines has long been handled by a central agency.

At six o'clock Evy Beck is to meet with the Laboratory Assistants Association in the Student Union's cellar taproom, which is rented to student groups. She's succeeded in getting the Labor-Management Committee to pay the rent. Evy Beck started out thirty years ago as a lab assistant—a helper for the researchers. It's still the lab assistants who have the closest contact with the experimental animals, just as in the hospital it's the nurses' aides who see the most of the patients, not the doctors. Everyone she's spoken with agrees that better care for the animals is to a great extent the same thing as better training for lab assistants. But two administrative obstacles have existed: cash is lacking and the working schedule for lab assistants leaves no time for further training.

She goes down to the lobby to see whether the Student Union's female custodian has turned up in the glass cage next to the lunchroom entrance. That, she has. Evy Beck is admonished sharply to pay ninety-four dollars in advance for the use of the room. She does. Out of her own pocket, for the time being.

There's one large room in the cellar and two smaller ones. They're poorly equipped for the evening's purpose. A few of the furnishings left over from the great days are cast up like driftwood: several foam rubber cushions right on the floor, a couple of wall-mounted ship's lanterns that spread a feeble light, and a hammock with a hole in the bottom.

At twenty past six she decides that the meeting will have to start. By then, five lab assistants have appeared, out of the Nobel Institutes' total of 1,400 or so. Two of the lab assistants are pregnant, in their eighth or ninth month. Another, Evy's already acquainted with in the girl's capacity as chairman of the Lab Assistants' Association. The two others have white coats on and may possibly have sneaked off for a few minutes from their evening duties.

"Hi," says Evy Beck. "I think it's just as well we got started."

For a moment she considers beginning with a few words about her own time as a lab assistant—to create a more comradely feeling—but she quickly decides to get right to the point.

"Anyone who goes over the problems of animal care and welfare that exist here at NMSI can't avoid running into the procedures for sacrificing animals. I mean, how one goes about taking the life of an experimental animal as quickly and neatly as possible . . . Have you had any training in that?"

"Oh, yes," says the chairman, a little offended. "That's one of the most important sections of our laboratory assistant training course."

"The theory of it, not the practice," says one of the white-coated girls.

"I suspect that when it comes to small and middle-sized

animals it's still true that you lab assistants handle the sacrificing yourselves. While with monkeys, dogs, and pigs it's another story?"

Someone giggles nervously.

"If we take rats, for example, the usual method is to put the rat in a bottle with ether-drenched cotton and then cut the head off with scissors or a decapitation device. Or else one breaks the neck by holding the throat between the thumb and forefinger of one hand, then yanking the tail with the other."

One of the pregnant lab assistants has fallen asleep lying uncomfortably on the cushions.

"But the trouble is, the rat wants to get away. And then you know the trick of taking the animal by the tail and twisting the tail between your fingers so that dizziness is induced?"

No one comments on these statements. They're self-evident to every laboratory assistant.

"I think that none of these methods is especially satisfactory," Evy Beck says.

"If the person who's doing the job is experienced, there's no problem," says the chairman of the association.

"What if you're not experienced, though?" asks the girl who pointed out earlier that the theoretical training is good.

"After a few weeks you get the knack of it."

"In our institute there's one girl who refuses. After five years!"

The discussion threatens to lead into the wrong problem area, though Evy Beck knows it's true that many of them have poor training in conventional techniques of sacrifice.

"I'm sure what you say is true. But maybe it's an exception."

"You've got to crawl before you can walk," says the chairman.

"If you look at the sacrifice situation," says Evy Beck, "you can distinguish two parts. The actual sacrifice, which I think is less of a problem; and the time before the sacrifice, I mean the time—hopefully, short—when the animal panics and tries to run away."

"It's no more than a few seconds," says the chairman.

Evy Beck knows that instead it can stretch out into minutes, but she says, "The ideal sacrifice procedure should be to induce instant unconsciousness in the animal before it has time to react with death-anxiety. And then sacrifice it."

"I don't quite get what you mean. D'you mean that the animals in a slaughterhouse are spared all fear?"

"I didn't say that."

"Then why all this clucking over our lab animals?"

"The Animal Welfare Law says that animals must not be exposed to unnecessary suffering."

"Yeah. Well, it's probably very much a question of opinion and taste."

"Nowadays it's technically possible to induce instant unconsciousness," Evy Beck says. "And right here is the device that will do it."

Out of her brief case she takes a laser-lamp no bigger than an ordinary bed lamp.

"This," she explains, "is Siemens' new Flicker-Laser. It's one of the few anesthetics that work through the sense of sight. You simply put the lamp in front of the animal—then turn it on. The Flicker-Laser gives out a high-frequency blinking laser beam. The animal looks at the light automatically—and within a second or two it's put into a hypnosislike sleep."

"I thought laser beams were dangerous to the eyes," says the pregnant lab assistant, the one who's awake, then stops with a giggle.

"Yes, they are," responds Evy Beck. "So this can't be used in cases where the animal is being used for eye experiments. Then, of course, the laser beam would spoil the experiment itself."

"But it must be harmful to humans too?" says the chairman.

"Yes. But protective goggles come with it."

She lets the Flicker-Laser be passed around. The sleeping lab assistant is discreetly passed by. Evy Beck feels very

153

guilty for having set up this meeting in the evening—but it was the only chance.

"Naturally the Safety Committee will have to take a position on this device," she adds.

"What's it cost?"

"Around two thousand."

The person who happens to be holding the lamp makes a face and passes it hastily to the next.

"One Flicker-Laser per institute ought to be enough," says Evy Beck.

Suddenly the cushion slides out from behind the sleeping lab assistant. She bumps the back of her head on the wall.

"I feel nauseated," she says.

They pull together several cushions so that she can rest a while.

"I have some literature here from Siemens," says Evy Beck. "You could each take one and show it to your bosses. Probably the only way to go about this is to get the researchers, who've got a little more clout, to start demanding lamps like this."

"We've probably got just as much clout through our association," says the chairman sharply. "When it comes to that."

One of the younger, white-coated ones giggles again.

"I'm approaching *you*," Evy Beck says, "because it's *you* who handle the sacrificing. It's in *your* interest for the technical aids that are available to get used."

"But two thousand dollars," says the chairman. "That means almost a quarter of a million for all the institutes. You'd like us to demand it . . . without having the least idea what we'll have to *give up instead!*"

154

MEMORANDUM TO ADP CENTRAL DATABANK
CLASSIFIED INFORMATION OFFICIAL USE ONLY
OBSERVER ASST ADMINISTR S HORRLIN NMSI
KEYWORD EVY INGA-BRITT BECK WOLMB
CONTINUOUS WORK REVIEW 4
VERBAL REPORT CONCERNING ACTIONS IN MARBUR
G EPIDEMIC SEE SPECIAL REPORT FROM PRODUC C
OMMITTEE B HAS OTHERWISE SHOWN HERSELF VE
RY ADAPTABLE BUT STILL OVERAMBITIOUS AND HA
S DIFFICULTIES LIMITING SCOPE OF WORK HAS
BEEN MOVED TO ADMINISTRATIONS OWN AREA TO
CLOSE UP RANKS RECENTLY MADE EXCELLENT APP
EARANCE BEFORE ANTIVIVISECTION LEAGUE SHOUL
D BE COMMENDED ON OWN INITIATIVE HELD MEET
ING LAB TECHNICIANS CLUB SHOULD BE REGARDED
USEFUL CONTACTMAKING BUT EVIDENTLY INTENDS
ENCOURAGE THEM INITIATE NEW ANIMAL TERMINA
TION PROCEDURES INVOLVING INCREASED COSTS
KEEP UNDER SPECIAL SURVEILLANCE FATHER LOTT
ED FOR PARLIAMENTARY ELECTION DESPITE SECURI
TY POLICE RECORD OVERAMBITION MUST DEFINITE
LY BE KEPT UNDER INCREASED SURVEILLANCE PRO
GNOSIS HARD TO JUDGE
RATING 1–5
COMPETENCE 4
ADAPTABILITY 3
SOLIDARITY 3
MOTIVATION 5
COST NONE

28

Bengt Orvarsson is Acting Head of the Institute of Clinical Psychology. The academic chair he holds is one of about a dozen positions at the Nobel Institutes that are donations pure and simple. Others are the Volvo Chair in Transportation Medicine, the Herman Miller Chair in Human Engineering, the Farben Chair in Toxicology, the Swedish Broadcasting Chair in Hypnosis Research, and the Hershey Chair in Diet Studies. The Chair in Clinical Psychology is paid for by the Personnel Administration Council and according to the donor's stipulation, is to "advance research into psychological stimulation in the working environment."

It is to Bengt Orvarsson that Evy Beck turns in her perplexity: to what extent do animals experience anxiety? Orvarsson gets quite stimulated by having the question put to him, and begins to run around the walls of his office at once, scribbling with magic markers on the enameled metal. After twenty years in the field of clinical psychology, Orvarsson ought to feel a certain fatigue and pessimism before such complex questions as this. But not he. He's like an overambitious student facing an examiner suspected of being senile. He looks her right in the eye, speaks loudly, slowly, and with exaggerated distinctness—meanwhile writing on the wall in an easy-to-read childish hand: DEFINITION? POSITIVE/NEGATIVE ANXIETY? DELIMITING THE PROBLEM? CHEMICAL EXPRESSIONS OF ANXIETY? HOW TO STIMULATE ANXIETY?

"Negative and *positive* anxiety?" she asks.

"Oh, yes. From working environment studies we know that stress in suitable doses will often have a positive effect, that is, it stimulates productivity. I'm completely convinced that anxiety functions in much the same way, that anxiety has really come into being because it serves man. The body can't afford to hold onto functions that are purely negative. Anx-

156

iety probably can be regarded as negative only when the biological system gets out of balance."

"But how can you distinguish between negative and positive anxiety?"

"By relating the anxiety to the situation. A physiological function first takes on meaning when it's placed in the total psychological context. That's the whole point of 'behavioral technology.' "

"What I'm after," she says, "is to find out roughly how much anxiety we subject our lab animals to, unnecessarily. Would you call that negative anxiety?"

"Like all intense experiences, anxiety develops the personality. What is experienced for the moment as a discomfort can, in the long view, be a psychological investment. A spiritual gain."

He ponders. The smudgy white coat hangs on his rangy frame like the shroud on a skeleton.

"Excuse me if I interrupt," she begins tentatively.

"It doesn't matter a bit . . . not a bit, d'you hear!"

"If an animal is going to die . . . and realizes it. Then the animal feels—one suspects—intense anxiety. But that anxiety can't ever be an investment."

He ponders again. She regrets having broken the flow of his enthusiasm; it would probably have been more instructive to let him go on.

"I thought you meant in human beings?" he says.

"What?"

"I thought you were asking about anxiety in animals so you could draw conclusions about anxiety in human beings."

"Well, look, I'm a veterinarian."

He laughs, a little embarrassed, looks at her, and scratches his head.

"You're not at all interested in making the step from animal to man?"

"In this case, no."

Slowly he writes on the white wall: ANIMAL ANXIETY????

"I came to you," she says, "to ask whether, as a by-product

of your work, you might have something to tell me about anxiety in animals."

"You've got me a little confused. You're putting the question backwards: you start with man and want to transfer human 'behavioral technology' to animals?"

"That's right."

"Then you really ought to go over to Stress Research, where they're torturing draftees. From your viewpoint, man is the experimental animal and the experimental animal is man."

"All I want to know is whether you've tried to measure anxiety in animals. I don't care a bit in what connection you've done it."

Orvarsson draws a cat and a rabbit on the wall. On the bodies of the animals he writes CAT and RABBIT, respectively. Under CAT he writes "anxiety over free fall" and under RABBIT, "chemical anxiety."

"Strictly speaking, we will never know whether animals experience either pain or anxiety. Not until we teach them to speak, anyway."

"Nevertheless, you're drawing a parallel with infants, that one causes them anxiety by letting them free fall?"

"Exactly."

"And chemical anxiety in rabbits?"

"It's induced by injecting the rabbit with phenylethylamine, which is like amphetamine but entirely lacking in amphetamine's euphoria. There's just the anxiety molecule left, you might say."

"Have you done such experiments?"

"No. But I thought I could whip up a couple of possible experiments for you."

"At the PA Council's expense?"

He goes back to his pictures and draws big talk-balloons coming from the cat and the rabbit. The sketch is beginning to resemble a comic strip. In the talk-balloons he writes "Free versus bound gamma in the noradrenalin fraction."

"We know that free and bound gamma are released by anxiety in man," says Orvarsson. "Therefore, it must be admissible to draw parallels with other mammals."

158

Suddenly he turns, puts down the marker, and looks at her.

"What the hell are you really trying to do?!"

"I've already told you: Find some kind of point of departure, some kind of objective basis for stating that animals feel anxiety. And if that's the case, that it's our humanitarian duty to minimize it."

"All you have to do is ask someone who owns a dog."

She doesn't answer. It would be completely useless to write to the Academic Council and state, *As every dog owner knows, dogs can experience pain, fear, and even anxiety. On the basis of that fact, 200,000 dollars is hereby requested for the immediate purchase of 100 Siemens Flicker-Lasers, Model S-320.*

Orvarsson has switched to writing out chemical formulas.

"We know that we have to reach the free and bound gamma during the anxiety reaction itself. When it's possible to measure them. After the anxiety goes into resting phase, there are the breakdown products left, of course, but they're not anxiety-specific."

Under the cat, he draws a long vertical arrow and writes FALL > 40 FEET. Then he draws a number of little cats that are falling along the arrow. The farther the cat falls, the bigger the talk-balloon gets.

"Exhaled breath is collected in a thin plastic bag," he explains. "The cat has to fall at least thirty-six feet because at the beginning of the fall it holds its breath by sheer reflex."

"Is forty feet really enough?"

He looks at her as if she were stupid.

"If you let the cat fall too far, the plastic bag will finally get so big that it begins to function as a parachute."

Quite a while back, Evy Beck realized that these experiments would be completely unrealistic for her. They would take time and money. Besides, she has no authority whatsoever to undertake her own research: it's not for the purpose of doing research that the Institutes have given her a job. What's left, then? Purely moralistic arguments? *Please, Academic Council: For ethico-humanitarian reasons, a quarter of a million dollars is hereby requested immediately!* There must be another way.

159

"Listen, Bengt, is it possible you've seen a similar experiment described somewhere in the literature?"

"Whenever I hit on something, I usually proceed on the assumption that it's my own idea," he answers, offended.

"Of course."

"Then we've got Peter Rabbit . . ." he says, and begins to draw a diagram of how one injects phenylethylamine into the rabbit's belly and then lets it pant into a plastic bag.

She's not watching any longer. She's disappointed in herself. When will you learn, Quotia? When will you learn not to run around, but instead to sit yourself down and *think?*

When Orvarsson has finished drawing, he points the marker at her and says accusingly, "Evy Beck, you're keeping two sets of books! If you're so hellishly sensitive about animals' feelings, then how can you allow anybody to induce such anxiety as this in animals?!"

After lunch, she goes to her office in the penthouse. A red bulb is shining by the tube outlet—the mail has come. She takes the transparent plastic cylinder out of the tube and with some difficulty succeeds in squeezing two fingers down into it. They haven't yet overcome the tendency of letters to adhere to the inside of the cylinder because of static electricity. She takes out some telephone messages, a postcard from Findus Pharmafarm that pictures the company's staff hotel in Gambia, and a little brown official envelope from the Labor Market Board.

She slits open the LMB envelope: *Your performance rating from the Alf. Nobel Med.-Surg. Institutes has arrived at the WOLMB Bureau. Since by this rating it appears that the NMSI Administration Department has given you the performance rating "Satisfactory," WOLMB does not for the present intend to make application to your employer for a permanent position until such a time as a further performance rating may be given from which it is evident that your performance has improved. Signed, Edgar Hultin, Chief Personnel Supvr.*

160

29

"You don't mean you're offended by this, for pete's sake?" says the head of the Administration Department, Håkan Rosenquist.

"I should think you could have shown me the performance rating before you sent it to WOLMB. We're on the same corridor, after all."

He hands back the little brown envelope. His office up here in the penthouse is markedly different from all the others. As a seasoned bureaucrat, he's acquainted with most of the other department heads at government agencies and institutions in Stockholm—when the various museums lend things out, Håkan Rosenquist is first in line. When the national portrait collection was transferred from Gripsholm Castle to the Wilhelmina, Rosenquist saw to it that two Roslin paintings got deposited with him. On his wall are hanging "Gustaf III in Coronation Regalia" from 1777 and "Bayreuth Police Prefect Justin de Rosny," probably from 1750. The rococo furniture comes from the Nordic Museum's storerooms in the Stockholm Palace and the rugs, from the Institute of Persian Handicrafts. The heavy crystal chandelier—which one has to detour around in order to avoid collision—hung in Haga Castle during Krushchev's visit in 1964.

"Sorry, Evy, really sorry," says Rosenquist, squirming behind Crown Prince Carl August's writing desk.

"It wasn't exactly apologies I was after. But why?"

"You mean the performance rating itself? But, Evy, you know very well nobody would think of calling you 'satisfactory'!"

"That's the way the letter reads."

"But don't you understand that this is simply a formality?!" he wriggles, and lets his wandering fingers find a haven in Axel von Fersen's traveling correspondence box, which looks like a coffee service for dolls.

"Excuse me, but I don't understand one iota."

Rosenquist takes a pinch of mint snuff out of Reuterholm's

ivory snuffbox before enumerating on his fingers.

"If we give you too high a rating, WOLMB says we'll have to hire you on a permanent basis. If we give you too low a rating, they'll send somebody else out to do your job. Actually, you're obviously worth the highest rating."

"Oh?"

"Yes, but I can't go to the Academic Council and tell them that NMSI's now going to take over paying your salary."

"So WOLMB has to think I'm just good enough so that they let me stay but don't demand that the Institutes pay my wages?"

"Exactly."

Mollified, she leans back in the visitor's chair and lets her eyes rest on the ceiling painting representing the Goddess of the Hunt waiting among pale blue clouds for the arrival of Aries. For some reason, an episode that took place when Erik was five comes to mind. She and Erik were out for a walk in the middle of winter. Erik had mittens on. Suddenly he said, "Mama, it's not fair that the thumb has its own case." She laughed as one does about little children's precociousnesses. Then Erik changed his mind, "No, Mama, the thumb ought to have it a little more comfortable because he's more useful than those other fingers."

Rosenquist tinkles a little bell brought home from China by the East India Company in 1762. She rises.

"No, no, I didn't want you to leave!" he says. "I was just ringing for my secretary."

She thanks him and goes into her own office to get her coat. It's four thirty. If one is Satisfactory, doesn't that mean that one goes home a little earlier?

When she gets home, she finds Papa in the kitchen. He's standing there staring apathetically out the window, the tubes hanging loose from his belly.

"But Papa!" she almost screams.

She leads him in to the bed and gets him to lie down.

"They took my liver," he says, as if in a trance.

She discovers that the night table is empty. The Auto-Hepar is gone!

"Who took your liver?!"

162

"Two . . . two . . . girls."

"They just walked in and took the liver away?!"

Papa succeeds in collecting himself a little: Two young women apparently got into the apartment while Papa was taking his midday nap. They disconnected him from the liver even though he woke up. Then they said, "So long!" and left the apartment, lugging the heavy machine along with them.

She first calls Roslagstull Hospital, where they promise to find a substitute liver by nightfall—otherwise Papa is welcome to a night in Detoxification.

Then she calls the police to report the burglary. The operator puts her in line for burglary reports. Nothing happens for two hours. She tries to put the receiver down and dial the number again, but it doesn't work. The phone is locked into the Police Station's exchange on "hold."

She warms up a mug of protein-free milk for Papa and then walks downstairs to a telephone booth to call the police, changing the report to "robbery of a life-supporting aid for a handicapped person." They put her on "hold." After twenty-five minutes, she goes to the next telephone booth, calls up the militia, and says that an "electronic instrument" has gone astray. When she returns to the apartment four minutes later, two plain-clothesmen from the militia are already standing at the doorstep.

"This visit will have to be treated as confidential," they say, and follow her in.

"I'll get Papa!"

"No. Don't bring in Rodion Beck," says one man, sitting down at the kitchen table with his hat still on.

The other man shuts the door to Papa's room and places himself in front of the keyhole.

"I shouldn't get my father? But he's the only eyewitness?"

"No."

She looks timidly at the man who guards the door and tries to smile, tries to take the bizarre situation with a grain of humor.

"So two younger women came in here and took your father's Auto-Hepar away with them?"

"But why don't you ask *him?*"

The chief interrogator doesn't answer the question, but instead looks around the kitchen like a sanitation inspector hunting for a dust ball or an overlooked spider web on the ceiling.

"Dr. Beck, we're pretty sure it was a couple of drug addicts who got in and stole the liver."

"Oh?"

"Would you please turn on the radio," says the man guarding the door.

She pushes the music-channel button on the transistor. If only Papa doesn't come roaring out here in a rage over "sour notes." But Papa's locked in.

"Drug addicts?" she says.

"These machines bring between 18 and 20,000 dollars on the black market," says the militiaman at the table. "Junkies use 'em instead of heroin. Hook themselves up to the liver and use the selector. Gives 'em a kick with the body's own substances."

She understands. If she can put Papa to sleep with the selector, then it obviously can be used to raise the level of natural psycho-stimulants in the blood.

"But their own livers, then?" she asks. "They can't get past their own livers, can they?"

"They make a shunt. Nowadays drug addicts are very technically savvy."

"I sure hope we'll have time to get a replacement machine before tonight," she says worriedly.

"Well, that's about it, then," says the man, and gets up from the table.

"But fingerprints? Or clues?"

"The fingerprints are sure to be falsified."

"Shouldn't you talk with Papa anyway? After all, he's *seen* them."

The men look at each other, then the one who seems to be in charge replies, "I'm sure you understand why, Dr. Beck. We're here in complete confidence."

She gets angry; why all this nonsense when it was an ordinary theft?

164

"I'm going to get my father," she says.

The militiaman grabs her arm.

"I wouldn't advise you to do that. I really wouldn't."

Out on the doorstep, he turns around and says with un-spoken meaning, "I'm sure you know about your father's background. His very special background."

She goes back inside and takes a glass of port wine. Seldom has she been so upset on his account. That people snigger behind his back because he rambles on about proofs of God's existence, she can bear. That he gets no preference on the waiting list for hospital care, she can understand. That be-cause of his political background militiamen won't even have him in the same room, maybe she can understand. But she absolutely cannot accept it.

It's half an hour till midnight. When she's almost coming apart with anxiety that Papa will go into another liver-coma, they come from Roslagstull with a new liver. It's not a West-inghouse Auto-Hepar. Instead, they drag in an oblong object as big as a piano. The blue-white enamel is chipped at the edges and one corner has been inexpertly repaired with plas-tic. The replacement liver is marked Singer Cyborg and is surely ten years old. In her contacts with the Institute of Transplantology at NMSI, she's learned that the model desig-nation Cyborg is a contraction of "cybernetic organism." If only Papa doesn't realize it! Realize, and misinterpret the concept as some kind of parasitism.

But Papa is apathetic now. His eyes have sunk back into their sockets and the pupils are parked on the ceiling.

"Well now, miss," says one of the five deliverymen when Papa has been connected. "Nobody's going to steal this mon-ster without a Mack truck and a crane!"

She has a hard time going to sleep. The Singer Cyborg sighs and groans like a prehistoric iron lung. When she finally succeeds in sinking down into the outermost layer of sleep, the telephone rings. There's a baboon at Nutritional Physi-ology that's got a tummy-ache. Evy Beck has to make her ninth night call this month.

30

The month changes its name and calls itself June —it happens suddenly and mechanically, as when the date indicator on a clock flips down a new panel. June comes on altogether too quickly; the time before the change of month gets absurdly jammed together. The birches have to leaf out, the tulips have to rise out of the flower beds, the fruit trees have to have time to bloom, the water must be warmed up for summer. She's always felt that May is the month that really needs six weeks. Time goes on flashing by—hardly have you had time to say First of June before it's time to say Midsummer.

After Midsummer, Papa has to go in for his second overhaul. He's as excited this time as he was at the end of March. The steam engine, as he calls the Singer Cyborg, doesn't have only disadvantages. The big, heavy, groaning machine evidently has an easier time keeping Papa's blood values stable than did the cute little Westinghouse Auto-Hepar. Papa's yellow skin is nearly normal now. First the yellow turned into bronze, and now he has faded and looks as though he came home from the Canary Islands ten or twelve days ago.

It's Sunday morning and they're sitting on the balcony, waiting for the radio worship service. Evy is sleepy. Papa woke her up at a quarter to three last night, declaring that he had heard "a mysterious hissing" from the steam engine; he wanted her to check. Till nearly three thirty she sat on Papa's bed and fought to keep her eyes open. He now recalls nothing of what happened.

"Papa," she says. "Soon you're going in for your checkup."

He doesn't answer. He sits there rotating the transistor's antenna through the air as if to feel out the best angle for radio reception, the little plastic box pressed against his ear all the while. But the radio isn't switched on.

"After Midsummer they have low-season rates for retirees."

"At Roslagstull?" he says, and taps lightly on the transistor

166

as if he expected the answer from it and not from Evy.

"People don't want to go into the hospital during their vacations."

"Want to get rid of me?" says Papa softly, and launches a thick gob of old man's spittle over the balcony railing.

"Papa!" she admonishes. "Papa, the people downstairs have . . ."

Papa immediately readies gob number two—draws his cheeks in hollow, pools and kneads the saliva, sucks in his underlip, and juts his neck forward: tfsss . . . He misfires, the gob never parts from its thick navel-string, but sails out, stops with a jerk, and drops on his knee. He wipes the string away with his arm.

"So now they're creeping to the cross," he says. "So now they want me at Roslagstull."

"You'd be able to stay there for two weeks. And you'd get gone-over very thoroughly."

"Two?"

"Ten days . . ."

"*Three* weeks. A so-called senior citizen can also need a little vacation from his relatives."

Evy feels guilty. She has deliberately tricked Papa, lured him into demanding three weeks in the hospital. On the sly, she looks at his profile for a long time—does she dare? Papa looks best in profile. Head-on, you're always thinking you'll cut yourself on him.

"Well, Papa. It's possible I may travel out of the country for a couple of weeks . . ."

Papa switches on the transistor, there's a Mozart matinee. He conducts with the antenna so that it whips through the pansies in the flower box.

". . . on a business trip to Gambia."

"Business trip?"

"NMSI gets some of its monkeys from there. From the Findus Pharmafarm."

"Can a person make a business trip when he's got no position?"

She picks up two beheaded pansy blossoms—a yellow one and a purple one—from the balcony floor.

167

"Why do you go on messing with those animals?" says Papa sarcastically, and pokes her in the right breast with the tip of the antenna.

That hurts. For the last two years, her breasts have been tender almost all the time—not, as before, just at menstruation.

"For two reasons," she says. "If the animals aren't looked after, we'll get poor results from the research. If we allow animals to suffer unnecessarily, we're behaving immorally."

"Poo!" he says, and whips the antenna around so that she just has time to duck her head. "Sentimentality!"

"How many thousands of animals do you think had to pay with their lives so that an artificial liver could be made?"

"For that, then. But the rest—poo!"

She mustn't get provoked now. She mustn't gamble with her vacation. Both she and Papa need to get away. If they're going to be able to endure the fall.

"Poo!!" says Papa, and tries to catch her eye.

"There's also a legal reason," she says, trying to divert the conflict onto a formal plane. "There's something called the Animal Welfare Law."

"You go around pampering rats while babies starve to death in Latin America, in Bangladesh, in Japan, in East Africa."

"The one doesn't exclude the other, Papa dear."

". . . While the lower class is tossed off to one side like human garbage because they're no longer needed on the farm. Because they just get in the way of the combines."

"You've always said that change has to begin *here.*"

". . . While the fascists pinch the fingers off Chile's communists with wire nippers!"

She gets up from the folding chair and goes inside. She's really not running away because she's afraid to collide with Papa. No, it's because she knows she can't handle this kind of discussion, because after a short time she feels herself logically overpowered, prepared to surrender and admit that her work with lab animals is silly in the face of human suffering.

She stops a little way inside the balcony door and looks at

168

the Singer Cyborg standing there with its side panel raised
so that it will cool off more quickly. I have accepted the fact
once and for all, she says to herself. Accepted countless animals' suffering and dying so that a seventy-nine-year-old man
without a liver will get to go on living for a few months more.
I accept mass death but I go cluck-cluck when I see a single
guinea pig tormented. What kind of logic is that, Quotia?

She prepares lunch and carries it out on a tray. She comes
out just in time to hear the closing hymn over the transistor,
"Spring Has Now Unwrapp'd the Flowers, Day is Now Reviv-
ing." Papa's sleeping in the sunshine. How many violated
arguments for the existence of God has he missed today?

"Papa," she says tentatively, and touches the antenna—he
has the radio on his knee.

He wakes on the sly. One might think he was still asleep
if his eyeballs didn't move under the lids.

"Spring has now unwrapp'd the flowers," says Papa.

They eat in silence. The weather has been perfect lately.
Yesterday they had dinner and then tea out here on the
balcony. You couldn't believe how Papa drops crumbs. The
crumbs stick to your shoes and get tracked into the apartment. She's certainly going to have to vacuum the balcony.
Actually, the sparrows did a lot of good in the past. At the
sidewalk cafés, the rats have taken over.

"Well, Papa," she says. "I really have to decide. Is it all
right with you if I go to Gambia while you're in Roslagstull?"

"Go to Gambia. I only hope you don't come home married
to a chimpanzee."

"It's settled, then, Papa?"

"Naturally you haven't considered the fact that you can't
take any money out," he says peevishly.

Then it hits her: anyone who's retired, sick, on relief, or
paid by the Labor Market Board has no right to exchange
money for foreign currency. Of course not. But maybe she
could talk to Erik. Maybe Erik could arrange something
. . . No! She's not going to mess things up for Erik. He absolutely must not risk getting the least blemish on him.

While Papa's having his midday dialysis, she calls up the
Findus manager, Pedersen. She has to hold her hand over

169

her left ear to shut out the steam engine's grinding and clanking.

"Greetings, Evy," says Pedersen brightly.

"I'd be delighted to accept two weeks at your staff hotel in Gambia," she says. "But there's this thing about exchanging . . ."

"There are really so many ways," says Pedersen.

"I hoped so."

"Really nothing to it. We'll arrange a short-term employment on our staff. The salary will be paid in Gambia."

31

While Evy Beck sits waiting in the bulletproof glass waiting room of the Passport Police, she tries to reconstruct what has happened this morning: Erik came to pick her up at ten o'clock sharp as she'd asked him to. Which didn't mean that she and Papa hadn't stood waiting at the door since twenty minutes till. Of course Papa rushed forward and worked himself into the front seat as soon as Erik stopped. She herself got to keep the baggage company in the back.

It was Papa's day. He babbled and gesticulated in the front seat until she began to worry about Erik. She usually would have enjoyed the drive out to Arlanda Airport, but now she was altogether too shattered by the impending trip. What did she—an old lady—have to do in Africa, really? And would Papa be able to make it—and Erik? Certainly Erik has made it through *every* problem, every tight spot since he was so little he could barely walk, but she lives with a continual and contradictory feeling about Erik: Erik is strong, Erik is superb, but his strength comes in some mysterious way from her. Nowadays she herself is only a dried-up and crumpled peel, the peel of the orange in which the seed once began to grow. At one and the same time, she is waste and power source.

Erik had reserved a table in the restaurant. Naturally she was a little worried about Papa. Papa could have started being difficult in two ways: either he could have displayed an exaggerated touchiness, demanding the food and commanding the cook, complaining that the food was cold or claiming that he was burned—or else Papa could have had a sudden attack of his old class solidarity, refusing to be waited on, stalking out to the kitchen to fraternize with the dishwashers. But he didn't do a thing. Papa was so enthralled with Erik that he only picked at his food. Even though she felt it was a shame for all the expense, she was just as glad he ate nothing. It was the wrong food for Papa.

It had been a long time since she ate real beef. It didn't really have any flavor—or else her throat was dry because of the trip. From the table they had a fantastic view over the runways. During dessert, Erik had suddenly cut Papa off for a few seconds and turned to her: "Mama, here comes your plane. A Concorde."

She had stared blankly at the plane, a long metal tube on high stilts with a mosquito nose dipping down so that the sting was imbedded in the asphalt. The plane was decorated in blue and white, with ITT TRANS WORLD AIRWAYS on the rudder. Actually, she hadn't seen the plane at all, she'd just let the word "Mama" slowly sink in and come to rest deep in her body. Erik hasn't called her anything but Evy since he started first grade.

They'd said good-bye at the lunch table so Papa could round off his coffee with brandy in peace and quiet; he would be going right to Roslagstull, and there they would take the brandy out of his blood pretty quickly. Erik had kissed her on the mouth. And Papa, Papa had risen slowly, solemnly stretched out his blue-veined hand with the twisted fingers, looked her right in the eye, and shaken hands.

Her luggage was already checked in, so she had walked right into Passport Control, shown her passport and travel permit from LMB, and had it exit-stamped. Then she'd sat, almost alone, in the departure lounge and looked at the great mass of people crowding up to the duty-free meat counter.

The loudspeaker had chimed and the number of her plane —IT 1027—had been projected on the white screen ceiling. She'd looked back one last time. But as agreed, Erik and Papa were not there. With her raincoat over her arm, she had walked out to the gate, handed over the boarding pass, and proceeded farther along the narrow tube that emptied directly into the cabin of the plane. Then, suddenly and firmly, she had decided: *I'm not going.*

She had tried to go upstream in the boarding tube, but that was impossible. She'd stirred an almost explosive irritation merely by standing still. When all the passengers had pushed by, she'd started back toward the gate. Almost at once the loudspeaker had begun to boom and echo: *Mrs. Evy Beck? Mrs. Evy Beck, passenger for Gambia?* At the gate, she had caused astonishment. Two attendants had to lift her up over the turnstile, which was set on Exit. Then there had been some palaver about the weight distribution on the airplane. They had weighed her again, and then said sourly that now all the passengers on the plane would have to change their seats: if a "weight" of 196 pounds was removed, it meant that all "weights" had to be redistributed. There was no question of getting her baggage back out of the hold of the plane; she was welcome to come back to Arlanda at six twenty-five this evening, when the Concorde was expected back from Gambia.

The real difficulties had begun when she tried to re-enter Sweden. One cannot enter at a passenger terminal that is built for exit. She had been questioned several times about her defection—was she ill? Stupidly, she had denied that she was. If she had said that she'd suddenly felt nauseated, she would have been able to get out through the first-aid station.

Now she's sitting in the waiting room of the Passport Police and saying to herself: You're just plain scared, Quotia. To call it fear of flying might possibly be comforting, but hardly true. I'm just scared.

She rises and goes over to the narrow rows of bulletproof bricks and tries to look out through the four-inch-thick glass shapes. Everything appears powerfully diminished: the giant gleaming airplanes drag themselves along the ground like wounded dragonflies and silverfish. They rock back and forth and crawl. They're drawn out into strings of spit when they're in the middle of a block. Where the blocks meet, they're squeezed together into coins. On fins, wings, and legs sit innumerable red and yellow lights that blink and pulse. The tank-trucks look like gaily colored larvae. She fills her lungs with air. One big puff would turn Arlanda into sticks and straws.

"Mrs. Beck!"

A passport officer is standing on the other side of the railing and waving at her.

"If you'll just go down the steps, a personnel bus will be leaving for the International Arrivals building in five minutes!"

"Thanks . . . thanks a lot!"

In the minibus sit a driver, two pilots in uniforms like admirals', a cleaning woman with kerchief knotted on her forehead and covered bucket, and a sky trooper with a submachine gun. The Passport Police have called ahead, so the officers at the Arrivals building give her no difficulty. She's told briskly that unfortunately the LMB travel clearance is forfeited even though she has traveled no farther than the departure lounge. Customs doesn't bother with her at all.

It's nearly two o'clock before she finds herself in Sweden again. Erik and Papa have surely left—she has no interest in going the three miles back to the Departures terminal to see if the car is still there. The simplest thing would be to wait for her baggage, which ought to be back in four and a half hours. But she doesn't want to have anything to do with her own suitcases. It's as if they belonged to somebody else.

She tries to buy a ticket at the bus counter to take the airlines limousine into Stockholm. But she has no papers that show she's an airline passenger, so it doesn't work. She's advised to take a taxi to Märsta.

It's the twenty-fifth of June and misting. Without really planning it, she finds herself walking in the direction of Stockholm. After a mile or so, the sidewalk peters out and she turns her steps onto a tractor track that winds through the birch- and bush-covered marshland.

The greenness is tender green no longer. The grass, dandelion leaves, pine needles, and birch leaves all have the same deep green hue. Rain-wet summer can be as monotonous as gray snow-fields on a misty morning in December. After a while, a breeze picks up, heavy drops are whipped from the trees. Suddenly she discovers it isn't raining any longer—the pattering sound comes instead from a grove of aspens through which the wind is blowing.

32

The afternoon is heavy, humid. The sun is frying the tops of leaden gray clouds that hang so low they make the woods into a hothouse. Evy Beck's white summer shoes are wet clear through the sole. As she walks, it squishes both under and inside the shoes. She sits down on a stone and slaps some mosquitoes, mostly just to have something to do. Then she takes off her shoes and stockings; the mosquitoes now attack her ankles. She slaps at her legs with her summer coat and gets up. The first barefoot steps feel chilly and risky. She walks as unsteadily as a tightrope walker, with the corners of her mouth drawn down and lower teeth bared.

After a few minutes, she falls back into her usual slightly rolling gait. She doesn't bother to stop any more and brush pine needles from her soles. But she keeps a sharp lookout for anthills. The woods thin out and she follows the pitch-black tractor trail over a bog that looks like a market place set with big brown cobblestones. On the other side of the sopping wet ground, the light-colored tracks meander up into a hill of juniper. There's a burnt smell in the air.

Right at the edge of the bog, she stumbles upon a grave: an oblong dug-up rectangle with a cross of birch, wired together with rusty baling wire. No name, no flowers. The smell of burnt leaves and burnt rubber gets stronger. On the little slope up toward the juniper grove, she gets short of breath.

From the top, she has a pretty ample view. Far to the north, she sees the control tower and radar antennas of Arlanda. In the east lies a lake or perhaps only a pool of water dammed up from the summer rain. To the west lies an extended clear-cutting—over an area of several square miles

174

the land has been brutally shaved. But the stubble has begun to grow out again: yard-high spruces with yellow tops, saplings, dogrose vines, birch, and burdock. To the south, on the other side of the hill, lies an old deserted farm. No, not really —in one corner of the obviously long-abandoned field lie a few small, irregularly cultivated pieces of land. They look completely out of place in the wilderness, as if an enormous steam shovel had scooped up a piece of the city gardens of her childhood, driven the fragment out here, and spilled out tomato beds, potato beds, pea and parsley and carrot plots higgledy-piggledy.

She tramps on along the tractor trail that has already begun to dry and crackle underfoot like some kind of light-brown lizard skin. The garden plots turn out to consist partly of some more professional elements, such as sugar beets, turnips, and a patch of four-inch-high broadleaf grass that must be wheat. A croaking call is heard from the edge of the woods. She stiffens and dares not breathe. There! A crow flaps lazily like a black flag between two birches.

Excited, she sneaks up to the birches—a wild crow so near town! Then a shotgun roars. Two crows fly right into the wind, turn, and sail away beyond the juniper grove. She gets terrifically angry and rushes stumbling in among the birches to catch whoever it was who shot.

Almost at once she catches sight of him. He stands calmly right in the middle of the tractor trail without making the slightest attempt to escape. He's a bearded man of indeterminate age. The baggy blue pants are shoved into a pair of big moss-green rubber boots with pink soles. On his torso he wears a tattered fishnet undershirt; the curly hair on his chest is white. On his head he has an old purple ski cap with visor. He gives a toothless grin and sniffs at the shotgun's muzzle.

"Gunpowder—Jesus don't she smell great!" he says, and holds out the gun as if inviting Evy to share.

"You must not shoot crows!" she says furiously. "They're protected by law."

Confusedly he puts the shotgun at parade-rest and picks his nose. The unsteady, squinting eyes no longer dare look at her.

175

"Don't you know they're protected?!"

He shrugs several times, wags his head about, and mutters to himself. Then he tries to look at her. It isn't bashfulness that makes his gaze unsteady—the man is drunk!

"Where does this path lead?" she asks.

He waves with exaggerated courtesy, trying all points of the compass, and says thickly, "Märsta, Norrsunda, Arlanda, Paris, New York, Tokyo . . ."

Then he does a surprisingly steady about-face, puts the shotgun at right-shoulder arms, and begins to stump away along the trail. She follows. From the rear, it looks as if he is sitting on an invisible rail even as he walks: his back is stooped, his rump hangs down, and his knees bend in the boots.

She follows him for at least a mile without either of them saying anything, or the man in the ski cap looking around a single time. They go through an abandoned gravel pit with a rusty conveyor that leans alarmingly, pass over a partly torn-up asphalt road where the dandelion leaves spread out like medallions between the barely discernible white center stripes. The road is maybe 150 feet long and chopped off at both ends by the gravel pit. By the side lies a gutted building with caved-in roof that was probably once a store, an upended gasoline pump, and a lead-pipe sign frame from which the bus schedules probably rotted away decades before.

She tries to keep just the right distance between herself and her guide. If she gets closer than fifteen feet, she has to walk in his exhaust, which stinks of urine, sweat, fusel, and gun oil. They wade over a shallow brook with a bottom of brown needles, and push on into a pine grove where some pullets are running loose. In among the pines stands an old army bus with wet Masonite over the windows and a black tin chimney whose peaked cap sticks up through the peeling roof.

"This's where we live," says her guide, and waves vaguely at the bus. " 'N' over there's the boiler!"

He points up toward the little hill where the chickens run, but evidently means the dilapidated cottage ninety degrees

176

south of the hill. It stinks from the "boiler"—a celluloselike odor that she realizes must be mash.

After that, they just stand there, fifteen feet apart, without really knowing what will happen next. The poacher with the sweeping gestures looks at the ground and picks his nose. Evy Beck looks around. There isn't much to look at; besides the bus, the cottage, and the hens, there is an old soaked-through living room suite in green cloth, a dish-drying rack made of sticks, a maroon motorbike, a plastic clothesline stretched between two pines—on the line sit blackened clothespins like little swallows with cloven tails. Twenty or thirty yards away, a trash pile and beyond that, a fruit orchard with trees so smothered in spider web and gray lichen that only a branch here and there has managed to raise a half-eaten leaf or two. The leaves are scalloped like the ears of cattle. She glimpses something white on the ground among the yard-high grass and fallen blackened branches between the fruit trees. It's a goat.

"May I step inside?" she asks cautiously, pointing to the bus.

The guide straightens up, bows from the waist, and makes a gesture of genteel invitation that sweeps beyond the trash pile. She lifts aside the burlap sack that serves for a door and clambers into the bus. It's murky—only the rear window seems to be intact and the light from that is in her eyes. The air in the bus is thick and has an odor like wet wool socks on a hot radiator. She accustoms her eyes to the murkiness: to the left—on top of the motor—stand a number of bottles, glasses, and plastic mugs. In the place where luggage racks must have been at one time stands a black cast-iron stove. In the body of the bus, a few rows of seats have been left intact but beyond that the fittings have been torn out and replaced with bunks made of planks. She goes along the middle aisle toward the sleeping quarters. Somebody—several bodies?—must be sleeping there. She hears snores, wheezing, and mumbling. A shy, ladylike little fart joins the chorus, and suddenly someone sits up with a howl, bangs his head on the bunk overhead, and howls again: "Goddamsonofabitching tooth-bastard!"

177

A gray face floats in the half-light, the skull darts forward, and she sees a bearded old man's face with an old curtain swathed around it.

"Oh, 'scuse me!" says the man, taking the finger out of his mouth and reaching out to introduce himself: George Krona.

"Evy Beck."

"A pleasure."

"Have you got a toothache?" she asks.

George Krona clambers out of his bunk, comes down into the aisle, spreads his mouth wide open with both index fingers, and says, probably, "Look."

It's entirely too dark, she can hardly tell his mouth from his eye sockets.

"Haven't you got a light?"

With his index fingers still hooked in his mouth, George Krona crowds by her and goes toward the door, shoves the sack aside with his head, and hops down to the ground. She follows.

Out in the light, she looks at George Krona curiously. He is maybe forty years old, short and fat, and has a crumpled boxer's nose that looks like it's been blown to one side by a high wind during a short but hectic sporting career. She takes hold of him by the curtain that swathes his head and turns his deep gullet toward the afternoon sun. His tongue flaps unhappily like a beached fish. He hasn't got many teeth left. Around the blackened ruins of one molar, the gums are swollen and inflamed.

"You must have that tooth pulled," she says, and dries her hands on her summer coat.

George Krona takes his fingers from his mouth and slumps. She turns around to look for the poacher, but he has disappeared.

"Okay," she says. "If you've got some kind of pliers, I'll take out that tooth for you."

He brightens and throws out his right fist to thank her— but changes his mind halfway and jams it into his pocket.

"Gunna hurt?" he asks with deep mistrust.

"Yes, it will. But it won't take long. Hopefully."

George Krona writhes in dread. He grinds his heels into

178

the carpet of needles and looks all around for a route of escape. Then he takes a deep breath, presses his nose together with two fingers, and thinks intently while his cheeks grow rounder and rounder and his face gets darker and darker. Then he exhales and says, "Guess I wanna talk it over with the Count first."

He goes back into the bus, apparently to talk with someone called the Count. Since the Count is probably sleeping and must be waked, she doesn't wait but instead walks down the narrow path between the nodding parasols of Queen Anne's Lace to the "boiler." The door stands ajar and she steps inside. Inside the cottage, the poacher is perched on a demijohn, smoking a wrinkled handmade cigarette. A very tall and fat man dressed in a blue nightshirt and with his bare legs thrust into a pair of huge rubber boots is working at a homemade distilling apparatus.

The big man stops and glares under his arm at her, then turns around and, advancing, greets her curtly: "Larsson!"

He goes back to his coiled pipes, but then stops to point to the poacher: "Pekka Fagerström!"

Anxiously she examines the floor for splinters before going half on tiptoe over to Fagerström and taking his limply offered hand. During these courtesies, he doesn't look at her but concentrates on stubbing out his cigarette.

She pushes aside a cobweb-swathed pile of corks on the window sill and seats herself. The men take no further notice of her. Larsson labors over the heat source, a bed of glowing pine cones. On a couple of occasions, Pekka Fagerström rises for no apparent reason, goes over to the coils, and whacks them a couple of times with a board—then he sits down again, like a cymbalist who has only a few bars to play during a whole symphony. Larsson puffs on the cone-fire and reads the thermometer with gaping mouth and squinting eyes.

She sits there for maybe an hour and watches how the men distill spirits. There's something highly sensual about their total submission to the process, their gloomy silence and concentration. Evy Beck hasn't so enjoyed seeing other people work since, as a child, she sat enthralled in the glassblower's shop at Skansen.

When the bottle has been filled, she goes out. She feels hypnotized by having stared at the water-clear drops that ran out of the copper coil. She has stared and stared, spell-bound, as when one watches an icicle melt in the heat of the day.

Outside the bus, two men are sitting deeply sunken into the green sofa: they are George Krona and a long gangly man with wavy silver hair and a thin hooked nose. When she comes up, the gangly man, who wears a light-gray but very soiled suit, rises, approaching her with floating step and head cocked slightly to one side. Silently he takes her hand between both of his, makes an elegant bow, and gives her hand the hint of a kiss before he lets her go. It has to be the Count.

She sits on the armrest of one of the chairs so as not to get her backside wet—the upholstery looks like a green bog. Krona and the Count sit close to each other on the sofa.

"I'm not a dentist, I'm a veterinarian," she says. "But I can probably get that tooth out. Of course, it would be better if Krona could go to the Public Dental Clinic."

Krona doesn't seem to hear, but the Count nods very reflectively over this information, and then says in a nasal voice that must be a combination of too-narrow nose, growing up in Stockholm, and striving for the aristocratic tone: "My friend here is not persuaded that he will feel welcome at the Public Dental Clinic." After a pause for effect, the Count adds: "And my friend is probably correct."

"Well then, if you've got the right tool," she says.

The Count rises from the sofa, floats over to the maroon motorbike, and takes a toolbox from the package rack. He puts the toolbox on the round, brown-polished parlor table that rests on a pedestal with tripod feet. Then he carefully sets the table with flat-nose pliers, wire pliers, round-end pliers, crescent wrench, screwdrivers, a spool of nylon cord, wire cutter, pipe wrench, drawing pliers, folding pliers, brewer's pliers, a watchmaker's loupe, and a sheath knife with sheath. He plucks out each tool with his fingertips, as if he was afraid to soil the instrument.

Krona hastily leans forward and points at the brewer's

pliers, then draws back at once with his head propped on his hands and his eyes on the ground.

Krona's right: the brewer's pliers, with adjustable jaws and knurled handgrips, are probably best for the job. She picks them out while the Count, with hands folded, hovers over her.

Without her noticing their coming, Pekka and Larsson now stand in back of the sofa. Larsson puts the filled bottle on the table and Pekka sets out five former mustard jars in varying sizes and designs. The glasses are filled in silence. Krona belts down his drink immediately and gets a refill at once without request. The others wait politely and then raise their glasses to Evy Beck. She nods encouragement at them —and dips the brewer's pliers in her own glass.

When everyone has finished his drink, she asks quietly if Krona feels ready.

"Sort of changed my mind," he squirms.

His friends look worried and then Larsson says, curtly and sourly, "Not another night of that howling!"

"I'm sure the doctor can guarantee that the pain will be relieved," says the Count.

All the men take a drink and deliberate. She herself feels a little hesitant on the patient's behalf; there is an obvious risk that Krona will be dead drunk before she even gets started. But probably he can handle quite a lot—and besides, old alcoholics seldom have any vomiting reflexes left.

"It's just as well we get going while there's daylight left," she proposes.

But at least forty-five minutes go by before she can set to work. First a suitable chair has to be found. The proposals are many and few of them realistic—finally she's able to get the men to fetch a plain Windsor chair from the boiler. Krona is placed astraddle the chair, but doesn't feel quite ready. A new discussion breaks out about the Public Dental Clinic's possible antipathy to Krona. Finally Larsson settles it: "Krona can't show himself in a decent place with as rotten a jaw as he's got!"

Krona is obliged to give in; he wouldn't be able to endure

the shame of nakedly exposing thirty years' neglect. Besides, he hasn't got a toothbrush. And one thing he remembers from dental hygiene drill at school: the last thing you do before going to the dentist is to brush your teeth.

When everyone has crowded around the kitchen chair, when Evy has wiped the sweat from her palms and grasped the pliers, and when Krona has had one last shot for the road —then Krona has to ask for a postponement so he can go behind the bus and take a leak.

"How about a little . . ." the Count suggests, raising the bottle, but before she has time to shake her head, he puts it down again with elaborate expressions of esteem. Krona marches with determined tread back around the bus. Buttoning his fly as he walks, he directs his firm gaze at some distant goal in the direction of the apple orchard. Larsson comes forward quickly and grips his arm. Robotlike, Krona comes along, seats himself astride the chair, clamps the bars of the chair back so that his knuckles whiten, and opens wide.

As soon as he feels the pliers against his lips, he attempts to wriggle free. But Evy Beck's entire dental experience is based on the treatment of horses. She swings her left arm around Krona's neck, drives her knee under his chin, has good luck, gets a purchase, and twists. Out glides the blackened tooth like a nail out of rotten wood. Afterward she takes a big drink.

33

The time is nearly eleven at night. The woods are black and still. But the sky is still so bright that she has to squint when she looks up. She takes several turns around the bus, breathing deeply at every step. She knows it's no use, you don't sober up by long walks and deep breathing exercises. But at least it feels a little better. Before she gets into the bus, she leans over the rain barrel and splashes her face.

She's greeted on her return by four outstretched arms. Pekka and the Count sit on the seat that runs lengthwise alongside the motor-box, while Larsson broods gloomily in the front seat, his forearm braced against the steering wheel. George Krona has said an early adieu—referring to his recent operation—and withdrawn to his bunk in the back of the bus.

"Hiya, boys," she says, and is pulled down on the seat between Pekka and the Count. A yellow-and-white striped oilcloth has been spread over the motor-box, and on that are laid out forks, glasses, gin, bread, tender carrots with their greens on, and a blackened pot filled with boiled turnips and sausage. Separate plates, there are none—one spears the chunks of sausage and turnip on one's fork and holds a bit of bread underneath so as not to drip too much.

"Well, well," says the Count, and puts his snaky arm around her waist.

Pekka starts giggling so hard he sprays out turnip gravy. He still has the ski cap on his head but has pulled off the fishnet undershirt. It's unbelievably hot in the bus—five candles and a kerosene lamp are shining. She looks at Pekka Fagerström in fascination. His deeply tanned torso is both emaciated and muscular. Not with a young man's bulging biceps, the arm one plastic unity. On Pekka you can see every separate muscle stretch like a rubber band under the thin skin. The corded muscles cross and recross each other, they interplay, pull, or poise, as in a complex mechanical counterbalance. As in a drawing by Leonardo da Vinci.

"Well," Larsson says darkly; he has drunk the most but doesn't show the least sign of intoxication—his heavy face is hard and composed. "Like I said, you mustn't think we're living here in some kind of goddam idyll!"

"Oh no, I never thought so."

"Yeah . . . maybe now, in the summertime. But otherwise it's a life for *pigs.*"

"That's right, dear Evy," says the Count, gazing down on her from above. "But now let us talk about something pleasanter. When ladies are present."

Pekka giggles so that his diaphragm skips up and down; the stomach muscles knead above the waistband of his pants.

"Yeah," says Larsson. "Wet and cold and always afraid of getting carbon monoxide poisoning from the stove."

"Larsson is a trained pharmacist," the Count explains.

183

"You are a pharmacist?" she exclaims with a surprise that immediately embarrasses her; a fallen pharmacist isn't so surprising—she's a veterinarian herself, and fallen right beside him.

"There's no decorum at all," Larsson continues. "My friends here drink like fish!"

Pekka's giggling has now reached such a pitch that he has to leave the room. Clumsily he climbs over her feet, slips, and drives a sharp elbow into her tender left breast.

"Beg the lady's pardon . . . !" the Count begins, but Pekka has already slunk out of the bus.

"How long have you lived here?" she asks.

"How long we've lived here?" begins Larsson ominously.

"Four years this August, for my part," says the Count, and pats her graciously on the hand.

"Like I said, we live here like pigs," Larsson repeats.

"Well, we are relatively independent, in any case," the Count says. "You understand, Evy, we're not subjected to any direct control here."

"Yeah, as long as we stay here!" Larsson says.

"What do the police say about your still?" she asks, and thinks maybe it's time to sip from the glass that the Count keeps continually refilling to the brim.

"If pigs pigify themselves, that's no concern of the police," answers Larsson.

"They make no trouble so long as we distill only for our own use," the Count explains.

"And don't sell it?" Evy interjects.

"Shit yes, we sell!" says Larsson. "How else could we get any cash for the necessities?"

Pekka comes back, pushes the Count aside, pivots heavily on one fist planted in Evy's pelvis, tramples on her feet, and falls back into his place. He has put on a cruel poker face for the purpose of giggle prevention.

"Don't trample the lady, you buffoon!" says the Count, waving Pekka off.

"Still . . . now, during the summer, you have it pretty nice out here," Evy says encouragingly.

"In wintertime the Red Cross helicopter drops a package

184

or two," says Pekka. "But never in the summer."

It's almost the first time this evening she's heard Pekka say anything. She leans toward him—to escape the Count's breath—and asks, "But the welfare people? Don't they ever come here?"

"Not since they got shot at," says Pekka, who has again reached the giggling point. Holding his hands over his mouth, he doubles over.

She looks at Pekka's skinny back. The shoulder blades have so little covering them that she's tempted to lift them up and see what's underneath.

"Yeah," says Larsson. "Living with that goddam wild west psychopath has its moments. Last spring he shot the porcelain insulators off the power line. *Then* we had the Märsta police on our backs the very same night!"

"We had to lie low for a while, so far as selling any gin," says the Count, and presses a skinny shoulder against her.

There's a little pause, with some eating and drinking. The spirits taste something like gin but don't smell very good. She's drunk now and feels that her face is completely stiff. She's hungry at the same time that the food repels her.

"I've been thinking," she says. "Krona really ought to have an antibiotic. He has an infection in his jaw."

"We can borrow penicillin over in the hollow," says Larsson.

"If our little doctor doesn't stay here with us!" says the Count hopefully, and strokes her again with his shoulder.

"In the hollow? Are there others living out here?"

"The woods are full of free men!" the Count exclaims, waving expansively clear up to the baggage rack.

"Yeah, quite a few people live in these parts," says Larsson. "Pioneers like us. This area used to lie right under Arlanda's flight path, with all that noise and vibration. Later on, the planners moved things around. But by that time, the land wasn't worth anything. The fields were all overgrown, the woods had closed in, the dikes had crumbled, the pipes had frozen. And the roads, yeah, the gravel company's dug them up, so you can't get in here by car either."

"A free life for tough, free men!" the Count cries, with his head thrown back and trembling with dramatic intensity.

"Hold your tongue, you goddam tailchaser!" says Larsson. "You get by because the rest of us take care of you. How things would go if everybody gave himself the airs you do, we needn't bring up."

Pekka Fagerström has straightened up again. Evy's alarmed—tears are dripping from the grooves in his gnarled face.

"In April, Bubba left us . . ."

She takes her handkerchief from her sleeve and dries his face.

"Your brother died here?"

"Pekka's brother, Kent Fagerström, passed away right here on the twenty-third day of the month of April," the Count informs her in a high official tone.

"Of what?" she asks.

"Of what! Of what!" Larsson cries. "We're alcoholics! We're undernourished! We freeze! We have vitamin deficiencies! The authorities don't give a shit about us!"

"Then we buried him over there in the field," Pekka says, and wipes his nose with his fist.

Drowsiness settles over her. She sits there blinking, trying to ease the prickly irritation in her eyes. The Count misinterprets the situation and gives her a great big theatrical wink in response.

"Perhaps it's time we broke up?" says the Count.

"*I* won't be able to sleep," snaps Larsson, angrily rocking the disconnected steering wheel back and forth.

"Where'll we put 'er?" wonders Pekka, pointing at Evy.

"I'll sleep outside," she says.

"Oh, no," says Larsson. "The mosquitoes will eat you alive."

"In the boiler, then . . . No," she changes her mind.

"You can take Bubba's bunk in the back end of the bus," says Pekka.

"Private room for the lady, private room for the lady," says the Count, swaying to his feet. "I hereby volunteer to carry a mattress to the boiler!"

But she's dead tired now. With some difficulty, she pulls

186

loose from the Count, goes outside, and squats down and pees. When she starts to get up, she falls forward on her knees. But she doesn't feel a thing. Now you're really pickled, Quotia . . . she thinks, perhaps aloud.

Five minutes later she falls asleep on the seat across the back of the bus without even having taken off her clothes.

She wakes up twice during the night. The first time, it is somebody clumsily taking her handbag, which she has been using for a pillow. She doesn't bother about that, but falls back to sleep at once with her nose in the seat upholstery which reeks of cigarette butts.

Next time, it's broad daylight outside and the sunshine is pouring in through the back window. Somebody's shaking her. She cannot lift her stone-heavy head and her mouth is as dry as a dried cod. The light stings her eyes and she can just force one eye open a crack.

It's the Count. He stands right by the seat, dressed in a shirt with sleeve-garters and a light-gray vest. Below that, he's naked. He holds the shirttails out primly, like a ballerina coming forward to curtsy. A narrow bright red penis wags in front of his navel. He leans over her and tries to get her to spread her legs.

She lies entirely still as if she weren't even involved. The Count kneels between her legs and starts tearing at her underclothes. Suddenly he starts rocking back and forth, his abdomen knotting and the doggy dick pumping. Out of it comes a little silvery drop no bigger than what comes out of the copper coil of the still. With a few tired shudders, his penis drops and hangs down like a string of dough over the low-dangling testicles.

"Pardón!" mumbles the Count, and glides away.

34

By the morning of the fifth day, Evy Beck has had enough of country life, of the blue-gleaming flies, the trash pile, the rats, the stink of mash, and the people-hating goat in the orchard. While the men are sleeping in their alcoholic stupor, she prepares for departure. She washes herself as well as she can at the rain barrel and winds a scarf around her stiff greasy hair. Then she pulls away the seat cushion of one of the rain-soaked armchairs and extracts the handbag they stole on the first night. The 250 dollars in cash are still there; she takes 50 for her own use and stuffs the handbag back under the cushion with 200 dollars in it.

Quietly she goes back into the bus and shakes Pekka Fagerström. The others, she doesn't want to meet; she'd rather avoid the depressive Larsson's reproachful glances, avoid George Krona's garrulous gratitude for the tooth treatment —and avoid seeing the Count's crushed pride and seeming fear that she will spread the word that he's impotent.

Pekka's the strongest of the men. Little and tough, uncommunicative, and without ties of human affection. Most of the time he's out with his shotgun and takes part in none of their activities except the boiler. He drinks a little more regularly than the others. While Larsson pours down a quart and a half in one evening without becoming a drop more cheerful, Pekka sits there sipping two or three shots altogether, handicapped all the time by his giggling.

Two minutes after waking, Pekka stands by the motorbike dressed in the fishnet undershirt and the ski cap with hanging ear flaps, and with his gun hung over his shoulder on a strap. He stamps on the starter-pedal and chokes the engine generously—all the time grinning toothlessly. And with his tongue showing, he looks for all the world like Dopey the dwarf in Disney's *Snow White*, Evy's first movie experience.

Oddly enough, Pekka gets the oil-soaked cylinder to fire. She takes a seat on the package rack and Pekka flips the motor into gear, so that the motorbike leaps. In fright, she throws her arms around Pekka and they bump away along the trail. At every unevenness in the ground, the rim thumps clear through the underinflated back tire, so that she thinks she'll break her tailbone.

They ride over gravelly ridges and through burnt fields. It's only now and then that they pass the ruins of a house, but often they ride through deserted orchards that have shed drifts of blossoms and set their fruit. The trail generally follows the power line right-of-way—civilization's closely guarded corridor through no-man's-land. When they see a good, smoothly paved road ahead, she takes a deep breath and again dares to lower her tender backside to the package rack—but Pekka drives right across the road and onto a trail through the woods on the other side.

They see only one single human being on the way to Märsta. In an overgrown meadow sits a woman in an improbable circus dress with several layers of skirts and a huge hat with plastic flowers twining around the crown. She has a long staff in her hand, and among the weeds are glimpses of a few sheep. Pekka slams on the brakes, slings his gun over from back to front, lets fly at the sky, and then drives on at once. The woman rises hastily and waves after them with a pink handkerchief.

Now they're approaching Märsta. Concrete towers shoot up out of the pine woods like some kind of giant fungus. Pekka slows down and drives carefully into an area where three-story multiple-family dwellings are dispersed over a field. The buildings are abandoned and badly dilapidated. The windows are either broken or clumsily boarded up, some of the balconies have weakened and hang down on the faded green façades. It's almost impossible to drive down the street between the buildings, the way is so littered with cement blocks, gravel, reinforcing rods, and uprooted curbstones. Here and there stand old automobile carcasses, wheelless. She's seen a few abandoned suburbs before. People don't want to live in Märsta, Jordbro, or Bålsta. Most of them want to live either in a real city or really out in the country.

They come to the end of the deserted structures. On the other side of a ridge rise buildings with shiny intact window panes. Pekka brakes to a stop before a half-ruined pavilion, apparently the area's former shopping center. Outside are a tethered pony and three battered motorbikes. A couple of gasoline drums are propped up on ramshackle wooden trestles.

"Over there's Märsta Station!" Pekka says, and points confusingly in the direction they've come from.

"Well. I want to thank you very much."

Pekka gets embarrassed, squirms, and puts his hand over his mouth to hide the wriggling tongue. Then he stumps into the store, pulling and pulling on the visor of the ski cap. She can't decide whether it's some kind of salute or it's just that he wants to pull the cap down over his eyes.

At 2:12 she steps off the commuter train at Karlberg Station. She has no thought of going home, but takes the express bus, instead to NMSI. It's the third of July and steamy hot. When she's showered and washed her hair, she goes into the Student Union restaurant and eats. She's alone and it takes more than a quarter of an hour for the soyburger to be ready at the pickup window.

Since she's really on vacation, she doesn't feel bound by any systematic work assignments. Instead, she strolls at random among the countless red brick institutes. Outside the Institute for Medical Ethology, she remembers that she's never actually been inside—for some reason, Ethology's never been included in any of her systematic sweeps. She goes up the short flight of stairs and puts her thumb against the lock. It opens—lawful territory.

Ethology looks much like all the other 107 institutes: a few floors with long corridors of researchers' offices, several names to a door. A thoroughly used course laboratory with tin lockers for the students. A lecture room that's become too cramped and been made over into a typing pool. In the cellar, storerooms, a dustbin, and some heavier equipment. The three-bladed warning symbol for radioactivity is on several of the cellar doors, so she doesn't go in. In the attic, up under the sloping roof, there are several overfurnished, mazelike laboratories, and built onto the building at one end, the animal quarters. Nowhere a human being.

She goes into the animal area. The whole bottom floor consists of a single huge room. When she opens the door, the powerful roar of fans nearly deafens her at the same time that a rank odor of rat assaults her nose. The huge room has no windows, but the ceiling is covered with floodlights which shine down into a kind of basin with glass walls. The basin is about fifty feet by seventy-five feet and filled with sand. Here and there, posts holding hoppers and trays for automatic feeding and watering stick up out of the sand. On the sand floor are crowded thousands of white rats.

She's read about this laboratory a number of times in the journals. Since the beginning of the sixties, the ethologists have allowed a strain of rats to reproduce freely and to maintain themselves. They are given water and food, but otherwise there is no human intervention in the basin except under the most exceptional circumstances. At first the rat population grew from one male and one female to over twelve thousand. Then a kind of stabilization took place and for many years the population figure has hovered around nine thousand rats. The long-term experiment is funded by EMRECOM, the Emergency Medical Relief Committee, which has access to the sought-after defense budget, in partnership with LERAD, the Law Enforcement Research and Development Council.

She tries to pick out the patterns in rat society. Large patches of sand are completely open. In other places the animals creep over each other in double and triple layers. Powerful social magnetic fields have created charmed circles. In several places the animal mass boils when the rats gorge themselves on some comrade who has become fair game, socially speaking. Big rat males lie here and there on the sand and sleep with a free zone all around them, or copulate rapidly and without interest. Nearly all the smaller rats are maimed in one way or another. Whole tails are unusual among them, as are two ears on the same individual. Despite the automatic feeding system, nearly all the animals seem scruffy, eczematous, and undernourished. In this rat hell the Animal Welfare Law is suspended, since the whole experiment depends on no human intervention.

Evy Beck is convinced that the experiment—called "packing"—is really unnecessary. For at least twenty-five years, a great many similar experiments have gone on around the world to find out what really happens in overpopulated societies. There could hardly be very much more to learn. But

191

continuing has become a kind of sport. A world's record competition among various universities to see which can hold out the longest.

She looks down into the stinking rat ghetto and thinks back to one of her all-too-hasty discussions with Erik. Erik doesn't understand her "clucking" over the animals at NMSI. Suffering can never be added up, Erik explained. From a logical standpoint, it's impossible. Therefore it's a matter of complete indifference whether one or ten thousand rats are afflicted. Each rat can only experience its own private affliction.

She feels an unpleasant heat well up in her chest, and undoing the top button of her blouse, she fans herself. From out of her blouse rises a sickening odor. It's as if she had not showered but instead had stored up the stench from the Arlanda woods in her own body heat: mash, sweat, urine, oil in gasoline, and a heavy odor of wet wool socks. She doubles over and vomits down into the rat basin. A troop of five white scouts detach themselves at once from a nearby rat community—a few seconds later, hundreds of rats make a shrieking feast upon the Student Union's soyburger.

MEMORANDUM TO ADP CENTRAL DATABANK
CLASSIFIED INFORMATION OFFICIAL USE ONLY
OBSERVER ACTING ASST ADMINISTR A LIDMAN NM
SI
KEYWORD EVY INGA-BRITT BECK WOLMB
CONTINUOUS WORK REVIEW 5
VERBAL REPORT B REACTED NEGATIVELY TO INSTIT
UTES OBJECTIVE PERFORMANCE REPORT TO LMB R
EPROACHING DEPARTMENT HEAD ROSENQUIST IN P
RIVATE CONVERSATION B HAS SUDDENLY INTERRU
PTED VACATION AND RETURNED TO HER WORKPLA
CE WITHOUT NOTIFYING ANYONE OF RESUMPTION
DUTIES GOING AROUND VARIOUS INSTITUTES FOR
PURPOSES UNKNOWN SEEMS TO DISPLAY ESPECIAL
LY STRONG INTEREST IN ETHOLOGICAL INST SEEMS
TO MISUNDERSTAND CONCEPT PREVENTIVE VETERI
NARY MEDICINE SEEMS TO HAVE POOR COMPREHE
NSION OF OWN LIMITATIONS
CLOSE UP RANKS CLOSE UP RANKS CLOSE UP RAN
KS CLOSE UP RANKS CLOSE UP
RATING 1-5
COMPETENCE 3
ADAPTABILITY 3
SOLIDARITY 3
MOTIVATION 5
COST NONE

35

It's the middle of July. She's standing on the balcony, which is steaming after a cloudburst, and looking into her apartment through the open French doors. Papa's at Roslagstull; the Singer Cyborg, they've taken away. Even Papa's ingenious bed has gone back to the bed depot. It's too costly to remain unused.

Carefully she lifts the heads of some flowers in the flower box—they got a knockout blow from the cloudburst. For the last week, Evy has felt split in two: she's on vacation, yet at the same time she spends the afternoons strolling around the vacant and deserted institutes. Nevertheless, she avoids going to her own office. She feels like a spy.

"Hasse?" she calls softly into the voice-tube that leads down through decades into her memory. "Hans-Olof, I should have stayed put at the Veterinary College. Should have stuck to doing research!"

More and more often she reproaches herself with this: that she didn't want to go on or didn't succeed in going on with research. To do research is to make a tiny, tiny piece of reality manageable. At the same time, she knows that she didn't enjoy the years that she wrote her dissertation. She felt boxed-in, oppressed—and then almost cheated when she saw how lightly the professor took the whole thing in the end. She didn't write the dissertation for her own sake, or for science. She wrote it for Hans-Olof. *On Cyclo-Metabolic Functions in Mammals,* the dissertation was called. On the flyleaf should have appeared "To H.-O. S." But she didn't dare.

Was it a good dissertation? The answer is as simple as it is brutal: No. From a good dissertation you get to be an instructor and get offered opportunities to continue research. *On Cyclo-Metabolic Functions in Mammals* resembles its originator to a T, she thinks: too fat, too ambitious, too honest.

For her dissertation subject she had chosen to chart some of the mechanisms of what is popularly termed the Biological

194

Clock. The subject wasn't original. During the seventies, research into the body's daily, weekly, and monthly rhythms had taken a sudden leap forward. To talk about the Biological Clock suddenly became as usual as talking about Stress—and just as misused. People blamed everything on disturbing man's natural rhythm: chest colds, erotic disorders, work performance, Weltschmerz, alienation. Leading politicians stood up in Parliament and said: The goal of our policy is to shape society in harmony with man's biological clock.

If she had been quick to maneuver, she could have ridden along on that wave. But she wasn't quick. She was slow, anxious, and lacking in what the professor called elegance of reasoning. Therefore her dissertation didn't come out until the general public—and the Research Council—had already half turned away from the Biological Clock in search of newer compasses.

"Have you read my dissertation, Hasse?" For the thousandth time she directs the question out toward Australia.

"An honest piece of work, Evy," Hasse answers. Has he really read it? She couldn't really send it to him after seventeen years. The address, she could always hunt up—but there's no reason to. Hasse knows nothing about Erik. On a couple of occasions in recent years she's nearly gone and told him that they have a son together. Not for her own sake and hardly for Erik's. But for Hasse's sake. She wouldn't at all begrudge Hasse the pride of having such a fine, successful son as Erik. The farthest she has gone is to make sure that two copies of the dissertation were sent to the faculties of veterinary medicine in Sydney and Canberra—precisely as it was sent to other universities around the world.

On the balcony floor, bread crumbs and potting soil have melted together in the rain. She scrapes up the tough mass with a dustpan and puts it into the flower box. A little bread and jam can't harm.

She goes into Papa's empty room. The parquet gleams. In the middle of the floor stands the Gambia luggage. She went out and fetched it yesterday but hasn't yet opened it. That was an idiotic notion, to jump off so suddenly. She'd really needed to get away for a while. Needed to refresh herself and get a little perspective on her existence. Besides, it could have been educational. Even if the trip was a kind of junket, nevertheless she had been invited to study the Pharmafarm conditioning facility for monkeys. She knows all too little about monkeys and about tropical animal diseases.

"Evy!" says Hasse so loudly it echoes around the walls. "It's not the monkeys that are the problem. Monkeys get the same care they'd get if they were private patients in Stockholm's best-known clinic."

To houseclean, sweep, scour, vacuum, mend, wash, iron—it's been many years since these were burdensome. On the contrary, they're a resource and a refuge. When she pulls on her old housecoat, it feels like when she was a child and took her place on the first hopscotch square.

"What d'you think, Hasse?" she asks. "Wouldn't it be just as well to pull out and spend my future on pension?"

"Why are you so afraid of punishment, Evy? You're strong. And steady. And secure."

It's never failed to amaze her: those around her consider her solid and harmonious—somebody you can depend on. She considers herself flabby, scatterbrained, gullible, and illogical.

"You're strong as a horse!" says Hans-Olof.

That's absolutely right! Horses, that is, being not especially strong. She knows that because it was horses she used for her dissertation. Few higher animals have as uneven an ability to perform as horses. Few animals are as extremely sensitive to disturbances of their natural rhythm. It's precisely that which puts the element of chance into all the horsy sports. When she published her dissertation, she was able to give ways of more easily smoothing out disturbances in horses' rhythm. That's how it is with you, Quotia, she accuses herself: the only real good you've done in the world is to give racing and trotting an undeserved boost.

When she's cleaned the whole apartment—for the third time this week—it's time to call the chief physician at Roslagstull. She's had to wait in line for a personal telephone appointment.

196

"Now my father's been in the hospital longer than expected. Has he gotten worse?"

"Not at all, Mrs. Beck. He's in excellent condition."

"Can I bring him home tonight?"

"I'm sorry."

"But he was just in for a little checkup?!"

"Your father feels fine. But just now we don't have the resources to make a portable liver available. So we'll just have to keep your father here. For the time being."

36

Several times during the following nights she is waked by the ringing of a telephone. But there's no second ring. When she lifts the receiver, nobody's there. She realizes that she's only dreaming that the telephone is ringing.

It's hard to get back to sleep. The first night, she sits in the bathroom for an hour with her feet in warm water. The second night, she tries to read. The third and fourth nights, she goes out and sits on the balcony in the soft night of late summer.

It's during the unreal quiet of the hours on the balcony that she comes to the decision to do something about the horrible packing experiment at Ethological. When she leans over and looks down into narrow Roslag Street, she seems to see thousands of white rats. Rats that chew on each other without a sound being heard.

At first, she tries to push this away as a stupid half-dream. But after a while she realizes that it's not dreams and flights from reality that she's experiencing every night—she's confronting her innermost conviction. That she must put a stop to this animal torture.

The fifth night, completely unable to sleep, she writes a letter to Erik. Why, she hardly knows. Maybe in a vague fear that the moment she pounds the table she will disappear, go up in smoke.

Dear Erik,
You advised me against continuing at NMSI. You suspected
I wouldn't make it. Sure enough, you were right, Erik. I've
gotten myself into a situation I can't handle. Now it's gone
so far that I must face the issue and really speak out. The
Institutes must take animal welfare seriously! I haven't
wished for this confrontation, Erik. I know that I'm not
strong enough, that I'm not a logical thinker, that I'm almost
always persuaded to take it back when I really speak out. But
I must do this! Even if it's without effect, Erik. I can't go
around despising myself. I'm not daffy, Erik. This decision
has been ripening for a long time.

> *Yours,*
> *Evy*

When she has written the letter, she sits there thinking about how it will be. How Nils Rosén is going to react. What Sundell's going to do. She realizes there's no point in trying to predict their reactions in detail. But she is anxious, and the anxiety is eased if she can sit there and imagine what's going to happen. That's the way it has always been when she faced a tough decision. First she experiences the decision or step before it is taken. Then she experiences the situation in reality. Afterward she goes over and over the events, again and again. It's very exhausting, and hardly conducive to taking the initiative.

On Saturday morning, she takes special pains with her morning toilet and even puts a touch of red on her lips. She props the letter to Erik against the pepper mill on the kitchen table. Before she leaves the apartment, she goes around one more time, making sure everything is closed and turned off.

37

An hour later, she's sitting with the three professors, Rosén, Sundell, and Orvarsson, in their Saturday morning meeting at Pharmacological. It's the first meeting of the new term. She has just said, *I demand that NMSI immediately stop the packing experiment with the nine thousand rats in Ethological.*

"But, Evy, you are a sensible person!" says Nils Rosén von Rosenstein.

"It seems to me she's leading up to something," says Sundell.

She looks out through the tinted windows. Looks at the Student Union, and at Chem, and glimpses the grove that surrounds Lindgården. On the other hand, she's almost uninterested in looking at the three professors. She already knows how they look. She's rehearsed the scene before her so often that she feels like she's seeing the same movie for the fourth time.

"Have I made myself sufficiently clear?" asks Rosén.

"The question is have *I* made myself sufficiently clear?" she says.

During the end of the summer she has gone through the literature, interviewed a number of experts by telephone, pondered, inspected Ethological again, and finally decided: the packing of nine thousand rats into the sand basin at Ethological is indefensible, the anticipated results approach zero, and no one seems to feel personally responsible for the decades-old experiment. It is systematic cruelty to animals without redeeming scientific value. The institute has changed director three times since the experiment got under way. The person who presently, on paper, is responsible for it is an associate professor who has not carried out his duties for eight months but instead is serving as an acting professor in Växjö.

"A sheer naked display of power," says Orvarsson.

"Let me turn the question around," she says. "Can any one of you give me a single argument for letting the ethologists go on with it?"

Nobody answers. During her imaginary rehearsals of this meeting, she has pictured to herself the following reactions from the three professors: First a momentary surprise, then a certain uneasiness and some hasty glances at watches. After that, the possibilities diverge. After additional explanations on her part she has expected: aggressiveness, passive resistance, diffuse interest, moves toward adjourning, a sudden enlarging of the problem with the effect of attenuating it—or the opposite: narrowing and specializing the problem. She's also looked for the kind of newly awakened interest one shows a child who suddenly says something both embarrassing and obvious. For example: Mommy, I don't want to die! At best, she has imagined a slowly building comprehension and some proposals of how one could go about quickly and neatly getting the ethologists to give up.

None of this happens. The three men simply cannot decide on any course—they spin their wheels in various directions but then roll back to their starting point: weariness and suppressed irritation. But she waits; they'll have to react soon. Yet so long as they don't react, she feels simply sleepy—can't they *get on with it!*

"None of us is a medical ethologist," Mats Sundell begins.

Evy Beck leans toward him and tries to look interested, but he just trails off. She looks at them one after another: Nils Rosén is looking at her warily, like a teacher regarding a favorite pupil who has suddenly come out with something unexpected. Mats Sundell is poking at his nose. Bengt Orvarsson is evading reality by test-driving his slide rule and calibrating it after its night-long disuse in his lab coat pocket.

"The packing experiment is paid for with money from the Emergency Medical Relief Committee, LERAD, and the National Medical Research Council," she says. "How many ethologists are on the boards of those organizations?"

The correct answer—strangely enough—is that no medical ethologist presently sits on the boards of EMRECOM, LERAD, or the Research Council.

"None," she says, answering herself.

"In principle, I can pretty well agree with you," says Nils Rosén. "Why don't you go right to the ethologists?"

"I? Alone? I, who haven't even got a job description? Not even employed by NMSI? Lack every means of putting pressure on?"

"I wouldn't look at it that way," says Sundell. "I'd consider it an advantage to be an outsider, unaffiliated, somebody able

200

to approach the problem from neutral ground."

She understands perfectly that he means precisely the opposite: if the professors in the Saturday morning bunch get mixed up in this, there'll be hell to pay. Just because they are part of NMSI, sit in the Academic Council, have a vote in the meetings, and apply pressure through the Research Council.

"Go to the police. Charge 'em with breaking the Animal Welfare Law," says Orvarsson as if any further discussion were superfluous: either the law's being broken or it isn't.

"What do you plan to do?" asks Rosén.

"What do *you* plan to do?"

Now she feels almost physically the breach widening between her and the three men. When she peers over toward them, it's as if they were floating away on their chairs, floating together, coalescing into a three-headed giant in a white lab coat sitting stiff-necked as an Egyptian god at the opposite end of the room. The question can no longer be brushed aside as a joke, an attack of momentary misanthropy, or a trial balloon. The lines have formed. It's now Evy Beck *versus* Nils Rosén, Mats Sundell, and Bengt Orvarsson.

"Close Ethological?" says Sundell. "And what if that saddles us with a precedent?"

"Of course that's what she's after," says Orvarsson.

"In *principle*, Evy, *yes*. But you're choosing the wrong approach!" says Rosén.

She looks Nils Rosén in the eye. The fact is that she has *not* chosen *any* approach. She's only laid out the problem: Rat-packing is indefensible. What to do?

"Let me put it this way," Rosén continues. "Naturally we don't know exactly how the future will shape up in this field. The commercial interests are already declaring that we're going to be able to go over to *synthetic* life in various forms. You've been to Findus Pharmafarm yourself. But of course they're ahead of their time. As usual. But looking at it in a somewhat longer perspective, development is naturally going to carry us right past these problems: just as, once, it became possible to exchange the plowhorse for a tractor."

"When?"

He looks at her as if she has asked an unusually dumb

201

question. No serious scientist can tell when man will first land on Venus, when man will be able to manipulate the genetic code, or when class distinctions in Sweden will be erased.

"I've got a proposal," she says. "One could apply PAB-REG."

"What?"

"One could make sure that the ethologists had to account for their activities according to the program of the Chancellor of Swedish Universities' Program Committee. You know: Goal Statement, Budget, Review, Accomplishment, and Effectiveness."

She meets with total noncomprehension.

"Well, look, ethologists have to state their goal just like anybody else," she continues. "The Research Council requires it. Even on a job as unimportant as mine."

They don't seem to be following her at all.

"P for Program, G for Goal Statement, B for Budget, R for Review, A for Accomplishment, E for Effectiveness!" she says.

Gradually Rosén's total lack of comprehension turns into a slow nodding that gains in speed. At last, in his eagerness, he holds up his hand like a traffic policeman to stop her: "Yes!"

Then he turns to his two colleagues.

"She means that CSUPC drivel we have to put the secretaries to work on every first of July!"

All three laugh amiably.

"Had no idea they plagued you with a *program,*" says Sundell.

"Why not?" she says, almost offended. "Is my work so insignificant it doesn't need to be accounted for?"

"Evy, you've evidently taken those CSUPC fellows a little too seriously," Rosén says. "*We* know what they're after. Sure, we have to scribble on their forms. But if we let ourselves be controlled by CSUPC we'd never get off the dime."

She feels at once relieved and betrayed. Relieved, because she really had worried over how to describe her work in PABREG terms when the day came for the required accounting. Betrayed, because she had invested energy in something that obviously no one else took seriously.

"That's right, Evy," says Sundell. "So maybe we can consider this matter closed?"

Now she gets really mad. You can't turn away from systematic, unjustified cruelty to animals just because it isn't practical to make the ethologists answer for it in PABREG terms.

"Fine. I'll press charges of cruelty to animals!"

Nobody leaps up and talks about scandal, blackmail, or overkill or accuses her of pure and simple childishness. Instead, all three look immensely weary and weighed down with responsibility.

"I think Evy and I will have a little chat about this," says Rosén.

The others rise, relieved, and bid her an unusually hearty adieu.

"You mustn't think I don't *understand* you," says Rosén, who remains sitting.

She doesn't answer. There's nothing to say. If Rosén says he understands, he's welcome to make specific proposals.

"Are you clear that I *understand?*"

She nods.

"Sometimes we human beings find ourselves in conflicts that are . . . yes, let's come right out and say it: *moral* conflicts."

She nods again.

"At times like these we face the problem of what to do. In the present case, you want to end an experiment that has been in progress for a very long time, that many people are involved in, that has had a lot written up about it, that money's been invested in . . . I can tell you in confidence that I happen to know that the ethologists have enough funds to keep the packing experiment going for—at the very least—two more years. So it's not as simple as you think just to *interrupt* it."

"No."

"First of all we have a moral duty to really think the thing through, so that we don't end up doing something hasty. Something unnecessary. Worsen matters instead of improving them."

"Yes."

"For that reason, Evy, I feel further thought would be appropriate. Before anybody gets things moving, so to say."

"Yeah."

"This isn't something you're going to be able to handle on your own. To develop a thought needs more than one mind."

"Yes."

He looks at her with irritation over her short answers.

"Well, haven't you got anything to *say?!*"

"So far I'm with you a hundred percent," she says.

"Evy, I think it would do you good to talk this over with someone who is, so to say, experienced at dealing with this kind of moral questioning."

"That's just what I'm trying to do. With you in the Saturday morning bunch."

"An acquaintance of mine comes to mind. You mustn't think I'm just trying to pacify you. But I think it would do you good to try the *Ethical Center.*"

"The Ethical Center?"

"Sometimes a person needs to get together with other people who are in a similar situation. The Ethical Center carries on that kind of discussion circle."

"Why can't *we ourselves* carry on these moral discussions, as you call them?"

"It's just to gain time, Evy! You can see for yourself that both Sundell and Orvarsson have a certain difficulty in *understanding.* It's not enough that just the two of us . . ."

"Well, just to gain some time, then," she says.

"I'll call there myself, Evy. I can tell you that the director of the Ethical Center has a *very* high reputation. It's a more or less open secret that several of our leading politicians go to Professor Morgan Fischer at the Ethical Center for a little ethical-ideological brush-up now and then. It's like having your windows cleaned."

When she gets home, she stuffs the letter to Erik in the incinerator.

EXTRA BULLETIN EXTRA BULLETIN EXTRA BULLETIN
EXTRA BULLETIN EXTRA BU
ADP CENTRAL DATABANK
CLASSIFIED INFORMATION OFFICIAL USE ONLY
OBSERVER ASST ADMINISTR S HORRLIN NMSI
KEYWORD EVY INGA-BRITT BECK WOLMB
EXTRA WORK REVIEW
VERBAL REPORT NOT ENTIRELY UNEXPECTEDLY B H
AS COMPLETELY DEVIATED FROM CHANNELS TAKE
N ACTION AGAINST ETHOLOGICAL INSTITUTE HAS
ATTEMPTED ENLIST ROSEN SUNDELL ORVARSSON C
LOSING UP RANKS APPARENTLY WITHOUT EFFECT I
T IS RECOMMENDED SHE SHARE OFFICE PROGNOSI
S PESSIMISTIC CANNOT FOR PRESENT RECOMMEND
ADDITIONAL TWELVE MONTHS ON WOLMB BUDGET
RATING 1–5
COMPETENCE 3
ADAPTABILITY 2
SOLIDARITY 2
MOTIVATION 5
COST NONE

38

She's sitting with Papa on the heights west of Roslagstull Hospital. They look out over Bellevue, Brunns Bay, and Haga Park. Papa has gained weight. He looks as if he has a thin layer of gingerbread dough right beneath his skin. It gives the skin a metallic sheen.

"But Papa . . ." she says. "We could just as easily go home a little while. You know it's just down the hill."

"Not on your life."

"What if we take a taxi?"

He slowly turns his trembling old man's face to her; his mouth starts kneading the words long before they're spoken.

"You can't trick me."

His eyes are dark and hard. Like looking into the lens of a camera.

"Just a little *change of scene,* Papa . . ."

"The nurse nags me too. She's just as fat as you. Go on home to your daughter, Mr. Beck! But I'm not stupid, d'you hear? I know."

"Know what?"

"That if I go home they'll take my bed away. Slip somebody else into my place."

"Not if you're away *a half-hour!*"

He doesn't deign to reply. Instead, he picks shakily at his narrow nose with the big nostrils. She's always thought that Papa had nostrils like a curious, sniffing dog. It's almost indecent.

"I'd intended to tell you in peace and quiet. At home. Now, don't you misunderstand me, Papa. But look, I've got an acquaintance at a place called Findus Pharmafarm. He can arrange for you to borrow one of his company's staff rooms at the Sophia Clinic. Your own room. Free."

"You sleeping with him?"

She's so startled that she probably looks guilty. Papa flicks his gaze at her. Then he sits there nodding and smacking.

"No."

"My answer's also *no,*" says Papa. "I don't intend to let anybody trick me into leaving Roslagstull."

"Your own liver, Papa dear . . . Not just a tube connected to Central Dialysis. Your own Auto-Hepar. The one you liked so much."

"I'm almost eighty. I say it's time that business and industry left me in peace."

She gives up. Somewhere deep inside, she's thankful—not for Papa's sake but for her own. If Papa had gone along with the proposition it would have been she who ended up under obligation.

"I want to write my will," says Papa, and strikes irritably with his cane at a caravan of ants that wind across the hot brink of the rocks.

"But Papa!" she begins, but realizes that for once he is being practical and logical; the chief physician has hinted at a few more months, at best.

"I want you to talk to the chief physician about them taking my body for transplantation. Whatever they want. Any part. But the legs, they ought to scrap. Because of the varicose veins."

She would like to say, Sure, Papa. Of course—if a man's a socialist, he's a socialist in death, too. But she has to be frank.

"Papa, I don't think . . ."

"Am I too old?!" he demands sternly, and starts to get up.

She supports him anxiously, making sure he gets a good purchase with the rubber tip of the cane. Bent-backed, he stands peering out over Bellevue's green hills. She tries to take him under the arm but is driven off with a hard blow from his sharp elbow.

"So I *am* too old," he says. "Then I want you to turn my body over to Anatomy instead. Let the students have a little practice material. It's a waste to be burned up. Or to fertilize the Forest Cemetery. Is cremation still required by law?"

"No. Now we have a surplus of graves."

"Fertilizer, I don't want to be!"

She's sorry for Papa's sake. During his whole adult life, it's been natural to him to look at death without sentimentality. It's just bad luck that he's apparently going to die right in the

207

middle of a fad for donating one's body to science, something to brag about in the obituary notice: "In accordance with the wishes of the deceased, the remains will be turned over to the Alfred Nobel Medical-Surgical Institutes."

"I don't want to just dump my proteins back into the dust," says Papa. "This old carcass has still got a million discoveries and secrets in it . . . How do the medical students measure up these days?"

"Very well," she says, though she knows better—she hasn't the heart to tell him how it really is: no really promising student studies medicine nowadays. They devote themselves —like Erik—to budgeting technique and administrative science.

Papa stumps down to the path and starts back in the direction of the hospital building. After a few yards, he stops and waves her forward with his stick. She must go *ahead* of him.

"But not to the Nobel Institutes. D'you hear? I want to be turned over to some medical faculty with at least a shred of reputation left. Medicine and dynamite don't mix."

"Of course, Papa."

"Now you get going, girl," he says, and smacks her backside with his stick.

It hurts a little, because Papa doesn't want to be suspected of tenderness. So as not to anger him, she doesn't turn around and wave as she goes down the hill.

39

The Vasatown Ethical Center is housed in a glass pavilion that was originally thrown together to be an in-town terminal for buses to Arlanda Airport. Evy comes walking down the path along the shore from the direction of Bellevue, but is halted by the high barbed-wire-topped wall around Stallmästaregården Country Club. There's a big German shepherd on the roof who barks at her; she makes an extra wide detour. When she reaches the Ethical Center, she's still almost twenty minutes too early—as usual.

She wanders around a little. Looks at the water in Brunns Bay, at the tennis courts on the outer edge of Haga Park, and at Haga Courthouse. A loop of highway holds the handsome yellow Jugend stil structure as in a snare.

At five of seven she steps inside the Ethical Center. On the glass door is stuck a crudely lettered cardboard sign: EVE-NING SESSIONS TONIGHT. Just inside the entrance is a reception desk, where a girl of Indian ancestry sits knitting away at an Icelandic sweater with metal needles as thick as pencils. Evy gives her I.D. card to the girl behind the glass barrier and has to pay $7.50; the Center is heavily subsidized by the county.

"Do you have a referral?" the receptionist asks.

"No. Well, I mean Professor Nils Rosén has spoken with Professor Fischer on the telephone."

The receptionist punches the buttons on the intercom one by one: "Morgan? Morgan? Morgan! Morgan? Morgan!"

The buttons have little typewritten labels taped to them: Office. Conference Room. Group Room. Coffee Room. Lounge.

"Sit down. Professor Fischer will be here shortly."

She seats herself on one of the metal-legged chairs with its bowl-shaped seat of thick, waxy tomato-red plastic. Nobody else is in the waiting room, which seems encouraging. It's stuffy. The late afternoon sun welds the aluminum window sill.

She'd really meant to call and cancel her appointment. She doesn't feel quite well today, feels stiff in the shoulders and a little bit dizzy, as if she's coming down with the flu. But she's been unable to detect any fever—and as long as you've got no fever, you're well. Just to be on the safe side, she takes her temperature once more: she holds the mirromometer before her eye. The mirromometer consists of narrow bands ranging from normal dullness to high-fever shininess. She compares the reflection of her own eye with the various bands. She hasn't any feverish luster in her eye this time either.

"Morgan? Morgan . . ." the receptionist cries into the intercom.

"Yes, Morgan here," an unusually high male voice responds.

"Finished your coffee break yet?"

The receptionist taps on the glass with the needles to get Evy Beck's attention.

"Third door to the right, please!"

She walks down the short hallway, knocks on Morgan Fischer's door, and steps inside. The room is small. The only furnishings are two swiveling armchairs and a little cart with intercom and dictaphone. Fine cracks run across the walls' battered gray plaster like the map of a river system. On the inside of the door, framed under glass, is an antique poster of Che Guevara. The window sill is cluttered with various souvenirs: an Indian brass lamp, a meerschaum pipe on a stand, a plastic penguin, an ebony monkey, a candle in the shape of a penis, an empty beer bottle, a model of the Tsar Bell in the Kremlin, and a peculiarly twisted divining rod that has been polished to a high sheen. In one swivel chair sits Professor Fischer. He has propped his feet, in half-boots, on the cart with the dictaphone.

"Welcome to a little intake interview," he says, waving her to the empty chair.

She sits down warily. Fascinated, she stares at the professor. He's dressed like some academic oddball who hasn't changed his style in twenty or thirty years. Short and thin, he's five-foot-three at most, and maybe fifty-five or fifty-six years old. His hair, which is steel-wool gray, reaches to his shoulders. Face, small and very suntanned. On his torso, a frayed, bleached-out blue-jeans jacket—unbuttoned, and he doesn't have a shirt on under it. The skinny brown chest is visible from collarbone to navel. Around his neck he has a number of ornaments on buckskin thongs: a peace symbol, a zodiac sign—Sagittarius—a beer can opener, a loupe, and a gold heart the size of a fingernail. His trousers are violet moleskin and the seam that runs their length is ornamented with a buckskin fringe. Around his middle he's got a six-inch-wide leather belt with a buckle in the shape of two interlocked stirrups. She's deeply impressed by a person so totally untouched by the shifts of fashion.

"You had some moral problems . . ." he begins cautiously in his almost womanishly high voice.

"I guess Rosén has called?"

"Right," he says, and looks at her with two bright little gray eyes.

"Before I start, I'd appreciate it if you'd tell me what this is all about?"

"Glad to," he says, smiling. His teeth are small and converge, rodentlike. "It's you yourself who proposes the problems and you yourself who solves them. Here in the Ethical Center, we sort of act as godfathers to the process you yourself subject your own identity to. Your conscience, to be blunt. In this preparatory interview, I try to judge whether you'll fit into a group. And if so, which of our ethico-therapeutic groups. It's in the group that you achieve insight."

"Does it take long?" she asks.

"Quick solutions are quack solutions. Only if you allow yourself time can you hope to reach a position that will hold for any length of time. A philosophy of life isn't picked up as easily as going into a store to buy new clothes," he says, and rubs the silver-star-studded half-boots against each other.

"Well, I don't know what Rosén has told you. He feels that I need to get a little perspective . . ."

"Uh-huh."

". . . on the problem."

"Oh?"

"I can't help it if I think animal welfare plays second fiddle at NMSI."

"Why do you say, 'I can't help it if I think'?"

She ponders. It's as though during the days she's spent waiting for an appointment at the Ethical Center, her resolve had begun leaking away. When she brought up the matter in the Saturday morning meeting and pounded the table, it cost her so much psychic energy that her involvement in the matter itself lost a little of its strength.

Morgan Fischer leans toward her; his back is very supple.

"You are not to *be ashamed of* your involvement!" he says. "Here at the Ethical Center, we take it as given that our clients are *dead serious.*"

"Yes, okay," she answers, takes a breath, and compels herself to continue: "NMSI is surely no worse than other research institutes, but it lacks any feeling of lab animals being living creatures."

"Why do you say 'surely no worse than'? Can't it actually be true that because of its size, NMSI has come to treat animals *worse* than other schools?"

"It's possible."

"Possible? *Is* it *so?*"

She mustn't let herself get pushed into a false position: Is there proof that NMSI is worst in any way?

"Maybe," she says very doubtfully. "Maybe bigness is bad in itself . . ."

"Let's go on. You're a person who wants to really know what you're talking about. So 'maybe' is a relevant answer."

"Well, I've tried to stop a very big ethological experiment that's called packing. But that's not it, really. I think I've gone around *looking* for a long time, looking for some example of cruelty to animals that was flagrant enough. I mean, all over NMSI there's unnecessary tormenting of animals, though in differing degrees."

"Do you agree with my putting it this way: you're objecting to a way of acting rather than to specific concrete acts of cruelty?"

"Yes," she says, and begins to feel glad, begins to experience real understanding.

"What *proof* have you got that animals really feel pain and anxiety?" he demands suddenly and fiercely.

She's confused—a moment ago she met with understanding.

"From a logical philosophical standpoint," he says gently, "you have no proof," and gestures with his little slender hands—he moves them around like someone singing "Itsy Bitsy Spider."

"I'm no philosopher," she says. "I'm an ordinary person."

"Pain and anxiety are subjective sensations," Fischer continues, while ascending and descending the waterspout with his clarifying hands. "Pain and anxiety are thus experiences of an altogether *private* nature, and so directly accessible only to one who is exposed to the experience himself. Through descriptive communication, we human beings can convince ourselves that experiences of pain are universal among humans. We lack the same possibilities of exchanging experiences with animals. Nevertheless, we suspect that even animals have similar abilities to experience pain. This suspicion can be supported with certain universal biological observations: the pain mechanism fulfills a purely life-protective function. The sensation of pain in a bodily part leads to its being relieved of work and protected. We know that people who lack the sense of pain find it difficult to survive. They ignore minor wounds, get infected, neglect their bodies. Therefore, it is reasonable to suspect that the ability to feel pain is of such fundamental importance to the continuance of life that pain must occur among most higher animals."

"Among rats too?"

He waves away this question of detail and proceeds with the principles: "The cerebral cortex of both animal and man shows the same basic pattern of signals when recorded at rest or at work, respectively. The neuro-anatomical similarities are also striking, as are the chemical. Therefore, on a practical plane, we ought to take as a starting point that animals do experience pain."

"I'm a veterinarian. I know."

Neither does this information deflect him; Itsy Bitsy Spider is climbing up the waterspout again.

"However, this does not prevent our interpreting scientific comparisons between animals' and human beings' experiences of pain very critically. For example, one should not be misled by the fact that decapitated animals can develop complex avoidance movements and even try to fly away or otherwise escape. We have good reason to believe that under such circumstances it is a question of nonconscious reflex movements."

"How about rats?"

"Good question. The spino-thalamic system, which is re-

213

garded as the conductor of pain signals through the spinal marrow and up to the brain's higher levels, is found both in the rodents and in our housepets. *But* their systems have not reached the same development as those of apes and men."

He leans back in his chair and stuffs his spidery hands in his jeans pockets. Apparently he expects her to present her own views, but she feels perfectly speechless. He leans forward again quickly.

"So it's not right for a person to imagine being in an animal's situation and then to try to imagine how it must feel. And one thing more: Research depends on quick growth and high productivity. So methods of handling animals that disturb them and don't serve their basic needs disappear automatically . . ."

Now Morgan Fischer is nearly eyeball-to-eyeball with her so as to study her reaction. She's curious herself about what she feels, but doesn't know.

"Conclusionwise," he says. "Conclusionwise, we can state that the question of animals' ability to feel pain and experience suffering is difficult to answer correctly from a strictly scientific point of view."

This last, she feels she can pretty well agree with. She licks her dry lips; does she have a fever after all?

"Evy Beck! Do you subscribe to what I've said?!"

The truth is that she's only heard part of what he's said— his spiderlike hands have gotten in the way and chopped up the argument.

"*No*, Evy Beck. You do *not* agree with me!" he says fiercely.

She opens her mouth to answer—but she has nothing to say, and so sits there with half-open mouth.

"All this stuff I've just reeled off. Do you know where it came from?"

She shakes her head.

"It's a quote from an old manual of experimental animal technique."

"Quote?"

"But you think otherwise. What you, Evy Beck, believe is that animals, like people, matter *in themselves*. That experi-

214

mental animals should be taken care of not because it will make them more productive for research, but because they're *alive*. You, Evy Beck, refuse to just sort out living things into higher and lower levels: for you, the costly chimpanzee has no more *worth* than a fifty-cent white mouse!"

"That's about right," she answers, a little bit scared. "I just haven't formulated my views as logically as you . . ."

"*Serious,*" he says. "Remember that within these walls everything is *dead serious.*"

"I appreciate that," she answers.

With the heel of his black glove-leather boot, Morgan Fischer punches the button marked "Receptionist" on the intercom.

"Helloo?!"

"Yes," says the receptionist.

"Set up Evy Beck in the Thursday group. Evening session."

40

It's been a tough day. The fall term, which had begun a trifle hesitantly and as if in jest, today came up to full speed. She's sitting at home by the kitchen table, licking the frost off a bottle of white port wine that's been lying in the refrigerator. Sweet white port wine has to be really cold—like putting your feet in cold water. It is invigorating.

Just before five Rosenquist, her department head, was in her office for a few minutes and announced that she probably couldn't count on having the room to herself for the whole fall. They'd probably be forced to have her share it at certain hours of the day with the curator they're considering employing. He's going to look after NMSI's oil paintings and sculptural adornments and last but not least, do the long-term planning for the Nobel Clock's eventual expansion.

She prides herself on not being totally dumb. In itself, having to share the room wouldn't necessarily have been a provocation, a vote of no confidence. But along with all the rest: canceled meetings, postponed inspections, and telephone calls that never got through; when she asks that a message be placed on somebody's desk, nobody calls back. She thinks: Okay, Quotia, this is how it feels when you've got the wind against you.

There's a ring at the front door. She shuffles out and opens it. The hour is almost 10:00 P.M.

"Erik!!"

She's so startled that she just stands there blocking the door.

"Mind if I step inside . . . ?"

She grips him by the shoulders and pulls him in. Worried, she peers up into his face, trying to decipher his expression. Is Papa dead?

"Just thought I'd look in," says Erik a little hesitantly.

"Thank God! I thought something had happened."

She follows him out into the kitchen and seats him at the table. Embarrassed, she slips the port wine bottle behind the window curtain. Erik doesn't drink alcoholic beverages. Slowly she sinks down opposite him. His face is tanned, lean, and streamlined. It's an unlined, handsome face. But the remarkable thing about Erik is that his face is so *concrete:* the mouth's a mouth, the forehead, a forehead, and the eyes express no obscure symbolism—they are just eyes.

"Evy . . . Are you having trouble?"

Slowly she lets go. A quiet happiness lights up inside her body—something like a drink taking hold. There's a pleasant tingle in her legs, her cheeks feel slightly stiff. She puts both her hands over his fine, suntanned hands.

"Erik! I am just so extremely happy that you've come here like this. Just dropped in."

In the midst of this, the telephone rings. She shuts her eyes and remains seated, hands outstretched to Erik: No, not now!

"Aren't you going to answer it?!"

She goes over and picks up the receiver. It's from NMSI, from the Institute of Experimental Thanatology. The duty animal caretaker is calling for help.

"Aren't you ever off duty?" asks Erik.

"There's nobody else, I'm afraid. I'm terribly sorry, Erik.

216

But I've *got to* go out. A chimpanzee who's got its jaw dislocated."

"Then I'll drive you."

When Erik's big black car pulls up before the institute, a woman in a flapping white lab coat is standing on the steps. She goes down the yard-wide, low steps like a bird wading into a stream. They greet one another. The woman is named Elisabet Skoglund, she's the lab animal caretaker on duty.

They enter the institute and go up to the third floor. In a large room with pale green walls stand four large plexiglass enclosures, extending out from the wall like sickbeds in a hospital room. In three of the plexiglass cages, chimpanzees are sleeping, one in each. In the cage nearest the door, a chimpanzee is sitting with its mouth open unnaturally wide. The ape has tears in its eyes as if it was choking with laughter.

"Here," says Elisabet Skoglund. "I don't know how long she's been sitting like this. When I made my rounds at eight o'clock, everything was normal."

"Why are the chimpanzees here?" Erik asks politely. "I mean, what's it all for?"

Elisabet Skoglund looks attentively at Erik, lifts one hand toward an explanation, and then stops herself, looking guiltily at Evy Beck.

"I wouldn't have called if it weren't acute," she says.

Evy Beck opens the latch and slides one plexiglass panel down toward the floor so that she can get at the chimpanzee. The chimp places both its hands around its jaw and wags its head in distress. Cautiously, Evy runs her fingertips lightly around the corners of the chimp's jaw.

"The jaw is dislocated," she says. "The tough part is, you can never tell whether something's been broken, too. How did this happen?!"

Instead of Elisabet Skoglund, it's the chimpanzee itself that now answers—not with words, but with a torrent of animated gestures in human deaf-mute sign language.

"What does that mean?" asks Erik. "Is it signaling?"

"Intelligent chimps can master several hundred deaf-mute

217

signs," Evy Beck explains—then turns to the caretaker: "What is it the animal is saying?"

The laboratory animal caretaker pretends ignorance, but she can't bring it off without reddening deeply.

"You most certainly know deaf-mute signs!" says Evy Beck, angered. "This chimpanzee hasn't been trained just for the fun of it!"

"Martha, that's what she's called—Martha says she laughed so hard that she couldn't shut her mouth afterward."

"Laughed?" says Erik, and laughs.

"Tell Martha I intend to pull her jaw back into place. It's going to hurt. But it'll be over as quickly as getting a tooth pulled."

Elisabet Skoglund gesticulates, strikes one hand against the other wrist, pats herself on the cheek, forms the word "hurt," and then signs emphatically the word "happiness" afterward. The ape nods attentively and then answers with several submissive gestures in slow motion.

"Martha says she's ready," the animal caretaker interprets.

"Nothing more? Didn't she say something else, too?" says Erik with sudden sharpness.

The animal caretaker reddens again and glances around the walls.

"Since we use deaf-mute signs in international data processing, I have an idea what the chimp is saying: It's got something to do with *death?*"

"The chimp is saying: I'm going to die soon, anyway."

"Tell me more," says Erik.

Evy Beck interrupts by bending over toward the chimpanzee, taking its hands away from its cheeks, and then getting a firm grip behind its jaws. She notices how she sticks out her tongue involuntarily and directs her own movements with the tip. If only it works! If she's inept, she can tear off the ligament or do harm to the jawbone's fragile stem. Quickly she presses the jaw downward, forward. Martha gives a shriek when the ends of the jawbone glide into their sockets. It worked!

"Beautiful, Evy!" says Erik. "I didn't dare to look."

She smiles at him. It is that one little weakness that makes

218

Erik human—that he's afraid of the hospital and can't bear to see blood.

"Well then, we can close up here," says Elisabet Skoglund, who seems to be in a hurry.

"Can't we hear a little more about the chimpanzees?" asks Erik.

"If you want any details, I'm afraid I'll have to refer you to my supervisor," says the caretaker sharply.

With a certain anxiety, Evy Beck sees Erik walk back to the chimpanzee Martha and awkwardly try to strike up a conversation in deaf-mute signs. She turns away, saying, "May I write out an x-ray referral some place? You must take a picture tomorrow morning. To make sure nothing's broken."

Reluctantly the animal caretaker leads the way to an office several doors away. Evy Beck sits down, gets the carbon paper in place, and begins printing a message to the X-Ray Department: "Jawbone luxation evening of Aug. 26. Manual reposition same evening. No clinical signs of fracture. Appreciate x-ray check. Fracture? Fissure? Malpositioning?"

When they return to the big room, Erik is still squatting in front of the chimpanzee enclosure. Each is signing slowly and overexplicitly to the other.

"I'm turning off the lights now!" announces Elisabet Skoglund.

"One minute, one minute . . ."

Nodding, Erik interprets a long sequence of movements by the ape. Afterward, both of them sit motionless and look at each other.

The animal caretaker turns off the ceiling light.

"Erik?!" Evy calls softly.

Finally he comes out in the corridor. They go back to the car. Elisabet Skoglund doesn't follow them out. In the car, Erik says, "Darned interesting. All four chimpanzees have leukemia. And know they're going to die."

She doesn't answer. Usually the duty animal caretaker would have been more than willing to describe the experiment to her, especially since she'd been called out late at night. It's only common courtesy to answer questions under such circumstances. But apparently not tonight. Elisabet

Skoglund must have been in contact with the institute director and been given orders: Not one unnecessary word to Evy Beck.

"Is this the sort of thing you do, Evy? Go out on call like any country doctor?"

He doesn't wait for an answer, but continues: "Did you know they'd come so far with chimpanzees? Inoculating them with leukemia and then following their psychological death processes?"

"Oh, yes," she answers wearily. "There's a fixed pattern of behavior in human beings who know they're about to die: First sorrow and depression—aggressiveness, maybe. Then repression, denying it's so. Then regression, that is, more or less childish behavior. Maybe aggression again—and finally resignation. When they've cut their emotional ties to life."

"Why use chimpanzees, then?"

"Because they haven't got any relatives to interfere."

They drive along the "outer ring," the freeway that runs along the boundary between Stockholm and Solna.

"Can we stop for a while?" she asks.

"No, Evy dear. One can't stop on a freeway."

She wants to talk with Eric in peace and quiet. It will soon be ten years since they really talked things over. But it used to be different: she remembers endless political, religious, and ethical discussions with Erik that began long before he reached his teens. They used to sit at the kitchen table. Long, enthusiastic evenings when Erik preached with glowing cheeks. In the beginning she dominated, but from the time he reached fourteen or fifteen, she fell back into a passive listening. Suddenly, when Erik was seventeen, the table talks stopped. His friends had begun to catch up with him and she was no longer needed.

"Can't you come up for a cup of tea?" she says when he brakes to a stop in front of her door.

"I can't park here either."

She puts her hand on his knee.

"If I pay the fine?"

Erik jumps, nearly standing right up in the car.

220

"Evy! You mustn't say things like that!"

While she's preparing the tea, she turns around several times just to look at Erik sitting at the kitchen table—as he used to.

"Erik, do you really understand what I'm doing at NMSI?"

"You're making an admirable contribution."

She takes the teapot to the table and sits down. She's a little worried that he'll avoid her eyes when she takes his hands. But Erik doesn't look away—nobody has a franker gaze than Erik.

"Erik, to put it plainly: I simply can't make it."

They sit quietly a few moments—then Erik frees his right hand and pours her tea.

"You've got to make it, Evy. They've got no one else to do it."

She begins to tell him about the packing experiment at Ethological, about the cold shoulder she got at the Saturday morning meeting, about the Ethical Center.

"I wonder if you *understand*, Erik?"

"To some extent, Evy."

She goes on. Telling him how she's begun to be afraid for herself, afraid for two completely conflicting reasons. Afraid because she hasn't succeeded in winning any real hearing for the idea that animals are living things and not expendable materials—and at the same time, afraid because she's able to go on with the work even though she feels completely torn in two.

"But that's a problem all human beings have, Evy. More or less. Maybe especially well-defined in your case. But we mustn't let ourselves be par-a-lyzed by it."

"What shall I do, then? Should the ethologists be allowed to go on with their experimental rat-hell?"

"Of course not. But you have to find *the proper channels,* Evy. Anyone who simply rushes straight ahead can end up beating his head against the wall. A medical school is a very elaborate and delicately balanced administrative system. Or to put it figuratively: a lot of interconnected *locks.* To open those locks, you've got to have the right key. It doesn't help a damn bit to stand there and kick the locks."

Of course Erik's right. Being impulsive won't get you anywhere.

"You're something like a surgeon, Evy, a surgeon who can't bear the sight of blood, who is horrified every time he cuts into a human being."

She feels comforted and crushed at the same time. Erik's right. But she still needs to *feel* that Erik's right.

"The right key and a well-oiled lock," says Erik.

When they've had their tea, she helps him on with the lightweight topcoat. He kisses her—as he used to—on the forehead. When she's closing the door of the elevator after him, he says, "That chimpanzee! To be doomed and yet laugh your jaw out of joint."

41

One Thursday evening in September, she goes to her first group session at the Vasatown Ethical Center. She's a little disappointed to find that the group is not led by Morgan Fischer but naturally, as director, he doesn't have time to do everything. The Thursday group is led by a married couple, Don and Doreen Hafez. Both are British citizens but have worked for a long time in Sweden. Don's a little over fifty, short and barrel-chested, carries his head high, and has a receding hairline and curly white hair. He has very dark eyes and a skin that looks like Papa's, grayish rather than olive-brown. Doreen's about ten years younger, slender, with shoulder-length, bright-red-tinted hair. She has the Englishwoman's typical habit of painting her lips too heavily and stickily. Doreen is lively, almost mercurial, while Don is more ponderous, but has a very impressive bearing.

Everyone starts by introducing himself—name, age, and problem:

Eifod Erlandsson, eighteen—conscientious objector.

Kerstin Wahlrot, thirty-nine—practical nurse in an Abortion Department.

Gustaf Strandberg, forty-seven—guard in a jail.

222

Wibeke Häll-Nordlund, forty-seven—responsible for an advice column in a weekly magazine.

Evy Beck, fifty-three—experimental animal veterinarian.

Hans Jönsson, twenty-nine—assistant pastor.

Wolfgang Widén, thirty-five—assistant administrator in the Swedish agency for aid to underdeveloped countries.

After this brief introduction—someone tries to elaborate on his problems but is stopped—the Hafezes take up the practical details. The room where they find themselves is bare and unfurnished except for the ten ordinary chairs that stand in a large circle. At the center is a brazier of black metal. Above it, an electrical smoke- and heat-absorbing filter is suspended from the ceiling.

"Please, everyone, sit down!" says Doreen.

When all are seated, some of them straightforwardly and others after furtively changing place, Doreen fetches a carton of charcoal briquettes.

"Notice how the charcoal tinkles like glass," she says, and ceremoniously pours the charcoal into the brazier.

Don comes up with a spray can of charcoal-lighter and sprays a shining cloud over the brazier. Doreen holds up a big box of fireplace matches and one of the twelve-inch-long matches.

"Every time," she explains, looking around to make sure everyone understands, "every time we begin by lighting our coals. When all the coals . . ." She looks around again: "When all the coals are turned to white ash, we stop. The burning time is almost exactly ninety minutes. The charcoal fire is our living timepiece!"

Don takes over the matchstick and matchbox and sets fire to the coals.

"This evening," he says, "we are just going to demonstrate the technique of ethico-therapy. Next time we will begin in earnest."

Taking an empty chair, Don sits down a few yards outside the circle of chairs.

"Don is director," Doreen explains. "It's he who leads. I—" she says, pointing to herself between the little pointed up-trussed breasts, "I'm co-director. I assist Don. Together, we conduct ethico-therapy. Who wants to start us off?"

No one wants to.

Smilingly, Doreen looks around. Then she goes up to the eighteen-year-old conscientious objector, Eifod Erlandsson, and takes his hand.

"Won't you begin?"

Eifod Erlandsson rises slowly and a little dreamily. Doreen faces him and grasps his hands.

"Now. Please tell us about the first time you ever said to anyone that you didn't want to bear arms?"

Erlandsson gazes into the fire and looks as though he would like to scratch himself but cannot because both his hands are being held. Instead, he wipes his nose on his sleeve.

"Don't be shy. We're all in the same boat," says Doreen.

"Well, it was the officer at the induction center, he referred me here . . ."

Doreen looks past Erlandsson at Don. Evidently she gets a sign from him, for she continues: "No, we won't talk about referrals now. When was the first time you ever told anybody you didn't want to bear arms?"

No answer. The tall, pimpled eighteen-year-old examines the ceiling, examines the brazier, and evinces a deep technical interest in the smoke-filter.

Suddenly Don strides into the circle, steps up behind Erlandsson, places his hands on his shoulders, and rises on tiptoe, saying over Erlandsson's shoulder, "I spoke with my father about two years ago . . ."

"Naw!" says Erlandsson sourly.

Doreen releases his hands, but Don keeps his hands on the conscientious objector's shoulders.

"What Don's doing now is called 'doubling.' It means that Don answers in Eifod's place. Eifod can either approve of the interpretation or reject it . . . Every one of you," she continues, pointing pedagogically at one after another: "every one of you can go up and 'double,' go up and say what you *think* Eifod really wants to say."

Once again Doreen grasps Eifod Erlandsson's heavy, unwilling hands. She looks at him in a friendly way and asks, "Why don't you want to bear arms?"

224

He doesn't answer this time either, but only takes a very deep breath so that his shoulders shoot up to his ears.

Suddenly Wibeke Häll-Nordlund rises, giggles a little, and goes to stand on tiptoe behind Eifod's back, taking a pinching grasp of his shoulders.

"Because I don't want to get killed myself!" she says shrilly.

Eifod again gazes up at the ceiling for help. Then he looks at Doreen and shakes his head.

"A typical beginner's mistake," Doreen says, "is not speaking but only shaking the head."

Don goes quickly into the ring, places himself behind Eifod, and says, "I refuse to kill that which God has created!"

"No," Eifod says firmly. "I'm a political objector. Not ethical!"

"Good!!" blurts Doreen, shaking his hands.

"Very good," says Don, and pats Eifod on both shoulders.

"Now we shall change roles," Don continues after leading Eifod back to his chair. "Evy Beck—will you please play Eifod's role?!"

She rises with difficulty; the hard chair has made her backside go numb. Quickly she dries her palms on her skirt and extends her hands to Doreen.

"Listen: Evy Beck is now taking Eifod's role. Now I ask you, *Eifod,* why don't you want to bear arms?"

"Should I answer as I feel . . . myself?"

Doreen nods encouragingly.

"Because I'm a political conscientious objector," says Evy.

Don strides into the ring and separates Evy and Doreen as if they were two prizefighters.

"You may answer just as you wish. But a little variation would be helpful."

"Should I pretend, then?"

Don nods, releases them, and returns to his observation post. Doreen looks at her again, smiles, and asks, emphasizing each word with a nod, "Why do you, Eifod, not wish to bear arms?"

Evy Beck ponders. Since she herself has never had to take a personal position on the matter, she tries to remember arguments she has heard or read.

225

"I refuse to be drafted because the system strengthens the class structure," she says, and thinks it sounds pretty dumb.

Don flies into the circle again: "Very appropriate. An excellent answer!"

Doreen reviews: "We've now learned to double and to assume roles. Now we'll learn to assume *opposing* roles."

She beckons forward the cleric, Hans Jönsson. Don gives Doreen a light pat on the forearm that could mean either "I go along with this" or "Go easy."

"Hans Jönsson is now *Eifod*. Evy Beck is the induction officer," Doreen says, laughing a little artificially. "Now, Eifod. Tell the induction officer why you refuse to bear arms."

Evy Beck looks at Hans Jönsson and tries to make eye contact, but he seems to be looking right at her breasts. She feels her palms again begin to ooze sweat. She tries to loosen Hans Jönsson's hands a little but he holds her in a cramping grip.

"I refuse to bear arms because God forbids us to kill!" says the clergyman firmly, staring her right in the eye.

Evy Beck becomes a little confused, she is suddenly unsure who she is.

"Speak up for the opposing role!" says Doreen encouragingly.

"Well, there are clergymen in the service too . . ." says Evy Beck.

"Superb!" says Don, stepping forward. "The purpose of the whole thing is for Eifod to see his problem from *outside.*"

Doreen chimes in as if following a prepared script: "The whole group takes part in Eifod's problem. Eifod solves his own problem. But it's the group that helps Eifod look for his solution."

"Now sit down, everyone," says Don, and remains standing alone by the brazier in the ring.

"I have a question," says Doreen, raising her hand as in school.

"Yes, Doreen?" answers Don.

"If Eifod gets unhappy, if he feels shaken by seeing himself from outside? Reaching insight is a very painful process for many. How do we help him?"

226

"A good question," says Don, and looks around the circle benevolently. "May I have your suggestions on how we should help Eifod?"

The members of the group are no longer looking shyly at the floor. Instead, they look at each other and whisper incomplete sentences, trying them out.

At a sign from Don, Doreen goes and sits beside Eifod on the same chair. For both to be able to remain there they must brace themselves and press their sides against each other. Don explains, "This is called 'sympathizing.'"

Doreen chimes in: "To sympathize means that anyone who takes the risk of opposing the group must never be left isolated. Therefore I go and sit by Eifod, I sit on the same chair as Eifod. I *sympathize* with Eifod."

"Are there more questions?" asks Don, but doesn't wait for an answer, leaving the ring to Doreen.

"Each time, we conclude by blowing on our living timepiece."

Doreen drops to her haunches and blows lightly on the charcoal fire. White and gray flakes whirl up. There's no longer an ember left to light.

"Come, everyone!" Doreen calls.

Hesitating and embarrassed, they all fall to their knees around the brazier. Simultaneously, at a sign from Doreen, they blow very lightly. A column rises from the bed of ashes. All must blow equally hard—otherwise the pillar of ashes may be driven into the eyes of one.

42

September's a tough month. Nothing gets done. She goes to the Ethical Center four times without feeling anything but strangeness. Nights, she's seldom allowed to sleep undisturbed: it's as though every night NMSI were seething with needs for help, and at the least sign of trouble everybody calls and wakes up Evy Beck. But not during the day. From nine to five the official Alfred Nobel Institutes evince not the slightest interest in their veterinary medical consultant.

When she comes into her office on the morning of October first, the room has been refurnished. Two desks stand in the room, and the white walls are covered with marker scrawls: Baroque—7, Neoclassic—18, Romantic—1, Realist—1, Impressionist—4, Postimpressionist—0, Surrealist—12, Concrete—9, Pragmatist—2.

" 'Morning, Evy Beck!" says someone behind her.

A man of around twenty-five stands in the doorway. He has a bright open face. His hair is chestnut brown, short, and parted in the middle. He's wearing a black double-breasted suit, a white shirt, and a dove-gray tie. On his feet are patent-leather shoes. His whole appearance fairly shouts out what he is: an artist!

"Welcome," she says, and goes up to shake hands. "I think you must be my new roommate."

"I'm August Klevberg," he introduces himself with a nearly imperceptible bow.

"Ah . . ." she says. "Well, let's hope we get along very well together."

"You bet!" says Klevberg cheerily.

Evy Beck sits down at her desk and Klevberg drops down at his. They look smilingly at each other.

"MELMB?" she asks.

"Never!" says Klevberg. "The department head here is a real art lover. Arranged for a civil service curatorial slot at once."

"What's all this on the wall?" she asks.

"That means I've gotten started trying to inventory the art holdings here at NMSI," he says. "It's amazing—*nobody knows* how many works of art are scattered around in the various institutes. There's no order to it at all. Some are lent, some purchased, others donated. There are pictures here that—well, nobody knows what they're doing here."

"Well then, it seems as though you're really needed. I mean, that's no way to handle things."

He leaps lithely up and comes around to lean over her, his knuckles on her desk.

228

"And now, Evy, you're going to show me around the place. Rosenquist says there's nobody who's pried into every nook and cranny as you have. So it would be damn nice . . ."

"Sure," she says.

All day she trots around among the NMSI buildings with Curator of Art August Klevberg. She feels cheered up—suddenly she is seeing the whole establishment with new eyes. Instead of going into Anatomy and nosing out how many guinea pigs they're keeping under the table in the darkroom of the photo lab, or how many forgotten carp gasp in cloudy glass jars in the loft, August Klevberg stalks right in to the professor's secretary and asks about Braque, Klee, Olle Olson-Hagalund, or Torsten Renquist.

The Anatomical Institute turns out to contain a large wall painting signed Orozco. It shows a few emaciated, naked people who stand looking down on a naked man who has fallen to the ground. Evy Beck thinks it looks like a memorial to concentration camp prisoners. A little metal plate dated 1960 says it is a donation from C.H. Boehringer Sohn of Ingelheim am Rhein, at that time manufacturer of the dieting preparation Preludin.

Klevberg has a little flash camera with him and takes a number of pictures of Orozco's work. He also writes a short description of the wall painting in his pocket notebook.

They then go on to the Institute of Forensic Medicine. They're shown first to the little museum, where among other things is a smallish display of tattooed human skins. These were collected during forensic medical autopsies done when the institute was located downtown right in the red-light district. But August Klevberg isn't especially interested and would just as soon assign these illustrated trollops' bellies to the category of curiosities. However, he changes his mind at the door and labels them "commercial folk art."

Then Klevberg asks the guard to show them to Bror Hjorth's great woodcarving in the chapel.

"Outsiders aren't allowed in there," says the guard. "Nobody's allowed into the autopsy department. When the old King was here on a visit in the fifties, even *he* wasn't allowed in there, they say. But of course he went in anyhow."

229

"Do you see this thumb?" says August Klevberg, holding up his right hand.

"Yes, it looks quite normal," says the guard.

"This is an A-thumb," says Klevberg.

Two minutes later, they've been piloted through the formaldehyde-reeking autopsy department, and stand before Bror Hjorth's great colorful wooden panel in the chapel.

During their lunch break, they survey the art in the Student Union. In the room with the wornout billiard table, where used textbooks and course outlines are sold, a smoke-darkened and stained Olle Bonniér is hanging.

"This one's got to go in for restoration," says Klevberg. "It's unique."

"Where do you get the money for such things?" she wonders.

He pretends not to hear the question. Instead, they go on to the library and look at some rather new paintings of the Pragmatist school. She doesn't like them. One is only two years old and is a copy from El Greco.

"Why do they only copy nowadays?" she asks.

August Klevberg gets very excited and gives her a long lecture on the function of art. She doesn't comprehend more than a fraction of what he says: One shouldn't stare oneself blind at a single, isolated work of art. The context in which the work has come into being is at least as important. Therefore, an El Greco painted today has a completely different function from an El Greco done in 1605.

They go on farther, to the Physiological Institute, and find a real treasure, a very early Picasso. The painting is a personal gift from the former Spanish Minister of Education and Science, José Luis Villar Palasí. It was presented to Physiological in 1973 when a Swedish physiologist was awarded the "doctor honoris causa" at the University of Madrid.

"How much can a Picasso like this be worth?" wonders Evy Beck.

August Klevberg looks it up in his little pocket listing: "They've gone down steadily in the last few years . . . 46,500 dollars."

Declining a cup of coffee at Physiological, they go on

230

toward the southeast corner of the NMSI grounds, where the dental institutes lie. The medical and odontological faculties have been united for a long time, but the dentists are still on an inferior footing and get treated somewhat like country cousins. The dental institutes took a giant step toward equalization, however, when Amalgam International donated a group of outdoor sculptures that, to the displeasure of the Buildings and Grounds Department, block off nearly half an acre of park area.

The sculpture group consists of over thirty pieces executed in brownish red marble. If you stand in the plot of park at its center, you feel you are in an ambitiously and artistically designed playground for preschool children, or perhaps an archeological dig. On the other hand, if like Evy Beck and August Klevberg you go to the roof of the Institute of Bite Analysis, you see that the sculptures together form an irregular bite of grotesque, brightly polished teeth—some with holes in them, others with bulbous abscesses and prolongations.

"This is Henry Moore's largest work outside England or the USA," the curator of art explains.

"Well, what's it worth?" asks Evy Beck, who's seized with the new-hatched collector's fixation on price.

August Klevberg flips back and forth through his well-thumbed pocket listing.

"Priceless. And at the same time, unsalable. Nobody's yet succeeded in selling a Henry Moore off its base."

The photographing and documenting of the Henry Moore takes time. It begins to drizzle and the metal roof gets treacherously slippery. Evy Beck is inclined to leave Klevberg and go back to her office to see whether any messages or announcements of inspections or meetings may be lying there. But she hesitates; it's been several weeks now since she received such an announcement.

"I'd really love to show you a Matisse," says Klevberg.

She decides to go along and see one more painting. Then, that's it.

"There're supposed to be two Matisses at the Institute of Medical Ethology . . ."

231

Evy Beck halts.

"No. That's enough for today."

He puts his arm around her cheerfully and draws her on.

"Matisse is extraordinarily well represented at NMSI. You must look! There was an art collector who deposited several Matisses here a long while back. And then he had to emigrate to Switzerland—in a helluva hurry. So now they're hanging here!"

Reluctantly she goes along with him into Ethological. That I should lack the least moral courage, she thinks. When I know I'm right about packing, I ought to have the guts to stride right in boldly . . . But her pulse speeds up and she puts a hand over her reddening throat.

She has never understood Matisse. They stand there staring at a huge painting hanging in the entrance. It is certainly fifteen feet by fifteen feet and consists of a number of scattered strokes and flowers sparsely disposed on a white background. In the middle is a stick figure that might conceivably represent a Chinese.

"Isn't it *subtle?*" says Klevberg.

She doesn't answer; she's never been much good at pretending. Instead, she stares at the painting and tries to look as though she's lost in thought.

"You asked earlier how we're getting money for conservation and restoration of the works of art," says the curator. "Well, I'll tell you: many of the works, like this Matisse for example, have been attached for debt by the District Marshal . . ."

August Klevberg breaks off when a man dressed in a rain hood comes in from outside and halts suddenly.

"Evy Beck?!" says the man brightly, pulling the hood back from his face.

She thinks she'll faint away: it's the one man she wants least of all to encounter: Professor Henrik Engquist, who's acting director here at Ethological.

Engquist advances and shakes hands.

"A fine Matisse, isn't it?"

"Subtle," says Klevberg.

"Well now, Evy Beck," says Engquist and takes her by the

arm: "You and I have a little something to talk over. You've started a campaign to stop this packing experiment of ours."

"I've got to try to follow my convictions," she says lamely.

"Absolutely! I want to tell you that I've labored for two years to put a stop to that mess. We can't have half our lab space tied up with that nuisance."

She doesn't understand at all. *Everyone* involved seems to be ready to stop the experiment—yet it can't be stopped.

"You see, Evy, the tough part is, we have such long, drawn-out *liquidation procedures,*" says Engquist, and points to the Matisse painting as though it were some kind of diagram of the institute's administrative processes.

"I don't understand," she gets out.

"Me neither! But there's the Research Council and there's EMRECOM. Yes, and LERAD. And then, especially, we have the people on our staff who'll lose their jobs if we stop ... There are so damn many obstacles, you see, that I'll be happy if I succeed in ending the nuisance within three years."

She's beginning to see what Erik meant about keys and well-oiled locks.

"Listen, sometimes I wonder if it wouldn't make more sense just to set fire to the whole mess!"

She giggles hopelessly, feeling exposed.

"But of course," Engquist says, "we'll have to make sure we've got time to lug this super-Matisse out first."

43

Not till November, when she goes to the Vasa-town Ethical Center for the eleventh time, does something begin to happen. As usual, she's the first to arrive and has to wait almost a quarter of an hour before all the others gather. Eifod Erlandsson is no longer with them; he dropped out after eight sessions. They have talked over Eifod Erlandsson in the group, and worked out that it was a mistake to take an eighteen-year-old into a group that otherwise consists of middle-aged people.

233

They seat themselves in a ring in their usual places. Doreen pours charcoal into the brazier—this always takes place in absolute silence. The charcoal tinkles. Then Doreen passes the fireplace matches to Don, who grasps a long matchstick right below the head. As if presenting her with a knife handle-first, Don gives the matchstick's white end to Evy Beck, bowing slightly.

She sits there a couple of seconds with the matchstick in her hand before she realizes that tonight is her night. The other ten evenings she's come here thinking: This time I won't get by, tonight it's going to be Quotia's turn. But today she's completely forgotten to worry about it. She repeats, now, the ceremony she's seen carried out ten times before. Rising, she goes forward to the brazier. Don lifts the spray can and sprays charcoal lighter over the coals. Evy Beck lights them. Then she waits till the long yellow flames shrink down and become blue.

With pounding heart, she says, "The first time I ever saw an animal killed, I was just six years old. We had a neighbor who kept rabbits. It was during the war. My playmate and I were going to watch when they slaughtered a white rabbit we'd been feeding dandelion leaves to all summer long. A man came and took the rabbit by its back legs and swung it around in the air. Then he beat its head against a cement block in the garden walk. When he lay the rabbit down on its back to cut it up, he pulled out its penis and said, 'Just like a little boy's.' "

She feels a pair of eager hands on her shoulders. Then she hears Wibeke Häll-Nordlund's contact-seeking voice.

"So I always associate animals and *smut!*"

She doesn't answer. She feels interrupted and doesn't want to lose the thread of what she was saying.

"Does Evy accept this interpretation?" Don asks.

"No."

She hears a disappointed sigh behind her as Wibeke Häll-Nordlund sits down.

Wolfgang Widén, the official of the overseas aid department who's sitting right in front of her, rises, nods encouragingly at her, goes around and lays his hands on her shoulders.

234

"It was then I decided to become a vet. Because I saw that the rabbit's penis was like my little brother's."

"I haven't got a brother," she says.

Closing her eyes, she searches for another early memory, one of those experiences in which she came to realize that the distinction between animal and man is false. But the picture of the cut-up rabbit lies in the way, as if its image had jammed in the projector: the shining moss-green intestines, the yellow fat, the brown heart that the slaughterer took on his palm to show them how it hopped like a little frog when you spat on it. The whole time, she had been saying to herself: *I* don't look like that inside.

Doreen has risen and grasped her hands.

"I am Evy!" says Doreen.

A little dispirited, Evy Beck goes to her seat. She looks at Doreen, at Doreen's sleek body, her waist, her thin wrists, her pointed fingers. Nothing fits.

"As a child, I got a shock. I realized that life was evil."

One after another they come forward, take Doreen's hands, and advance various more or less plausible interpretations of Evy Beck's childhood experiences. After a few minutes, she notices that she's not listening, that it is as if she were sitting in the semidarkness of a theater and watching something going on far away. She hardly even notices when people change place.

"Gustaf, would you play Evy's role now," Don requests from his director's chair.

Gustaf Strandberg, a guard in the pretrial detention jail, gets up. For the last three sessions, the group has worked intensively on Gustaf's inability to use violence—he was referred to the Ethical Center because he has repeatedly reported sick rather than lay hands on violent prisoners. In the beginning, Gustaf maintained that violence was irreconcilable with his views on human rights. The group has given him perspective on the situation by showing that he is really afraid of his own aggressiveness, of being unable to master his emotions. In fact, his whole upbringing has been based on this: mastering emotions. Since Gustaf has realized this, it has been possible to proceed with getting him to accept the necessity of "measured violence"—meaning certain essential and closely controlled forcible measures that a democratic society must resort to in order to protect its existence. Gustaf has also come to accept this.

Last Thursday, he declared that he was proud that society had had the confidence to choose him for such a touchy assignment. They have all endorsed his conclusion: It is wrong of Sweden to look down on her legitimized practitioners of violence, the police and the military. They are the ones who take upon themselves the thankless job that benefits the whole society—but that almost no one wants to acknowledge: the tremendous trust of practicing necessary violence.

Evy Beck looks at her new identity: Gustaf suits the role better than Doreen. Gustaf is short of stature, has hunched-up shoulders that do not slope, heavy arms, a large belly, and short bowed legs. Gustaf could have been my brother, Evy thinks.

"I am against vivisection because it is an attack on the defenseless," Gustaf says quickly and firmly.

Evy Beck nods: as a matter of fact, that is how she feels.

"Actually, I am opposed to *all* animal experiments!" says Gustaf.

"No," she says. "No I'm not."

"Please don't interrupt Gustaf," Don says gently.

Now Gustaf begins pacing around the brazier. This is called "circling" and is a way of showing that one does not wish to be interrupted.

"I say that I accept essential animal experiments. But actually, I accept *none*. As soon as I've gotten into the right position at the Nobel Institutes, I'm going to forbid all experimentation with animals."

"No!" she nearly shouts.

Doreen lightly covers Evy's mouth with her hand, and calmingly strokes her brow.

"Man is an animal species!" thunders Gustaf. "No animal has the right to oppress any other!"

Evy Beck howls like a whipped dog.

"I have realized, you see," Gustaf continues, "that man keeps animals *not* primarily because they are useful. No. But

236

to show he's *master!* To show that he himself is really not an animal. The main purpose of all the millions of animals being held in captivity in Sweden is to turn men's aggressiveness away from other men. Man is the cruelest animal in creation. Just so that we won't kill each other, we have to unfeelingly beat down defenseless animals. It is necessary for our self-esteem!"

"No, no, no . . ." wails Evy Beck, nearly biting Doreen's hand.

Gustaf has come to a stop right in front of her, thrusts his heavy, callous face at her, and shouts, "To kill! Cut up! Rape! Decapitate! Chloroform! To wring their necks . . . beat their brains out on the drainboard!!"

She falls to weeping. She bites her own hand and weeps without restraint. It has been at least a year since she cried last—but then it was only a few silent tears when she learned that Papa's liver was finished. Now she cries as if she was being hunted, as if mean boys were hunting her through a thicket and whipping her bare legs with thorny switches.

Doreen seats herself by Evy on the chair; embarrassed, she shrinks away and goes on crying because she is so fat, so ugly. Don comes over and takes her hands.

"Weep," he says in a caressing voice. "Weep. Cleanse yourself."

She doesn't regain control of herself until it is time for everyone to fall on their knees and blow in the ashes. But she's so stopped up by all the crying that she blows too feebly. She can't hold her own. She feels the flakes of ash strike her cheeks and stick to the half-dried tears.

When they're leaving the Ethical Center, Gustaf comes up and smiles at her in a friendly way. Then they stand silently for almost five minutes pressing their backs together. That's called "relaxation" and is recommended after sharp personal confrontations between two group members.

Don and Doreen follow her to the taxi that's been called for her. She waves to them gratefully through the back window. During the short ride home to Roslag Street she is filled with a tired happiness, like an athlete after a winning game. Or a person tormented for a long time by a knotty problem

—who at last *understands.* Or someone who has asked for-
giveness. And has been embraced.

44

It's not yet six o'clock on the morning of December second. The night has been cold and clear. But no snow
has fallen yet. Evy Beck balances on the frozen light-brown
ridges of earth between the deep imprinted ruts of tractor
treads. NMSI's southwest corner is uprooted and riven
around the "new building"—that newly built pedagogical
complex which has now been in use for over ten years without money being found to plow and landscape around it. The
little money available has been used instead to stifle the spon-
taneous growth, to dig up and poison nature's own unhesitat-
ing attempts to introduce sprouts, shoots, and saplings of
birch, hazel, and dogrose.

Approaching the huge educational complex of liver-col-
ored brick, she meets a few people on their way home. They
become more and more numerous. Hunched over against
the cold, they trail long streamers of steamy breath. They are
file clerks and students who dropped out. Over 1,300 file
clerks are employed in the Nobel Institutes. More than half
of them have permanent night duty; were all the file clerks
to work day shift, there would be no space for them. But
Papa, who misinterprets nearly everything, declares that the
night duty is a way of tucking the file clerks away out of sight
—so ordinary people won't be upset.

She steps aside to let them go by. Many are young. These
are students who for various reasons have dropped out of the
regular course schedules. They get instruction at night, when
the lecture halls would otherwise stand empty.

Evy Beck feels thankful. She herself belongs to the aristoc-
racy of the less productive—even gets to work in daylight,
gets to work in her own field. She starts counting the people
passing. The stream doesn't slacken before she has counted
long past two hundred. What are all these people being used
for? A few have qualified assignments that really should be

238

THE ANIMAL DOCTOR

paid for in the usual way. Some are seriously ill, hurt, or so deviant that they come here mostly as a kind of therapy. But most of them? Most are invited to find their motivation in meaningless cataloguing, record searching, attic cleaning, and inventory taking. The alternative is no work at all.

She looks after the last of them, thinking: What a terrible waste of human capacity. If a computer stands unused overnight, there is uproar and inquisition. But no one seems to react to there being more than a million human beings of normal ability standing idle. Could one pool this unused brainpower, how many Einsteins might one crystallize from it?

Foolish whimsies. You must be happy and thankful, Quotia! And the way to show you're thankful is not hair-splitting and storms of conscience, like another princess-and-the-pea. One thing you owe all these people with meaningless assignments: you have the obligation to carry out your work carefully and industriously. Anything less would be a betrayal of those who don't get to work, don't get to use their capacity.

And one more thing, Quotia! There are quite enough clever and qualified people who ponder and plan, who think their way through moral and political tangles, who invest all their integrity and effort in making a better society. You're not one of them, Quotia. Instead, you're one of those who can do a fine veterinary job, if only you want to. While the high-level thinkers think, somebody's got to keep the wheels turning.

The last stragglers of the night people disappear around the hill next to Pharmacological. Another thought strikes her: If all of them joined forces—if all the file clerks, all the early retirees, all the retired people in general, all the quota people joined together *against* the favored and productive people. Would society make it through? If all of them went and stood in one corner of Sweden, wouldn't the whole country tip over?

She feels a little ashamed. Why think *they?* She herself is a quota person. Why not *we?* Then she realizes how childish it is to think like that—all Swedes are *we*, whether we are

239

quota people or sound, productive citizens. You must look at it that way. Must you? Whoa, Quotia, she thinks, don't get started on that again, flopping here and there like a duck full of buckshot. I'll turn the question over to Erik! she decides, and marches on toward the big classroom building.

She passes the large kidney-shaped basin in front of the building, the basin that has never had its finish coat of cement, but has become instead a fireproof brazier for Stockholm's largest Walpurgisnacht bonfire. Even now, in December, piles of trash, smashed furniture, plaster-clotted boards, twigs, and paper lie there waiting for spring.

Stepping into the vestibule, she presses her thumb in the hole below the time clock. It shows 6:03:59. Nearly the whole ground floor is one extended hall. In the center is a glass booth, something like the control tower at an airport. It's the information booth, but this early in the morning it's empty. Around the hall stand several hundred plain plastic chairs, a few tables, and a long row of automatic machines vending coffee, soft drinks, snuff, sandwiches, soyburgers, and candy. In the inner reaches of the hall loom long green-painted banks of lockers for the students' coats and books.

In the whole hall there is not a single flower, not a potted plant or even a cactus. Instead, they've tried to brighten the chilly atmosphere by exhibiting some items from the old anatomical museum. Half a hundred skeletons of various ages and showing the most varied skeletal anomalies are prettily arranged in little groups or in different movements. Evy Beck pauses to look. She thinks each time she goes by that it's like stepping into a wax museum that has suddenly been heated up, pasteurized, so that all the wax has boiled away.

She tears herself away from the skeletons and begins trotting across the stone floor toward the elevators. Her steps ring so hard it makes her teeth ache. She steps into the elevator and says, "The animal runway!"

The twenty-four-passenger elevator carries her below ground. A speaker in the ceiling announces every floor: "Minus One: osteology, embryology, and microscopy. Minus Two: muscles, tendons, and ligaments. Minus Three: intes-

240

tines, circulatory system, and nervous system. Minus Four: animal runway and bomb shelter."

She goes into the animal runway and hangs up her coat. The runway itself consists of an x-ray fluoroscope that the animals—mostly mice and guinea pigs—have to crawl through in order to get through the runway. The procedure is effective for screening out animals with diseases that x-rays can detect. The regulations prescribe that before the animals can be given out to the students in the various lab courses, they must be checked for contagious diseases. She closes the main circuit-breaker of the x-ray runway. While the big machine warms up, she gets a cup of coffee out of the automat behind her.

In a few minutes, the first roentgen tube lights up and the fans get going. The little green window at eye level before her seat slowly brightens like a wintry dawn. She focuses the picture and presses the input control button. After a few seconds, the first mouse comes creeping through the runway with nose wiggling. The rest come crowding after, nose to tail. All the mice are seen in cross-section, the whiskers bent by the walls of the tube, the nearly white blob of the heart pumping eagerly—and the long tail containing a glowing green twig of bamboo.

She keeps her right foot on a cast-iron pedal in the floor. As soon as an animal with suspicious shadows in its lungs or odd kinks in its skeleton comes into the picture, she presses the pedal and the animal disappears instantly. She dislikes this cruel work in the runway, yet at the same time she knows it is important and meaningful. A qualified veterinary assignment that protects the health of the students while ensuring that they are able to work with good experimental animals. Animals that give them essential knowledge of how to save the lives of folks of all ages.

MEMORANDUM TO ADP CENTRAL DATABANK
CLASSIFIED INFORMATION OFFICIAL USE ONLY
OBSERVER ASST ADMINISTR S HORRLIN NMSI
KEYWORD EVY INGA-BRITT BECK WOLMB
CONTINUOUS WORK REVIEW 6
VERBAL REPORT B HAS RECOVERED WELL ACCORDI
NG SPECIAL REPORT VASATOWN ETHICAL CENTER
SHOULD HOWEVER UNDERGO CONTINUATION COUR
SE SINCE DISTURBANCE IS MODERATE TO SEVERE
B WILL IN FUTURE BE ASSIGNED HIGHLY STRUCTUR
ED DUTIES MUST NOT BE PERMITTED TO DRIFT OU
GHT NOT BE CONSIDERED FOR REGULAR EMPLOYM
ENT ON NMSI STAFF HOWEVER AFTER FURTHER OB
SERVATION PROBABLE RECOMMENDATION FOR WO
LMB MANY USERS SATISFIED ESPEC WITH NIGHT E
MERGENCY CALL SERVICES
RATING 1–5
COMPETENCE 3
ADAPTABILITY 2
SOLIDARITY 3
MOTIVATION 4
COST NONE

45

It's eleven o'clock at night when she comes hurrying over the little triangular park at Roslagstull and up toward the hospital. The office building façades at the end of Valhalla Street are covered with an enormous animated neon sign. First, the Co-Op's infinity symbol in bright shining blue. In the next second, bright red flashing out THOUGHT FOR THE MONTH. Then the sign turns a radiant orange and declares in yard-high letters LOVE THY NEIGHBOR— IT'S GOOD MANAGEMENT.

The gates of Roslagstull Hospital open just as she comes puffing up the hill. Fifty or so visitors stream in, none of them carrying flowers or bags of grapes. She follows the straggling crowd to the Dialysis Ward.

The visiting room in the Dialysis Ward is divided down the middle by a thick, greenish-tinged plexiglass wall. In the big aquarium inside are patients waiting for their relatives. A few stand with their foreheads leaning on the glass, some sit in wheelchairs, and ten or so are lying in their big hospital beds, which have been driven up and parked with the foot against the glass. The patients here in the Dialysis Ward lack either liver or kidneys. A mild infection, such as a head cold or stomach flu, would mean death for many of them. So they have to be hermetically sealed off from the outside world.

Papa's not really awake yet, he's sitting there in the wheelchair with his head drooping. She has to knock several times on the glass before he lifts his eyelids and sleepily gropes for the telephone receiver. She unhooks her own receiver and says as cheerfully as she can, "G'morning, Papa! Have you slept well?"

"Slept?" he says confusedly. "What time is it?"

"Ten past eleven."

Nowadays Papa's on the night shift. All day long he sleeps in his bed with his tubes connected to the hospital's central dialysis installation, the "mother liver." A million-dollar in-

243

stallation that the county can't afford to have standing unused for even one hour of the day.

A nurse's aide in ankle-length dark green coat, cloth cap, transparent plastic face mask, and elbow-length rubber gloves comes up to Papa with his breakfast tray. Smiling at him, she clamps the tray into the wheelchair tray-holder. Papa yawns and rubs his eyes.

"Take a little juice and you'll wake up," she suggests.

He stretches out a trembling hand toward the juice mug. But a completely normal phenomenon hinders him: a person who's not quite awake can't grasp things firmly.

She looks away. She's seen these scenes re-enacted on twenty-five or thirty nights. Night-weary relatives who tap their telephone receivers on the glass to waken morning-drowsy patients.

"How's Erik?" asks Papa.

Since he's got the receiver nearly two feet away from his face, she doesn't really hear what he is saying, but she watches his lips. Besides, she knows Papa always starts out asking about Erik.

"I'm sure he's fine!" she says soothingly.

"Sure??" grunts Papa.

He has the receiver nearer his lips now. While talking, he doesn't look through the glass at her face, but instead looks slantwise down at the receiver's mouthpiece, as if he were talking into an ordinary telephone. His gaze is empty, as if there were miles and miles of telephone wire separating them.

"Don't you worry about Erik, Papa dear. He's just so aw-fully busy. He's preparing his trial lecture for a professorate."

"He's going to go far, that boy," Papa says, pleased, to himself, and indulges himself in a smile at the breakfast tray.

"I'm proud too."

"You?!" he grunts sourly, but then quickly softens and says absently, "Yes, yes."

She wonders if she dares tell Papa that she's been in touch with the chief physician again about taking him home. Or at least getting him transferred to a ward that has individual liver dialysis at night, so that Papa can be awake in the day-

THE ANIMAL DOCTOR

time like other people. But Papa seems to have read her thoughts already by holding the other end of the spiral telephone wire in his fist—he twitches the wire delicately, as if it were a fishing line.

"They aren't giving me a new Auto-Hepar," he says as if the matter didn't really concern him. "You should have made sure there was a seven-tumbler lock on the outer door!"

He's not really accusing her, but nevertheless she feels a deep guilt. Of course she should have foreseen that the artificial liver could be stolen. When one can't leave an ordinary telephone unwatched at NMSI, it's sheer madness to practically offer a 20,000-dollar Auto-Hepar. Now, in retrospect, she understands full well why insurance companies refuse to insure any kind of electronic instrument kept in the home.

Papa takes out a thin newspaper he's kept tucked away in his robe. Holding the telephone receiver between his shoulder and his jaw, he begins to unfold the pages. Papa's in a relatively good humor tonight. On other nights, he's quite simply dropped the receiver on the floor when he thinks it's time to take out the newspaper. She doesn't feel hurt that he reads during visiting hours. She agrees with Papa that if they were sitting at home instead, it would have been perfectly natural for him to leaf through the paper while they chatted.

Now, while Papa's absorbed in the paper, which is printed in the hospital under sterile conditions, she dares to look at him closely. He's gained weight these last months. But it's not healthy weight. It's as though water has run out into his arms and legs and made his skin look padded and puffy. Each night she thinks: This is the last time I'll see Papa. But she's repeated it to herself so many times that the thought has lost most of its anxiety for her. The ethico-therapy that she's just gone through has also given her a more matter-of-fact view of Papa: I have to accept Papa's dying—and my own moving up to the front lines. The front lines, where one can foresee one's own death in the dust on the other side of the battlefield.

Suddenly Papa mumbles something into the receiver that she doesn't quite hear: ". . . lonely!"

245

A sob stops up her nose so that she has to gasp for breath. This, Papa has never admitted before: that he must feel enormously lonely. Guilt climbs back onto her shoulders like a fifty-pound pack. She collapses and gropes for the handkerchief in her sleeve. If only I'd had the good sense to lock up the Auto-Hepar, Papa could still be living at home!

"I can come twice a day, Papa," she whispers into the receiver. "I promise I'll come during the second visiting hour too, between four and five in the morning."

"What the hell are you talking about?" says Papa sharply.

He has dropped the newspaper on the vegetarian breakfast omelet and is staring her sternly right in the eye.

"I don't want you to feel lonely, Papa . . ."

"Me? Lonely?!"

She stares at him, frightened. Is he so senile or so badly dialyzed that he doesn't remember from one second to the next?

"What the hell are you talking about?" he repeats, and leans forward so that the newspaper is pressed right down on the omelet. "I'm not lonely. Not for a second. I've got a full-time job keeping track of all my ideas and speculations!"

Then Papa almost smiles, and says amiably, "It's you who's lonely, Evy. But you mustn't be. It's time now you were a big girl and stood on your own two feet."

Then he does something that shakes her completely. He reaches out to pat her on the cheek. He rests his fingertips on the glass so that little haloes of moisture form around them. He doesn't smile. Rather, he looks at her a little sternly, as if he intended to tousle her hair.

46

On Lucia Day, Evy Beck and Nils Rosén von Rosenstein are invited to lunch at the Stallmästaregården Country Club. Since the restaurant was converted into a private club, it has had a thorough shaking up. By enclosing the eighteenth-century buildings with a twenty-foot concrete wall, the architect has succeeded in screening the old

246

tavern from its inauspicious surroundings: the high railroad embankment, the six-lane superhighway, and the tacky pleasure-boat marina. Within the walls, the low yellow buildings lie surrounded by a bright, luxuriant winter garden. Plexiglass screens and forced-hot-air curtains make possible a constant Mediterranean climate. Lemon and mimosa bloom above the close-growing lawn, which is decorated here and there with old water wheels, carriages, an Apollo and Venus in simulated marble, little rock gardens, and fountains. Above the flower beds' fireworks display hover dozens of hummingbirds, each no bigger than a bumble bee.

Evy Beck and Nils Rosén are led to a white-painted cast-iron settee facing an antique sundial. An unseen light turns with extreme slowness, timed to the movement of the sun so as to make a natural shadow-hand move around the sundial's roman numerals. The headwaiter serves them two gin fizzes and the head gardener, in ankle-length blue apron and big wooden shoes, ceremoniously presents Evy Beck with a rose. Blue lights play on the condensed-air layer twenty feet above their heads, so that the heavens beam as clear and bright as on an early morning in summer.

Mr. Pedersen, the manager of Findus Pharmafarm, comes hurrying down the garden path of red and white pebbles. When he walks on it, it doesn't crunch. His step is moccasin-soft, as if he were on wall-to-wall carpet.

"Hello there!" he puffs. "Very sorry to be late!"

They shake hands and Pedersen roguishly sniffs the rose that Evy has placed in a buttonhole on the jacket of her suit. The headwaiter turns up with a glass of varnish-colored bourbon, presenting them at the same time with the bill of fare, as big as a newspaper. The head gardener toddles rustically over with slivers of raw carrot, tender spring onions, and black olives still on their twigs.

The drinks begin to take hold and Evy Beck relaxes a bit. By old tradition, most NMSI professors and administrators eat Lucia Day lunch at Stallmästaregården. She realizes that it's a great honor for her to be there. That Pedersen has invited Rosén and her is very surprising—Findus Pharmafarm invites only two guests every Lucia Day. Last year,

Rosén has told her, the guests were the president of NMSI and the chairman of personnel, Edwin Karlsson.

When they've finished their drinks, Pedersen helps them out of a real dilemma: he himself suggests what they should have for appetizer, main course, and dessert. When the wine steward, in a peaked cap, comes over with the Wine of the Month in a little keg, Pedersen waves away the invitation to taste it and asks, instead, that two bottles be brought up from Findus's own wine collection.

Fifteen minutes later, the headwaiter leads them to their table. In the restaurant are many whose faces are known to Evy Beck. There are few among the patrons Evy doesn't recognize from her tours of the institutes.

"I've really and truly been looking forward to this," Gorm Pedersen says. "For a very special reason."

"I can well imagine," pops out of Evy, who feels a heedless intoxication blooming on her cheeks and throat.

"Are you crazy about the history of medicine too?" Pedersen asks, restraining his surprise.

"The history of medicine?"

"No?" answers Pedersen, and looks laughingly at Rosén.

"Y'know, Evy," Rosén says, "Gorm Pedersen and I are cooking up secret plans for getting Findus and NMSI to invest some money in a museum of medical history. The history of disease has been at least as significant as political history in man's development through the centuries."

"Yes, Evy. Of that you can be sure!"

"But me? Why am I invited?"

"You?!" says Pedersen, lifting his glass to her. "Because we really and truly like you!"

"Because we're treating medical history as a unified whole," explains Nils Rosén. "It would be wrong to limit the museum to human medicine. We must span the entire field."

"Here's to animal medicine!"

Evy and Nils Rosén raise their scarcely three-quarters-full melon-sized wine glasses toward their host.

"We thought we'd begin by taking over the medical history collections on Åsö Street," says Rosén. "The present sponsor's been nationalized and can't keep them up any longer."

"And Evy . . ." giggles Gorm Pedersen. "Y'know what? Y'know who's going to be head of that museum? When he retires?"

She looks at Nils Rosén, who smiles brightly and boldly.

"We're scheming right out loud, Evy!" he says.

"And I?" she asks.

"You?" says Pedersen.

"It's not all that easy!" says Rosén with mock severity. "We can't undertake to arrange for a chair in the History of Veterinary Medicine overnight. You're to be a consultant."

Suddenly she feels a hand on her shoulder. Startled, she turns her head and her mouth contacts the hair of Rosenquist, her department head, who's bending over her.

"Evy . . ." he whispers when she's adjusted matters so that her ear contacts his hair instead. "Today, right during the holiday, I've sent a new performance rating in to WOLMB. I want you to know that just now we're very pleased with you!"

Before she has time to answer, her department head straightens up and slowly and seriously toasts all three. Then he walks silently back to his own table, where she has glimpsed her officemate, August Klevberg, Assistant Administrator Hörrlin, and a couple of others from Administration.

Some silent minutes ensue, during which they slice into their four-inch-thick steaks with surgeonly concentration. She hasn't eaten real meat since the farewell lunch at Arlanda. But this is something else entirely. Erik once remarked that the Stallmästare Club has Scandinavia's best kitchen.

"Truly a pity you didn't go to Gambia, Evy," says Pedersen.

"My father got sick."

"Maybe there will be another chance," Rosén says.

"No, one can't really be sure of that," Pedersen answers, and actually looks worried.

"Yes . . ." says Rosén. "I heard a rumor about that—that you're considering shutting down?"

"Right. Honestly, there's hardly a cent of profit in it. These chimpanzees. They have to be transported by air like first-class passengers. Otherwise they get sick. We're moving the whole operation to Poland. The Poles have vast experience in raising horses. We think they'll be able to handle the chimps extremely well."

"Is it true you've come so far you can take the minds right out of animals?" asks Rosén.

"Minds? Do you mean consciousness?"

"I mean suppressing the development of certain parts of the cerebral cortex," Rosén explains. "Taking away the possibility of pain and anxiety in experimental animals?"

"No, not in chimpanzees . . ."

"In which animals, then?" Evy asks.

"Can't talk about that!"

"Are you afraid you'll have an ethico-moral debate on your hands?"

"No!" chuckles Pedersen, and snaps his fingers for the wine steward to come and refill the glasses. Then he leans over to them and says with a wink, "Secrets of the trade."

Now Evy Beck feels she's had too much wine. Her actions are preceding her thoughts. Before she's had time to think, May I put my elbows on the table, she's sitting there with her chin in her hands, feeling that her mouth is smiling.

"Now we won't have any more shop talk!" says Pedersen, gripping Evy and Rosén by the arm. "Now we'll discuss our museum of medical history!"

They sit there at the lunch table till three thirty. Then Rosén has to head for home to prepare the speech he'll give that same evening in the Student Union to this year's newly chosen Nobel prizewinners in medicine. The restaurant manager himself comes with the check, which he doesn't unfold. Without even looking at the folded check, Gorm Pedersen presses his thumbprint onto one corner.

250

47

During the evenings that follow, Evy Beck sits scribbling away at a Christmas letter to Erik—who is devoting the last part of December to a combined vacation and study tour of New Zealand. She writes:

Dear Erik,
Thanks for the postcard! Since you left, there's been no real change in Grandfather's condition. He is still unconscious. Yesterday I sat a while by the oxygen tent but he never knew I was there. The chief physician thinks that we can hardly expect Rodion to regain consciousness. But how long he can go on lying there nobody knows. It might take months.

As for me, I'm doing fine now. You mustn't worry about me. It's amazing how much I have to do at NMSI. And Erik! I feel I'm making a real contribution.

I haven't wanted to burden you with my petty troubles but now, in retrospect, I feel the need of telling you a little about them. You know, I've brooded quite a bit over what happened to me last summer, when I "dropped out" at Arlanda and then, later, got a little off the track or something. For a while, I really thought I'd been sick. But no matter how I turn or twist what I did, I keep coming back to the fact that what followed, I mean the fuss over "packing" and the rest, was deeply and honestly felt on my part. Erik, I wasn't "play-acting," as you used to call it when you were a boy.

Now that it's past, I prefer to look at it this way: the pressure got too high. I was simply not strong enough or mature enough to cope with the moral dilemmas I got into. Whether to go on working as before or to speak out. I'm still not sure. Should I have avoided a fuss? Probably the mistake was that your clumsy Mama spoke out in the wrong way. You're absolutely right, of course, about keys and locks—as you tried several times to get me to understand. I kicked the lock instead, and that's something I've regretted, Erik.

I owe Nils Rosén my deepest thanks, he was so kind and arranged for me to have ethico-therapy. Sure, I was skeptical at first! You wouldn't guess how many times I was ready to drop out and give up. It wasn't till I'd been there ten times that I began to understand, to realize that they all wished me well. I was really suspicious. To think how one never learns to trust people—just because they look strange, talk strangely, or behave a little oddly.

I don't know whether your mother has impressed you as someone kind and tolerant. Others have had that impression, I know. So have I. But now I've realized that it's probably not true in all respects. On the contrary, I have quite a lot of prejudices and intolerance in me, which I need to come to terms with. So I've applied for a continuation course next spring at the Ethical Center. Though of course one can't be sure of being accepted. And I wouldn't want anyone with more serious problems, who really needs the therapy more than I do, to miss out on my account.

Did you have time to see the Thought for the Month before you left? "Love thy neighbor—it's good management." I can't help being a little annoyed by that. You wouldn't have put it so crudely, Erik! Neither you nor I would say that management ought to be put ahead of everything else, that good management is the real goal to strive for. Management is only a means to an end. Right, Erik? Say that Mama's got it right! Management is one of those keys we need in order to advance ourselves toward a better life. Though I understand that this isn't so awfully much to fuss about either. Can't make a fuss about everything. One must be positive. Whoever wrote the Thought for the Month surely wished the best for everyone.

Believe me, I've read your article in "Business Week" very, very closely. You write so clearly, so lightly! And so wittily. That's the first time I've heard anybody called a "hyperhuman" instead of a "bleeding heart" as we used to say in the past. In particular, your discussion of "the great goal and the small" strikes me as being especially directed to me. All of us who are entrusted with our little means must, of course, subordinate ourselves to the great, long-range ends. Poor at-

THE ANIMAL DOCTOR

tention to animal welfare mustn't lead a person to throw a monkey wrench into the whole operation of NMSI.

I wonder what Grandfather would have said if he'd been able to read what you write about socialism and bureaucracy. Maybe he would have agreed with you, Erik! You mustn't underestimate him. You write that control of the means of production is only one of the very first steps in development. That for far too long, we've stared ourselves blind at that. Instead, we must first and foremost set to work on the great problem of our time—how organizations and administrative systems can be utilized and controlled. That's so! When I was growing up, I came in contact through Papa with many socialists and communists. And they got caught in bureaucracy's net, they like all the others. And the knots didn't untie themselves!

Finally, about "lock-oil," as you call it. I know I can do it, Erik! I can say the right words, the ones that calm things down for the moment so that we gain the strength and the time to go on working in peace and quiet for what we want to reach at longer range. One mustn't be "hyperhuman" like those escapist anti-vivisectionists. Otherwise one may fall into bad company. As you express it in "Business Week," nothing is truly one hundred percent when it comes to assigning priorities. It's a matter of weighing pros and cons. A person has to be able to choose the argument that is weightiest, even if the difference in weight between the various views is small.

I notice I'm getting a little blurry. I'll bet you've guessed that I've got a little glass of port wine beside me at the desk. Ethico-therapy has taught me not to feel guilty about it! It's silly, Erik. Now, in my fifty-fourth year, I finally begin to feel I've come of age.

Before I close, I've got to tell you what Nils Rosén hinted at today. He states positively that they are saying in the inner circles that you're going to get your professorate. Don't tell me you already know. I suspect so.

And Erik! Let me brag a little. The department head, Rosenquist, said quite unexpectedly the other day that they are going to give me a fine performance rating with WOLMB.

That will almost surely lead to a real, permanent NMSI position! So Mama's getting straightened out. Last fall I was quite sure I'd have to resign and take out my pension in advance.

Well, Mama's going off to bed now. Hope I get to sleep tonight. There have been many night calls lately. Fatiguing, of course, but one's doing some good! The suspicion of me seems nearly gone now. You mustn't think they're usually as unkind as on the night you drove me to the Thanatological Institute. As a matter of fact, I think I've now rehabilitated myself. In other words, NMSI and I know where we have each other.

Finally, I wish you a very Merry Christmas and a Happy New Year. I wish you the same from Grandfather, though it has to be "by proxy," so to speak.

Yours,
Evy

CONCLUSION

1

The highest distinction a doctor can ever hope to receive is not the Nobel Prize. Rather, it is to get a disease named after him. Prizewinners are often forgotten as quickly as last year's reigning film star. But practically all diseases remain. Not only remain, but increase. The more billions of human beings born on earth, the more possibilities for disease. Medical science can't keep up when every year many new millions swarm into that snakepit where over seven thousand different WHO-registered and numbered diseases await.

Thus one who, like Friedrich Daniel von Recklinghausen, succeeds in getting no less than three different diseases named after him isn't going to be forgotten so long as mankind continues on earth.

Other ways do exist to honor those who ought to be honored. In the past, when white spaces still remained on the anatomical charts, outstanding researchers could get newly discovered organs and body parts named after them. On the other hand, famous faculties and clinics such as Stanford University or the Mayo Clinic have taken their names from their founders or benefactors.

A somewhat more limited distinction is to get to bestow your name on an individual laboratory animal. In the Osmosis Laboratory's animal room stands a little plywood hut the size of a playhouse. Over the door hangs a sign with a message in hard-to-read gothic characters. The capitals are painted in red, the small letters in black. Some style-crazed

257

amateur must have fussed for weeks over the sign, which
bears the text:

*Euer wird keiner im hintersten Winkel bleiben, an den nicht
die Hunde scheissen werden. Ich sage euch, mein Gauchhaar
im Gnick weiss mehr, denn ihr und all' eure Scribenten, und
meine Schurinken seindt gelehrter, denn euer Galenos und
Avicenna.*

—Paracelsus

Not by chance does this quotation hang on the little house.
The house's tenant is a middle-aged goat who answers to the
name Paracelsus. The historical Paracelsus, who's sometimes
called the Luther of medical science, spent many years as a
vagabond and quack healer before accepting a professorship
in Basel in 1526. Paracelsus taught that it is experience,
rather than the scholastic texts, which is essential for medicine.

The goat Paracelsus is also distinguished from the mass of
goats by an altogether special ability. In his brain Paracelsus
the goat has a thin wire of silver. The silver wire runs from
a banana plug in his forehead and hits Paracelsus right in the
middle of the thirst center. If Paracelsus is connected to an
ordinary 1.5-volt battery, the goat will start drinking like a
Birmingham coal-heaver. Paracelsus's own personal record is
twenty-five quarts of water for breakfast.

The connection between the goat Paracelsus and the Luther of medicine is not immediately apparent. Often one
finds that there is a notably firmer connection between a
famous researcher and the laboratory animal that bears his
name. In the Endocrinological Institute there is a thirteen-
year-old turkey named Ivar Sandström. The turkey has had
its parathyroid glands removed and thereby owes its thanks
to the man who discovered these organs. Ivar Sandström was
associate professor of anatomy at Uppsala, lost his mind and
died at the age of thirty-seven in 1889.

Had Sandström instead had the advantage of living during
the second half of the twentieth century, perhaps he would
have been spared immense suffering thanks to the freshwa-
ter dolphin Anne in Neurophysiological. Anne is named after

258

the famous psychiatric clinic St. Anne in Paris, where chlorpromazine was first introduced. This preparation was revolutionary in its day and radically improved the possibility of treating acute anxieties and chronic psychoses.

Had Ivar Sandström been unable to profit by the results achieved with the dolphin Anne, he might instead have received the same help as one of NMSI's most valuable gorillas. This gorilla, which answers to the name of Moniz, is the only survivor of a small tribe of gorillas that were first made schizophrenic and then underwent lobotomy. The gorilla Moniz is named after the father of psychosurgery, E. Moniz, who discovered lobotomy and was honored with the Nobel Prize.

An experimental animal very popular among the students is the hog Handlebar, named after an examiner and chromosome investigator much feared in his time, who despite his nickname never wore a mustache. Handlebar is now the Western world's oldest living pig, and still does a good day's work in the service of medical research into senility. In recent times, Handlebar has become something of an animal symbol for NMSI—more or less like Rome and its she-wolf—and feeds upon the student restaurant's scraps.

That this wantonly uncontrolled application to animals of the names of prominent medical investigators should have been allowed to continue so long must be regarded as irresponsible. The auditors of the Nobel Institutes have, very rightly, begun to examine this name-giving from the standpoint of effectiveness. The auditors' interest is dictated by economic factors. It is rumored that the Nobel Institutes' benefactors have felt themselves slighted. Why, in the world of science, are internationally famous experimental animals named only after researchers? True, there formerly was a dog at Pharmacological named Maecenas—but that applied altogether too generally for any of the benefactors to be able to feel himself personally honored.

The problem has not been so simple to solve. One must begin with the assumption that other legitimate name-interests may exist besides researchers and benefactors. Politicians or leading figures in popular causes obviously cannot be excluded without closer examination. There are other hidden reefs and shoals: The Institutes would not willingly repeat the mistake the directorship of the Caroline Hospital once made. When that research institution, founded by Gustav V, was going to celebrate its fortieth anniversary, it came out that for many years they had had a rheumatoid ram around the place who, more or less officially, was called Gussie Vee. The revelation led to an acid commentary from the Keeper of the Privy Purse.

The Institutes can no longer allow the nomenclature problem to drift at loose ends. The already established Task Force for Experimental Animal Nomenclature must be taken in hand and made effective, so that in the future animal naming will take place under more stringent conditions—and so that the procedure may yield the Institutes' budget ready money.

2

The first meeting of the Academic Council after Nobel Day, the tenth of December, is held in a rather slack mood. All during the fall, the famous Nobel Clock has been being rebuilt. Yet, despite very firm promises from Buildings Management, the clock was not ready on the tenth of December, nor was it ready for the traditional ceremonies on Lucia Eve. When the year's five prizewinners in medicine should, according to plan, have advanced with solemn tread into the Institutes' courtyard and engraved their signatures on the silver vanes, there were no silver vanes available. The Nobel Clock stood in the December gloom shrouded in a plastic sheet like some kind of tender cherry or mimosa tree. It was necessary to trot out a big guestbook in great haste for the five prizewinners. This year, the prize was divided among the Russians O. Jefimov, L. Mandel, and M. Vartanian and the Japanese Ito Agaki and Eleonore Sasebo. All five contributed to the so-called antibodybody theory of the cause of schizophrenia.

The NMSI experts in that field did not wish to have as many as five prizewinners. They wanted to reward only a single scientist, as in past years. They reasoned that if the prize is spread among several, an inflation in honorary distinctions can easily occur. Yet something very odd has happened at NMSI this year: the theoretical professors with seats nearest the long green conference table have had to share their power. Not with their clinical colleagues in the outer circle nor with the proletarian representatives of industrial hygiene and child psychiatry on the window sills. The power has moved over instead to the newly named Budget Director of the Nobel Institutes, Håkan Rosenquist, who formerly had been attending the Academic Council only in an advisory capacity. Not even the representative of personnel, Edwin Karlsson, has been able to intervene in this redistribution of power. From the highest levels of the Department of Education, a ukase has come: in the future, the awarding of the Nobel Prize shall not be based only on scientific merit. The national economic situation demands that consideration also be given to international relations in general, to how Sweden's position in the world can most effectively be strengthened. This autumn, the Department of Commerce has proposed that three fingers be outstretched to the Soviet Union and two to Japan.

The meetings after Nobel Day usually open under a pall of fatigue. In the afternoon, distraction takes over, and something that might be described as paralysis of action. It's as if old horses can't find their way to the stall. The president goes and sits at the wrong end of the table and the professor of thoracic surgery walks right through the conference room like a sleepwalker and drops into Forensic Psychiatry's armchair in the corner beside the fire exit. Only the brightly varnished long-dead-and-gone, who hang at several levels on the walls, sourly maintain their locked-in positions without a tremor of their pince-nez or confused plucking of hairs from their white coats.

With a weary gesture the president raises the gavel like a white flag—then allows the gilded thighbone to fall on rather than strike the table: "The meeting is called to order!"

Then the president glances hesitatingly in the direction of Budget Director Rosenquist. The budget director grins immodestly with his nicotine-yellow teeth, and teeters on the back legs of his chair so that it groans.

"Item two!" the president continues: "Giving out this year's Nobel medallions."

Two attendants who had been poised near the door now advance. They are loaded down with small casques of imitation-grain leather, which they carry in as if they were stacks of hymnbooks. Each member is to have five. In every casque rests a medallion with one of this year's Nobel prizewinners in profile. The medallions really should have been distributed at the last meeting, but the Bureau of the Mint couldn't handle such a big order on such short notice. Listlessly a member here and there opens a casque and yawningly scans the snows of yesteryear.

"Item three!" says the president when the dull distribution appears to be complete, at least within the inner circle. "Item three: The budget director's proposal-in-principle that next year's Nobel Prize in medicine be divided among at least *seven* recipients."

Nobody raises his hand. The president surveys the old habitués around the table with the practiced eye of an auctioneer. The tremble of anyone's nostril, a shadow in the corner of someone's eye, or a half-evidenced front tooth suffices . . . But all of them are staring down at the piles of hymnbooks on the table, like a congregation in silent prayer awaiting the text for the day.

Only the budget director speaks up—without asking to speak: "It's foolish to put all your eggs in one basket."

The congregation broods a while over this biblical quotation. Then Nils Rosén von Rosenstein clears his throat and proposes: "It will be hard to find *seven* qualified prizewinners who've all worked on the very same problem."

"Not at all!" says Rosenquist. "More and more, research is becoming teamwork."

"Well, I was thinking . . ." says the president.

"Yes?" Rosenquist encourages.

"—that maybe other persons could be included besides just the researchers who work on a specific project."

"We can't just sit here at the table and okay that for the

262

union!" mutters Edwin Karlsson. "Sure as hell the employer's going to want something back in exchange!"

"Oh no, I wasn't thinking mainly about laboratory animal caretakers and lab assistants," the president continues. "Surely nothing would be more natural than to widen the circle to include benefactors? Those whose economic sacrifices have made a scientific breakthrough possible."

"Small change as thanks for big money?" wonders Rosenquist.

"As a matter of fact, I was thinking chiefly of the honor," says the president.

"Good proposal otherwise," says Rosenquist with satisfaction. "Would reinforce the giving motive. So far as Sweden is concerned, it might also mean that the Nobel prize money went right back into the Treasury."

No debate develops. No one feels himself powerful enough to rise in opposition. The insecurity is great. The old foxes suspect that their poverty-stricken colleagues on the window sills might have something to gain by the dividing of the Nobel Prize among at least seven persons. Within the socially oriented areas of medicine, it seldom happens that a single person is struck with an epochal inspiration one dark night at the scanning electron microscope. Social medicine generally progresses through the labor of many.

"Item four," says the president: "The Institutes' art holdings."

Budget Director Rosenquist has the floor.

"As the Council is aware, this fall an art curator was hired to put this matter in order. Since all the works of art in the Institutes have been attached for debt by the District Marshal, our next move is to get the District Marshal to stand the expense of maintenance and repairs. These works, worth millions, simply cannot be left to rack and ruin. Further, we plan to initiate art tours for the interested public . . ."

"And for the personnel," says Edwin Karlsson.

". . . and for NMSI personnel."

"Probably one might expect a little revenue from these art tours?" the president asks.

"Obviously," says Rosenquist.

Item five on the agenda concerns the Administration's longtime uneasiness over the fact that experimental animals —animals that become internationally known through journal articles and dissertations—are getting named just higgledy-piggledy. As an example, Rosenquist brings up the goat Paracelsus. The Administration hasn't been able to find in the literature any clear connection between the concept goat, the concept artificial thirst, and the concept Paracelsus.

The redness of embarrassment spreads like measles among the professors. Somebody turns furtively toward the only empty window sill, way down at the end of the room. But it's been several years since the NMSI chair in Medical History was occupied.

"Well, well," says the president. "But Rosenquist, I have the feeling that you already have a concrete proposal to advance?"

"I propose that we establish a new and more effective Task Force for Experimental Animal Nomenclature, with centralized power of decision in all naming questions."

The president sneaks another look at a piece of paper— then he quits faking and reads directly from the paper Rosenquist has slipped him.

"As members of this task force I wish to propose Edwin Karlsson, Art Curator August Klevberg, and as chairman, Rosenquist."

Nobody objects, which is equivalent to consent.

The next-to-last item—number six—concerns the establishment of new positions. Rosenquist reads out the Administration's proposal from a list. Five bookkeepers, three programmers, three research engineers, and a Chief Supervisory Inspector of the cleaning force are to be hired. The president has already raised his shining decision-stick in the air when Nils Rosén asks, "And Evy Beck?"

"The question is only what persons are to be employed in those positions already on the list," the president points out.

"As a matter of fact, I'd intended to bring up Evy Beck under Other Business," says Rosenquist. "But maybe it fits in here?"

"Go ahead."

"As you know, Evy Beck is a female veterinarian whom we've had here for the past year on the WOLMB budget. Only in the most exceptional circumstances can such a person be transferred to regular employment."

"What's the difference where the salary comes from," says the professor of thoracic surgery. "The main thing is for a person to have a job. And to make himself useful."

"She certainly does," says Professor Nilson-Roth from the Physicum. "Evy Beck got us through that Marburg epidemic."

Rosenquist takes in enough air to fill his tanks for a real declamation.

"First we let her wander around on her own. There really wasn't anyone who had time to give her any detailed guidance. She got to walk around and find her own assignments. Well, it went all right for a while. Animal welfare probably hasn't been given priority everywhere. Sure, we got help. Especially at night she turned out to be useful. I think plenty of you sitting here at this table can confirm that?"

A few professors nod feebly; one looks at his watch.

"Well, there you are. Veterinary service on call is something that's needed. But now, look here, when it comes to this preventive business: Am I all alone in having the feeling that such a veterinary consultant can put obstacles in the way of the Institutes' *freedom of action?* I mean, how can we have a person running around making demands that completely upset our cost calculations?"

Three or four professors nod—not so feebly this time.

Suddenly Nils Rosén leaps up, tipping over his chair so that the back bounces on the floor.

"Evy Beck has really struggled to do her best. I've followed her work closely, and I can testify that better manpower would be hard to find. Besides, she's more or less been promised a position."

"We-e-ell, promised?" says Rosenquist. "She'll get a good performance rating. But we simply haven't got any night positions."

265

Rosén gets his chair set up again and sits down heavily.

"She herself understood it as a firm promise. Besides, who says she's only to work at night?"

Now Edwin Karlsson asks for the floor, hooks his thumbs round his belt, and hoists his belly into place.

"This matter of night and day positions has long-standing traditions. The Labor Market Board usually covers night positions. Besides that, I have to remind you that there have been some small controversies. Not just about protecting animals. But also about protecting workers. I don't think she's shown very sound judgment in making these difficult distinctions . . ."

"Somebody's seen her going to the Vasatown Ethical Center," the president suggests.

"That's all over and done with," says Rosén. "I must express my deep disappointment if the Council should not see its way clear to giving Evy Beck a position."

"Should a hundred institute directors be sitting here babbling about this the whole afternoon?" says the professor of internal medicine.

"We'll have to see what we can do in next year's budget," says Rosenquist. "For the present, she knows we appreciate her. Very much. So much that she's going to get to keep her office in our Administration Building."

"May we proceed to Item Seven?" asks the president.

Nils Rosén rises again, more carefully this time.

"Evy Beck has done extraordinary work in preventive animal care. Now that she's gotten herself on the right track, so to speak, I'm convinced she's going to be extraordinarily useful to the Institutes."

"She's got the whole night every night," says Edwin Karlsson. "Why can't college graduates be allowed to work night shift?"

The discussion is derailed again. Nils Rosén sinks down in his chair and puts his big handsome head in his hands.

The president devotes one moment of silent thought to the problem, then raises his gavel to give the starting shot for item seven.

"Wait!" says Budget Director Rosenquist. "Wait. If this

266

question is so sensitive . . . Let me offer the following proposal: In our new Task Force for more effective Experimental Animal Nomenclature, we not only lack expertise in medical history. Since it is animals that are to be named, it would be extremely appropriate if we could have a veterinarian in the group too. So I propose that besides her night duties, Evy Beck also be called to our meetings. In an advisory capacity."

"Does the Council accept this proposal?" asks the president.

Nobody answers or raises his hand—which is tantamount to consent.

A few minutes later, those members of the Academic Council who haven't sneaked away gather around the Nobel Clock. One week late, the clock can be unveiled. Item seven on the agenda is the inspection of the new Nobel Clock. Forty-three men and two ladies of the Council station themselves in irregular rings around the wide rim of the stone basin.

The people from Buildings Management pull away the black plastic. Formerly the clock consisted of a number of vertical rods with several vanes on each. Now the clock has been supplemented with intersecting bands of thin silverplate, a sphere of intersecting haloes. In every circle, an astrological or animal sign can move. The clock can stand in the sign of Cancer or in the Year of the Pig. The world-famous mobile now functions not only as a weather vane, a · timepiece, and a compass—but also as a horoscope.